SHADOWS OF
DECEIT

SHADOWS OF
DECEIT

A HAMILTON ST. JAMES MYSTERY

PETER CLEVELAND

IGUANA

Copyright © 2025 Peter Cleveland
Published by Iguana Books
720 Bathurst Street
Toronto, ON M5S 2R4

Publisher: Cheryl Hawley
Editor: Lee Parpart
Front cover design: Nadine Buckley, mcgillbuckley.com

ISBN 978-1-77180-735-7 (paperback)
ISBN 978-1-77180-734-0 (epub)

This is an original print edition of *Shadows of Deceit*.

OTHER BOOKS IN THE

HAMILTON ST. JAMES MYSTERY

SERIES

Double Shot of Scotch (2020)

Gobsmacked! (2022)

PROLOGUE

Several months ago...

Russell Allaband sat behind his dark walnut desk, the rich wood a stark contrast to the pale-yellow walls of his converted home office. Dressed in a grey tracksuit, he ran a hand through his thinning salt-and-pepper hair, each strand a testament to the stress of managing his own private investment firm. Years of financial turbulence had etched deep lines into his face. Now, disbelief settled over him like a dense fog, his thoughts confronting a new unforeseen challenge.

Allaband was fixated on a video call with a Costa Rican Registry official who struggled to maintain his composure amidst rising tension in the virtual room.

"Mr. Allaband, our records indicate no outstanding property taxes are owed," the agent repeated.

Allaband's hand shook, his jaw tightening as he struggled to contain his rising anger. "I haven't paid last year's taxes yet! And you're telling me I don't owe anything?"

The official grimaced, his face flickering on the monitor. Apprehension crept into his voice. "You sold your home to Gael Vargas several months ago, so you don't owe tax," he asserted.

Allaband squirmed in his chair. "I did no such thing! I never sold that house to anyone!"

The bureaucrat trembled as he tried to calm the situation. "Sir, the transfer papers are in order. Carlos Sánchez, your notary, signed them on your behalf."

"I didn't authorize a sale, I tell you!" Allaband articulated each word slowly as if addressing a child. His hands clenched into fists.

Ed, Allaband's golden lab, lay at his feet. The dog's ears perked. He shifted closer, pressing his body against his master's leg, whimpering, sensing distress.

"We didn't create this problem," the bureaucrat announced. "The matter lies between you and Mr. Sánchez. We're not involved."

Allaband clicked off the call without another word and closed his laptop. He stared at the screen until his meticulously organized desktop morphed into a video of sequoia trees slowly encircled by early morning mist. The screen saver, which had often soothed his mind, suddenly seemed fake and offensive, like a product of AI. *What could be happening? Was anything real?* He rose from his black leather chair and paced the room, massaging his neck, cursing under his breath as heat rushed to his face.

He stared at Ed in stunned silence, frustration and disbelief churning in his mind. His chest tightened as he considered the possibility of losing his cherished property.

Ed nudged Allaband's hand with a cold, wet nose.

"Don't know a Gael Vargas, Ed," Allaband murmured. "And I sure as hell didn't sell my house. I think I would have remembered that." Ed let out a soft whimper, and Allaband ruffled the fur on his head.

A thought pierced his confusion. *What if Sánchez forged my signature?* Allaband rushed back to open his computer and slammed his hands on the keyboard. Each keystroke followed the rising storm of thoughts as he demanded proof of the property transfer from the Costa Rican Registry.

Allaband buried his head in both hands.

Losing his vacation home — the one place Allaband could genuinely unwind — was unthinkable.

He glanced at Ed, who looked back at him with trusting and worried eyes.

"We'll figure this out," he said, stroking the dog's head. "I'll spare no expense to get justice!"

CHAPTER 1

The Boeing 737 nudged Liberia's Daniel Oduber Quirós International Airport bridge in Costa Rica, and the seat belt signs turned off.

Excitement stirred among the passengers as they scrambled to retrieve their carry-on bags from overhead compartments — a race for space in the aisle.

Struggling with an overstuffed carry-on and a computer bag that he hadn't even been sure he would bring until the last minute, Louis Smythe stood, glancing at his reflection in the airplane window.

He wore three types of mismatched plaid — an eye-popping mix of blues, whites, pinks, and purples. Since founding his niche computer company specializing in high-level financial fraud, clashing plaid had become his signature look. He thought anyone who wanted to work with an eccentric genius would be drawn to his style. Conventional clients would steer clear.

As he fumbled to adjust his combover, his computer bag swung across his body and grazed an elderly woman who remained seated beside him, disturbing her snow-white hair.

The lady shot Smythe an enraged look and shifted her hair into place.

Smythe immediately apologized, but the woman glared at him and hissed, "You could have knocked me out with that thing!"

Smythe raised his hands in surrender. "Ma'am, it was an accident, truly. I didn't mean to—"

The woman held his stare and muttered, "Carelessness!"

Smythe clutched his computer bag and moved further into the aisle, seeking a less hostile position.

A few feet away, Dozer White rose out of his seat, filling the cabin, and reached for his carry-on bag. Dozer was thanking his dapper seatmate for the engaging conversation. "I hate long flights," he told the man, his deep voice swelling the cabin. "This one went faster with our conversation. Thank you."

The gentleman beside him, a calm presence dressed in a tailored black suit, smiled politely. "The pleasure was all mine."

Dozer's imposing figure shoved Smythe aside, further infringing upon the irate woman's space.

"Stop pushing, you big galoot!" she snapped.

Dozer shook off the complaint without a word. He eyed Hamilton St. James, three rows ahead, adeptly navigating the sea of bodies. Next to him, Anna pulled a silk eye mask over her blonde hair, which was a little rumpled after the flight.

With one hand resting on Anna's arm, St. James turned and called out to Smythe and Dozer. "Meet you at baggage claim!"

Dozer waved back as he pushed past the congestion.

When the bridge crew swung open the heavy door, the passengers were hit with a wall of humid air as they disembarked — a stark transition from the cool plane. Relief came from the air conditioning at the top of the bridge.

The passengers filed into the immigration line, a serpentine mix of citizens from many countries, including excited tourists and business travellers. Costa Ricans returning home were funneled through an express lane.

The airport was small and clean, with high ceilings and whirling fans strategically placed for even air circulation. The structure resembled an industrial warehouse. Natural light streamed through the expansive windows.

All around the terminal, posters of sun-soaked beaches, magnificent wildlife, and lush jungles offered a snapshot of what Costa Rica had to offer.

Passenger lines led to two customs officers manning separate stations.

The officer on the left wore a name tag that read Rafael. A short Peter Sellers look-alike with a pointed nose, he fixed his dark, insinuating eyes straight ahead, ready to trip up any passenger who might intend to make false declarations.

The queue moved steadily, and Dozer soon found himself facing Rafael, or rather looking down on him from what felt like too great a height. The officer regarded him with a professional detachment that made him uncomfortable. Dozer was conscious of being the only Black man in the line.

"Passport?" Rafael said.

Dozer handed over his travel document and willed himself to stay calm.

Rafael studied the document, his manner inscrutable, before looking up. "Name?"

"Erasmus White."

Rafael frowned. "I see the word 'Dozer' here in brackets. What's that mean?"

"Oh, that's just a nickname," Dozer said, trying to sound casual. When the agent looked at him blankly, Dozer added, "From my football days."

A commotion suddenly erupted down the line: three men arguing over who was next. Two uniformed security guards rushed to break up the dispute.

Rafael watched the scuffle evenly, then turned back to Dozer and smiled. "Glad I never had to face you on the football field."

Dozer offered a faint smile in return.

Rafael's look shifted once more as he studied Dozer's face. "Sir, you look familiar."

Dozer tried to brush off the comment. "I hear that a lot."

Rafael's tone returned to formal. "Business or pleasure?"

"Relaxation."

Rafael slid the passport through the scanner, his eyes still fixed on the large passenger seeking entry into Costa Rica. Dozer could feel his heart pumping wildly. He was sure he would be searched.

This seemed to go on for an eternity until Rafael suddenly relaxed his gaze, stamped Dozer's passport, and handed it back to him. "Hope you find the peace you're seeking, Mr. White."

Dozer was surprised. "Thank you, Sir," he said, the words expressed with an unexpected sense of relief.

Rafael turned to the next passenger. Smythe moved forward, his eyes encountering Rafael's with irritation.

"Name?"

Smythe directed Rafael to his passport. "Right there."

Rafael's eyes narrowed as he insisted, "Please state your name."

Smythe made no attempt to hide his frustration. "Why?"

Rafael lowered the document onto his desk and glared at Smythe. "Are you going to make this difficult?"

Smythe, not wanting to create further aggravation, hiked his eyebrows and blurted, "Louis Smythe."

Rafael nodded. "Better."

He proceeded with questions, and Smythe answered each one succinctly. Rafael ran Smythe's passport through the scanner.

"I'm accustomed to seeing colourful attire. Never all plaid. Any reason?" Rafael's voice carried a hint of condescension.

"Specialize in computer fraud."

Rafael's smirk faded. "Causing it?"

"Detecting it."

Rafael's amusement gave way to confusion. "What does that have to do with how you dress?"

"I wanted a distinctive look."

Rafael's brow furrowed as he observed Smythe, head to toe. After a moment of consideration, he waved two immigration agents over to his desk. The authorities approached, their presence creating a stir.

Fear rippled through the line as the agents escorted Smythe to a private room. Murmurs of concern grew louder.

"Hey! What's going on?" Smythe yelled. "I answered all your questions, didn't I?"

Rafael's expression was impassive. "Next."

CHAPTER 2

Dozer trailed St. James and Anna to the busy baggage claim, where they waited for a conveyor belt to activate.

The conveyor creaked, suitcases dropped and began marching around.

St. James snatched a suitcase.

Anna pointed to a light blue Pullman. "That's mine," she said, and St. James retrieved it for her, eliciting a playful "Thank you, kind Sir" from its owner.

People of all nationalities swarmed the conveyor belts, determined to grab their bags on first passing.

Anna moved closer to St. James and ran a simply manicured finger across his smooth white shirt and stylish blazer.

"Are you always this unrumpled after an international flight?"

"Only when I have the world's best seatmate."

"That's right, Hamilton — lay it on with a trowel," Anna said dryly, getting a laugh.

Dozer was approaching them when St. James looked at Anna and said, "Have you seen Louis?"

Dozer rotated, searching the crowd. "Behind me a few minutes ago."

St. James yanked Smythe's bag from the belt. It was the only plaid weekender in the place.

Pink sunglasses and a beige fedora gave Anna's slim figure a flair. "He'll show up soon, I imagine."

The three hurried to where drivers stood, displaying printed name signs.

Dozer beckoned to a man holding a *St. James* sign. "There he is."

The man introduced himself as Emiliano Rojas Rodríguez. "Welcome to Costa Rica," he said in a marked Spanish accent.

James shook Rodríguez's hand. "Muchas gracias."

Bulging biceps suggested to Dozer that weightlifting might be Rodríguez's regular exercise.

Anna gestured to Rodríguez. "We're missing a travel companion."

"No problem, Señorita. We will wait. Please stay here while I grab baggage carts."

As Rodríguez walked away, Anna spotted Smythe manoeuvring through the crowd.

He was more dishevelled than usual, with his blue-and-white plaid tie loosened and his unbuttoned pink and purple shirt ruffled.

Anna took in Smythe's haggard state. "What happened to you?"

"You don't want to know," Smythe said, readjusting the belt buckle on his pants.

Anna grimaced and let it go.

Rodríguez returned with two carts and, with a nod to Smythe, began loading them with suitcases. He and Dozer pushed the carts from the airport to the parking area. Rodríguez led them to a faded white Hyundai Tucson bearing a grey sign that read *Rodríguez Tours*. The rear passenger door was dented, and the front bumper was missing. Other than that, the vehicle looked passable to St. James.

The sun's intense rays reminded Anna of sunscreen. She applied some to her face and hands and passed the bottle around to the others. The faint odour of her mineral sunscreen mingled with a woodsy aroma left by an overnight rain.

For a second, Anna thought of friends back home who longed for a Costa Rican climate in winter but complained of the heat when they actually went someplace warm. Anna silently vowed not to be a tourist who could never be pleased.

Rodríguez struggled to load the bags in the rear of the Tucson. St. James took the front seat while the others climbed in the back, bantering about expectations for the Tamarindo holiday.

Smythe eyed the countryside as Rodríguez pulled away from the airport. "How far to Tamarindo?"

Rodríguez hung his cap on a grey metal hook behind his head. "The most direct route is about seventy-eight kilometres, but the traffic can be heavy through some of the small villages along the route. Makes the journey seem longer."

Dozer turned to his travelling companions. "Feels like a long way from Gundelsheim." Everyone laughed in relieved agreement, causing Rodríguez to peer at them curiously from the rearview mirror.

St. James caught the questioning look. "We've just finished a big case," he explained.

Rodríguez nodded, impressed. "You all work together? And vacation together?"

"Only when we're overdue for a team getaway."

Without going into all the details, St. James explained the team had just cracked a massive fraud case in Gundelsheim, Germany, two weeks earlier. They'd recovered millions of dollars for hundreds of global companies, and the mastermind was now serving twenty-five years in a German prison.

"Sounds intense," Rodríguez said, glancing between the road and St. James.

"Oh, it was. A gruelling investigation, followed by multiple court battles that will continue for months. Our plan now is to relax, rejuvenate, and celebrate our hard-earned victory."

"Well, you've picked the perfect place to unwind," Rodríguez said.

St. James nodded and turned to the others. "The man's right. We're in paradise. Let's not talk about work for the next two weeks."

"We won't even think about it," Anna chimed in, to a round of approvals.

Rodríguez adjusted the air-conditioning. "Temperature okay?"

A chorus of yeses drifted from the seats behind.

Smythe took in the tropical scenery as the SUV approached the town of Comunidad. His eyes lit up at the sight of a rider crossing a green field on horseback. "Can't wait to try that. I've wanted riding lessons ever since I was a kid."

"Mom and Dad never gave you a pony?" Dozer teased, and Smythe shook his head in mock woe.

Rodríguez negotiated a turn. "Lots of stables near Tamarindo."

Dozer grinned at Smythe, who had removed his plaid jacket and laid it over his plaid pants. "Think they have plaid horse blankets, Louis?"

Smythe raised an eyebrow, lips curling into a dry smile. "Well, Dozer, I'm sure they've got it all — plaid blankets for the horses and pink neon bridles to match your socks."

Dozer raised one pant leg to reveal neon yellow socks, not pink, and Smythe shielded his eyes with his hands, saying, "It burns."

"Boys, boys," Anna scolded, rolling her eyes.

St. James smiled to himself and gazed out the window at Guanacaste's serene countryside, with its rolling hills and lush pastures. Pointedly changing the subject, he said, "What's the crime like in Costa Rica, Rodríguez?"

Under his breath, Smythe said, "So much for not talking about work."

Anna let out a minor chuckle and St. James bristled good-naturedly. "What? I'm just curious."

Rodríguez smiled at the light-hearted bickering and checked the mirrors for traffic. "Used to be minor, petty stuff when I was a kid."

Dozer perked up. "Used to be?"

"It's become more sophisticated in recent years — more organized. More like a steady business than random acts by individuals. It got worse during COVID."

The exchange caught Smythe's attention. "What type of crime?"

"Thought you didn't want to know," St. James chided, prompting a shrug from Smythe.

Rodríguez eased the gas to let a car pass. "The usual telephone and credit card fraud, identity theft. That sort of thing."

St. James remained focused on the scenery. "Corporate fraud?"

"More corporate stuff reported now."

"Interesting," St. James mused.

Quaint villages popped up between sugar cane fields as Rodríguez drove on.

Anna was following along on her cell phone, trying to pronounce the names and learn a little about each place. "Cañas Dulces village appears larger than the one we just passed. What's the population?"

"Cañas Dulces is actually a district with a population of about thirty-five hundred. It's mostly agriculture and tourism. Visitors love volcanic landscapes. And it's a service centre for surrounding farms."

Smythe leaned forward, pointing at a large field filled with unusual vegetation. "What's that?"

Rodríguez slowed for traffic ahead. "That's a savanna. We have a lot of them. Grasslands, shrubs, and scattered trees adapted to drier conditions."

Smythe nodded. "I see."

"No palm trees?" Dozer asked.

"Not along this route. It's too dry. They're more common in wetter areas, near resorts."

Dozer watched a farmer poking along on an ancient red tractor. "Makes sense. More water to soak up."

Anna smiled as she looked all around. "This is like stepping into a postcard."

Rodríguez's face glowed. "Yes, we have some of the most diverse ecosystems in the world. Everything from pristine beaches to dense jungles. And we have a wide array of flora and fauna."

As if on cue, a pair of brightly coloured birds shot through the dense foliage of one tree and landed on a nearby branch. St. James watched in amazement. "Those toucans?"

Anna's eyes sparkled. "So beautiful."

Rodríguez cast a quick look as they drove past the scene. "No. Aracari. Like toucans but smaller."

Smythe couldn't take in everything fast enough. Pointing at a sign leading into a forested area, he asked, "Is that a national park?"

"Rincón de la Vieja," Rodríguez said. "It's a vast volcano and national park. Locals refer to it as the Colossus of Guanacaste."

Anna quickly called it up on her phone. "Says here it has nine volcanic craters and at least thirty-two rivers flow down, bridging the Continental Divide: rainforests, hot springs, and mud pots."

Rodríguez nodded. "Then there are the hiking trails — some moderate, others more challenging. And it has magnificent waterfalls. You can feel the energy from the volcano."

Dozer perked up. "Like to do some hiking while I'm here."

Smythe leered. "Wanted you to take a hike for some time."

Anna laughed.

Dozer ignored Smythe's dig.

St. James rolled his eyes and returned his focus to Rodríguez. "What's the wildlife like?"

Rodríguez described howlers, parakeets, giant iguanas, pumas, and peccaries, and proudly announced that the country hosts "over three hundred types of birds."

Smythe's forehead lined. "What's a puma?"

Dozer's eyes twinkled. "Like a cougar, dummy."

Rodríguez stopped to allow a herd of sheep to pass in front. "We do jungle tours if you're interested."

Anna admired sugar cane fields drifting by. "Jumping in the swimming pool as soon as we arrive."

St. James leaned over the headrest. "What about you, Dozer? What do you want to do?"

"Guzzle beer to celebrate not having to protect your sorry ass while we're here."

St. James smiled. "Now, is that any way to talk to your most prized client?"

"What makes you think you're my favourite?"

"I pay you more than anyone else. And then there's the fact that even though we're not supposed to be thinking about work, we've somehow all ended up on vacation together."

"How did that happen again?" Dozer laughed.

"Could be Stockholm's Syndrome," Smythe said dryly.

Dozer glared at Smythe. "What's Stockholm's Syndrome?"

Smythe laughed. "Developing an ability to cope with people who abuse you. Like vacationing with the very people you need a vacation from, dummy."

Dozer shrugged and said, "Touché."

Anna laughed while St. James shook his head, amused and resistant.

"Oh well," Dozer said, "better make the best of it. I'd like to try deep-sea fishing."

Anna lowered the window and waved to a group of schoolchildren standing by the roadside. "Sounds like fun, Dozer." The kids smiled and waved back.

Smythe joined in. "What about you two lovebirds?"

St. James exchanged a glance with Anna.

"Hamilton and I haven't discussed it. I wouldn't mind a few snorkelling lessons. What do you think, Hamilton?"

"I'll think about it. Anything but work."

CHAPTER 3

The afternoon sun began to fade as Rodríguez pulled the SUV into the Tamarindo Diria Beach Resort.

Enchanted by the breathtaking view, Anna sprang from the vehicle as soon as Rodríguez shifted into Park. She stood on the curved driveway and turned around slowly, taking in the sprawling compound with its palm trees, whitewashed buildings and bright green lawns.

She looked at St. James. "Mind if I take a look around while you boys get the luggage?" She was already darting toward the main entrance when St. James laughed and said, "Oh sure, it's all women's lib until there are bags to carry."

Anna turned around and winked at St. James. "No one says 'women's lib' anymore." Then she disappeared through the front door of the main building.

The open entrance from Diria Boulevard to the oceanside permitted the warm Pacific air to pass freely through reception.

Anna fixed her gaze on the rich-looking reception desk to the right of the entrance. Embedded in its dark wood was the most beautiful porcelain flower.

To the left, a woman with a welcoming smile sat at a desk, arranging tours for guests lined in front. Straight ahead, a swimming pool was jammed between the Brisa bar, children's pool, and ground-floor rooms.

A soft breeze carried the intoxicating fragrance of blooming hibiscus. A sense of tranquility washed over Anna as she inhaled the fresh Pacific air, and she began wandering around the hotel lobby, ending up outside.

On the beach side, in front of the bar, she spotted an unusual tree that seemed to be growing in all directions. She opened a flora app and pointed her phone at it and marvelled at the quick reply. "Matapalo tree," she read. "'Spanish fig, known for enveloping its host tree and eventually killing it.'" She shuddered at the violent image, even as she imagined herself sitting under its meandering canopy with St. James, savouring drinks.

She was gone by the time St. James, Dozer and Smythe carried the bags through the entrance and made their way to the front desk. A cheerful young man at reception looked up from his computer to greet the three men. St. James handed over his credit card and asked that all team expenses be charged to him.

St. James smiled and read the badge on his shirt. "Carlos, is it?"

"That's right, Sir."

"Impressive resort."

"Hope you enjoy it, Sir."

"I'm sure we will."

Dozer filled in the registration form and handed Carlos his passport. He looked around at the spacious lobby, with its views of palm trees and bright green lawns just outside. "A talking parrot is the only thing missing here."

Carlos's eyes twinkled. "Oh, we had one, Sir."

Smythe was intrigued. "What happened?"

Carlos grinned. "A few drunken military guys thought it would be funny to teach Harold, the parrot, some colourful language. It was funny until Harold welcomed a busload of older ladies with some rather suggestive remarks."

St. James laughed.

"The ladies were not amused," Carlos said, smiling. "They refused to check in and the manager had to give them a free night to calm them down. Let's just say Harold left town early the next day."

The guys laughed.

Anna flounced over, beaming with delight. "This is incredible! There are swimming pools — plural — and bars and restaurants all over the place. The grounds are pristine. I can't wait to explore everything!"

St. James smiled. "Chill, Anna."

"Can't help it. It exceeds all my expectations."

"There'll be plenty of time to see everything." St. James glanced at Dozer and Smythe. "Meet us at the bar in an hour?"

They agreed and headed to their rooms.

St. James and Anna had little trouble finding their top-floor accommodation. St. James entered the door code, and they stepped into a spacious oceanfront suite with a king-size bed butted up against a turquoise wall on the left. The other walls bore brightly coloured artwork and textiles, infusing the space with warmth.

Anna's gaze lingered over two white wicker chairs flanked by a matching loveseat and a wooden coffee table that brought a touch of rustic elegance. She slipped off her sandals near the door and stepped onto the cool softness of a handwoven rug anchoring the room. "Gorgeous," she said, kneeling down to inspect the piece, with its soft blue background and bright orange details. "This feels like traditional Costa Rican craftsmanship."

St. James opened the sliding door to reveal their balcony and spectacular ocean view. Below their room was a well-kept lawn, edged to accommodate a ribbon of concrete walkways extending in all directions. Lush palms, ferns and other flora, golden sand and waves completed the picture.

Anna padded out onto the balcony and stood next to him. "It's stunning," she said. "You've outdone yourself."

"I made sure we got the best ocean view in the place," St. James mumbled.

Anna peeked at her watch. "Think I'll go for a swim before drinks."

St. James looked surprised. "You always want to unpack first."

"Not this time, darling. I'm on holiday. Can't be like any other case trip."

Anna poked St. James gently on the arm and walked back into the suite to find the bathroom. Once there she piled her long blond hair into a loose bun and changed into a blue bikini. She grabbed her sunglasses, kissed St. James quickly on the cheek, and headed for the pool.

St. James whispered, "Guess I'm stuck emptying the cases."

Anna turned and levelled him with her gaze. "Up to you. We can always take care of it together later."

"That's okay."

Anna took him at his word and disappeared out the door. She was not going to sacrifice the one thing she most wanted at the end of a long day of travel: a refreshing swim.

Thirty minutes later, damp but happy, Anna slipped back into the suite and had a quick shower. Then she changed into a milky white jumpsuit with low-heeled gold sandals. She and St. James headed downstairs to the bar, where they found Smythe and Dozer sitting by the pool, getting a head start on drinks.

Dozer's seersucker suit and bright Hawaiian shirt made him look right at home. He was leaning back on a lounge chair when he saw St. James and Anna approaching. Dozer held up what remained of an Imperial beer, as if to toast his employer. "Fabulous place, Hamilton. Nicely done."

St. James smiled and motioned for the server. "You earned it. Germany was intense."

Dozer, Smythe, and Anna all nodded in agreement at the memory of their last case. German criminal gangs, British grocery store tycoons, and a conspiracy to embezzle wads and wads of cash had made for an especially complex case. They all needed a real vacation.

Anna glanced over at the pool next to the bar and lowered her sunglasses. St. James followed her sightline all the way to a handsome young body-builder type, bouncing on the end of a diving board before diving into the water.

"Be a little more obvious, won't you, Anna?" St. James scolded, but she just smiled and slipped her hand into his.

"You told me I've earned a vacation. Can't a girl admire the scenery?"

Smythe seemed to find this amusing. He laughed and raised a glass of wine and said, "You go, girl." Anna curtsied and lowered herself onto a chair, still grasping one of St. James's fingers in her petite hand.

Smythe, who had changed into long shorts and a linen shirt, again in mismatched plaid, directed his question at Anna. "Apart from gawking at boys, how do you plan to recover from the rigours of the German case?"

"Oh, there's a delightful pool on the other side of the resort. I think I'll sunbathe there tomorrow. Maybe lounge around on a day bed in one of the curtained cabanas and read a mystery."

Dozer smiled and drank the rest of his Imperial and set his glass down on a table. "I seem to be out of beer," he said, leaning one arm against the recliner.

Anna laughed. "We'll have to take care of that." She raised one arm to attract the attention of a waiter, then closed her eyes dreamily as a warm breeze passed through the happy group. "This place is a welcome relief."

Smythe nodded and swirled his wine in his glass. "You can say that again. Can't see myself going back to Germany again — ever."

Anna opened one eye at him. "You can't write off a whole country just because we caught one difficult case."

"Nein. I suppose not."

Drinks arrived for St. James and Anna, along with another Imperial for Dozer.

As they sipped their drinks, Anna noticed a subtle change in Smythe's demeanour. "Louis, you seem a bit off. Is something wrong?"

"This is like a dream. I'm afraid I'll wake up, and it'll all be gone."

Dozer wagged a finger in Smythe's direction. "No, don't you jinx us. I've been looking forward to this vacation for weeks. I'm not letting one of your spooky premonitions destroy it."

Smythe frowned. "I don't want anything to wreck it either."

Now Anna looked concerned. "What could ruin it?"

Smythe shrugged. "Don't know. Just a feeling."

CHAPTER 4

Anna reached across the bed, searching for St. James, only to be greeted by a pillow. She surveyed the room — no Hamilton.

The morning sun beamed in from the balcony, creating a surreal, almost biblical illumination. The sultry air carried a strong floral fragrance. Anna inhaled deeply, with eyes closed, and tried to place the tropical scent. Finally, she smiled to herself. "Plumeria."

Anna rose, pulled on a cover-up, and walked out onto the balcony. A fresh ocean breeze washed over her as she let her gaze wander from the manicured lawns to the tall palm trees and the magnificent gardens beyond.

Gradually, she became aware of a peculiar sound floating in from behind the complex. It started at a low volume and grew to a harsh cacophony of wails, hoots, and cackles. Anna thought of the howler monkeys that Rodríguez described, but the resort seemed too far from the jungle for them.

Astonishment swept across Anna's face as the scene on the lawn came into focus. St. James stood below, invigorated from a morning swim, grinning ear to ear. Beside him, Smythe and Dozer mirrored his electrified expression, their excitement nearly as vivid.

Early morning runners whisked down paths. Hotel guests gathered in small groups, discussing plans for the day.

Anna's heart raced as she looked around, trying to make sense of the unfolding scene. Then her eyes darted from St. James to an unusual sight.

At first, it looked like a mirage — a splash of vibrant yellow against the green lawn. She squinted, and suddenly she could see a panorama. More than a hundred — a thousand? — ripened bananas had been laid out on the grass, forming giant letters. The letters cohered into a short sentence, ending in a question mark.

Anna's hands flew to her face. Her body tensed with shock and exhilaration.

She had to read it again to be sure she wasn't hallucinating.

But no. There it was, in yellow on green: *Will you marry me?*

St. James gave a signal, and music blasted from a hidden speaker. Voices began warbling up from the space below. Hotel staff singing, "I hear those church bells ringing..."

Anna's pale complexion shifted to a radiant flush as her eyes welled up with tears. Everything about the sight before her — St. James's hopeful, adoring gaze and the unexpected cascade of bananas — threatened to overwhelm her senses.

A loud, jubilant squeal burst from her lips.

As the song played on and the moment lingered, Anna's tears of joy mingled with her beaming smile.

The surrounding laughter and applause only added to the euphoria.

"How is she taking it?" Dozer sounded as if the bananas had just delivered bad news.

St. James appeared nervous. "Can't tell. Crying can mean many things to Anna. Maybe I went too far."

Smythe considered the lengths St. James had gone to propose. "Geez, and they call me eccentric."

Dozer grinned. "Someone like you is just nuts. Crazy."

Smythe shot Dozer a penetrating look.

Parakeets, with their tufted orange chest feathers, chirped musical sounds from a nearby tree.

Swimmers screeched above the sound of crashing waves.

Anna disappeared from the balcony. She was carrying her sandals, wearing only her cover-up and a pair of silk sleeping shorts, when she sprinted across the lawn and leapt into St. James's arms, almost toppling him.

"Does this mean—"

"Yes! The answer is yes." Anna's tear-streaked face was inches from his. "It would be an honour to be Mrs. Hamilton St. James!"

Cheers erupted around the grounds. An elderly groundskeeper stood still, pressing his hat against his white shirt.

"Phew! I was worried I'd spent a fortune on these bananas for nothing."

Laughing, Anna gave him a fake slap. "Sweetest, most creative proposal ever." She clapped her hands together in glee.

Dozer smirked. "Don't forget — insane."

Smythe said, "Bananas."

Anna, ignoring their banter, threw her slender arms around St. James's neck and said, "You've made me the happiest woman in the world."

Smythe homed in on Anna. "This fiancé of yours forced Dozer and me out of bed in the middle of the night. Do you have any idea how hard it is to spell with fruit at three in the morning?"

St. James laughed. "Quit stewing, Louis. You know you had fun. And for once in your life, you got to see the sunrise."

Smythe's look softened. "I did, you know. Enjoy it. And the sunrise wasn't horrible."

"Admit it," said Dozer. "You'd have been hurt if you hadn't been included."

"Probably."

St. James trained his gaze on his friends. "Couldn't leave out either of my two best men."

Smythe looked at him, astonished. "Two best men?"

St. James grinned. "Yes, I want you and Dozer to be in the wedding party."

Dozer raised an eyebrow. "Can you have two?"

St. James's eyes twinkled. "I think so, but if not, Louis will make a helluva flower boy."

Smythe laughed along with the others.

Anna, who was still recovering from the surprise, clung to St. James like he was about to fall off a cliff.

Dozer was eager to celebrate, but St. James just winked at him.

"Nine thirty in the morning, Dozer. Perhaps we should wait a bit."

St. James's phone buzzed. He glanced at the number on his cell and looked stricken. "Oh no! Not now! Dammit."

CHAPTER 5

St. James didn't even say hello. He pressed Talk and started talking. "I'm on a two-week holiday, and just this minute, I became engaged to Anna. Please tell me you're not going to spoil it."

DeSilva was unaffected by his plea. "Congratulations, Hamilton. Anna's a lovely woman."

St. James pictured DeSilva, with her uncanny ability to shut out everything when she wanted something else. He was vaguely impressed that she had enough presence of mind to congratulate him.

Dozer and Smythe realized who it was. Dozer shook his head. "Told you not to jinx this vacation!"

Smythe winced. "I didn't tell DeSilva to call him."

Dozer mumbled something under his breath.

A small group of singers approached them and started to serenade Anna, but St. James held up his hand and they dispersed.

Mary DeSilva, Global Insurance's senior vice president, engaged St. James to investigate substantial insurance claims she found questionable. A call from her could mean only one thing: work, or a work-related problem that couldn't wait.

"Where are you, Hamilton?"

"Costa Rica."

"Oh, God! I can't believe it," DeSilva yelled.

St. James yanked the cell from his ear.

A group of shrieking teenagers hijacked the pool and jumped in, cannonball style.

The Righteous Brothers singing "You've Lost That Lovin' Feelin'" blared from outdoor speakers.

Dozer had arranged with the hotel for some local kids to take the bananas after St. James proposed to Anna. Several children rushed toward the fruit, competing to gather the most.

Dozer and Smythe retreated to their rooms, hoping Global wouldn't ruin their vacation.

St. James wanted a quieter place. "Too much noise here, Mary. I'll call you back from the room."

The remaining singers offered their congratulations and left. Anna looked at St. James. "What is it?"

St. James put an arm around her. "Let's go to the room, and I'll reconnect with DeSilva. See what she wants."

Anna covered her face with both hands — new tears, less happy ones, welling in her eyes. "I was afraid of this! DeSilva only calls when she wants you to drop everything. Never a social call. Did she even say congratulations?"

"She did, actually."

"That's a shocker."

St. James held her hand. "Believe me, dear, I don't want anything to shatter this precious moment."

Then why did you take the call, Anna wanted to ask. Instead, she followed him mutely back to their room. Without another word to her, St. James grabbed a pen and some paper, sat down at a desk, and returned DeSilva's call.

Anna kicked off her shoes and flopped on the bed, bitterly burying her nose in a book, while listening with one ear.

"What's this about, Mary?"

"Claims from Costa Rica."

St. James couldn't believe the coincidence. "Shit!"

DeSilva didn't understand St. James's response. "Yes, it's shit."

St. James sighed. "Okay, what do we know?"

Anna fumed into her book. She knew that sigh. She knew what that question meant. *What do we know* could only mean that Hamilton intended to take this case, whatever it might be — engagement be damned. And he hadn't even talked to her. Not a word. He'd barely offered any resistance.

St. James sat with his back to Anna, oblivious, while he listened to DeSilva.

"Three notaries have allegations against them regarding real estate title issues. We negotiated smaller ones that were not worth the legal fees. Now, the claims are growing. I'm hoping to prevent them from escalating."

"So you're assuming they're fraudulent?"

DeSilva ignored his comment. "I'm counting on you proving they're fraudulent."

"Haven't you set a precedent by paying some?"

"Lawyers say each claim stands on its merit."

"Police?"

"The OIJ handles such matters."

"Costa Rica's FBI," St. James said.

"Right. There's a Captain Jiménez heading up the investigation. I'll email everything to you. I have to go now, Hamilton. I'm swamped." DeSilva ended the call, leaving St. James staring at his phone.

It stunned him how completely Global had managed to overshadow the euphoria of his engagement.

Anna put her book aside, a tear rolling down her cheek. "Well?"

St. James sat down next to her on the bed and repeated his conversation with DeSilva. Everything he was saying confirmed to Anna that he meant to take the job. DeSilva had told him to jump, and he was asking, *how high*?

Anna rolled away from St. James and stood next to the bed with her arms crossed. She glared at him, and he looked back at her, confused.

"No. No way!" she shouted.

"What—"

"This is the most important day of my life — of *our* lives. I don't want it ruined with work."

"But—"

"You're going ahead with DeSilva without any consideration for my feelings."

"I don't know that! I haven't promised her anything yet."

"Yes, but all signs point to yes. You took the call, you marched up here to get some quiet, and you let her explain the details of the case. How are you going to back out now?"

St. James looked uncertain.

"I would think that a man who proposed as creatively as you just did would know that marriage is a union of two partners. Partners who make major decisions together." She hung near his face and pointed at him, then herself. Then she stood up straight and turned away. "You're treating me as a researcher, not a future wife."

St. James turned red. For once, he had no idea what to say.

His inability to respond made Anna more upset. She gave him a few more seconds to defend himself. When no words came, she walked out and slammed the door behind her.

***

Scouring the hotel from top to bottom, St. James eventually found Anna sitting at the Brisa Bar, sipping a vodka martini. He climbed onto the stool next to her and ordered a double Macallan. They sat in silence for a time.

St. James turned to her. "I am so sorry, Anna. The last thing I want is to hurt you."

Anna said nothing — her hurt obvious.

"I have no excuse," he said after a sip of scotch. "It's just that I've been dealing with DeSilva on my own for so long that my responses to her are automatic. But it was thoughtless of me." Anna raised her head, and he tried to meet her eyes. "I should have said a firm *no* before she even got started. I shouldn't have even taken the call."

Anna nodded and took a sip. "I suppose, on some level, I understand all of that," she whispered. "I'm just disappointed because I thought this day would be as important to you as it was for me."

"It is! I assure you. You're the only person I've ever had a serious relationship with. No one else has had a chance to train me."

Anna laughed at that. "You consider yourself trainable?"

St. James shrugged. "Maybe."

A faint smile flickered and disappeared from the corner of her mouth. "Let's face it, you love to work." St. James looked at her guiltily, and she met his eyes. "And if I'm honest, it's one of the things I love about you."

St. James smiled at her gratefully, but she returned his gaze with a stern look.

"When I say partners, I don't mean just in life. I mean in investigations, too."

St. James listened and nodded. "I promise to be more sensitive to us being partners in every way. Honestly, I thought that's what I was doing. I could never have solved the German case without your brilliant research. You were with me every step of the way. Essential to our success. I didn't say that enough." St. James drank more scotch, waiting for Anna's reaction.

Anna finished her martini, contemplating St. James's words. "Maybe I overreacted," she offered softly.

"No! You didn't. I needed a wake-up call, and you gave it to me."

Anna smiled at his confession.

St. James leaned in and touched her arm. "So, partner, what do you think we should do about DeSilva's offer?"

Anna paused. "I think we should find out more and probably take it. Might as well make hay while we can."

"Maybe it'll be an easy case, and we can get back to vacationing in a few days."

Anna laughed and said, "Maybe."

St. James raised his hand to order another round of drinks. "You know, I've been told San José is one of the best places in the world to buy an engagement ring. That's the first thing we'll do when we arrive."

Anna's anger was slowly backing off. "Something to look forward to, I guess."

St. James stared off, anxious to change the subject. "Remember what Rodríguez said?"

Anna's eyes had turned red when tears of happiness blended with tears of disappointment. "What?"

"The increase in organized crime, corporate fraud. DeSilva's call could be something to do with that."

"Could be," Anna said, dabbing her eyes with a cocktail napkin.

"I should contact this Captain Jiménez to see what we're up against before I talk to Dozer and Louis."

"Makes sense."

***

When Anna and St. James returned to the suite, Anna's frosty view of St. James's behaviour had thawed.

His cell buzzed with DeSilva's emails listing contact details for everyone involved in the files she wanted investigated. He saved everything on his laptop.

St. James emailed Jiménez asking for a meeting. Jiménez refused, wanting nothing to do with a private detective from up north. "Investigations are going well. Don't need help from anyone who hasn't sworn allegiance to Costa Rican law."

DeSilva would never accept him giving up, so St. James persisted. After several polite requests for a Zoom session, Jiménez finally relented. "I'll give you fifteen minutes, not a second more."

An hour later, the two sat face-to-face by computer.

St. James gave a quick summary of his professional life up to that point, recounting his work with global law enforcement, responsibilities, diverse skills, and efforts to expedite criminal justice.

Jiménez continued to refuse help.

A muscular man in a black suit, his strong, square jawline and deep Spanish accent lent him a touch of authority.

"I'm not here to question your work," St. James assured. "Just to recover assets for Global. We would pool information. Expedite a successful conclusion to your criminal case and my recovery objective. Minimize duplication."

Jiménez lit a Delta cigarette and studied St. James. Then he shook his head. "Relentless determination!" He took a puff. "Okay, I'll reserve my decision until I've made a few inquiries."

Jiménez stroked his pencil-thin moustache. "I'm not committing to anything other than a review of your past work relationships. Nothing more."

"Fair enough. Would you like some references?"

Jiménez bent forward to flick ashes in a glass tray. "No!"

St. James frowned.

Jiménez cast a cunning smile. "I find contacts provided by people I'm investigating tend to weigh in their favour. I prefer my own sources. I'll contact you with my decision once I've made it. Whatever it is, it will be final. Understand?"

"Yes, Sir. Thank you."

Jiménez ended the meeting.

Anna inserted a bookmark in the mystery she was reading. "How'd it go?"

"Not sure."

CHAPTER 6

Smythe shook his head and downed his cabernet. "I knew damn well this was too good to be true!"

Dozer took a long pull of his Imperial and sighed.

St. James drummed his fingers on the table. "This is one of the most beautiful places in the world. Anna and I are happy and engaged, yet we're all acting like we just came from a wake. I don't know about you, but I intend to enjoy myself. Global be damned."

Dozer reflected on St. James's words. "Acting like kids who didn't get their way." He made an imaginary sweep of the grounds. "But let's not forget, Global makes all this possible. The money's incredible, and the perks … well, just look around."

Smythe gave Dozer a look. "What church are you preaching in?"

Dozer grinned. "The church of, 'I don't give a damn.'"

Anna's face lit up. "Right. Moping is a waste of energy. Hamilton and I have our whole lives ahead of us, and so do you two sad sacks."

"Hey," Smythe protested, but Dozer laughed and said, "The lady has a point."

St. James smiled and leaned back, considering the OIJ. "Hard to say when I'll hear from Jiménez. It might take a day or two for him to decide if we're worthy. So, let's have a proper celebration."

Anna sounded more upbeat. "Wonderful!"

"Why don't we ask Rodríguez about a tour for tomorrow?" Smythe suggested. "We don't have to jump even if the OIJ decides it'll work with us. Let's take a couple of days to unwind."

Dozer took a swig of his Imperial and grinned. "For the first time, I agree with you, Louis."

St. James signalled for another round. "Let's do it!"

Dozer grabbed his cell and returned to a website he'd seen earlier. "Think I found us the perfect restaurant."

Anna drained her first pinot grigio before the second arrived.

"El Pelicano. Terrific menu — seafood, something for everyone," Dozer read aloud. "Hey, listen to this. It's right across the street. Part of the resort."

Anna smiled. "Clinches it for me."

St. James rimmed his glass with a forefinger. "Me too."

Smythe left the table to phone Rodríguez. Dozer crossed the lawn to request a reservation for six-thirty at El Pelicano.

The second round of drinks arrived just as Dozer returned.

St. James sipped his Macallan and looked at Smythe. "What about our tour?"

"Too late for tomorrow. All booked up. Rodríguez is trying to fit us in for the day after."

Anna glanced at Smythe. "Thursday?"

"Yes."

Anna thought about the change. "I'll do tomorrow what I had planned for today," she said, snuggling closer to St. James, "before this handsome man made my dreams come true."

Smythe rolled his eyes and faked a gag with his forefinger.

Anna scrunched her nose at Smythe in mock protest and St. James laughed into his whiskey before taking a sip.

***

El Pelicano's open-air setup absorbed Diria's traffic noise and welcomed refreshing breezes. As they entered the restaurant, Dozer slipped the manager a fifty for permission to announce St. James's and Anna's engagement.

Smythe looked around the restaurant approvingly. "Excellent choice, Dozer."

Dozer's eyes followed a tall, attractive woman as she glided by.

A young dark-haired server introduced himself as Nicolás and escorted them to a white linen table under soft-glowing lanterns.

Nicolás wore a polite smile.

Anna eyed the drink menu and ordered a vodka martini.

St. James didn't wait. "Double shot of your best single malt."

"Imperial for me," said Dozer.

Nicolás turned to Smythe.

"Red wine of some sort."

Nicolás smiled. "Les Petite Jamelle, Languedoc grenache?"

"Sure." Smythe had no idea what he'd just agreed to.

Minutes later, with drinks in hand, they began to settle in. Dozer stood up, holding his Imperial, and studied the room. As St. James eyed him curiously, Dozer waited for a few more people to drift in from Diria Boulevard. Then he picked up a small salad fork from the table and clinked his bottle.

"Ladies and gentlemen, may I have your attention?"

Silverware clinked on plates as almost everyone in the place turned to look at Dozer. Only a couple of servers continued to move among the tables.

Dozer motioned toward the engaged couple with a sweeping gesture. "My two dearest friends here became engaged this morning. I'd like to propose a toast to their future."

Several people cupped their ears, signalling an inability to hear over the traffic noise. Dozer repeated himself in a louder voice.

Everyone clapped.

"I have watched Hamilton and Anna together for some time now; they are the very definition of love. Please join me in wishing the soon-to-be Mr. and Mrs. Hamilton St. James a lifetime of happiness!"

A chorus of "hear, hear" swept the room, along with the tinkling of glasses.

Anna turned beet red as she smiled bashfully around the room. St. James raised his glass in Dozer's direction to thank him for his kind words.

Dozer sat back down with a satisfied nod. "You are most welcome."

Nicolás came around again, with a complimentary bottle of wine sent over by the manager, and the four thanked him profusely and gave their food choices.

For the rest of the evening, the team immersed themselves in a seafood extravaganza. They feasted on giant shrimp, yellowfin tuna, and a beautiful ceviche of mahi-mahi and sea bass, washing it all down with three bottles of a crisp, refreshing 2018 chardonnay from the Alma Fría Campbell Ranch.

The air filled with the energetic strumming of guitars of a mariachi band from Nicoya. Dressed in colourful charros and wide-brimmed sombreros, they serenaded the team with traditional Mexican music.

St. James paid the bill at ten o'clock, and they went down the steps to the crosswalk. Streams of scooters and cars prevented them from crossing to the resort. A kind security guard rescued them, halting traffic to let them pass.

Unlocking the door to their suite, St. James's phone buzzed with a text from Captain Jiménez: *Call me!*

CHAPTER 7

Wednesday morning, Anna rose at six, preparing for a day at the pool. While St. James slept, she changed into a bikini and left a note explaining her whereabouts.

St. James woke at seven, shaved, showered, and dressed in a white Greg Norman golf shirt and black shorts. After slipping into canvas deck shoes, he headed to the dining room. Composing emails and texts, he paused periodically to sip coffee and enjoy bacon and eggs.

Dozer texted that he'd chartered a fishing boat for the day. Smythe let the group know he'd booked a horseback riding lesson at the stables Rodríguez mentioned near the Diria resort.

St. James planned his day: documents to review and a call with Jiménez to schedule. He texted Jiménez to arrange a video conference.

Jiménez was unavailable for half an hour. St. James used the time to peruse insurance claims until he connected with the captain forty minutes later.

"Saw your text late at night," St. James began. "Seemed rude to call then."

"Wasn't urgent. Just wanted to give you the feedback from my sources."

St. James smiled. "Did I make the cut?"

"I talked with several authorities in our network. They agreed you contributed to their investigations without interfering. You're well-regarded." A faint smile crept over Jiménez's face. "Though they mentioned that you're arrogant."

The words hung there, but before St. James could reply, Jiménez smiled and added, "That's not a problem for me."

St. James looked puzzled. Jiménez beamed, pointing to himself. "I'm arrogant, too."

St. James smiled. "Does this mean we can work together?"

"Means I'll give it a try. There are a few rules."

St. James raised his brow as Jiménez continued. "Don't keep anything from me. Don't take the law into your hands like you did with Scotland Yard. We have regular sessions to update each other on everything, no matter what. And you don't undermine my command with subordinates."

St. James smiled. "The person you talked with at Scotland Yard?"

"DI Phyllis Joy."

St. James beamed. "Bet that was a colourful conversation."

Jiménez grinned and picked up a notebook from his desk. "Colourful enough for me to jot down a few notes."

"This should be interesting."

"It is. She said, and I quote, 'St. James is the most annoying, arrogant, tantalizing son-of-a-bitch I've ever worked with.'"

St. James laughed. "Tantalizing. Curious word choice. She say anything else?"

Jiménez flipped to the next page. "Just that you're 'the best God-damned detective she's ever been paired with,' that you solved a 'difficult multinational fraud,' and that I'd be a 'damn fool' not to have you on my team."

St. James shook his head. "Speaks her mind."

"She does, indeed. So — do you accept my terms?"

St. James countered. "Only if you accept mine."

Jiménez scowled.

St. James smiled. "You don't keep anything from me. You take no action that jeopardizes my ability to recover assets. Update me on everything, no matter what. And don't undermine my relationship with Global Insurance."

Jiménez laughed. "See, we are like-minded, Mr. St. James."

St. James smirked. "Like-minded, arrogant, and perhaps, a little blunt."

"Could be the beginning of a beautiful relationship."

St. James returned the captain's smile. "Or the worst we've ever experienced."

Jiménez shrugged.

St. James cleared his throat. "So, what can you tell me?"

Jiménez lit a Delta, took a few puffs, and opened a dossier.

"Five years ago, all our efforts were focused entirely on Italian, Mexican, and Colombian cocaine traffickers. Most of those resources are still in place. The focus on these traffickers means our current fraud investigations are intertwined with longstanding efforts against major criminal organizations."

St. James shrugged. "The mob?"

Jiménez took another puff of his Delta. "No such thing as one mob. There's competition for where the money is. We're dealing with a complex web of criminal activity, not a single, monolithic organization."

"These groups mainly local or international?"

"Some Tico-run, some multinational, with Tico frontmen and foot soldiers."

"Tico?"

Jiménez looked surprised. "Tico. It's the term Costa Ricans use to refer to themselves. Like 'Kiwi' for New Zealanders or 'Aussie' for Australians."

"Ah," St. James said. "Any Tico mob bosses in your sights?"

"There've been a few. Probably the most colourful is Baca. Carlos Baca. Patterns himself after a figure named Elfego Baca. Even calls himself Elfego when he wants to convince people he's a stone-cold killer."

St. James thought. "Where does the word Tico come from?"

"From the way Costa Ricans often add 'tico' to words, as a diminutive. Like 'chiquitico' for something small, or 'hermanitico,' for little brother."

"That's cute." St. James turned back to business. "I'll bet Baca's cute, too."

"Cute as a pit viper."

"What can you tell me about the cocaine trade?"

Jiménez nodded. "Still the highest margin crime. But there are more scams now. Criminals are diversifying, adapting to changing circumstances."

St. James hiked his eyebrows. "Something different?"

"New fraud schemes grew during COVID, for obvious reasons. People conducted activities online from home. In-person appointments like doctor and dentist visits were postponed when possible."

St. James gave a nonchalant gesture. "Same as everywhere else in the world."

"Yes. Some Costa Rican laws make certain frauds attractive here. Changes in travel patterns also brought greater opportunities for criminal activities. Real estate fraud has taken off in the past three years. We know the mob's involved, but we can't prove anything."

St. James paused. "Informants?"

Jiménez nodded. "Too scared to talk. Penalty for snitching is death, or worse — torture and maiming while still alive."

St. James winced. "Worked a case like that in England. Hideous."

Jiménez showed indifference. "Crooks ensure layers of accountants, lawyers, and representatives between themselves and their victims. Hands are never dirty enough to lay successful charges. We've tried to connect with the abused many times to gather evidence, but luck hasn't been on our side."

"Hmm." St. James rubbed his square jaw. "I'll read Global's insurance claim files over the next few days. Then I'll come to San José and work through yours. That should bring me up to speed enough to be of some help."

"Sensible approach, St. James. The word *enough* is critical. We haven't been able to gather enough substance to move forward. Maybe we'll finally change that."

"Understand. Do you recommend a place to stay in San José?"

"The hotels are all reasonable in the downtown core. My personal favourite is the Presidente. Small. Older. Well-maintained. Rates are competitive. Close to the courthouse, where my office is."

"Hotel Presidente it is."

The computer display fluttered as the consultation ended.

St. James only needed a half day to finish Global's claims, but time was essential to cushion the team's disappointment. The team's holiday was not supposed to include work, so he would need more than a dinner to soften the bad news.

By midday, he had waded through three-quarters of DeSilva's files. Familiar boilerplate paragraphs enabled him to skim through the pages. They described various fraud schemes and how they might relate to the cases in Costa Rica.

At twelve-thirty, St. James found Anna lounging on a beige chaise by the pool, nose in a mystery novel.

He leaned down and kissed her, then sat down. "Fun morning?"

Anna smiled. "Terrific. I've been in and out of the pool twice and I'm reading a wonderful book. My idea of heaven. What about you?"

St. James recounted his discussion with Jiménez and the highlights of the claims he'd read.

"You have strange ways of relaxing."

"I realize that."

"Got a sense of what we're dealing with?"

"Not yet. Won't know until we meet Jiménez on Monday or Tuesday."

Anna sat up and gathered her things. "I'm famished. Let's have lunch."

After they'd enjoyed Caesar salads and pinot grigio, Anna returned to her lounge, and St. James strolled to the room to finish reading DeSilva's claims.

At three-thirty, when he passed the final page, he reflected on what he'd read: case after case of distraught clients suing notaries for corrupting their land titles. Specifics were scarce. The notaries had all filed insurance claims with Global to cover liabilities arising from client lawsuits.

St. James poured a coffee, went out on the balcony, and stared out at paradise. With his eyes fixed on the gently rolling ocean, he thought about what he had read, possible theories forming in his mind.

"There's a pattern."

CHAPTER 8

Alajuela, Costa Rica

Carlos Sánchez slid open the glass door that separated his family room from the deck encircling a kidney-shaped swimming pool.

Tall, thin and bald, he wore a red-and-white beach cover-up and slip-on sandals. He strode onto the deck, turned slowly, and surveyed the dense thicket of trees surrounding his property. The Guácimo trees pleased him. Tall, statuesque Cedro Espinos — Spanish cedars, with their trunks and branches covered in giant thorns — enhanced his feeling of security and seclusion.

Nearby, a stand of Guanacaste trees, Costa Rica's national symbol, stood guard. Their broad canopies and flat, elephant-ear-shaped seed pods added to the fortress effect, deterring potential threats. The living wall between his house and the world had been his vision — a testament to his will to survive.

Sánchez scanned the periphery, listening closely for any for any signs of disturbance. The slightest movement took on a threatening quality, as each flutter of leaves or snapping of a twig amplified his paranoia.

He forced himself to focus, but an unsettling emotion gnawed at him. At last, he retreated inside his upscale white stucco bungalow. He brewed a fresh black coffee, grabbed the day's newspaper, and headed back out to the swimming pool.

He positioned himself in one of eight rainbow-coloured hammock chairs that looked like they belonged on a movie set. Sipping coffee, he admired the manicured gardens. The sun climbed higher in the sky, casting shimmering reflections on the pool's surface.

Sánchez contemplated the life he had created. His legal career afforded him luxuries and freedoms that many would envy. But at what cost? The unease that had begun to creep in seemed to intensify with each passing moment.

His thoughts drifted to his three wives: Maria, his young love, who left when his dedication to law eclipsed their life together. Anxious, sensitive Isabella, who couldn't bear the constant threat of violence that went hand-in-hand with his job. And then there was beautiful, rudderless Elena — the bottomless pit of need who ensnared him in his thirties. He'd been obsessed with her for a time, but in the end, like Maria, she couldn't stay with a husband who seemed more married to his businesses than to her.

Had they even been different women? Their stories, their complaints, even their appearance had begun to merge. Together, they told a story of personal failure, all pointing back to him.

Work was no easier. It was only a matter of time before the Boss became unhappy with him. He knew how that would end. He also knew the time was approaching.

The solitude at home was both a refuge and a reminder of the void left by his failed marriages. Once a lavish retreat secluded in nature, his estate had become a sanctuary from the world's relentless criminal pursuits.

Yet, even in this serene setting, danger loomed. Shadows seemed to grow darker, the rustling in the trees more deliberate, as though something unseen waited beyond his line of sight.

The offer from the OIJ beckoned to him like a distant lighthouse in a stormy sea. Witness protection in the United States, the promise of safety and anonymity, a chance to start anew, without the constant threat of reprisal. He'd contemplated it for months, wrestling with the fear that had become an unwelcome and ever-present companion.

Talking to the OIJ would be treason in the Boss's eyes and would be treated as such. Sánchez shuddered at the thought of the torments that would be visited upon him if anyone learned of his conversations with the agency.

As the morning wore on, the shadows across the deck seemed to lengthen, and Sánchez began to feel as though someone else was in the house with him, standing at his elbow, full of silent menace.

Echoes of past decisions mingled with the uncertainty of the future. Combined, they amounted to a symphony of doubt and dread.

His intense look darted toward the edges of the property. He felt it now — something was out there, ready to breach his oasis. Something or someone.

Sánchez sighed, leaned back in his chair, and closed his eyes. An old mantra from a meditation class he once took floated through his thoughts. Focusing on it now, he tried to let himself be enveloped by the moment's serenity.

The world outside could wait. Yet, the thought of the OIJ's offer and his growing paranoia were inescapable.

His thoughts shifted from safety to wealth and back again. What good was wealth without someone to share it with? Inviting another person into his world was impossible. His three ex-wives were proof of that. Leaving it all was now a more attractive option.

Sánchez stood, frustrated by the endless loop of worry. His eyes scanned the pool, the water inviting. Perhaps a swim would free his mind and bring him relief.

He removed the cover-up, tossing it onto a chair. His movements were jittery and unsteady.

He climbed onto the diving board, the surface bouncing beneath him. He jumped once. Twice. The water below rippled, serene, but the air around him felt heavy and oppressive.

Arms outstretched, Sánchez took one final leap, launching himself toward the pool's deep end. A loud crack echoed the moment he hit the water, followed by a sickening thud. His head exploded on impact, brain matter spraying over the shallow end. Blood fanned out in ripples across the pool, mingling with the water carrying his lifeless body.

CHAPTER 9

Smythe shifted in his chair, wincing. "My ass is so sore!"

Anna burst into uncontrollable laughter. "So much for childhood dreams, Louis," she hooted.

Dozer's eyes sparkled with amusement. "Not quite the horseback adventure you imagined, huh, Louis?"

Smythe smirked, shaking his head. "Catherine wouldn't stop, no matter how loud I hollered. We galloped along the entire beach — at least three kilometres."

St. James raised an eyebrow. "Catherine?"

Smythe shook his head. "Camp's chief torturer."

Laughter rippled around the table.

The team sat at the Brisa restaurant, savouring succulent lobster. The crashing waves created a soothing backdrop as the sun dipped lower.

Thiago, a portly waiter, arrived with a smile and placed three bottles of Yao Ming Cabernet Sauvignon 2018 in front of St. James.

Thiago uncorked one bottle, poured a small sample, and watched St. James swirl the glass and savour the aroma. When St. James nodded approval, Thiago topped each glass and retreated to the bar.

St. James broke the brief stillness as the crystal glasses clinked in a toast. "We must have something better to talk about than Louis's backside."

Dozer smiled broadly as he slid a photograph across the table.

St. James's eyes widened as he took in the image. "Look at that yellowfin! Must be at least two hundred and fifty pounds."

"Three hundred," Dozer corrected with a satisfied grin.

The photo circulated, each person murmuring their amazement.

Smythe squinted at the image. "Beginner's luck."

Dozer cast him a look. "You wish!"

Anna held the photo up to the fading light. "Beautiful fish, but what do you do with something that size? You'd need an army to eat it before it spoiled."

Still excited, Dozer said, "The captain handles everything — cleans the fish and sells the meat to local restaurants."

St. James leaned back, twirling his wine glass. "How long did it take to land him?"

"About two hours. A brutal fight." Dozer flexed his arms as if still sore. "Thought my arms would fall off before I got him on board."

Anna beamed. "Sounds like you've found a new passion."

"Without a doubt. Thrill of a lifetime."

Smythe turned to Anna, shifting the focus. "What about you? What adventure did you have today?"

Anna twirled a piece of lobster on her fork. "Oh, nothing as thrilling as Dozer's epic battle. Just swimming — enjoying the quiet. Boring."

Dozer snorted. "Boring, my foot. That's what you came for."

Anna laughed, her eyes sparkling as she took a bite. "I also reviewed Hamilton's notes from his review of solicitor claims filed with DeSilva."

Smythe looked thoughtful as he addressed St. James. "And you? Busy with work as usual?"

St. James sighed, shaking his head. "Of course. Spent most of the day going through legal documents and organized a Zoom call with Jiménez."

Dozer groaned. "So, what's the latest? Fill us in?"

St. James swirled his glass. "All tangled in legalities, land titles, and trouble with Spanish gangs. I don't think you and Louis need to be involved."

Smythe perked up with a grin. "Suits me. Rather stay here, away from messes."

Dozer frowned. "Spanish gangs mean I'm in. Can't risk you getting shot like in Ottawa. You came close to meeting the devil. Might not be so lucky next time. I'd hate to lose my cash flow."

St. James smiled. "Your concern for my well-being is touching, Dozer."

Anna glanced at Smythe. "Have a tour planned for tomorrow, don't we?"

Smythe nodded. "Yep, Rodríguez is picking us up early. We'll drive through Tamarindo, head up the coast, visit some small villages, and enter the rainforest. There's tubing, a swim in the Rio Celeste, and lunch. Don't forget comfortable shoes — there's a bit of hiking involved."

Anna lit up. "Sounds amazing. Always wanted to experience a rainforest."

Dozer leaned back in his chair. "Looking forward to learning more about the country. There must be more than drinking and fishing," Dozer grinned, "not that there's anything wrong with that."

St. James agreed. "Thanks for setting that up, Louis."

The conversation waned. St. James's phone buzzed. He checked the screen — Captain Jiménez. "What can I do for you, Captain?"

"Carlos Sánchez was found dead this morning. Floating in his pool."

St. James stiffened, gripping the phone tightly. "Dead? How?"

"Shot in the head."

A chill spread over the table as St. James's face darkened, and he ended the call. His voice dropped to a strained whisper. "Shit."

Dozer's grin vanished. Anna set her fork down. Her eyes turned to Smythe, who sat frozen with the sudden news.

St. James stared off. "We lost a key source of information. Sánchez was found dead in his pool. Shot in the head."

Smythe's forehead creased. "Suspects?"

St. James shook his head. "Too soon."

Anna reached for her wine glass, her earlier excitement gone. "Think it's connected to the Spanish gangs?"

St. James hesitated, his mind racing. "Possibly. This could be bigger than I thought."

"Bigger and more dangerous," Dozer said. "We can't ignore this, Hamilton. Not now."

St. James exhaled slowly. "No, we can't."

CHAPTER 10

Thursday, Rodríguez arrived at the Diria resort at seven, and for the next twelve hours, he led the team through an unforgettable adventure.

They experienced the iconic Volcán Arenal and gaped, spellbound, at the sight of lava trickling from its summit. Then they went to La Fortuna for a traditional midday meal of rice and beans, succulent grilled meats, and fresh tropical fruits. While tubing down the sky-blue waters of the Celeste, Smythe fell out of the raft. Dozer grumbled over Smythe's carelessness as he fished him out.

They walked along a well-marked trail through the lush rainforest, crossing suspension bridges before relaxing in the rejuvenating hot springs. Rodríguez pointed out toucans, howler monkeys, sloths, and vibrant butterflies.

For dinner, the team enjoyed a three-course meal at the Brisa restaurant. Lively conversation quieted as the day's excitement gave way to a more reflective mood. St. James, preoccupied with Carlos Sánchez's death, retreated to his room to review plans.

**

St. James sat alone on the balcony early Friday morning, savouring the tranquil time.

Watching a ride-on mower cross the lawn, his thoughts drifted to Sánchez's murder. He opened his laptop, accessed the Costa Rica file, and scrolled to Sánchez's section. Below him, teens tossed a frisbee around, and morning swimmers rushed to claim lounge chairs by the pool.

He read Sánchez's first claim three times, learning nothing more the third time than the first.

Russell Allaband from Greenwich Village, New York, owned beachfront real estate north of Tamarindo. While Allaband was in the U.S., he accused Sánchez of misconduct. The details were unclear. Sánchez denied the allegations but faced a lawsuit from Allaband.

Sánchez's insurance claim showed Allaband instructed the property transfer to Gael Vargas, a public accountant in San José. The claim didn't detail the transfer price, but Allaband's $995,000 lawsuit hinted at high stakes.

St. James found little else of substance in the documents, making it apparent why DeSilva requested the investigation.

He poured another coffee and dialled Allaband's New York number. It rang twice before a strong New England accent answered.

"So, you're validating that son-of-a-bitch's insurance claim?" he growled.

St. James's tone was deliberately calm. "Not sure."

"What do you mean?"

Sánchez isn't with us anymore."

"What do you mean?" Allaband repeated.

"He was murdered."

There was a pause, and then Allaband's voice dropped. "Jesus! I didn't know that. What do I do now?"

"Nothing. Your lawyer will name Sánchez's estate as the defendant."

Allaband's irritation heightened. "Shit. More legal fees."

St. James could hear the rustle of papers. The habit of an anxious man trying to organize his way out of chaos, he thought.

St. James said, "Afraid I have a few questions."

"What do you want to know?"

"When were you in Costa Rica last?"

"Almost three years ago, I think. Before COVID. From February to May."

"How often did you travel back and forth?"

"About four times." His tone carried a hint of defensiveness as if he was worried about where St. James was leading.

"Do you have documentation to support all the trips?"

"Yes, I'll send you the summary."

"Did anyone ask about your house while you were there?"

"Nothing that stood out."

Something about the way he spoke made St. James doubt Allaband's answer.

"Did you meet with Sánchez during any of those trips?"

"Not for business. Played golf."

"Did you go to his office or sign anything?"

"I think I signed something about property taxes — an objection to an assessment."

St. James made a note. "Have a copy?"

"Yes. I'll send it."

"Did Sánchez handle any other legal work for you?"

"No." The denial was almost too quick.

"How would you describe your relationship with him?"

"Just lawyer-client. Professional."

St. James noted the underlying uncertainty. "But you golfed together."

"Not often."

"Did you entertain at your place?"

"Couple of cocktail parties."

"How many people?"

"Thirty or so."

"Sánchez came to both?"

"Yes."

"How did he act?"

Allaband wavered, a slight crack in his otherwise steady demeanour. "Strange question to ask."

St. James smiled to himself. "Goes to the heart of behavioural change — worry, stress, anything that might indicate he could be threatened."

"He was normal. Calm. Friendly. Same as always."

"Did anyone spend an unusual amount of time with him?"

"No. A few seemed interested in his opinions, but nothing unusual."

"Did Sánchez ever mention personal conflicts or client disputes?"

"No, he kept things professional. Never anything personal."

"Any known enemies?"

"None that I'm aware of."

"Anything unusual happen at the parties?"

"Just the usual chaos. One guest tried to enter a private room, but I think they were just curious."

"Did you take any security precautions for these gatherings?"

"I had security staff at the entrance. Nothing elaborate."

"Did Sánchez mention any business deals or investments?"

Allaband thought for a moment. "He mentioned a new venture, but it was only in the planning stages."

"What was the new venture?"

"Something to do with technology; nothing real estate related."

"Do you remember if any guest focused more on Sánchez than anyone else?"

"There was one, but I don't remember anything specific. They talked a lot."

"Did you notice any changes in Sánchez's behaviour?"

Allaband pondered this. "Hard to say. I suppose he seemed a bit more reserved than in our previous encounters."

St. James scribbled notes, his mind racing. "Can you text me the names of the attendees along with the other documents you mentioned? Someone might remember more."

"As soon as we finish the call."

"Did you know every guest personally?"

"All except two. Companions of other guests."

"When you send the list, please identify those you didn't know personally and those who spent the most time with Sánchez."

"Okay."

"Did Sánchez do any real estate work for you before?"

"Yes, he helped me sell another home further inland."

"And that went well?"

"No issues."

"What about the oceanfront parcel? Did you authorize him to sell it?"

Allaband's voice rose, anger simmering just beneath the surface. "No!"

St. James noticed the shift in tone. More defensive. "What happened with the real estate?"

"I stayed in New York after my trips that year. I was unsure of my Costa Rican property tax assessment, so I called the National Registry. They informed me that no taxes were owed, and that Gael Vargas now owned my residence."

"Did you contact Vargas?"

"I tried calling him several times, but his voicemail said he's in conference."

"What about Sánchez?"

"I tried him too, but he wouldn't take my calls when I demanded an explanation."

"And you're sure he facilitated the property transfer?"

"According to the Registry, he did."

"When did you check with the Registry?"

"Mid-August of that year."

"Mr. Allaband, please double-check your records and send me everything related to this."

"All right."

"One final thing — how was your experience with the OIJ?"

"I gave a statement to Captain Jiménez when I hired a lawyer to sue Sánchez, but nothing came of it. Jiménez said it could take ten years for a case to be resolved. And I didn't have a hope in hell of getting any money or my property back."

CHAPTER 11

St. James was still interviewing Allaband when Anna came back from breakfast, changed quickly, and then left again for the pool at ten o'clock.

The sun shone brightly in the cloudless sky. The air was warm and mixed with the faint scent of coconut sunscreen and the salty tang of the ocean. Sounds of laughter and splashing water floated in from the swimming pool.

"Everyone's having fun but me," St. James mumbled. He scanned the attendee lists for the house parties Allaband had mentioned. As he read through the names, he couldn't shake the feeling that he was peering into a hidden world.

He didn't expect the names on the list to reveal much, but it was a necessary step for a credible investigation.

"Most seem to be couples," he said, his voice barely above a whisper.

Forty-one attended the first, thirty-eight the second. "Slightly more than Allaband's estimate," he murmured. St. James ran his finger down both lists, picturing the social dynamics at the parties. He could almost see the wine flowing and hear the play of Spanish and English as Ticos and ex-pats mingled over plates of giant shrimp and other delicacies.

Anna returned from the pool around noon, damp hair glistening. She plopped into a chair and felt the warm, sun-drenched fabric against her skin. "I decided to take a break from the heat. Afraid of getting burned, even smeared with sunblock."

St. James smiled. "Can't have a crispy fiancée."

"What have you been up to?"

"Work, work, and more work."

"Oh? Plotting another brilliant exposé?"

St. James leaned back in his chair. "Maybe. Had a good chat with Russell Allaband."

"The one who had his house stolen?"

"That's the one."

"Find out much?"

"Well, he hosted a couple of parties when he was here. A mix of local elites and expatriates. He sent the guest lists for both gatherings."

"And?"

"And … since we're partners, I thought you could investigate the people on the lists."

Anna gave him a look. "Is this for real, or are you patronizing me because of our argument?"

St. James's look was inscrutable. "You gave me a wake-up call, remember? This is my way of showing I got the message."

Anna studied St. James for several seconds, then said, "Okay. I planned on staying in this afternoon anyway. Let's grab lunch first, and then I'll start."

"Deal."

For the next half hour, they shared a simple lunch of salad with roasted chicken in the cool of the air-conditioned suite. As the room service trays were being removed, St. James began pulling on his shoes.

"Where do you think you're going?" Anna asked, in a tone half spritely, half piqued.

St. James leaned over and gave her a quick kiss. "Into town. I've been here all day. Thought I'd give you some space and enjoy a little foot tour."

"Suit yourself."

Anna was climbing onto the bed with her laptop when St. James slipped out. For the next two hours, she worked through the lists, searching each name and following out leads to websites, registries, and databases all over Costa Rica.

She found a cell number for a Juan Arnez, who'd attended both Allaband parties and texted him to ask for a meeting. She explained she and St. James were investigating Allaband's property theft on behalf of Global Insurance.

Arnez didn't have time for a meeting but would accept a brief phone call.

Anna agreed, dialled the number, and introduced herself.

"Mr. Arnez, thank you for meeting. I'll get right into it. How long have you known Russell Allaband?"

Arnez paused to think. "About five years, I think."

Anna wasn't expecting such a high-pitched voice.

"How did you two meet?"

"At a fundraising dinner for the less fortunate. Allaband and I were assigned to the same table. I was interested in his investment activities, and he wanted to know about the challenges of growing and managing a chain of convenience stores. We hit it off and kept in touch."

"I see. Did you engage in any business activities after that?"

"No. Our businesses are mutually exclusive. There's no overlap."

"No common real estate interests?" Anna pressed.

"None whatsoever."

Anna could see the interview wasn't going to bear fruit, so she politely ended the call, thanking Arnez for his time — but not before feigning interest in his stores.

Anna then turned her attention to a man named Roberto Salazar, who also attended both Allaband parties. Salazar answered Anna's call, but only after three attempts. She asked similar questions to the Arnez call with the same conclusion. He would be no help to the case.

Having struck out with the first two interviews, she turned her attention back to public records, digging into the backgrounds and business activities of several other guests.

When St. James breezed back in at five, Anna barely noticed him. She jumped when he leaned down to kiss her.

"Deep into the research?" He lingered near her, noting the scent of sunscreen still on her skin.

Anna mumbled distractedly. Then she yelped and grabbed her foot and started working her fingers along the arch in a panic.

"Pins and needles?"

"I haven't moved from this spot since you left."

St. James sat next to her on the bed and wrapped his hands around her slender foot. "Good for you. So diligent." He leaned forward on his elbows and pressed into the arch of her foot with both hands. "Find anything useful?"

"I think so, but I didn't get far," she said, recovering. "How was your walk?"

"Excellent. Temperature was perfect for most of the time, and the afternoon shower held off. What did you find?"

Anna retrieved her foot with a smile of thanks for the mini massage. She leaned back into a big pile of pillows. "The first interesting thing was that only four names were common to both parties."

St. James rose from the bed and plunked himself down on a chair, the better to focus on her words and not her bare, shapely feet. "Which ones?"

"Carlos Sánchez. No surprise there. Mr. and Mrs. Jaun Arnez. Mr. and Mrs. Ramón Mora and Mr. and Mrs. Roberto Salazar."

Anna turned to her computer screen, her fingers dancing over the keys. "Got a little way with Jaun Arnez and Roberto Salazar."

"And…?"

Anna scrolled. "Arnez owns a franchise for ten AM/PM stores. Typical twenty-four-hour convenience stores."

St. James grinned. "Probably why they're called AM/PM stores."

Anna's eyes were dancing. "Suppose you think you're smart?"

"Crossed my mind," St. James said, though he looked less sure.

"Not this time, sweetheart," she said, grinning. "Arnez borrowed the acronym AM/PM from the hotel industry. It stands for 'Abierto Más, Precio Menor.'" Anna struggled with the pronunciation. "Translates into Open More, Lower Price."

"How does that relate to the hotel industry?"

"The policy allowed hotels to adjust room prices depending on demand, local events, or other factors. By having more pricing options at the same time, hotels could attract more customers, even price-sensitive ones. Arnez thought he could adapt the strategy somehow to prices for goods sold in his stores."

St. James rose out of the chair and threw himself on the bed next to Anna. "What about Salazar?"

"He owns several fast-food outlets. He and Allaband have been seen at charity events together, but I couldn't find a solid connection beyond that."

St. James pondered this. Sounds of the bustling lobby filtered in through the open window. "Hmm. What's their connection to Allaband besides friendship?"

"I'm not sure they are friends. Could be neighbours or have a common business interest."

"Could be." St. James shifted onto his back and stared at the ceiling. "What about Mora?"

"Lawyer. Haven't spoken to him. Research reveals no connection to Allaband other than social."

St. James shrugged.

"I'll keep going until I've covered everything." Anna smiled as she tapped the computer keys. "Must be a weasel in here somewhere. We'll find him."

St. James felt a surge of pride. She wasn't just assisting anymore; she was owning the investigation along with him — chasing leads, ready to sit across from suspects and draw out the truth on her own. She was becoming everything he'd hopes for — and more.

CHAPTER 12

On Friday morning, St. James and Anna strolled along the beach, hand in hand, carrying their sandals. They paused now and then to watch surfers and happened upon an older fisher preparing his weathered dory for the day.

St. James's curiosity got the best of him. "What are you fishing for, Sir?"

The angler turned from his grey boat to face the couple, squinting through the morning sun. "Oh, just wahoo, grouper, snapper. Whatever's close to shore."

"Well-maintained boat," St. James said.

The old man patted the bow. "Been my faithful companion for thirty years." His warm smile revealed a missing tooth.

St. James and Anna waved to the man and continued their walk. When they reached an unpaved parking lot, they brushed sand from their feet and slipped on the sandals to take in Tamarindo's shopping area.

Anna scheduled a hair appointment at a quaint Plaza Conchal salon for Saturday morning. St. James steered them into a leather shop and bought a sleek attaché for the investigation.

"Admit it — you're glad you left your briefcase at home," Anna chided.

St. James stroked the soft leather and looked at her innocently. "I had no choice."

After a delightful seafood lunch at Nogui's Restaurant, they strolled toward the resort.

Anna swept sand from her shirt. "How's Jackie making out with the class?"

"We emailed a bit yesterday. She's doing well — high student ratings and keeping up with the curriculum."

"Wonderful," Anna said. Then her eyes twinkled, and she poked his arm lightly. "Good of the dean to let you skip off to Costa Rica in the middle of the semester."

St. James bristled slightly. "The university knew what they were getting when they hired me. I can't be in Ottawa all the time. I have to be solving cases. It's part of me."

"I know, sweetheart. I was only teasing," Anna said. "They're lucky to have you. You're not some dusty professor teaching the same old case studies year after year. You bring that fraud course to life."

"Exactly what the chair said when they offered me the job," said St. James. "The students don't like it when I'm not there to teach, but they always appreciate a fresh case when I come back."

"I know they do. And you're lucky to have a PhD student as good as Jackie Corning covering for you."

"True." St. James took Anna's hand as they climbed onto the resort lawn.

***

The following day, while Anna was at the hairdresser, St. James booked an afternoon Sansa flight to San José and reserved a room at the Hotel Presidente. He texted the itinerary to Jiménez, then went for a long walk.

As mud-covered SUVs and passenger trucks rumbled past him, he hugged the side of the road and thought about his call with Allaband. He replayed every detail of their conversation, looking for the clue that would help him understand the feeling in his gut that something was off about the man. It was subtle but unmistakable, and St. James couldn't dismiss the possibility that Allaband had colluded with Sánchez to facilitate the fraudulent property transaction.

When he finally circled back to the resort, St. James looked down at his linen shorts and shirt and realized that he was coated in a fine layer of dust. *The price of a walk-and-think*, he thought.

He found Anna by the pool, stretched out on a lounge chair, staring at her iPad.

"Still hunting down information about the party guests?"

Anna looked up and smiled. "Yes, Sir. How was your walk?"

"Refreshing. And productive."

Anna reached out and shook a little cloud of dust from the hem of his shirt. "Looks like you've been on a nature hike."

He laughed without explaining and pulled a chair next to her lounge. "Any sign of Dozer and Smythe?"

Anna produced a yellow sticky note from inside her iPad cover. St. James recognized Louis's messy scrawl. *Dozer touring Volcano Brewing Co. I'm at a foodie show. See you 2nite.*

"Well, I'm glad they're enjoying themselves," St. James said. "That's what I wanted."

***

At breakfast the next day, Dozer eyed St. James. "Flying to San José?"

"Yep." St. James nibbled scrambled eggs. "Leaving this afternoon."

Dozer frowned. "Shouldn't I be there for protection?"

"Not yet. Stay here. Have fun. How much trouble can we get into?"

"That depends."

Smythe perked up. "Need me for anything?"

"Not unless a complex computer issue arises. For now, no."

Smythe grinned. "Fine with me."

Dozer's forehead creased. "Not thrilled about you going there without me."

St. James frowned. "Why?"

Smythe glanced at a woman at the next table. She was sitting by herself, working on a laptop. Her hair and glasses were both a little askew, but she had that look that Smythe could never resist: pale and brainy, with clear skin, minimal makeup, and unpainted nails.

The woman got up to refill a small plate from a buffet table across the room. As she walked past their table and then back to her own, Smythe noticed a small tattoo on the inside of her wrist. It flashed by quickly, but it looked like a QR code.

Anna poked Louis on the forearm and whispered, "Why don't you go talk to her?"

His face reddened as he shook his head. Reluctantly, Anna decided to drop her matchmaking.

Dozer had watched all of this and waited until Louis was paying attention before speaking softly to St. James. "We don't know if the mob's involved. Promise you'll call if you get even a hint that things could turn rough?" His eyes searched St. James's for reassurance.

"I promise."

***

Later that day, at five o'clock, St. James and Anna arrived at Hotel Presidente in San José. The room was simple, with a king-sized bed, one large dresser, and a desk by the window.

"Bit more modest than the Diria," Anna said.

"I like it. Has a casual, Spanish vibe." St. James sat his attaché on the desk and started going through the contents.

Anna turned to a suitcase. "I'll unpack. What are you doing?"

"Setting up our temporary headquarters."

He emailed Dozer and Smythe with the agenda for the OIJ meeting. Then he scheduled a 9 a.m. session with Jiménez, who confirmed a meeting room at the courthouse in González Lahmann.

St. James watched Anna hang clothes in the closet and arrange folded shirts and tops in bureau drawers. "I'm all set," he said. "Let's find a bar."

Anna found a brochure for Azotea Calle 7, the hotel's rooftop bar, on a bedside night table. "Let's see what that's like."

They climbed a red spiral staircase to the bar's open-air terrace and settled at a white cast-iron table surrounded by lush vegetation. Bougainvillea plants burst with fuchsia blossoms, and citrus trees and tropical ornamentals spilled out of large pots.

Anna breathed in the scent of a nearby lime tree and closed her eyes. "The ambience is wonderful."

St. James folded his hands over hers. "Feels like we're sitting in someone's backyard."

A tall server with thick, black glasses approached and introduced himself as Mateo. Anna ordered a pinot grigio, St. James his usual double Macallan.

Anna tapped the table in time to the Spanish music in the background. "How should we play tomorrow?"

"Listen to what Jiménez has to say. We'll figure out how to tackle the investigation after that."

Anna nodded. "Did Sánchez represent other property owners?"

"Yes. There are five other claims for a total of six million."

"Small compared to DeSilva's usual dollars," Anna said.

"Two other notaries have larger claims — Samuel Hernández — thirty million and Nicolás González — twenty million."

Anna watched two middle-aged couples looking for a free table. "So, including Sánchez's, we're at fifty-six million?"

"Yes."

"And Global paid nineteen million in claims before DeSilva called you?"

"Yep."

"So, DeSilva wants us to find out if the remaining thirty-seven million is legitimate."

Mateo arrived with drinks.

St. James took a sip of Macallan before answering. "Yep. After tomorrow's meeting, I'll review Jiménez's files, and you can investigate any leads he provides. We should have a clearer picture by the end of the day."

"Can't know less."

Anna leaned back, swirling her wine. "What's the common thread among Sánchez, Hernández, and González?"

"DeSilva suspects fraud similar to each of their claims." St. James took another sip of the golden liquid. "If her suspicions are correct, the implications for Global could be dire. It's not just about money. If it comes out that Global missed extensive fraudulent activity, it could undermine their reputation and affect shareholder trust in the company."

Anna grimaced. "Big challenge."

"One we're more than capable of handling."

Anna grinned at his officiousness. "True."

St. James's eyes gleamed with tenacity. "Tomorrow, we begin unravelling everything."

CHAPTER 13

On Monday morning, at 8:30, St. James and Anna stood in front of the Hotel Presidente, waiting for a taxi to the courthouse. The sky was blue, and the temperature was expected to climb to a stifling 32°C by midday.

A taxi skidded to a stop in front of the hotel. The driver's reckless entry tempted St. James to reject the ride, but they were running late for the meeting, so he decided to take the chance. The ride was just as St. James feared. Sudden lane changes and speeding through intersections seemed to be this driver's *modus operandi*.

Anna looked at St. James nervously. "Slow down!" he growled from the back seat, but the driver just smiled and continued risking their lives for ten more minutes.

When at last they pulled up to the courthouse in one piece, they encountered a stately concrete building, with the colourful blue, white, and red of the Costa Rican flag standing guard over the entrance.

Inside, they were met by Jiménez's executive assistant, Luciana Cortez, a plump, friendly woman in her early forties. Cortez escorted them into a spacious boardroom filled with dark birch and mahogany furniture. A large conference table, surrounded by high-backed leather chairs, dominated the space.

The walls showcased Costa Rican scenes: a painting of Fortuna Waterfall, and photographs of the lush Monteverde Cloud Forest and the vibrant Parque Nacional Manuel Antonio. Potted plants added a touch of greenery, and a modern credenza held a selection of coffees and teas.

Cortez smiled as she departed. "Captain Jiménez will be with you shortly."

Jiménez arrived moments later, dressed in a black business suit. He shook St. James's hand heartily, then paused before Anna's outstretched hand and smiled. "Señorita," he said, giving her hand a gentle squeeze.

"Anna."

Jiménez guided them to their seats and took his place at the head of the table. He paused and twitched his thin moustache. "I didn't realize until you sent your itinerary that you would bring a woman."

St. James bristled. "I fail to see—"

Anna cut him off, addressing Jiménez. "You have a problem with me?"

Jiménez raised his shoulders. "No, you misunderstand. The Agency is focused on anti-discrimination."

"Could have fooled me!" Anna said.

"Believe me, it is. The United Nations commended Costa Rica for advancing women and combating stereotypes."

St. James's face clouded. "You mentioned Anna as if you don't approve."

Jiménez smiled. "First blunt exchange between two blunt men."

"Oh, there we go," Anna said, directing a weary gaze out the window.

St. James stabbed the top of the table with one finger as he spoke. "Anna is my partner, and the cleverest investigator I know. I don't work without her."

Jiménez eyed Anna and raised his hand. "I didn't mean to offend, Anna. I'm very supportive of OIJ policy and proud of our female agents. They allowed me to sever poor male performers. We're dealing with dangerous people who could put you at risk. OIJ provides advanced training for female agents, which you may not have."

St. James frowned. "I understand the concern. If trouble arises, my bodyguard will come from Tamarindo to shadow her."

Jiménez paused and stared at them for longer than St. James liked. He smiled and pulled out a pack of Delta cigarettes. "Very well. Mind if I smoke?"

Anna's head quickly lifted. "I do mind, yes."

Jiménez's look of surprise turned into a smile. "You speak your mind, Anna. I like that. Perhaps I'll wait for a suitable time to take a break outside."

Anna smiled. "Thank you."

St. James was eager to proceed. "Can we begin?"

"By all means." Jiménez's voice was steady as he observed St. James and Anna. "We generally discussed Sánchez's insurance claim, but there's more to uncover for your investigation. I can also provide details about Hernández and González, the other notaries who filed claims with your client."

St. James nodded. "I'll review your files later. For now, can we delve deeper into the Sánchez-Allaband situation?"

Anna pulled a notepad from her travel bag to take notes.

Jiménez raised an eyebrow. "I'm surprised to see a young person relying on a notepad instead of a laptop."

Anna grinned. "My shorthand's faster."

Jiménez smiled. "Fair enough."

He turned to St. James. "Our investigation revealed Sánchez transferred Allaband's land to Gael Vargas. Allaband filed a complaint with us and informed me that he was suing Sánchez."

St. James's look was intense. "Did Allaband give his consent for this transfer?"

Jiménez shook his head. "He says no. Allaband discovered the transfer when he inquired about his property taxes with the Registry."

Just then, St. James's phone buzzed with texts containing the documentation he'd requested from Allaband. He glanced at the screen before looking back at Jiménez. "So, what are your thoughts on why Sánchez was murdered?"

Jiménez's manner darkened. "We believe the Spanish mob knew we were trying to turn Sánchez. Intended to place him in the witness protection program with our American friends."

Anna frowned. "Would you have succeeded using his testimony if he'd survived?"

Jiménez shook his head, a pained look crossing his face. "We were getting close. Sánchez's death was a major setback."

Jiménez stood and announced that he was going for a cigarette. Anna continued to flesh out her notes, and St. James jotted down initial thoughts.

Five minutes later, Jiménez returned, reeking of tobacco smoke. "You know about the Protocolo?" he said, as soon as he sat down.

St. James and Anna looked up from their notes and stared at him.

Anna spoke up first. "Is it like a protocol? As in, a system of rules?"

"Not quite."

"Go on," St. James said, struggling to hide his impatience.

Jiménez directed his words to St. James. "Every notary in Costa Rica must maintain a book referred to as a Protocolo. This is where all public instruments created by the notary are recorded."

Anna, who had been writing again, looked up. "Public instruments?"

"Affidavits, wills, mortgages, civil marriages, real estate transfers, and powers of attorney. That sort of thing."

St. James looked intrigued. "A giant paper trail. The complete record of a notary's work, all in one place."

"Correct," said Jiménez.

Anna smiled. "So, if we could see Sánchez's Protocolo, we could find a clue to Allaband's deed transfer."

St. James leaned across the table. "Have you seen Sánchez's Protocolo?"

"I have."

"What does it say?"

"It contains a letter of consent allowing him to act on behalf of Allaband."

Anna and St. James stared at Jiménez. St. James finally spoke. "Does this letter of consent give Sánchez specific authority to sell Allaband's real estate?"

Jiménez shook his head again. "It's a general authorization for Sánchez to act on Allaband's behalf in various matters."

Anna pressed for clarification. "So, Sánchez could represent Allaband in any matter?"

Jiménez nodded. "Exactly. As long as Allaband's instructions are given in advance. Preapproval is required for any action."

As he took this in, St. James couldn't shake the feeling that they were merely scratching the surface.

CHAPTER 14

Anna paused. "So, Sánchez could sell Allaband's real estate once he'd been instructed to do so? No further approvals or signatures required?"

"Correct," Jiménez confirmed. "Anyone purchasing real estate based on the strength of Sánchez's signature would assume Allaband's signed deed was maintained in Sánchez's Protocolo."

Anna was puzzled. "Sánchez could forge Allaband's signature on a deed in his Protocolo to give the appearance that the sale of Allaband's land was legitimate."

Jiménez agreed. "Yes, he could."

St. James frowned. "And this could happen without anyone checking?"

"Also correct. But the Notary Directorate can audit a notary's Protocolo at any time, which could expose such forgeries."

St. James hesitated. "So, Sánchez wouldn't have to file Allaband's power of attorney and the deed with the Registry to transfer the title?"

"No. The transfer is valid as long as Sánchez's signature is on the documents."

Anna's forehead creased. "How would someone searching the Registry know if a house sale has been approved by its rightful owner?"

"They wouldn't."

"That sounds like chaos."

"Perhaps, but in Costa Rica, a notary is entrusted with something called Public Faith. This means that the notary's signature and the documents they handle are considered authoritative under the law. The public trusts that the notary has conformed to proper procedures."

Anna looked curiously at Jiménez. "What happens if a notary abuses the trust placed in them, say, by transferring a deed on behalf of their client, without preapproval?"

"Well, that is, as you say up north, a pickle. The only way to challenge such a sale is through the court system."

St. James frowned. "So, if I'm a notary and sell a property by certifying a title change without the owner's consent, it's accepted as valid due to this Public Faith? The purchaser believes the owner's signature is on an actual deed in my Protocolo, albeit it could be forged?"

"Correct," Jiménez said. "A legitimate owner might never realize the fraud occurred unless they check the Registry or wished to sell the property themselves."

Anna's eyes widened in disbelief. "How is that possible?"

Jiménez shrugged his shoulders. "The Registry doesn't notify owners if their real estate has been transferred. Owners only find out if they check the Registry themselves. How many people do that unless they're suspicious or planning to sell?"

"Wow!" Anna exclaimed. "That leaves the system open for abuse by crooked notaries."

"Yes, it does," Jiménez agreed. "The system relies on the integrity of the notary."

"It's a design flaw, for sure," St. James said. "But it also seems risky for the criminals. Real owners could show up any time and catch them in the act."

Jiménez's tone was thoughtful. "That's where the pandemic comes in. During COVID-19, homeowners weren't travelling. Borders were closed, and foreigners couldn't enter the country. Homes were often left unattended, making them prime targets for fraud."

"But travel restrictions came and went," Anna said. "How would criminals know when homeowners were coming and going?"

"Arrivals and departures are made public. Anyone can access that information — including a corrupt notary."

St. James grimaced. "So, a foreigner returns after many months and finds someone has built on their lot, or taken over the deed to their house, and their only option is to sue?"

"Correct. And if the property has been transferred multiple times or mortgaged to a third party, it can take years to untangle the legal issues."

"You'd need deep pockets and unlimited time just to have a hope of winning back your own property," St. James said.

Anna's curiosity was piqued. "What does a notary gain from destroying his credibility?"

Jiménez twisted the end of his moustache. "A big payout and a lifetime position with the mob. The key is to stay loyal to the mob. Anyone who doesn't ends up like Sánchez."

St. James looked pained. "Why didn't you arrest Sánchez if you knew all this?"

"Sánchez's associates wouldn't cooperate, even under interrogation."

"The mob got to them?"

"That, and there was not enough evidence for a successful arrest. Sánchez's lawyer would have him out on the street the same day. That's why we opted for witness protection — to get his testimony and move him out of the country."

"Did you get what you needed to apprehend the leader?"

Jiménez shook his head, his frustration evident. "Not before they killed Sánchez. We could have everything we needed if he'd survived."

Anna interjected. "What about the transferee, Gael Vargas?"

Jiménez's countenance was grim. "He's with the mob, too."

St. James wanted more. "And Vargas's lawyer?"

"A man named Ramón Mora."

Anna gave St. James a knowing glance when she heard Mora's name.

St. James took a moment to consider. "Is he straight — I mean, is he on the up and up?"

Jiménez's smile was thin and unconvincing. "Straight as a ninety-degree turn."

Anna struggled to grasp the situation. "So, everyone involved in these transactions is connected to organized crime?"

"Exactly," Jiménez confirmed. "One person lies, another documents it, and a third swears to it. And it can be even more complex than that."

St. James was skeptical. "How?"

Jiménez's frustration was evident. "If someone buys the property from Vargas, the title becomes more complicated. Takes a long time to prove whether the buyer is innocent. Never easy."

St. James thought for a moment. "So, the mob tries to create as many fraudulent transactions as possible after stealing the title from the real owner?"

"Pretty much. The more cryptic the ownership trail, the better their chances of getting away with it." Jiménez looked disgusted. "And with every fraudulent transaction, the rightful owner's chance of getting their property back shrinks."

Anna shook her head in disbelief. "It sounds diabolical — and almost impossible to fight."

Jiménez nodded and twisted his mustache again. "And there are so many ways for them to pull this off."

"What's another one you've seen?" St. James asked.

"Well, there's foreclosure fraud. That's a popular one."

"How does that work?" Anna asked.

"Let's say the second buyer is also part of the mob. He takes out a huge mortgage on the property and pockets the money, never intending to pay down the mortgage. When he defaults on the mortgage, the mortgage lender, probably another gang-related party, forecloses. They end up with clear ownership of the property. The mob gets what it wants, and the real owner loses everything."

Anna, still in shock, wanted to make sure she understood. "So, the system is designed in such a way that lets criminals take advantage, and the real owners get stuck in a long, difficult legal battle?"

"Yes. The mob uses these loopholes and delays to their advantage. Every new transaction makes it harder for law enforcement and the actual owners to regain their property. The government is working on new laws to stop all this."

St. James leaned back in his chair. "It's a sophisticated operation. And I'm guessing it's not just about money. It's also about power and control."

Jiménez's face hardened. "Exactly. The mob is basically laughing at us. These scams will continue to damage public trust in our legal system unless we can disrupt their operations and improve the laws."

St. James felt the weight of Jiménez's words. The question was, who could be trusted?

CHAPTER 15

St. James grinned. "Mary, I have good news and bad news. What would you like first?"

St. James and Anna sat in the Hotel Presidente room after breakfast on Tuesday morning. St. James had organized a Zoom call with DeSilva to give her a progress report. He wore the cheap black headset they'd given him on the plane, so as not to bother Anna, who was reading on the bed.

"Surprise me," she said.

"Following Monday's meeting with Jiménez, we reviewed OIJ's files related to González, Hernández, and Sánchez, the three notaries who filed claims with you. The claims were all like the Sánchez-Allaband case. In every situation, the notary certified that they possessed the signatures of the relevant parties on the appropriate documents in their Protocolo. Public faith entrusted in a licensed notary is enough for the National Registry to trust their word."

Anna was knee-deep in research on the three notaries and the three unknown couples at Allaband's parties. No need for her to spend time on Sánchez. She examined their professional histories and educational qualifications and cross-referenced their previous transactions and legal cases.

She combed through their personal and professional connections, searching for links to criminal activity or suspicious patterns in their conduct. She also delved into their roles within the notarial system, scrutinizing past certifications for anomalies or irregularities in their Protocolos. Her goal was to uncover collusion if it existed. Reveal how they facilitated fraudulent transfers.

DeSilva was impatient. "Remind me again what OIJ stands for?"

"You're the one who told me what it meant during our first phone call!"

DeSilva ignored his response.

St. James shook his head. "OIJ stands for Organismo de Investigación Judicial, the Spanish acronym for the Judicial Investigation Police. Costa Rica's equivalent to the FBI."

"Why didn't you say that in the first place? I'm acronymed to death."

"Just trying to expand your knowledge, Mary," St. James poked.

"Don't play with me, St. James. I'm busy. Give me what you've got."

"Total claims by all three notaries are fifty-six million USD. You negotiated settlements for nineteen million dollars' worth of those claims. That leaves thirty-seven-million dollars' worth of claims still to adjudicate. The good news is you don't have to pay the thirty-seven million. The claims are all fraudulent. The bad news is you didn't have to pay the nineteen million either. The mob runs the whole operation. Notaries facilitated the frauds by transferring real estate without the owner's consent."

DeSilva's breathing was laboured. "Jesus!"

"Thought you would be pleased. Shortest time to solve a case for you."

"That 'Jesus' was for us paying out nineteen million dollars when we didn't have to."

DeSilva's gaze floated to the ceiling as she reeled from the revelation. "Okay, St. James. Walk me through how these properties were stolen."

St. James adjusted in his seat. "The scheme revolved around manipulating Costa Rica's land registration system and exploiting the role of notaries.

Notaries create and maintain Protocolos — official record books that log all public documents they produce, like deeds and transfers. Protocolos serve as a detailed ledger for processed transactions.

Notaries hold a position of trust, but some of them are on the take. They get hooked into the mob and they forge sale agreements and create fake documents that look like the original owner signed. The aim is to make the fakes indistinguishable from actual documents in the bureaucratic records."

DeSilva listened intently.

"Once fraudulent documents are registered and thefts discovered, the legitimate property owners file lawsuits against the notaries. In response, corrupt notaries file insurance claims with you and use the proceeds to pay for lawsuits.

After transferring ownership, crooked notaries sell the stolen real estate and divert the proceeds into mob bank accounts. Various methods of laundering the proceeds make it impossible for the original owners to trace the money. They funnel the proceeds through a network of shell companies that look legitimate but function only to transfer proceeds through complex transactions. Illicit funds are invested in high-value assets like new real estate or businesses, which are then sold or restructured to obscure the source of the money further."

"Go on," DeSilva said, looking crestfallen.

"Once a property is transferred, crooked notaries manipulate the records to make everything look legitimate. They forge documents in their Protocolo to back up the fraudulent transactions, and no one checks."

"Wouldn't the authorities flag these transactions?"

St. James shook his head. "The system relies on something called Public Faith in notaries. The Registry doesn't notify owners of transfers, so unless an owner checks, they might not realize their property was stolen until it has changed hands several more times. By then it's basically too late."

DeSilva's appearance hardened. "And the insurance claims?"

"Notaries facilitate fraudulent transfers with fictitious buyers within their criminal network," St. James explained. "Then they file inflated insurance claims based on the fake transactions, claiming losses and damages that never occurred."

DeSilva caught her breath. "How did they avoid the law for so long?"

St. James sighed. "A combination of factors: the complexity of the transactions, the trust placed in notaries, and the fact that that trust is being exploited by the mob. They make sure anyone questioning the transactions faces intimidation or worse. The government is creating legislation to prevent all this abuse."

DeSilva sat back, absorbing the gravity of the situation. "So, we resolved nineteen million dollars' worth of claims without knowing they were fraudulent."

St. James nodded. "A calculated decision based on the information available to you at the time. Litigating each claim would have been expensive and time-consuming."

"Doesn't help, Hamilton. I should have known better."

St. James was quiet for a moment.

"Got any bright ideas?"

"Yes. I'll see if I can do something about the claims you paid."

"Do that, and I'll kiss your ass in Times Square."

St. James laughed. "Careful what you promise, Mary."

DeSilva briefly raised her chin in place of a goodbye and clicked off the Zoom call.

Anna laid down her book. "How did it go?"

"DeSilva's upset that she settled claims she didn't have to."

"Understandably. What'd she say?"

"Jesus."

Anna scrunched her face. "Huh?"

"That was her response when I told her the nineteen million didn't have to be paid."

Anna looked bewildered. "That's it?"

"No. She said she'd kiss my ass in Times Square."

Anna's impatience was growing. "Hamilton, you're being tiring."

"Get her nineteen million back, and that's what she would do — kiss my ass in Times Square."

Anna calmed. "Can't wait to see that."

St. James peered off for a moment. "I have to figure out how to tackle a recovery involving the mob — that is and stay alive."

Anna shook her head. "Why take the risk? You've earned ten percent of thirty-seven million dollars in less than two days. Is that not good enough for you?"

"It's not just about the money. There's a contract obligation, and I want to rectify the situation for DeSilva. Solving the case was just the first step. There's ensuring the fraudsters are held accountable."

"I know that, Hamilton. Why not quit while you're ahead!"

"Point well taken. I told DeSilva I would try."

Anna was already fuming. "Just how do you propose to do that?"

"Wish I knew," St. James admitted with a sigh.

CHAPTER 16

St. James shook Anna's shoulder. "Wake up, sweetheart. We'll be late for the appointment."

"What?" Anna mumbled, struggling to wake from a deep sleep.

St. James placed a cup of coffee on the night table. "Drink this. It's almost ten o'clock. You need to shower and dress."

Anna rose onto her elbows, took the mug, and sipped coffee. "What appointment?"

"What did I say we would do in San José?"

"Meet Captain Jiménez."

St. James laughed. "No, no. Nothing related to business."

"Still half asleep, Hamilton. Cut me some slack."

"Shop for an engagement ring."

Anna's eyes popped open, and she let out a yelp. After taking two sips of coffee, she jumped out of bed and ran to the shower. "Why didn't you tell me?" she called from the bathroom.

"Just did."

"When did you book the appointment?"

"Yesterday."

"You're being annoying again, Hamilton. Where are we going?"

"The concierge recommended Tiffany's in Multiplaza Escazú. A cab ride away. You need to hurry — it's nine-fifteen."

Fifteen minutes later, Anna emerged from the bathroom dressed in a light blue pantsuit showcasing her slim, sculpted figure. A gleaming silver bracelet that St. James had given her for Christmas complemented the outfit.

Anna noticed St. James staring at her and looked at him with a hint of worry. "What's wrong? Don't you like it?"

St. James walked to her and gazed into her eyes. "You are stunning."

Anna blushed and moved closer to him. They shared a tender moment, holding each other without speaking, until Anna broke their embrace.

"Let's go, let's go!" she said, pulling St. James out the door.

***

St. James was at his wits' end. Anna tried on every Tiffany engagement ring as if it was a lifesaving decision. Eventually, she chose the most expensive one in the store.

As they left, she waved her ring around, catching the sunlight. "Hamilton, I'm thrilled! Let's celebrate with a splendid lunch."

"Great idea. There's a restaurant," he said, pausing to check his phone. "Tenedor Argentino. Let's try that."

Anna, lost in her world, didn't respond. She walked with her left arm stretched out in front of her, admiring her gorgeous new rock in its white gold setting.

"Earth to Anna," St. James said. She giggled and grabbed his arm.

Several minutes later, they were seated in a charming Argentinian restaurant filled with vibrant prints, colourful tables, and lush greenery. St. James enjoyed an Imperial while Anna sipped pinot.

Her attention was still on the ring. "I cannot believe how pretty it is. What a wonderful morning."

St. James shared her joy, but as they worked their way through lunch, he said less and less.

When he ignored an offer to taste her entrée, Anna set down her pinot. "Earth to Hamilton."

"What's that? Oh, sorry, Anna."

"What's wrong?" She suddenly looked worried. "Did we spend too much on the ring? We did, didn't we—"

"No! Not at all."

"What, then?"

"It does have to do with money, but not ours. My mind's on recovering the nineteen million." He looked at her guilty. "Here I go, ruining our celebration—"

Anna reached across the table. "It's all right, Hamilton. I know who I'm marrying. Let's finish our lunch so you can focus on your work."

St. James lifted her hands and kissed them. "You get me, don't you?"

"I do."

"Keep practicing that phrase —you're going to need it."

***

By mid-afternoon, St. James was sitting at his temporary workspace back in the hotel room, beginning his investigation of DeSilva's $19 million loss. Anna relaxed on the bed, reliving the morning and admiring her diamond ring.

St. James remembered their encounter with Jiménez. "Neither of us missed Jiménez's reference to Vargas's lawyer, Ramón Mora. Have you gotten to that name for research yet?"

"Not yet. Tomorrow morning."

"Okay."

St. James realized he needed information he didn't have. He called DeSilva.

"Mary, I need the list of claims you settled and contact information for the property owners."

DeSilva hesitated. "Don't know where to lay my hands on that."

"Your claims manager can find it."

DeSilva's frustration was evident. "Do you think I have nothing else to do?"

"I'm trying to haul your ass out of the fire before Global's next board meeting. It's critical information to avoid reporting claims paid that you didn't have to pay."

"Good thing I like you, St. James. I'll see what I can do." DeSilva abruptly ended the call.

St. James spent hours exploring ways to recover homes transferred by corrupt notaries but could think of no method to avoid retaliation from the mob. He knew the fact that the mob was involved meant that he should be calling Dozer in, but he decided to call Jiménez first. He would leave Dozer out of it for a while longer. Let him recover from the mess in Germany before pulling him into another fray.

"We need a planning session, Jiménez."

"Why?"

St. James heard a puff on a cigarette. "We have to figure out how you can make a solid arrest, and how I can recover Global's loss."

Jiménez took another drag. "Without sparking a war with the mob."

"That's why we need a planning meeting."

Jiménez butted out the Delta in an ashtray. "Let me first understand how Global's claim settlements are managed."

"Okay," St. James said.

"Here's what I think happens," Jiménez began. "Global gives the money to the notary's lawyer, who then sends it to the property owner's lawyer to settle the lawsuit he filed against the notary. The idea is to make sure the notary doesn't misuse the money. The funds move through trusted lawyers to ensure they're used for their intended purpose — settling the claim."

"Almost, but not quite," St. James said. "Global's cheques are made payable jointly to both the notary's lawyer and the property owner's lawyer. That way, neither party can cash the cheque alone, preventing either from diverting the money."

"So, to divert the funds, the notary's lawyer would need to gain full control of the cheque?"

"Exactly. And there are only two ways that could happen. The first is absurd: the property owner instructs their lawyer to endorse the cheque over to the notary's lawyer."

Jiménez frowned. "Why would they ever do that?"

"They wouldn't. Makes no sense to enrich the same notary they just sued."

"And the second way?"

"If the property owner's lawyer is also corrupt. They could endorse the cheque to the notary's lawyer without the owner's knowledge or consent."

"Meaning both lawyers are in on the fraud?"

"Yes. Two crooked lawyers — one suing, one defending — in the same case. A tangled web of deceit."

Jiménez nodded. "I'll compile a list of the lawyers representing the property owners."

"That would be helpful. Anna will start investigating them."

"Alejandro can assist."

"Alejandro?"

"Alejandro Montero. One of my agents."

St. James shrugged. "In any case, Global's money is long gone. Without those funds, the legitimate property owners are left with unresolved claims. And we'll be forced to gain control of the stolen real estate and liquidate it to recover Global's nineteen million."

Jiménez looked skeptical. "If you recover the titles, aren't you legally obligated to return them to the original owners?"

"No. The original owners have legal claims against the notaries, not the current holders of the properties. The properties may have changed hands multiple times. Proving original ownership would be time-consuming, expensive, and likely to fail in court."

Jiménez absorbed this. "So the mob now owns the properties stolen by the notaries. And the same notaries file insurance claims with Global to cover liabilities from the lawsuits by defrauded owners?"

"That's right. If Global honoured all the claims, those criminals would've collected fifty-six million dollars in settlements — on top of over fifty-six million in stolen property."

Jiménez whistled softly. "Over one hundred and twelve million dollars."

"We were fortunate to uncover the fraud before they could collect the remaining thirty-seven million in pending claims," St. James said.

Jiménez leaned back. "I definitely see the need for a planning meeting now. Nine o'clock tomorrow?"

"Sounds good."

CHAPTER 17

On Wednesday evening, St. James and Anna sat at La Criollita, a cozy restaurant a short walk from the Hotel Presidente. A middled-aged woman in a powder blue dress — name tag Consuela — crossed the gleaming white floor, past walls covered in photographs of regular patrons, to deliver their drinks.

Anna rested her elbow on the table to show off her engagement ring. "I can't believe how many emails I've gotten congratulating me on this beautiful ring. Even Dozer and Louis sent notes."

St. James grinned. "Texted a picture, I assume?"

"Yep — to the whole world."

Anna sipped her pinot and looked around the restaurant. "So, how are we going to handle this case?"

"Jiménez's team is dealing with the thefts. Our job is to make sure Global gets its nineteen million back." St. James pulled a folder from the case he carried. "Here's what DeSilva sent — claims settled and the lawyers we need to check. Jiménez is adding a list as well."

Anna scanned the documents. "For the nineteen million?"

"Yep."

Consuela came by to take their food orders — chicken fajitas and pork chops — and hurried off.

Anna looked at St. James. "I've been checking into the notaries."

"Tell me what you found out about Ramón Mora first."

"Okay. We already know he's Vargas's lawyer. He's not the high-fee, big-name kind of guy. He usually works with clients like Vargas — people with lower reputations. He's a bottom feeder."

St. James drank Macallan. "Probably too sleazy to attract better clients."

Anna considered this. "Then why was he at Allaband's parties? We haven't met Allaband, but everything I've read suggests he's a respectable, successful businessman. Not the kind of person you'd expect to associate with someone like Mora or Vargas."

St. James nodded. "Mora could be the link between Allaband, Vargas, Sánchez, and Baca."

"Carlos Baca? The mob Boss Jiménez told you about?"

"That's the one."

"Mora was at Allaband's parties, and so was Sánchez," Anna mused, trying to work out St. James's logic. "Mora is Vargas's lawyer, and Vargas is Baca's accountant."

"So Mora could have helped set up the theft of Allaband's Costa Rica home using those connections."

"It's possible."

St. James texted Allaband, suggesting he ask his lawyer to follow up. "The other notaries?"

"Hernández graduated top of his class and has a reputation for handling high-profile, high-value transactions. Major real estate deals and corporate settlements. He has a strong finance and real estate network and could be a key player here."

St. James was quiet. Thinking.

"González's academic record was average. He built a solid local practice. Recent work involved real estate transactions and small business disputes. Some issues with his documentation might suggest negligence or problems."

"Sánchez started his practice after graduation, focusing on property and estate law. His practice is more independent. Involved in cases that resolved quickly."

Anna thought for a moment. "What do you think we'll learn from all this?"

"Probably nothing. But if we're lucky, we might uncover a connection between the lawyers for the property owners and the notaries they're suing. They could be working together to cheat clients out of what they're owed."

"How will you manage that?"

St. James grinned. "I won't — you will!"

Anna frowned. "Should have seen that coming. How many lawyers are we talking about?"

"Twelve."

"Time-consuming."

"Did they graduate the same year?"

"No, a couple of years apart."

Consuela returned with their food. "Is there anything else I can bring for you?"

St. James smiled. "Bottle of your best Rioja red."

"Of course." Consuela departed.

St. James turned back to Anna. "Any sign of collaboration among the notaries?"

"Nothing visible. Could be colluding off the grid."

"What about recent changes in business practices or significant lifestyle changes? Anyone suddenly able to buy a yacht or a mansion?"

Anna bit into her fajita. "Nothing popped up."

"Ongoing or recent litigation? Patterns or connections in the types of cases they handle?"

Anna sipped her pinot and shook her head. "Nothing unusual."

St. James rubbed his temples in frustration. "Dead end. I hate dead ends."

CHAPTER 18

Thursday morning, San José was grey and overcast. Heavy clouds cast a dim, muted pall over the city — a fitting backdrop for the difficult discussions they were about to have at the OIJ, St. James thought.

Anna looked down at their nearly matching outfits: colourful shorts and pair of golf shirts. "Think this'll pass for business casual in Costa Rica?"

"I think we look great. A bright spot on a drizzly day."

At nine, they met Luciana Cortez again, and she guided them to their seats in the familiar room. Jiménez was already seated at the head of the table. He looked refreshed in a light-brown coat and cream chinos, moustache neatly trimmed. He stood up briefly to welcome them, then excused himself and went back to reading a report.

A tall man in plain clothes entered the room and sat next to Anna, nodding to her as he took his seat. He had dark skin, close-cut blond hair, and a scar on his left cheek. Jiménez put aside his reading and introduced him as Agent Alejandro Montero.

After they had all exchanged pleasantries, Jiménez turned to St. James. "Montero is up to speed, so we can begin."

"Great." St. James rose and walked to the whiteboard. He addressed his host as he gestured to the board. "Do you mind? It helps me think."

"Be my guest."

St. James addressed the room. "I like to start by determining what everyone in the room wants."

When everyone nodded, St. James continued. "Agent Montero, what's the OIJ's objective?"

Jiménez talked over Montero. "Create a set of actions to arrest these criminals."

St. James paused briefly before writing *ARREST CRIMINALS* at the top of the whiteboard. Then he turned to the group and said, "Global's goal is to find nineteen million dollars in real estate to compensate for its losses. Any objections?"

Jiménez twisted the end of his moustache. "Not as long as everything's legal."

Montero squinted in a way that distorted his scar as he mulled over these potentially conflicting goals.

St. James wrote *RECOVER $19 MILLION IN REAL ESTATE* below Jiménez's goal.

Anna thought about the goals. "Common ground between the two?"

Montero brushed his hand through his short hair. "Just the obvious one — the mob."

A collective nod rippled around the table as St. James wrote *THE MOB* on the board.

Anna suggested: "Notaries and lawyers."

"Right." St. James added the second commonality to the whiteboard. *NOTARIES AND LAWYERS.*

Montero stared off. "Real estate must be a third. A crucial element in laundering money."

Jiménez stood up and began pacing. His irritation was obvious. "St. James, is this how you envision the day unfolding? We're just listing the obvious."

St. James wanted to appear open-minded. "What do you suggest? Are there other connections we should explore?"

Jiménez stopped and met St. James's eyes. "Feels like we're wasting time on givens. We need actionable intelligence."

St. James gestured to the whiteboard. "I disagree. These givens, as you refer to them, form the basis for a strategy to achieve both goals. We need to understand how these elements interact before developing a plan."

Anna tilted her head, her air thoughtful. "Are we missing something?"

St. James stared off. "Possibly. Commonalities suggest the two goals could be linked."

Jiménez sighed. "I've seen too many cases go south. We need a clear strategy, not just a list of commonalities."

St. James wanted to move on. "How would we coordinate an arrest?"

Cortez entered with a tray of coffee and served each participant before making her discreet exit.

Montero's manner soured as he reflected on the question. "Need to catch them in the act, committing a crime red-handed. Anything less won't hold up in court."

Jiménez shook his head. "This is the challenge we face every time. The criminals are always one step ahead."

Montero loosened his black tie. "Never a chance to make a solid arrest."

St. James eyed the paintings around the room. "So, you always wait for them to make the first move?"

Jiménez frowned. "We can't exactly ask them for their theft schedule."

Anna smiled and took a sip of coffee.

St. James turned to Jiménez. "Not what I meant. Why can't we make the first move?"

Frustrated, Montero snapped, "Just how would we do that?"

"Provoke them," St. James suggested. "Create a scenario where they would be compelled to act. Perhaps by making them think they're losing something."

Jiménez raised his eyebrows. "How?"

Anna swept her long blonde hair back over her shoulders. "Could an undercover cop facilitate something? Infiltrate their operations to gather intel?"

Montero frowned. "Too risky. It takes months for an undercover to be accepted and trusted. And there's always the risk of them blowing their cover."

"What about the mob's notaries?" Anna countered. "Could we use them to run interference? Offer immunity or protection in exchange for cooperation?"

Montero opened his hands. "They'd report us to their boss. They're too entrenched and have too much to lose."

Jiménez agreed. "Montero is right. They'd sabotage us to protect themselves."

St. James glanced out the window at the busy parking lot below. He twirled a marker through his fingers like a seasoned card dealer shuffling a deck with one hand. His mind raced through potential scenarios.

Jiménez rested his arms on the table. "What are you thinking, St. James?"

St. James turned to the group. "What if we took something from them — something valuable enough the mob would come after it?"

Jiménez struggled to imagine this. "Like what? They have connections everywhere and could trace that back to us."

St. James thought for a moment. "Maybe this is where our two goals join up. Suppose a notary transferred property back from the crooks. That would provoke them. Make them mad enough to come after whoever did it."

Jiménez's eyes narrowed. "A judge is the only one who can transfer without consent. Has to be a legal process."

St. James persisted. "Okay, let's assume a notary made the transfers, legal or not. The mob would feel their grip slipping away. They might act out of anger. Desperation."

Jiménez stared at St. James. "The notary would be dead before the day was out. The mob doesn't tolerate thefts against them."

St. James took his seat. "We could protect the notary, secure them in a safe location, and use the ensuing chaos to set our trap. High-risk strategy, but it might be our best chance."

Jiménez frowned, his voice rising. "You don't know these people. Disloyalty means death. I've dealt with organized crime here for a long time. OIJ is bound by strict rules. The mob is not. We're talking about risking lives."

St. James grew impatient. "I know that. I'm suggesting we try something different. Something innovative. Don't you want to get these bastards?"

Jiménez's frown persisted. "Of course I do, but what you're proposing is against the law and about as dangerous as it gets. There's no precedent for this kind of operation."

Montero was staring at the painting of the Turrialba Volcano on the far wall, considering St. James's suggestion. He looked at Jiménez. "What harm would it do to run the idea by the Director? We'd need his approval for any operation this risky."

Jiménez eyed Montero in disbelief. "He would question our sanity, whether we're fit to serve."

St. James contemplated Jiménez's response. "Not if we present a well-thought-out scheme. Show how we could disrupt their operations in a way that would lead to arrests."

Jiménez's surprise was evident. "No such thing as a solid plan with the mob. They have moles everywhere. Their intelligence is better than ours!"

Anna wanted to refocus. "Does the Agency have trustworthy notaries to work with us?"

Montero rubbed his neck. "Access to them, yes."

"How confident are you that they're honest?" St. James pressed.

"Very," Montero said. "Some of them are working hard with the Costa Rican Legislature on enhancing laws that demand greater notary disclosure of client transactions. If they were crooked, they'd be trying to keep the legal loopholes just as they are."

St. James considered the risk. "Does the government conduct background checks before hiring them?"

Jiménez was surprised at the juvenile-level question. "Of course. Standard procedure. We do our own checks. Our notaries are well-vetted."

Anna jumped in. "So, you're confident they can be trusted?"

Jiménez didn't hesitate. "Yes."

"Good. An honest notary is a must, no matter what," St. James said. "We need someone reliable to handle the documentation."

Montero looked at the table, his mind far away. "We would need a complete list of the property claims Global has settled. Legal descriptions, everything for transfers. Have to be meticulous."

"Already in our files," Anna said.

Montero smiled. "That's a start. We'll need to prepare for potential fallout around all this if we actually go ahead."

Jiménez looked at St. James and Montero with skepticism. "All right, let's proceed with caution. If we do this, we must prepare for every eventuality."

St. James felt a renewed sense of purpose. "Agreed. Let's draft an outline and see if we can convince the Director. It's taking a big risk, but it might be our best chance."

Jiménez began to show interest in the idea. "Montero, see if Alana's available."

Anna glanced at Jiménez. "Alana?"

"Alana Segura. Forgery expert."

Anna made a note.

Montero left the meeting in search of Segura.

St. James noticed a gradual change in Jiménez. The man was conflicted. Eliminating the worst threat to society was appealing. But it could become the worst career decision he ever made. One that could cost lives.

St. James looked at Jiménez. "What is it?"

"There's merit in what you're proposing, St. James. For it to work, the Agency would have to become a thief to catch a thief. I don't know if we can live with that."

CHAPTER 19

It wasn't long before Montero returned with Segura and Jiménez, who used Montero's absence to sneak in a quick smoke. St. James fleshed out the steps he'd refined during the recess. At the same time, Anna expanded the list of actions for them to consider.

The short, plain-looking Segura sat beside St. James, scribbling notes as Jiménez explained the case.

Segura waited for Jiménez to finish before asking, "So, what would you like me to do, Sir?"

Jiménez gestured to St. James, who took the question. "We're hoping you can help us retrieve the properties."

Segura opened her hands in a dismissive gesture. "How?"

Montero interjected. "Explain how you discover forgeries, and we'll take it from there."

Segura looked at Jiménez, who nodded. "Okay. Some signatures are forged without the forger ever seeing the real one. This method works only if the intended target of the forgery hasn't seen the authentic signature either. A risky approach because the forger can never be sure who might have seen the genuine signature."

Jiménez smiled. "Called blind forgeries."

Anna was eager to understand. "What's an example?"

"In a car theft, the thief might forge the owner's signature to make a sale seem legitimate."

Anna smiled.

"Another type is a trace-over forgery. The forger traces over the real signature, as the name suggests. These can be convincing on the surface, but they often lack the fluidity of the authentic signature if the forger stops and starts midway through the signature."

St. James was focused. "How do you catch a well-executed forgery?"

Segura stood to use the whiteboard. St. James handed her a marker.

Anna observed Segura as she talked, noting her pale complexion and lack of makeup. Her plain appearance struck Anna as deliberately understated — a way of blending into the background and letting her expertise take centre stage.

Segura continued. "Several factors can reveal a forgery. One of those is pen pressure. We search for deviations in three ways: pressure on part of a letter, pressure on the entire letter, and pressure on the entire signature. Inconsistent pressure in any of these areas can be a red flag."

Anna interrupted, "So, three levels of pressure differences?"

"Yes. To analyze a signature, we break it down into individual letters and then group them by first name, middle name, and family name. A skilled forger matches the pressure used on each letter to avoid detection. Detecting a forgery involves studying a signature's composition to reveal even the smallest deviation."

Segura demonstrated her points on the whiteboard with various examples, showing the nuances of different forgeries. "Speed, acceleration, and smoothness of execution — any of these, if poorly formed, can give a forger away."

St. James was intrigued. "How?"

"People tend to start signatures slow. The first letter often receives the most attention. Subsequent letters are usually executed more quickly. That's where we find most deviations from a real signature."

Anna's interest was piqued. "Can you illustrate?"

"Of course. Each letter can be executed with a heavier or lighter hand, as I said. Some letters, like P, O, or C, might have exaggerated loops. The letter C in an authentic signature might be heavier and wider at the top, while a less skilled forger might place greater emphasis on the middle or bottom of a letter. A sharp eye, patience, and precision are essential for detecting well-executed forgeries."

Segura wrapped up her explanation and returned to her seat.

Anna turned toward her. "What about the use of software, Segura?"

"Fraud detection software is constantly improving. OIJ is testing AI tools like SignatureXpert. As technology advances, software will replace more manual work, but we're not ready to rely entirely on digital tools yet. I think we're gradually moving toward a synergistic approach where technology enhances the skilled judgment of forensic experts, without replacing it."

St. James took all this in. "Are you able to forge signatures yourself? Perfectly, I mean."

Segura's eyes searched Jiménez's for guidance. Jiménez gave a slight nod.

Segura turned to St. James. "Given sufficient time to practice, yes."

"Excellent."

Cortez entered the room and cleared the coffee pot, cups, and napkins. "Sir, I've taken the liberty of arranging lunch. Hope that's all right?"

Montero glanced at his watch. Eleven-fifteen.

Jiménez smiled. "Thank you, Luciana."

Cortez juggled a tray of dirty dishes. "Everything is set up for twelve-thirty in the next room."

St. James moved to the whiteboard. "Very helpful, Segura. Thank you."

Segura, oblivious to St. James's compliment, did not respond.

St. James raised a hand. "I would like to cover one more thing before lunch."

Jiménez's forehead lined. "What?"

"The notary the Agency uses."

Montero turned to St. James. "The one we use most often is Saúl Madrigal. Good man to work with."

"Trust him?"

Jiménez was annoyed by St. James's repetitive question. "He's one of the advisors to the government I mentioned earlier."

Anna jumped in. "Can we include him in this discussion?"

Jiménez hesitated, but said, "Don't see why not, since we're planning for planning's sake. I'm texting to see if he's available."

Ten minutes later, a compact man with unremarkable facial features and shoulders like a pop bottle entered the room, carrying a laptop. Montero introduced him as Notary Madrigal.

When Jiménez mentioned transferring real estate from the mob, horror crossed Madrigal's face. "Jesus, you're kidding! That's against the law. I was under the impression we were the good guys."

St. James grinned at Madrigal's exaggerated response.

Anna appeared puzzled by Madrigal's behaviour.

"Take it easy, Madrigal," Jiménez said. "This is an exploratory conversation. Nobody is running off half-cocked."

Madrigal's panic retreated, but a hint of apprehension remained in his eyes.

St. James explained. "We're considering transferring property from the mob to cover Global Insurance's losses caused by fraudulent claims filed by dishonest notaries associated with the mob. The theory is to lure them into the open, catch them committing a crime, and make arrests. We want to do to the mob what they've been doing to innocent Costa Ricans: turn them into victims instead of predators."

Madrigal shook his head. "What notary would be foolish enough to do that?"

***

After lunch, they reconvened in the meeting room.

"This is a fascinating exercise, St. James," Jiménez concluded. "I admit I'm enjoying it. But I doubt we'll be able to sell it to the higher-ups. It's still stealing holdings, even if we're stealing from crooks."

"You don't think they'll see the distinction?"

"Oh, they'll see it, but they'll be afraid of blowback. The higher we go in the OIJ, the more politics and image are involved in decision-making."

St. James deliberated over this. "Doesn't it depend on how we present it? Could be convincing if we outline everyone's role and tie it into an arrest plan."

Jiménez shook his head. "Too much can go wrong."

Madrigal was emphatic. "I'm not sticking my neck out to transfer land from the mob. No, siree!"

St. James grinned. "You may not have to."

Jiménez reconsidered the strategy, eyeing Montero. "Let's assume we're planning a takedown. Who would you suggest lead it?"

Montero didn't hesitate. "García."

Anna wrote the name on her pad.

Segura sat stone-faced.

St. James hiked his forehead. "Why García?"

Montero smiled. "He's a good strategist. The agents respect him, and he's effective in planning and execution."

Jiménez agreed.

Anna's concern was evident. "How will you convince the Director your people wouldn't be harmed?"

Jiménez gave a sombre half shrug. "No point even trying. Going against the mob puts us in harm's way. That's what we're paid to do. The only non-OIJ personnel in danger would be the notary."

Madrigal's agitation welled up. "I want no part in this."

Everyone ignored Madrigal's drama.

St. James turned to Montero. "How long would it take you and García to prepare a detailed arrest plan?"

Montero lifted his eyes to the high ceiling. "A day." He sounded as if he was trying to convince himself.

Jiménez winced. "I would say two or more."

Montero was reluctant to agree. "I suppose."

St. James sought agreement. "Combining all this into a detailed strategy might convince Director Ramírez."

"I doubt it," said Jiménez. "But it might be worth a try."

Anna tried to conceal her amazement at Jiménez's about-face on the idea of a plan. She knew what she would say to her betrothed on the way back to the hotel: "How in the hell did you get that done, Hamilton St. James?"

CHAPTER 20

Planning concluded around three-thirty, with Montero and García assigned the task of developing an arrest strategy. St. James and Anna stayed as the others filed out, seizing the moment to strategize their next steps.

Everyone agreed to reconvene on Monday to review the plan, address potential weaknesses, and reinforce necessary solutions. The stakes were high — there was only one chance to secure the Director's approval for such a risky mission. Even if they managed to get the green light, the odds of success hovered around fifty-fifty.

During the planning meeting, Jiménez had sat rigidly, fingers tapping a restless rhythm against the tabletop. It was painfully clear, he had not fully committed to the process.

St. James noticed the anxiety on Jiménez's face, his forehead puckered as if he were wrestling with an unseen demon. Torn between duty and risk, Jiménez wanted to do the right thing, but his worry about failure loomed larger than his ambition. St. James realized Jiménez's lack of conviction would not win the group the Director's support if he continued with ambivalence.

St. James felt it necessary to be present when the presentation was made to the Director. Jiménez might falter without his support. The idea of a mission failing to receive approval without clear support from Jiménez gnawed at him. Yet, pushing Jiménez too hard could backfire and complicate matters further.

Anna's voice broke through his thoughts. "What's on your mind?"

St. James sighed, shaking his head slightly. "It's Jiménez. I can't help but worry. If he doesn't believe in this, it's not going to work."

Concern overtook Anna. "He needs to see that this isn't just another job; it's a chance to make a real impact — rid the country of a major threat. We're in trouble if Jiménez doesn't believe that. Might as well quit now."

"Exactly. We must make him see that. How can he rally the Director if he can't rally himself?"

***

Anna sat opposite St. James on the Azotea Calle 7 bar, sipping Las Moras pinot grigio. "Segura is quite a strange character, don't you think?"

St. James sipped Macallan next to one of the bar's bright bougainvilleas. "She'd have to be, to spend her days hunched over a light table, comparing pressure points on the top of an S and the bottom of an E."

"You have a point there. But she was impressive, wasn't she?"

St. James nodded as neutrally as possible, not wanting to seem too taken with the only other woman on the team. But he had been impressed by Segura's clear explanations and knowledge of her field.

Anna swirled her glass. "What did you think of Montero?"

"Seems capable enough."

"My thought, too."

St. James grinned into his glass. "The devil in me wants to tell Madrigal he'll be the one to transfer property from the mob."

Anna burst into laughter, spewing white wine through her nose. "Oh my gosh, no, Hamilton, you'll give him a heart attack."

St. James laughed and handed her his clean dinner napkin.

Anna dabbed her eyes and nose and willed herself to stop imagining the little pear-shaped Madrigal going berserk at their next meeting.

"You can't," she said through spasms of laughter.

"No, I'd better not."

As she recovered, Anna's thoughts drifted to the case. "So, how do you think we should approach this?"

"Tomorrow, I'll explain the scheme to DeSilva."

"Think she'll approve it?"

"For sure. If there's a chance to recover her nineteen million, she won't sweat the details."

"Suppose I didn't need to ask."

"I'll have DeSilva incorporate a subsidiary here in Costa Rica."

"Where the landholdings will be transferred."

"Yes."

Anna observed a young couple hugging at a nearby table. "What prevents the mob from reclaiming the assets once we transfer them to DeSilva's subsidiary?"

"Nothing," St. James said, leaning back. "Here's the thing — if they transfer the titles back to themselves, the properties will have been stripped of nineteen million in equity. That money will be diverted to cover Global's insurance loss."

Anna furrowed her forehead. "Interesting approach."

"Once we transfer the real estate to her subsidiary, DeSilva will mortgage the property for nineteen million. Then, the subsidiary transfers the nineteen million to Global, eliminating its insurance loss and reducing the subsidiary's equity in the property by the same amount. Even if the mob reclaims the titles, it won't matter. Global will have already recovered its losses."

St. James took another sip of scotch, his expression thoughtful. "The mob will retaliate. Protection will be necessary."

Anna raised an eyebrow. "You think protection will be enough to deter them?"

St. James finished his scotch, a shadow of a smile crossing his lips. "We'll handle whatever comes."

CHAPTER 21

Despite the sweltering thirty-four-degree heat on Saturday, St. James and Anna ventured into the heart of San José's sprawling central market, determined to sightsee on their day off.

A labyrinth of vibrant stalls, the market offered colourful fabrics and clothing, handcrafted goods, gleaming glassware, and delectable local food.

Anna paused at a stall draped with colourful woven textiles, admiring the patterns as she ran her fingers over the fabric. "Exquisite."

The owner, an older woman with a warm smile, beamed with pride. "Gracias, Señorita. Artisans from Indigenous communities handcrafted each piece."

St. James was nearby, taking in a display of carved wooden masks. He picked up an ornate piece, marvelling at its delicate craftsmanship, and turned to the elderly man behind the counter. "This is beautiful."

The vendor pointed to the crafts. "These masks represent ancient traditions and stories passed down through generations."

St. James smiled. "They're wonderful."

Navigating through the crowded aisles was challenging. People moved like swarms of bees.

"No place for a claustrophobic," St. James mumbled.

The enticing aroma of cooked empanadas wafted through the air, and St. James glanced at Anna with a raised eyebrow. "Shall we try one?"

Anna smiled. "Why not?"

At a bustling food stall, a jovial vendor greeted them warmly. "Bienvenidos! What can I prepare for you today?"

St. James ordered a chicken empanada for them to share. They passed the golden crescent back and forth and finished it off in a couple of bites each, which only whetted their appetite for lunch.

Following a delightful midday meal at the Capital Grill, they retreated to the Hotel Presidente and spent a relaxing afternoon in their air-conditioned suite, reading. At one point St. James fell asleep on Anna's arm. When he got too heavy for her, she gently slid out from under him and covered him with a light blanket.

On Sunday, they joined a guided tour of San José, eager to immerse themselves in the city's rich cultural tapestry. Anna's eyes sparkled, her excitement apparent as they walked through the bustling streets.

The original international airport was now a stunning Museum of Art filled with contemporary masterpieces and timeless classics. St. James was drawn to a floor-to-ceiling mural depicting Costa Rican history from pre-Columbian times to 1940, while Anna was taken by the rounded human figures in the sculpture garden.

"So different from classical European sculpture, and so powerful in its own way," Anna said.

"Art in its purest form," St. James mused.

Anna was breathless as they walked into the opulent halls of the National Theatre. "Just imagine the stories these walls could tell," she whispered, her eyes bright with wonder.

Next they visited the Pre-Colombian Gold Museum — a modern marvel of ancient artefacts. As they meandered through the exhibits, Anna whispered, "These artefacts are like whispers from the past, telling tales of a world long gone."

St. James nodded. "Like witnessing history come alive."

On the way back to the hotel, the couple walked together in silence, humbled by a sense of their own smallness, of their place in the sweep of human history.

St. James's thoughts were different than they had been that morning. He pondered all the ways humans had found to survive and leave their mark on the world, not just in that moment, or even during his lifetime, but across time.

He thought of the way people took care of themselves and their families, sometimes with honour, sometimes through deceit. The whole of human industry seemed to be pressing on him. How would history record his attempts to right the wrongs of this world? Would history notice him at all?

Anna looked down at her ring. For a moment, she glimpsed her connection to every other woman who had ever been in love. All of them, across time!

She thought of women like herself who had tied their fates to men of great skill, ambition, and integrity. Men like St. James. And what of the other women, the luckless or reckless ones, who stumbled into lives with men of far lower quality? Dishonest men. Men capable of deceit, even cruelty. What of them?

St. James squeezed her arm that was wrapped around his. "You seem lost in thought," he said.

Anna wanted to ask him if he thought they would be happy. Whether they would make something lasting and valuable of their time together.

She pulled them to a stop under a streetlamp that illuminated St. James's puzzled face. "Do you ever think of all the people who came before us?"

St. James nodded at his betrothed and smiled at her, as though he knew exactly what she meant. "I do."

***

On Monday morning, everyone gathered at the courthouse as planned. Agent García, a tall man with a weathered face, bulging eyes, and a red beard that gave him a Viking-like presence, seemed displeased to be there.

García and Montero sat to the right of Jiménez, with Segura on his left. Madrigal fidgeted in his seat, visibly nervous. St. James could easily guess that he had spent a tough weekend worrying that Jiménez would pressure him to transfer property from the mob. St. James and Anna took their seats next to Madrigal.

"Good morning, everyone," Jiménez said, opening the meeting. "St. James and Anna, I hear you've been taking in some of our local culture. I trust you had an uplifting tour."

"How—" Anna began.

Jiménez wiggled his fingers in the air. "We have eyes everywhere."

"You had someone follow us?" St. James was incredulous. "Why—"

Jiménez roared back with laughter, amused by his own joke. Finally, he folded his hands on the table and stifled a last laugh. "My cousin owns the tour company. I happened to mention you were in San José. It was purely by accident that he even noticed your names." Jiménez waited for any reaction and finally said, "How would you like to begin?"

St. James shook off his bemusement and gazed at his host. "Do you still have access to Carlos Sánchez's house?"

"Yes, it remains a crime scene. Sánchez lived alone. No one pressuring us for access."

"Where is it?"

"Escazú. Upscale neighbourhood west of the city centre. Why?"

"That's where we should execute our strategy."

Montero raised an eyebrow.

García rolled his eyes.

Jiménez looked puzzled. "Why there?"

St. James smiled. "That's where our notary lives."

Noticing Anna's disapproving eye, St. James adopted a more earnest tone. "Carlos Sánchez is the notary we should use to make the transfers."

Montero looked incredulous. "Thought he was dead."

García was confused. "He is."

"Here's my suggestion. Set up Sánchez's computer at his house exactly as it was when your agents found it. Segura, you'll become an expert at forging Sánchez's signature."

Segura remained emotionless.

St. James turned to Madrigal. "Madrigal, you'll prepare the legal documentation on Sánchez's computer to transfer the land from the mob. Once you've finished, Segura will forge his signature. I have all the legal descriptions needed. Global will incorporate a subsidiary in San José where the realty titles will be transferred."

All the blood seemed to have drained out of Madrigal's face. St. James looked at him and tried to sound reassuring. "Don't worry, Madrigal. Everything will be in Sánchez's name. There'll be no trace of you in the documentation. It will be as if Sánchez were alive and handling it himself."

Madrigal's bearing changed from terrified to somewhat concerned but still unconvinced. He began to speak tentatively. "But won't they … I mean, won't they know he's dead? I mean, they killed him?"

St. James was nodding at Madrigal when Jiménez, who had barely heard Madrigal, interjected. "It's brilliant."

Montero grinned. "It has a certain kamikaze charm. Leaves no trace of us. Done by someone dead. It's just crazy enough to confuse the hell out of them."

García frowned. "Can't the mob just transfer it back right away?"

St. James turned to García. "Yes, they can. Anna and I discussed this over the weekend. Here's the plan: Global will incorporate a Costa Rican subsidiary, Reclamation Properties Inc., which will own the lands we transfer from the mob. Reclamation will mortgage them through Global Finance, Global Insurance's New York-based finance company, for nineteen million dollars. Reclamation will use those funds to repay Global for its loss. All before the mob realizes the assets have been taken."

García understood the potential. "So, if the mob transfers them back to themselves, they'll inherit the mortgage obligations."

Montero jumped in. "Exactly. The mob discovers the mortgages when they do property searches."

St. James shook his head. "I don't think they'll do searches right away. They'll be in such a rush to transfer the real estate back, they'll move titles first and worry about searches later. Titles are out of mob hands for only a few days. It won't occur to them that someone would have time to abscond with equity. They'll assume property titles are the same as when they stole them from legitimate owners."

García appeared puzzled. "How can you be so sure?"

"Global Finance can process mortgages in no time. Unlike most finance companies that take several days to handle such transactions, Global can complete everything in less than a day. The mob won't suspect there's time for anything to be amiss. Too fast for normal mortgages to be approved and registered."

"So, we'll just have the advantage of time?" García said. "That seems far too simple. Dangerously so."

"But time is not just time," St. James protested. "It's what you can and can't do in the time you have that makes the plan work."

Madrigal looked helplessly at Jiménez, his anxiety reactivated. Segura lifted one eyebrow — the most change she showed all morning.

St. James backed up and tried again. "Most borrowers deal with independent mortgage companies with strict procedures — evaluating the borrower's creditworthiness, appraising the real estate, conducting title searches. All this takes time. Global Finance only needs a directive from DeSilva, which takes seconds, not days. The mob won't know what hit them because they won't know about DeSilva or her influence over a finance company's ability to act immediately."

Madrigal was listening too intently to fidget or protest.

It was Montero who finally spoke. "Not all the land might be mortgage-free."

"Only need about thirty properties with enough free equity to mortgage to cover Global's loss of nineteen million," St. James figured. "You can check for mortgages on that many properties in a day. Besides, if your intel is correct, the mob holds more than thirty properties. There's likely plenty of equity to cover Global's loss."

Everyone silently contemplated the feasibility.

Jiménez cogitated on all this. "What happens when the mob defaults on the mortgages?"

St. James grinned. "That's the best part. Global Finance will initiate foreclosure proceedings against Reclamation. Force the sale of property to recover the unpaid mortgages. The mob will have two choices: let the ownership go to foreclosure or pay off the debt. They'll never pay the mortgages. Probably argue that Reclamation should be responsible for the debt. By then, Global Insurance will have recouped its nineteen million from the mortgage proceeds."

García was curious. "What happens after the foreclosures?"

Montero elaborated. "If a third party doesn't buy the assets during foreclosure, Global will sell them to recover the delinquent mortgages."

St. James agreed. "Exactly. The current situation has the mob with stolen real estate and Global's nineteen million insurance payments. Once the strategy is executed, Global will end up owning the land and the nineteen million, effectively turning the tables on the mob.

Jiménez smiled. "Scam the scammers. I like it."

St. James turned to Jiménez. "You didn't expect the OIJ would resort to such tactics."

Jiménez's smile was wry. "Didn't say we would do it. I just liked the idea."

St. James beamed. "You're enjoying this more than you let on."

Jiménez ignored St. James, but his small smile gave him away.

St. James moved on. "What do we know about the mob Boss?"

Jiménez twisted the end of his moustache. "He thinks of himself as a Mexican strongman — instills fear in his men. 'Loyalty or death' is his motto, as we've seen with Sánchez. He has a huge ego and is insecure and spontaneous, which makes him more dangerous."

St. James winced. "Where is your intel on him coming from?"

Jiménez smiled. "Many sources over several years."

Montero cleared his throat. "Carlos Baca is from Mexico City. He's supposed to be this big, intimidating figure, but he's just an average-looking guy — in his early forties, under six feet tall. Mob bosses often have to show strength, even if they don't have it. Intimidation is critical in his line of work."

St. James mused, "So he's an average man playing a big role in a violent world."

Jiménez smiled. "About right."

Anna considered Montero's words. "I can see how that would fuel paranoia."

St. James nodded. "Stronger men beneath him, nipping at his heels for the top job, wouldn't help his stability."

Anna looked away. "How did he become Boss if that's the case?"

Jiménez looked at Anna. "He was like a son to his predecessor. On his deathbed, the predecessor gathered all senior mob members and ordered them to accept Baca as his successor."

St. James scowled. "Wouldn't last long after the old man died."

Jiménez leaned forward and placed his elbows on the table. "He was smart. He knew the others would kill Baca as soon as he died, so he put out a contract against anyone who would try to harm Baca — left the contract with an anonymous lawyer to be activated if anything happened. Then he told all the men. They didn't want to risk eliminating Baca with a potential hit order hanging over their heads. So, they left Baca in place and worked around him."

St. James smiled. "Didn't have to be a mob member who killed him. Could be any hitman outside the mob."

García became more serious. "There's something else you should know."

CHAPTER 22

St. James's eyes narrowed as he examined a black-and-white photograph Jiménez placed on the table. "Who's that?"

The man in the picture wore a stern expression framed by a wide-brimmed hat and a formidable moustache. The yellowed photograph captured an era long past.

Jiménez's finger glided along the edge of the photo as if seeking to draw the past into the present. "That's Elfego Baca. Ever heard of him?"

Anna's curiosity was piqued. "No." She bit her lip, her gaze locked on the photo.

With a slight tilt of his head, Jiménez's tone switched, a note of reverence creeping in. "Baca was a notorious figure in the early 1890s — a lawman, lawyer, and later a politician in New Mexico. He made a name for himself by eliminating criminals. Intimidation was his weapon. If that didn't work, he made good on his threats."

St. James mulled over Jiménez's story. "So, it was 'clean up your act or face the consequences.'"

"Exactly." Jiménez's eyes darkened as he relived the history. "He survived multiple shootouts. His most famous was holding off an attack by several gunmen for over thirty hours. They fired more than four thousand rounds into the wooden jail Baca was holed up in. Legend has it he escaped through the floorboards. Died of natural causes in New Mexico at eighty."

St. James raised an eyebrow. "Mob Boss's relative?"

Montero shrugged, disdain in his eyes. "That's what Baca wants us to believe." He crossed his arms defensively as if the idea was absurd. "No evidence to support it."

St. James thought about the implications. "So, what's the takeaway?"

Jiménez leaned back, the leather chair creaking beneath him. His gaze lingered on each face as he surveyed the room. "Baca projects himself as a descendant of Elfego Baca — rugged, ruthless, unbeatable. He demands respect, embodying the traits of his alleged legendary ancestor."

"Sounds like he's concocted quite a fantasy," Anna said.

Montero laughed, shaking his head, the corner of his mouth twitching in a knowing smile. "Baca's the only one who believes it. They say his men joke about it behind his back."

St. James glanced out the window. "So, he's compensating for insecurities with an imaginary persona?"

"Yes." Jiménez grinned as he recognized the truth. "Classic overcompensation."

Jiménez glanced at his watch. "Would you mind if I took a smoke break?"

A chorus of "no" echoed in response.

When they reconvened, García's voice pierced the silence. "One final detail about Baca."

Anna straightened in her seat. "What's that?"

"A few years ago, he changed his name from Carlos to Elfego to complete his rebranding." García's fingers steepled, emphasizing the stupidity of the revelation.

St. James smiled. "I like it."

Jiménez glanced at St. James. "Why?"

"An audacious yet fragile personality like Baca's is easily provoked." St. James's tone was measured, a glint of mischief in his eyes. "Using Sánchez's name to transfer land will make Baca more paranoid. He'll rush Sánchez's house, seeking revenge."

Montero raised an eyebrow. "So, you're betting on his ego being his undoing?"

"Precisely." A confident smile crept across St. James' face. "The more threatened he feels, the more likely he is to slip up."

St. James turned to García, "We're counting on your team to act when the mob enters Sánchez's house."

García scratched his red beard, his demeanour sharpening. "That can be arranged. Once the land is transferred, we can station twenty-five special agents around Sánchez's neighbourhood."

Anna's eyes narrowed. "What's going to be the biggest challenge?"

García's expression hardened. "Keeping our agents hidden. It's a quiet neighbourhood. Too many agents would attract unwanted attention."

Montero stood up. "Let's take a break. I know some retired agents in Escazú. I'll ask how we can discreetly move enforcement officials."

St. James felt the momentum building. "Okay. Anna and I will go out for fresh air while you make calls."

Jiménez stood and glanced at Madrigal. The nervous notary was fidgeting with a pen, one leg bouncing. Segura remained stoic, unreadable. "I'm heading to my office to return messages," Jiménez said.

Thirty minutes later, they reassembled.

Jiménez scanned the group. "How'd it go?"

Montero shrugged. "Better than expected. A retired agent, Henry Araya, lives near Sánchez's house. His place is more modest but close enough in distance."

García approved. "Excellent! Araya's a good man."

Montero was optimistic. "Araya's enthusiastic about helping. His living area is enormous. He's willing to host thirty agents. We can blend in if the people arrive in small numbers and dress casually. It'll look like a retirement get-together."

St. James smiled. "I like it. Move them at night to minimize visibility."

Anna brightened, her earlier confidence returning. "Sounds solid."

The group fell into a contemplative silence.

Anna scanned the room, sensing uncertainty. "What are we forgetting?"

Everyone pondered the question, their faces reflecting a mix of concentration and unease.

Jiménez's frown appeared thoughtful. "Can't think of anything major at the moment, but I'm sure Director Ramírez will have plenty to say."

Montero's look was steady but fringed with concern. "Are we ready for Director Ramírez?"

Jiménez tapped his fingers on the table, the sound a steady rhythm. "No. The Director will expect a complete plan with every conceivable detail worked out. What we have is an outline. A concept. I don't want to put much time into preparing a detailed plan if he doesn't approve the concept."

CHAPTER 23

Director Ramírez's tone was laced with skepticism as he leaned back in his chair. "So you want to take on the mob, Jiménez?"

Jiménez squinted, burdened by the weight of the question. "Sir, I would prefer to think of it as addressing real estate thefts."

Ramírez chewed on an unlit cigar, his appearance hardening. "You believe the mob orchestrates the thefts?"

"Yes, Sir."

"Then you're taking on the mob."

"Sir, what we are presenting here is an outline of a detailed plan yet to be prepared," Jiménez advised.

Ramírez scowled. "How do you expect me to respond to an outline?"

"We are looking for approval of a mission in principle. I didn't want to waste manpower if there was no appetite for any plan."

Ramírez grunted. "Proceed, but I'll be adding my thoughts on what a plan should include as if that's what you're presenting."

Jiménez didn't like that. It meant the Director would compare their outline to a plan as if they should be the same. Jiménez gave his team a knowing look, hoping they picked up the same nuance.

Jiménez introduced St. James and Anna, explaining their role in the investigation. Ramírez acknowledged them with a curt nod, then gestured to a woman in a dark blue suit, seated next to him. "I've asked María Chávez, head of the Prosecutor's Specialized Fraud Unit, to join us — our equivalent of the U.S. Attorney General," he explained for the benefit of St. James and Anna. "She will ensure whatever we discuss is legal."

Peering over her half glasses, Chávez made a blunt point for St. James and Anna. "*Sticking to established legal procedures minimizes issues later on.*"

"Take us through your outline, Jiménez," the Director ordered, his eyes narrowing with scrutiny.

Jiménez gestured to St. James. "Hamilton St. James developed the strategy. I'll let him explain."

Ramírez raised an eyebrow. "Why is a Canadian consultant crafting strategies for the OIJ?" he said bluntly.

Jiménez quickly detailed St. James's background, emphasizing his law enforcement experience and connection with Global Insurance. Ramírez listened carefully.

"Very well. Proceed," he instructed.

St. James outlined the plan: securing Sánchez's home, Segura's forgeries, Madrigal's legal documents, and Global Finance's foreclosures. He answered several questions as he went along. "Sir, executing the rest of the strategy rests with Montero and García."

"Thank you, Señor St. James. Montero?"

Montero and García described their roles: deploying hidden agents, dispersing them around Sánchez's estate at night, positioning them strategically, guarding entrances, and managing arrests.

Ramírez paused. "Is this legal, María?"

Chávez reflected on the question. "Depends."

Ramírez frowned. "What do you mean — depends?"

Chávez took a deep breath and explained. "If you induce someone to commit a crime they wouldn't have committed otherwise, it could be interpreted as instigating. This may not directly apply to the mob, but they would argue that the OIJ instigated the crime by using a deceased person's signature to flush them out. To ensure a judge doesn't accept that argument, you must demonstrate that the mob was the one who initiated the criminal activity that necessitated the flushing out."

Anna interjected, "What about entrapment?"

Chávez's voice was authoritative. "Entrapment involves the intent to commit a crime originating with the accused, not being instigated by others. In this case, the mob's criminal activity originates with them, so entrapment by the OIJ could be interpreted as acceptable procedure."

Frustration crept into Jiménez's voice. "That's exactly what we're proposing. Why can't we be more decisive?"

"Property transferred from a person without their consent can complicate the matter," Chávez countered.

Jiménez turned to Chávez. "How?"

"Judges interpret testimony and facts their way. There's always a risk they won't view it from our side — that everything originated with the mob."

St. James crossed his arms, dissatisfied. "Great."

"María, discuss this with your colleagues and come back to me with a final position," Ramírez said, his tone brooking no argument.

"Of course, Sir." Chávez stood and left the room.

Ramírez turned to the remaining men. "How much blood?"

Jiménez appeared puzzled. "Sir?"

"How much blood will be spilled?"

The men exchanged uncertain glances. García frowned, hesitating. "Haven't thought about that, Sir."

Ramírez's voice turned abrupt. "Why?"

Montero pulled a handkerchief from his pocket, wiping his forehead as the stress thickened. "How could we, Sir?"

Ramírez turned the cigar to a fresh side and bit down, his frustration evident. "An estimate is better than nothing."

Jiménez's voice lowered. "We can't anticipate every outcome, Sir."

Ramírez's gaze was piercing. "You're not going to pull off an operation of this magnitude without risk of violence. We need to assess the potential loss of human resources."

García's demeanour reflected defensiveness. "We're aware of that, Sir."

Ramírez's disapproval was palpable. "How many men will Baca deploy once he realizes his real estate is gone?"

"Can't be sure," Montero admitted.

"Then how did you decide on twenty-five agents?"

Jiménez felt cornered. "Can't imagine he would send an army just for reconnaissance."

Ramírez began gnawing on a fresh cigar. "You're assuming Baca won't expect a trap."

The men observed Ramírez, realization dawning on them.

"If a notary you knew was dead and property was transferred away from you by him, wouldn't you be suspicious?" Ramírez's voice was steady but intense.

García looked uncomfortable.

Ramírez chomped on his cigar. "How do you intend to secure cooperation from local law enforcement?"

García blinked, surprised by the directness of the question. "We'll arrange a meeting with the local police chief. We're concerned some force members may be on Baca's payroll."

Ramírez grunted. "You can say the same about us."

Anna's cell vibrated with a text.

Ramírez squinted at the group. "What contingency plans do you have if agents are compromised?"

Jiménez's face turned pale. "That will be in our fully developed plan, Sir."

Ramírez snorted. "You're proposing to walk into a potential hornet's nest without considering all the repercussions. Have you assessed the financial impact of the operation on our resources — budget and manpower?"

Uneasy glances floated around the table.

Ramírez rose and began to pace. "And what about collateral damage? Have you considered innocent bystanders caught in the crossfire? You can't just charge into a residential enclave with guns blazing and hope for the best!" He slammed his hand on the table, fluttering papers. "What if we end up sparking a national incident? The implications would be catastrophic."

Everyone was beginning to look demoralized.

Montero cleared his throat. "Didn't consider that, Sir. We'll need to incorporate those measures into our draft plan."

Director Ramírez shook his head in disgust. "What about surveillance? Have you thought of electronic monitoring or counter-surveillance? The mob has resources — they might be watching, listening — using drones to spy on us."

"Yes. We've debated all that, Sir," Jiménez assured.

Ramírez's eyes reflected a more significant storm brewing. "How about coordination with other government agencies? The operation might require joint efforts from customs, immigration, or even military units if things escalate. Have you considered red tape and jurisdictional issues?"

Jiménez shook his head. "We've been focusing on tactical issues. I suppose we should consider the need for other agencies."

"Suppose? We're not talking about an afterthought," Ramírez snapped. "You need clear lines of communication and coordination with every relevant department. If the operation is compromised and becomes public, the fallout could be enormous. You're risking a political scandal that would destroy the OIJ's reputation."

St. James agreed. "A crisis communication plan is necessary to address potentially leaked details."

Ramírez's deportment hardened. "How will you handle legal objections? What measures are in place to ensure every action is within the law?"

"We'll have a detailed legal protocol and documentation for every aspect of the operation. I'll ensure it's reviewed with Chávez before we proceed," Jiménez said.

"What about your exit strategy? If the operation goes sideways, how will you extract your agents safely? And what if you can't capture all the suspects?"

García's face paled. "Haven't developed a comprehensive exit strategy yet. That needs to be created and integrated into the plan."

Ramírez glared at him, his disappointment apparent. "You need more than a generic exit strategy. To have a hope in hell of succeeding, you'll need to consider every possible scenario — hostile responses, ambushes, even hostage situations. Ensure you have contingency plans for each one."

Everyone displayed trepidation.

Ramírez's voice thundered in the tense room. "This plan is no plan at all! It's a recipe for disaster! I expect better from my team. Go back to work, and don't come back until you have something worth considering. Your outline, as you call it, has more holes than my target range — too many even to qualify for an outline."

CHAPTER 24

Alajuela

"Jiménez hired an advisor," announced Eduardo, a tall, thin Tico with smooth, dark skin and a love of well-made shirts. His voice carried urgency as he strode into Baca's dimly lit office.

Baca's eyes narrowed. "Who?"

"Detective from up north."

"Where?"

"Canada."

Baca assessed this unexpected development. "What do we know?"

"His name is Hamilton St. James. Has a partner. Erasmus White, who goes by Dozer. And there's a woman."

Baca raised an eyebrow. "Dozer? What kind of name is that? Is he sleepy? Narcoleptic?"

Eduardo indulged his Boss's joke with a chortle. "I believe it's a football reference."

"Someone who bulldozes through the other team."

Eduardo nodded.

"And the woman?"

"St. James's fiancée, Anna Strauss. A researcher."

Baca absorbed the information, his mind racing. *An odd combination for Jiménez. What's he up to?* "What else?"

"That's all our informant knew."

"Get back to them. I want to know everything about Jiménez's new people. Tell our researcher to do the same."

Eduardo nodded and quickly exited the room, leaving Baca alone with his rising paranoia. Already, on his hard, square face, the little diamond-shaped scar below his lower lip was beginning to do its telltale dance. A gift from a knife fight, it became more pronounced when he was enraged and retreated in times of calm.

He paced the room on short, muscular legs, trying to think through this unexpected challenge. Why would Jimenez, a man he had been dancing around for years, suddenly bring in a group of investigators from, of all places, Canada? What could this possibly mean? No matter how hard he tried, he couldn't stop his mind from racing in all directions. As he passed the room's only mirror, he lifted his wide-brimmed Mexican hat — the one that he insisted belonged to the legendary Elfego Baca — and ran his hand over his receding hairline.

Half an hour later, Eduardo returned, looking subdued. "Our informant had little more to offer," he said, "but our researcher uncovered some intriguing details."

"Go on."

"Hamilton St. James is a fraud detective with an impeccable record. He's known for solving difficult cases, and for his determination. I'm told he has an annoying habit of never giving up." Eduardo glanced at Baca for his reaction.

Perfect, Baca thought. *Just what we need right now.* "And this Dozer?"

"Erasmus White owns an investigation firm in Toronto. He handles security for St. James and is reputed to be a dangerous adversary."

Baca's forehead furrowed. "Strauss?"

"Not much is known about her. She's a partner, working with St. James. Thought to be a top-notch researcher."

Baca reflected on the implications. *Another unknown. Not just a team — a potential threat.* He leaned closer, his dark eyes piercing. "What about St. James's methods? Past cases?"

Eduardo flipped through his notes. "Known for going off the grid, pursuing leads others think irrelevant or too risky. Some say he's reckless, but those who've worked with him admire his tenacity."

Baca exploded in anger, wiping a small pile of paper off his desk. "My God, man, did you get this off their website? Give me something I can work with, please. These sound like client testimonials. I need to know their weaknesses!"

Eduardo stumbled on his words. "I'm sorry, Boss. This is what came back from the researcher. We'll try to find out more."

"All right, all right." Baca rubbed his stubble, attempting to calm himself. "What makes Dozer so dangerous?"

Eduardo hesitated. "Dozer has a security background, and he isn't afraid to use intimidation tactics."

Baca smirked. The information fed his mental image of the trio. "If they're so formidable, why haven't they made a move?"

Eduardo shook his head. "That's what worries me. St. James is also known for patience. He waits for the right moment to strike — meticulously."

Baca's stomach churned. He ran a hand through what was left of his hair, contemplating potential fallout.

"Anna Strauss? Any dirt?"

Eduardo steadied his voice. "Not much. She keeps a low profile, but whispers suggest she may be a key strategist."

Baca processed the implications. *Jiménez is upping his game. Not a game of cat and mouse now; we're playing chess.* "We need to be prepared for anything."

Eduardo paused for a moment to think all this through. "I'll have our researcher dig deeper into Strauss's background."

"Good. And let's consider the possibility that Jiménez might use this team as a diversion." Baca continued pacing. *What else is Jiménez hiding?* "Keep an eye on Jiménez's other activities."

"I'll prioritize it."

Baca's jaw tightened. "Can't show weakness. We need to be smarter and quicker. Anticipate their moves. Be one step ahead."

Eduardo's eyes reflected a hint of admiration. "You've always been one step ahead. I'll make sure we stay that way."

"Good. Keep me updated." Baca's tone was firm. "And Eduardo?"

"Yes?"

"Make sure our informant knows we mean business. If they hold back information, it won't end well for them."

Eduardo swallowed hard. "I'll make it clear."

When Eduardo exited, Baca continued to pace. The stakes were higher now. *We have to outthink these people before they turn the tables on us, whatever that might involve.* He stopped and stared out the window at industrial truck traffic. *Every detail matters. One misstep can mean disaster.*

CHAPTER 25

St. James sat in their brightly lit hotel room in San José, taking a moment to admire its high ceilings and large windows overlooking the bustling city. He glanced at his laptop as it buzzed with a video call from Dozer.

Dozer's familiar, rugged face filled most of the screen. Behind him was a sun-soaked beach scene in Tamarindo.

"Hamilton, you won't believe it!"

St. James moved closer to the computer. "Believe what?"

"Louis has a girlfriend!"

"What! You're kidding!"

Dozer grinned. "Nope."

"Who is she? I'm scared to ask how she dresses. Mismatched paisley? Clashing polka dots?"

Dozer laughed. "Not that I've seen. She's a guest at the hotel. Visiting from California."

"How did they meet?"

"We actually saw her the other morning at breakfast, when you and Anna were still here. Louis noticed her at the time, and Anna tried to get him to talk to her, but he chickened out. Then they ran into each other again two days ago and she wound up talking to him."

"I don't remember any of that. Can you text me a picture?"

Dozer grinned. "Way ahead of you. Check your phone."

St. James grabbed his cell and opened Dozer's text. "My God, she looks normal. Not bad looking, either. Got a picture of them together?"

"Should be coming through now."

St. James's phone buzzed with Dozer's new message. He burst into laughter. "Oh my God! I've never seen him in a regular shirt and tie — without plaid."

Dozer laughed, enjoying St. James's reaction. "He bought that in Tamarindo. They're a sight to behold. Not a bad-looking couple once you get past the initial shock."

St. James studied the picture. Louis was dressed in a crisp, tightly fitted light suit, standing next to a well-dressed woman with a warm smile. She was fair-skinned and taller than Smythe, with short black hair. "Must be quite a woman for him to give up his plaid. What's her name?"

"Sandy Bradshaw."

St. James was puzzled. "Trying to figure out what she sees in him. What's the attraction?"

Dozer's eyes wandered the room behind St. James on his screen. "Brains, I think."

"Brains?"

"Sandy's into computers too. She handles app design and programming for a major tech company in California."

St. James smiled. "Nerds in love."

Dozer shot him a look. "Nerd is a compliment these days."

"As it should be," St. James conceded. "Good for Louis."

Dozer took a sip of coffee. "How's the investigation going?"

"I need you."

Dozer let out a long sigh. "Thank Christ."

St. James laughed. "Getting antsy? Too much R&R?"

"You know me. Can't sit on my hands for long. What's up?"

"Remember when you made me promise to call at the first smell of trouble?"

"Yep."

"Well, it's become a stench."

"What happened?"

St. James outlined everything since they arrived in San José: mob involvement, stolen real estate, high-stakes meetings, planning sessions, and ongoing investigation and research.

Dozer listened carefully and paused after St. James finished. "How long have you known that the mob was involved?"

"A couple of days."

"I should have been on a flight to San José the minute you heard."

"We're fine," St. James reassured him. "But it's time."

Dozer's expression turned grave. "Stealing real estate from the mob won't win you many friends."

"I'm guessing none."

"And you don't have a game plan approved yet?"

"It's in the works."

"What's the team like?"

"Solid, I think. The OIJ is committed, but their methods are still a mystery to me, and I don't really know these guys or their capabilities. I need your eyes on them now, while they're revising their tactics, not after."

Dozer's mood lifted. "Sweet. One final question."

"What?"

"You solved the case and made almost four million in two days. Why are you risking your skin and what's left of your holiday for less money?"

St. James grinned at his bodyguard, a mischievous glint in his eye. "Let's just put it down to eccentricity," he said, ending the call before Dozer could respond.

St. James contemplated the blank screen. The gravity of the situation weighed on him, but Dozer's arrival promised a much-needed boost. He began preparing for the next day, knowing a revised strategy could make or break their chances.

In Tamarindo, Dozer leaned back in his chair, a smile tugging at the corners of his mouth. The serene rhythm of the waves lapping at the shore was about to be drowned out by a different kind of energy — the chaos he craved.

CHAPTER 26

Dozer grabbed his bag from the carousel and headed for the airport exit, where he summoned a taxi for the ride into downtown San José.

The young Mexican driver chatted incessantly during the cab ride. Dozer lied; he was in Costa Rica for an aunt's funeral, hoping that would signal the driver to be quiet. Instead, the driver launched into tales of funerals he attended.

"Will you please stop talking?" Dozer said, unable to take it any longer.

The driver was quiet for a moment, then grinned in the rearview mirror. "Guess I inherited the talking gene from my family. My Uncle Rodríguez —"

Dozer had had enough. He grabbed the door handle while the car was still moving. "Let me out here!"

The driver protested. "We're not at the Hotel Presidente yet!"

Dozer tossed money over the front seat to cover the fare. "I'll walk the rest of the way."

The driver glanced at the bill, then back at Dozer through the rearview mirror. "You sure? It's a long way."

Dozer gritted his teeth, fighting the urge to snap. "I've got it from here."

The driver pulled to the curb and popped the trunk. "Suit yourself, mister." He watched Dozer yank his bag from the trunk and slam the trunk closed.

It was a fifteen-minute walk to the Hotel Presidente, which only heightened Dozer's frustration. After checking in and unpacking, he headed down the hall and knocked on St. James's door.

Anna welcomed Dozer. "I'd know that banging anywhere."

Dozer smiled. "You should. I've perfected it since we met."

St. James emerged from behind the desk. "Ah, the cavalry has arrived. Cavalry of one, that is. Come in, Dozer. We have a lot to talk about."

Dozer flopped onto the bed. "I've been expecting one of your case dumps. I even played it out in my head during the flight."

Anna smiled. "You know him well."

Setting aside the playful dig, St. James painted a vivid portrait of each OIJ official, delving into their personalities and analyzing what he thought were their strengths and weaknesses.

Dozer showed particular interest in the mob Boss Baca and St. James's discussion with Director Ramírez. "The Director was wise to push back. Baca won't come with just a couple of bodyguards. He'll bring a small army."

"Most likely," St. James agreed. "That's why I wanted you involved in the next phase."

Anna piped up. "I wanted you here to protect my fiancé."

Dozer winked at her.

St. James sat behind the desk. "I'm emailing Jiménez to let him know you're here and want to be part of the planning revisions."

Dozer smiled. "Great. Is there a bar nearby?"

Anna rolled her eyes toward the ceiling. "On the roof. The Azotea Calle 7. Opens at four."

Dozer checked his watch. "Fifteen minutes from now. Think I can hang on until then."

St. James detailed his findings from Jiménez's files, and Dozer sought more information on how the property frauds were conducted — timing, execution, notaries, lawyers, and the involvement of mob buyers.

St. James's phone buzzed. He read it and smiled. "Email from Jiménez. Says he doesn't need your help, Dozer. Then he says, *you'll argue the point, no matter what I say, so bring him anyway.*"

Dozer laughed. "You've only been here a couple of days and already you're annoying people."

St. James chuckled at the dig and sat down to reply to Jiménez.

Anna's enthusiasm bubbled over. "Dozer, I need to know more about this Sandy person who has captured Louis's heart. What's her background? Where does she live? How does she dress? Her mannerisms and personality — everything! Go!"

Dozer held up his palm to fend her off. "Anna, you're machine-gunning questions I can't answer!"

Anna was incredulous. "Didn't you ask her anything?"

"No! The conversation was all about computers. Couldn't squeeze in a word."

"Okay, but what about her clothing? Is she stylish? Attractive?"

"She wore —" Dozer struggled. "Some sort of sun dress."

Anna glared. "A sun dress? Is that all you've got?"

Dozer searched his memory. "She may have been wearing a straw hat."

Anna was fuming and laughing at the same time. "You know, for someone who has to pay attention to the details of criminal cases, you're not very good at this."

"I can say, confidently, that there were no fashion crimes committed by Sandy. Or none that I noticed." Dozer looked down at his simple cotton shorts and taupe golf shirt that had seen a few too many washes. "Then again, do you really want a wardrobe report from me?"

"Fair," Anna said, giving up in amused frustration. "I'll research her myself."

***

The following day, St. James, Anna, and Dozer arrived at the courthouse and headed to the usual room where the OIJ participants had gathered.

St. James entered first. "Apologies for being late. This is my bodyguard, Erasmus White — he prefers Dozer, a moniker from his university football days."

Dozer smiled at the law enforcement agents who eyed his imposing figure.

St. James gestured toward Jiménez. "Dozer, this is Captain Jiménez, who leads operations here."

Jiménez rose, extending his hand for Dozer to shake.

St. James introduced Dozer around the table.

Jiménez brought the meeting to order. "The Director sent us back to create a detailed plan and address unknowns regarding the takedown of Baca's mob. Montero and García prepared the approach. Montero, you begin."

Montero moved to the whiteboard. "Initially, we thought twenty-five men and women would suffice. The Director questioned that number. We thought using Sánchez's name would enrage Baca, prompting him to rush to Sánchez's house."

Dozer interrupted. "Since I'm new, may I ask questions?"

Montero looked put out. "Go ahead."

"Thank you. How many men does Baca have?"

García squinted. "Don't know for certain, but estimates put it at around fifty to sixty."

Dozer turned to Jiménez. "How many field agents can you assemble on short notice?"

Jiménez gestured for García to answer. "About forty."

Anna interjected. "How much notice?"

Jiménez twisted the end of his thin moustache. "A day, if I push it."

"Longer," Montero added. "Some would have to disengage from current assignments and travel from the borders."

Dozer turned to García. "I assume you've scoped out Sánchez's house?"

"Of course. Several times. We got security codes from the alarm company. Took pictures inside and out, noting potential ambush locations."

Dozer paused and then said, "I'd like to do another sweep of Sánchez's house if that's all right. With you there, of course."

García flushed slightly and his jaw tightened, but he said, "Happy to."

"Okay. Was there forced entry when Sánchez was murdered?"

Jiménez twisted the end of his mustache. "No. The shooter made the hit from a roof three houses over. No evidence anyone but Sánchez was in the house."

Dozer rubbed his smooth, hairless head. "So, Baca has sharpshooters?"

Jiménez nodded. "Intelligence says five."

Dozer frowned. "That changes things. We'd need agents on roofs around Sánchez's to counter them."

Montero's irritation grew with each interruption, until he cast a questioning glance at Jiménez.

Jiménez's piercing eyes gave Montero a warning.

García agreed. "We'd notify the owners that we'd need access to their homes."

Dozer frowned. "Not until the last minute. Some might be on Baca's payroll."

Now it was Jiménez who looked frustrated. "Easy to say. But when is the last minute?"

St. James shook his head. "The million-dollar question — when will Baca show up?"

Dozer's thoughts raced. "Are we planning to forge Sánchez's signature for the realty transfers?"

Jiménez glanced at Segura. "Yes. Segura is the expert on that."

Dozer nodded in Segura's direction and paused to consider his next question. "How will Baca learn about the missing real estate?"

Jiménez stoked his square jaw. "The ministry doesn't notify owners of changes in ownership. We'll send an anonymous email using Sánchez's computer, telling Baca his property has been stolen, without specifying which properties or who stole them — just enough information to drive him crazy. Without this, Baca wouldn't know his property had disappeared until he checked the property registry."

"But Baca may not have a reason to confirm his tax obligations in the short term," Montero cautioned. "We need him enraged on cue, so he attacks Sánchez's house immediately. If we wait, the operation fails."

Dozer's forehead creased. "So, you're using the dead guy's name for the transfers and to inform Baca of his loss?"

"Yes," Jiménez confirmed.

Dozer shook his head. "Who suggested using a dead man as the notary?"

"That would be me," St. James admitted, pride evident in his voice.

Dozer frowned. "That's stupid, Hamilton. You know better than that."

Jiménez was astonished. "I thought using Sánchez's name was smart."

"Might have been if Sánchez wasn't dead," Dozer argued. "His name signals a trap is certain. Baca will do one of two things."

"Being…?" Anna prompted.

"Storm the place with fifty men or send a scout to watch it for as long as necessary to figure out what to expect."

The room fell silent.

Montero pondered. "How do we lure Baca to Sánchez's house if we don't use his name?"

Dozer's confidence surged. "By using another Baca notary's name for the transfers — one that's still alive. Baca receives the email, becomes enraged, and contacts the Registry office to find out which land has been transferred and the name of the living notary. With no one living in Sánchez's house, Baca will think his notary is using Sánchez's computer and house for the thefts. Sánchez's name on the email means someone is impersonating a dead man. If he thinks it's an unknown person setting him up, he'll come prepared for anything — bring an army. Using a living notary means Baca has someone to target. He might send fewer men to eliminate a single person."

St. James looked simultaneously proud and like he'd had the stuffing knocked out of him. "Well, folks, this is why we pay Dozer the big bucks. When I look at it now, it's obvious. A living target makes more sense. Short-sighted on my part."

Anna touched St. James's arm in support.

García's embarrassment was evident. "Short-sighted on all our parts."

Montero looked troubled. "What if Baca sends a scout first, as you suggested?"

"We'll prepare for that scenario, too," García said.

Montero grimaced. "We'll need a surveillance team in case of scouts. I can organize that. Ensure they're intercepted before they can report back to Baca."

Jiménez wanted to move on. "What does using a living notary do to our personnel count?"

Dozer's eyes took in the agents. "Twenty-five is a good estimate if we use a living notary's name. It's not nearly enough if we use Sánchez's."

"Shit!" García exclaimed. "We've gone through all this just to end up with the same number we started with."

Jiménez frowned. "That's not what Dozer is saying. He's saying we decided on twenty-five without considering Baca's emotional response to hearing from a notary he's already killed."

Montero frowned. "Probably what the Director was trying to tell us."

St. James looked curious. "Who do you suggest play the notary, then?"

Segura spoke up for the first time. "What about Héctor Pérez?"

Montero didn't hesitate. "Good suggestion. We have a file on him."

St. James turned to Montero. "What does that tell us?"

"Pérez has been Baca's notary for about ten years. Charged with real estate fraud five years ago, but a lawyer got him off on a technicality. No doubt he was guilty as hell."

Dozer smiled. "Sounds like the perfect candidate."

CHAPTER 27

Alajuela

Eduardo sat across the table from Baca in the dimly lit warehouse part of Baca's office building. The air was thick with the metallic scent of oil and rust. Massive metal beams loomed overhead, casting jagged shadows on the floor. The faint sound of dripping water resonated, each drop marking time like the tick of a clock.

"St. James specializes in fraud-related crimes." Eduardo's voice was steady, though a slight tremor in his hands betrayed his nerves. Despite his years of service, Baca's right-hand man still felt his Boss's glares like a vise. "He's well-known by law enforcement worldwide. Investigates defrauded corporations — highly regarded and relentless. Not a man to be trifled with."

Baca slanted back in his chair, arms crossed, muscles tensing under his fitted shirt. The chair's creaking punctuated his stillness as his narrowed eyes assessed Eduardo's every word.

Eduardo maintained his composure. "Besides running an investigation agency in Toronto, Dozer acts as St. James's bodyguard. They tackle fraud cases together. The Strauss woman — Anna — is supposed to be a crack researcher. There's also a fourth man, Smythe, a computer expert, but he's not tied to Jiménez."

Silence hung thick as Baca absorbed the information.

"St. James has an MBA from Harvard and a CPA. Dozer's a muscle-bound Black man with a black belt in karate."

"Karate?" Baca's disbelief was apparent. He tilted forward, fingers tapping rhythmically on the table. "Muscle used to be all you needed back in the day. Doesn't seem to be enough today. What else do we know about St. James?"

"He solved a major case in Germany, where several companies were defrauded. The ringleader's in prison. He also collaborated with Washington D.C. police on a hidden cash case in Grand Cayman."

Baca's jaw tightened, a muscle jumping in his cheek. "Get Jimmy to tail them. I want to know where they go and who they talk to."

"Certainly, Sir. But—"

"But what?" Baca's voice lowered, an undercurrent sharp as glass.

"I want to ensure we're not overextending ourselves. St. James has connections. If they catch wind of our interest—"

Baca cut him off, leaning forward until the table groaned under his weight. "Do you think I care what they think? We're not the ones who should be scared. This is our territory. I want them to feel that."

Eduardo swallowed hard as sweat beaded on his face. He had witnessed what happened to those who didn't follow Baca's orders — stories of violence that still haunted him. "Of course. I'll have Jimmy start surveillance immediately. Gather intelligence on their every move." He tried to project confidence, but the knot in his stomach tightened.

Baca's eyes darkened, and he interlaced his fingers. "What vulnerabilities do they have?"

Eduardo took a deep breath. "St. James is emotionally attached to the woman. Strauss could be leverage if we need it." He caught the intent of Baca's sharp look.

Baca's grin was devoid of warmth, like a wolf sensing weakness. "And Dozer? What about him?"

"There's something wrong with his brother — mentally challenged. If we can find a way to exploit that…" Eduardo let the suggestion linger, watching for Baca's reaction.

Baca let out an icy snicker. "A bodyguard with a soft spot. How convenient." He leaned back, a glint in his eye, revelling in the potential chaos.

Eduardo shifted. "We should also consider Smythe. He could pose a risk. Computer experts can unearth many things from afar."

"What do you know about him?"

"Not much. He's a tech wizard, specializing in financial fraud. The only computer guy on St. James's team."

Baca's look darkened further. "Keep tabs on him, too." His voice was cold, measured, like the steel of a knife. "We could become exposed if we don't nip this in the bud."

"Understood. We must be careful about how we handle Strauss. If St. James realizes we're targeting her, he'll be unpredictable."

"Then we tread lightly. Let them think they're safe until it's too late." His lips curled as if relishing the impending confrontation.

Baca's voice cut through the tension as Eduardo stood to leave. "And Eduardo — if things get out of hand, I don't want any loose ends. Make it clean."

"Of course, Sir." Eduardo forced a confident smile, knowing Baca's gaze remained on him.

Outside, the setting sun cast an orange glow across the sky. Eduardo climbed into his car, his mind consumed by his heavy conversation with Baca.

The stakes were higher — and with them came danger. As he drove through the city, thoughts of St. James's team swirled. Formidable opponents, but Baca was not to be underestimated.

Back in the warehouse, Baca remained seated, eyes fixed on the far wall, envisioning his next move. The faint water drip tormented the silence. A predatory smile crept across his face as he contemplated the chaos he would create.

CHAPTER 28

St. James stood before a small grocery store on Calle 5, three blocks from San José's Aurola Holiday Inn. The faint scent of stale bread and old fruit wafted through the open door. One window of the red-brick building was boarded up. Above it, the second floor housed the cramped offices of struggling professionals catering to clients who couldn't afford better.

Pulling open a dented metal door to the left of the grocery store entrance, St. James stepped into a tiny landing that stunk of mildew and ammonia. He climbed the narrow staircase, past dull brown walls that seemed to sag under their own grime, and ended up on the second floor.

Flickering fluorescent lights hummed overhead. Four doors lined the left side of the hallway, each likely leading to dank, suffocating offices. The third door bore a tarnished copper sign that read: *Gael Vargas, Accounting Services*.

St. James knocked. After some shuffling sounds, the door creaked open to reveal a small, stooped man in ill-fitting black trousers and wire-rimmed glasses. Sweat stains darkened the underarms of his rumpled dress shirt. A vague, slightly puffy appearance around his eyes and a crease along his cheek suggested to St. James that he might have been napping.

"Can I help you?"

"Are you Gael Vargas?"

"Yes," he said. "Who are you?" He was awake now, his voice sharp.

"A friend of Elfego."

Vargas narrowed his eyes, assessing the six-foot-tall figure before him. "Never seen you before."

St. James grinned. "We've had no reason to meet until now."

Vargas hesitated, forehead furrowing. "Name?"

"Carlos."

"Carlos what?"

"Simpson. Carlos Simpson."

"What do you want?"

"Elfego said you could help me."

"With what?"

"I'm looking to buy a winter home here. Elfego said you could help find a property."

"The hell he did!" Vargas exploded, his face flushing. "Baca wouldn't send anyone to me without calling first. You're a fraud — and a rotten one. Get lost!"

St. James grinned. "Thanks for confirming you're Baca's crooked accountant."

Vargas's fists clenched, his knuckles cracking in the tense silence. "Leave, or I'll call the police!"

"Don't think so, Gael. That'll bring the roof down on Baca." St. James rested one hand on the door frame and leaned in. "How do you think he would take that?"

Vargas's expression changed from rage to concern, then angst. St. James savoured the impact of his words, noting the slight tremor in Vargas's body.

Rethinking his position, Vargas took a deep breath. "What do you want?"

"A few minutes of your time."

Vargas weighed the risk, unease creeping in as the oppressive heat from the air-conditionless room bore down. Curiosity got the better of him, and he moved aside to let St. James enter.

St. James moved through a thick haze of cigar smoke and sat in a creaky wooden chair that groaned under his weight. Vargas took his place behind a makeshift desk cluttered with crumpled papers and empty paper coffee cups, disdain radiating from him.

St. James broke the silence. "Why work in a dump like this if you're making good money as Baca's accountant?"

Vargas snapped back, "Don't make much."

St. James's tone was playful yet probing. "Find that hard to believe."

"Don't care what you believe!"

St. James scanned faded pictures of Presidents Nixon and Reagan hanging on the walls, their frames a depository of dust. The grimy window let in little light, casting eerie shadows across the room. "Carlos Sánchez transferred a waterfront estate owned by Russell Allaband to you without permission. Did you keep it?"

"No!" Vargas snapped, eyes darting away.

"You must've gotten something for it. You don't shelter Baca's stolen property for nothing. What does he pay for your risk?"

Vargas looked haunted by the thought of Baca's wrath. *If Baca knew I talked to this guy, I'd be dead.*

Letting the silence hang, St. James weighed his options. Vargas returned to the present, beads of sweat forming on his face. He forced himself to engage. "What do you want?"

"Answers, in exchange for my silence."

"What silence?"

"The silence I'll maintain if you cooperate. Emailing Baca about this chat could shorten your life."

Vargas's voice quivered. "How do I know I can trust you?"

A smile played on St. James's lips. "You don't."

Vargas frowned. "Guess I don't have much choice."

"No, you don't. I need you alive — and I need your help. I have no interest in seeing you dead, harmed, or arrested. Unless you lie to me, then it's on you. You would have to take your chances with Baca."

Vargas thought about this, the faint ticking of a clock in the background. Resignation crept in. "What's your real name?"

"St. James."

"Figures. A pushy, bloody arrogant Brit."

"No. A pushy, bloody arrogant Canadian!" Amusement coloured St. James's tone.

"What do you want to know?"

"How many men does Baca have?"

Vargas thought about the risk of answering, then squinted. "Sixty or sixty-five."

"Does that include the crooked notaries?"

"No. They're part-timers."

St. James snickered, narrowing his eyes.

Vargas's face clouded. "What's so funny about that?"

"The irony of the mob saving on costs. Thought you just stole more to cover increases."

Vargas's eyes projected defiance. "It's a business. Gotta watch the bottom line."

"What do the sixty men do?"

"Manage day-to-day operations. Keep the rest of us in check. Make sure we don't defect or cheat. Real estate is just one of Baca's businesses."

"What else is he into?"

Vargas hesitated, wary of where the conversation was heading.

"What else?" St. James's tone was sharp.

Vargas's words spilled out. "Drugs, telephone scams, prostitution, identity theft and some others."

"How does he maintain loyalty from all you guys?"

Vargas laughed quietly and picked up a letter opener on his desk. "How does any kingpin maintain loyalty? Terror and reward. Lucrative incentives for the faithful. Violence and intimidation for those who stray."

"Was Sánchez murdered because Baca thought he defected?"

"Baca discovered the OIJ was putting him into witness protection if he agreed to testify against him. Baca doesn't tolerate betrayal. Acts fast against threats to the 'company,' as he calls it."

"How would he know?"

"Has eyes everywhere."

St. James smirked. "A lot of eyes, and a lot of part-time mouths to feed?"

Vargas opened his hands.

"How does he choose land to steal?"

"His scouts research that."

"What's the criteria?"

Vargas hesitated, intimidated by St. James's gaze. "Starts with a list of foreign property owners. Mostly Americans. The wealthiest. His contacts at the National Registry provide the intelligence."

"Then what?"

"Absentee owners who stay away from Costa Rica the longest move to the top of the list. Less chance of being surprised mid-theft."

"How does he know this?"

"Easy. His men monitor comings and goings through airport travel lists. He figures out who's away, then he re-ranks by value. Most expensive land moves to the top."

"Smart. What if an owner returns earlier than expected?"

"Travel list is checked every day."

"What happens when an owner discovers his real estate's been stolen?"

Vargas's discomfort grew. "Reports it to the OIJ and hires a lawyer to get the property back. Real estate can only be returned legally by court order. Not much the OIJ can do except monitor cases."

St. James paused, weighing Vargas's responses. "You didn't answer my first question."

"What?"

"Why are you working out of this dump?"

Vargas forced a smile. "A front. I have a modern office where I live, in a more affluent part of the city. Baca thought a space like this would draw less attention." Vargas made a sweeping motion with an arm. "Does this place look profitable?"

"That's why you dress like a bum?"

Vargas shrugged. "What can I say? I'm a method accountant."

"Cute," St. James said dryly. "What about firearms?"

"There's an arsenal in a small warehouse."

St. James's forehead creased. "Arsenal?"

Vargas sat very still. He had a sudden vision of himself dead in a ditch, and his cheek began to twitch.

Impatience crept into St. James's voice. "Come on, Vargas. I don't have all day."

When Vargas did speak, it was in a whisper. "Several hundred weapons — handguns, rifles, dynamite, and some grenades."

St. James grimaced. "What's the security like?"

"Tight."

"What's the system?"

Vargas glanced at a picture of President Reagan, stalling, his pulse quickening. "Not at liberty to say."

St. James's tone turned steely, each word deliberate. "Then I'm not at liberty to keep quiet!"

Vargas focused on him, assessing St. James's sincerity. "Why do you want to know?"

"Writing a book on organized crime. This is part of my research."

Vargas scoffed. "Bullshit! I already told you too much."

St. James's voice was firm. "You're already in too deep. May as well keep going. You won't be in any more trouble with Baca than you're in right now."

Vargas hesitated but relented. "Surveillance. Armed men. Strict access controls to prevent infiltration and sabotage."

St. James pulled a small notebook and a pen from his pocket. "What about alliances or conflicts with other criminal organizations?"

Vargas stared at him. "Jesus, maybe you are writing a book." He unscrewed an old thermos on his desk and took a drink of water, making a point of not answering.

St. James levelled him with his gaze. "If you want to cut this short I'm happy to let Baca know all about our conversation so far."

Vargas raised a hand in surrender. "Alliances for mutual benefit. Turf wars with rivals over territory and power."

St. James jotted notes. "Are the men armed all the time?"

"No one's allowed to carry unless Baca authorizes it. And then only during specific actions for short periods."

"Seems odd."

"Baca doesn't want his men walking around armed. Too many questions if they get stopped. After a mission, weapons are returned to the armoury."

"Who has access to the armoury?"

Vargas's voice tightened. Anxiety crept back in. "Four people — Baca himself and three senior members."

St. James's tensity thickened. "Does Baca have anyone from the OIJ in his pocket?"

Vargas removed his glasses, cleaning the lenses with trembling hands, trying to buy time. "Have no way of knowing."

St. James saw through the lie but chose to let it go. "Where is Baca's headquarters?"

"Never been there."

"Didn't ask if you were there. I asked where it is."

Vargas's voice lowered. "Very few know where it is. Not even all his men. There's only a handful of members to interrogate if someone squeals. Wouldn't take long for him to reach me."

St. James's stare was intense. "Where is it?"

Vargas shook, alarm in his eyes. "Warehouse in Alajuela."

"Where in Alajuela?"

Vargas hesitated, shifting his gaze as if searching for an escape. "Not sure of the exact address. It's kept secret."

"You expect me to believe that you, Baca's trusted accountant, have no idea where his headquarters are?"

Vargas swallowed hard, beads of sweat trickling down his forehead. "I swear, I only know what I've been told. Baca doesn't share that information, even with his closest associates."

"How does he have meetings if men don't know where the HQ is?"

Vargas's anxiety crept back in. "Zoom."

Leaning back in his chair, St. James let out a long sigh. "All right, let's move on. Tell me about Baca's operations. Any specific territories he controls?"

Vargas found some relief in the changing topic. "Several key territories under his influence: downtown San José, parts of Alajuela, and some coastal regions like Jacó and Quepos."

St. James made notes. "What about law enforcement? Any notable ties or conflicts?"

Vargas glanced around, lowering his voice as if the walls had ears. "There have been rumours of corruption within the local police force. Some federal agents ignore Baca's activities."

St. James raised an eyebrow. "Interesting. What about his relationship with government officials?"

Vargas chose his words carefully. "Baca cultivates relationships with certain politicians and bureaucrats to protect his interests."

St. James weighed the implications. "All right, Vargas, that's enough for now. Remember, our conversation never happened. Understand?"

The fear of Baca's wrath was etched all over Vargas's face.

St. James stood, tucked his notebook into a pocket, and glanced at Vargas. With a final nod, he opened the door and walked into the dull hallway, leaving Vargas to ponder the implications of their conversation.

CHAPTER 29

Dozer could only see the top of García's head beyond a stand of trees as they walked the perimeter of Sánchez's land, dressed in worn shorts and faded T-shirts. Dense foliage surrounded them. Each step was a reminder of the confrontation that lay ahead.

The grounds were immaculate. The grass was perfectly mowed, well-watered, and neatly edged. Vibrant flower gardens showcased heliconia, hot lip plants, purple passion, and Dutchman's pipe flowers — all maintained to *Home & Garden* standards. It struck Dozer as a cruel joke that so much beauty sprouted from the dirt of crime.

"Must have spent a fortune on gardeners," he mused.

"All it takes is money." García pushed aside a branch — his voice edged with bitterness. Dozer sensed his partner struggled with the morality of it all.

"Stolen money," Dozer noted. He thought about the families torn apart by Sánchez's greed. "Blood money. How many lives that money could've saved."

"Flowers don't care if it's stolen," García countered, parting the bushes ahead.

Dozer's face puckered as an unpleasant odour wafted through the air. "What's that smell?"

"Volcanic ash from Turrialba, northeast of here. Torments communities around San José when the wind blows." García's irritation seeped into his tone.

"Must be close," Dozer remarked, the smell wrinkling his nose.

García's focus was sharp. "About fifty kilometres."

Dozer shook his head. "Sure would turn a fellow off barbecuing."

García scanned the estate, instincts on high alert. "That's why I don't own barbecue."

Dozer looked up at cameras embedded in the eaves of the house. "Let's make a note to have someone from the alarm company on standby. A malfunction could give us away."

"Good suggestion. Montero will have a small backup team ready for unexpected interference. Keep curious onlookers out of harm's way. Madrigal is organizing medical support."

"Excellent." Dozer surveyed the thick row of trees. They lined the cracked concrete driveway, stretching about 160 metres from the street to Sánchez's front door. A challenge they would have to navigate — both physically and mentally.

The branches knitted together, forming a lush canopy — a perfect arch, high overhead, which shaded the grounds beneath.

Standing in front of Sánchez's house, Dozer looked down the drive. "See the natural cover? The second and third rows of trees fill the gaps in the first, creating a wall of greenery. No one from the street can see through."

García stretched for a better view. "Let's test it. I'll take the left; you take the right."

Dozer pushed through the branches, estimating he was halfway to the street. García mirrored him on the left.

"Can't see the driveway, let alone you," Dozer yelled.

García shouted. "Same here!"

Dozer glanced around. "Great. Let's go around back and see what we have there." There was an urgency in his tone. He needed to see everything — to make sure nothing was overlooked.

Sánchez's residence loomed ahead — a vast white stucco bungalow with a red-tiled roof. Nestled on what Dozer thought to be a half-acre lot, a half-hour drive from downtown San José.

Dozer pushed through the underbrush. "The guy sure liked his privacy."

"A fat lot of good it did him," García yelled back. "Killed anyway."

As they rounded the corner of the house, García's eyes narrowed at the sight of more security cameras. "These could provide valuable intel during the operation. We need someone to monitor them in real-time."

"Do we have anyone with the technical expertise for that?"

"I'll look into it."

The two turned the back corners of the house simultaneously. "The trees back here are thicker than in front," Dozer observed.

"Better cover." García scanned the terrain. "A tactical advantage, but every advantage comes with a danger."

"True." Dozer contemplated the thick foliage surrounding them and wondered if it would be enough.

García glanced at the shimmering swimming pool. "Not big enough for laps. Good for cooling off after a hot day, though."

Dozer took in the pool. "Inviting."

A far-reaching wooden deck surrounded the pool and connected to a multi-section sliding glass door that opened into a beautifully decorated living room. Imported grey sofas, a black granite coffee table, and exquisite paintings of historical Spanish buildings — all spoke of a life fueled by ill-gotten gains, Dozer thought.

García grinned. "Want a tour?"

"Appreciate it."

García unlocked a solid imported oak door at the side of the house and turned off the alarm system. Dozer followed García inside.

As they moved through the rooms, they noted the elaborate mahogany cupboards and fine furniture.

Dozer surveyed the space. Admiration and disdain swirled within him. "Wonderful decorating ideas here," he said sarcastically.

Noticing no significant obstacles to a takedown and arrest plan, they ventured outdoors and around the perimeter, where the land met the neighbouring houses.

García made an imaginary sweep of the premises. "Let's check out the houses around this."

The two men walked the four streets surrounding Sánchez's, jotting down addresses and descriptions and discussing where to place sharpshooters during the mission.

Satisfied they had gathered what they needed, they returned to Sánchez's driveway for a final assessment.

Dozer didn't want surprises. "What about reliable communications during the mission?"

"We have a guy organizing encrypted radios."

García turned to Dozer. "I think we're as prepared as we can be."

"Dense foliage and trees offer several protection ideas," Dozer mused.

García agreed.

Dozer lowered his voice. "Trouble is they're as much an advantage for Baca as for us."

García nodded. "You think Baca has men hidden here now, watching us?"

Dozer scanned the property one final time. "Assume the worst. Awareness is the difference between life and death."

CHAPTER 30

Jiménez, Montero, García, and Dozer sat in a bland, windowless meeting room of the courthouse, revising the first draft of the takedown. Doubts crept into Jiménez's mind as he watched García sketch a rudimentary layout of Sánchez's land on the whiteboard.

The captain's eyes darted around the room, searching for reassurance. "We've assumed Hector Pérez's name will drive Baca to send only three or four men to kill him. Is that still a valid assumption?"

Dozer rubbed his bald head, a habitual gesture. "Fair assumption." A hint of hesitation cracked his facade.

"Fair?" Jiménez raised an eyebrow. "You were more certain last week."

Dozer crossed his arms defensively as if bracing against an unseen threat. "That was before García and I surveyed the land and refined our estimates."

García moved closer to the whiteboard. "Sánchez's property is a lush wonderland. The greenery offers perfect cover for our team. But it also gives Baca options. We must prepare for each one." A gnawing worry made their preparation seem inadequate.

Dozer frowned. "Baca knows the area, too. Estimating how many men he'll bring is trickier than we thought a few days ago."

Jiménez couldn't shake the thought they were underestimating Baca's capability. "Why is that?"

"Sánchez was murdered by a shooter Baca placed on a rooftop three houses away. He did that to avoid the exposure of a direct approach. Too easy to be ambushed with a direct strategy." Dozer's voice was low but firm. "He's no fool."

Montero stared off thoughtfully. "If Baca wants to kill Pérez inside Sánchez's house, how would he do it?"

"Likely by hiding men along the drive and behind the bushes at the back." Dozer's tone was grim. "Well-concealed, surrounding Sánchez's house. Pick us off one by one without exposing himself."

Jiménez contemplated this. "Then we need to arrive there first."

García frowned. "And do what?"

Montero opened his hands. "Ambush them." His tone suggested García's question was stupid.

"How would you know when they're coming?" García countered.

Jiménez glanced at García. "We'll have men watching the place."

Disbelief washed over García's features. "Around the clock, seven days a week?"

Dozer evaluated the situation, the enormity of the task dawning on him. "Baca will probably approach from behind the trees once we're in position, potentially ambushing us instead."

Montero grew more perplexed. "How would we manage the logistical challenges of surveillance shifts?"

Jiménez turned to Montero. "Coordinate with local law enforcement to ensure adequate coverage. But we don't know when Baca will come."

Concern was chiseled on Montero's face. "Without a clear timeframe, scheduling becomes a nightmare. We can't afford surveillance gaps, nor can we keep personnel on standby indefinitely."

García added, "If Baca's arrival is unpredictable, we may have to stay vigilant for a long time. That complicates scheduling even more."

Jiménez broke the stalemate. "Let's put the timing issue aside for the moment and focus on the strategy itself." The group reluctantly agreed, shifting their attention back to the task.

They debated every aspect of the amended scheme for two hours, finishing at four o'clock. As they left, Dozer felt uneasy. Dread and determination swirled in his mind.

***

The Hotel Presidente's bartender, Sergio, recommended Restaurante Silvestre. The grey and white concrete building resembled an embassy anticipating a siege — windows reinforced with iron bars and imposing gates at the entrance. Inside, the elegant dining room featured rich red and gold wallpaper, an elaborate crystal chandelier, and dark wood flooring. The dinner menu offered an eight-course table d'hôte and the finest wines from France. The ambience far surpassed Sergio's assessment, Anna thought.

They were seated shortly after six. Hanna, a short, thin lady with a warm demeanour, rushed to ask for drink preferences.

Anna felt adventurous. "I would like to try something local. What do you recommend, Hanna?"

"The most popular local drink is Guaro."

Anna was intrigued. "What's that?"

"A clear liquor, much sweeter than vodka, made from sugar cane. Quite strong, so new drinkers should be careful. We recommend no more than two."

"Sounds interesting. What do you mix it with?"

Hanna smiled. "Different juices. My favourite is Guaro Sour."

Dozer raised an eyebrow. "What's the mix?"

"Guaro, club soda, fresh lime, and raw sugar. Our bartender adds other ingredients to make it extra sour."

"Count me in," Anna decided, uncertain but willing to try.

Her milky white jumpsuit and understated makeup added to her elegance, complemented by a necklace of tiny gold rings and a matching bracelet.

St. James was staring across at her when Hanna interrupted his reverie to ask for his order.

"Macallan on ice." St. James's eyes wandered the room, observing how other men were dressed. He was glad he'd chosen his pastel-coloured suit and white linen shirt for the evening. Anything else would have left him feeling underdressed.

Dozer was clad in black leather, accentuating his muscular build. "Imperial."

While St. James and Anna listened, Dozer recounted his day with the OIJ senior agents, describing changes to the draft and disagreements over details. There was still ongoing uncertainty about when Baca might come to kill Hector Pérez.

Once Dozer finished, St. James scratched his head. "Poses a problem, doesn't it?"

Hanna returned five minutes later with their drinks.

Dozer gazed at St. James. "What about you?"

"I've been listening to you and wondering how I would recount my day. Bizarre, to say the least."

Anna sampled the Guaro Sour. Her expression morphed as her lips puckered, and her eyes squinted and widened in surprise.

St. James noticed her reaction. "Are you all right?"

Unable to respond, Anna choked and struggled to catch her breath. St. James rushed to her side and began patting her on the back. When her misery continued, two other people rushed from nearby tables to help, and the maître d' hurried to her side. It took five minutes for Anna to regain her composure. As he took his seat, St. James thanked everyone for their concern.

"Don't think this drink's for me." Anna's voice came out a gurgle.

"No kidding," Dozer exclaimed. "You scared the hell out of us."

St. James held her hand reassuringly. "Guess experience is what you get when looking for something else, sweetheart."

Dozer grinned. "Want another one?"

Anna hit back with a steel-melting look.

St. James got back to his day. "What I'm about to tell you cannot be repeated until I give the okay."

Dozer's forehead creased. "Now you have my attention."

Hanna returned. "So sorry, señorita. Can I arrange something else?"

"Just water for now." Anna shook her head. "I thought it was supposed to be sweet."

Hanna smiled. "Guaro alone is, but you drank our sour version. It packs a greater wallop."

St. James detailed his unusual meeting with Vargas — how the man shifted from aggression to divulging information, realizing that calling the police would bring Baca down on him.

"The guy went from wanting to throw me out to telling me most everything I wanted to know, all in about fifteen minutes."

Dozer's skepticism was evident. "Were you not worried he would tell Baca?"

"No. I threatened to tell Baca we met if he didn't answer my questions."

"You could have done the same with a Baca notary," Dozer challenged.

"Not the same. Vargas is Baca's accountant. He has to know everything — much more than a notary ever would. Notaries handle individual transactions and rarely grasp the full picture of a business. Baca would keep them in the dark to minimize risk. The accountant must be in every corner of the business."

Dozer pondered this. "Vargas's biggest mistake was opening the door to you."

"Sounds to me like he was terrified before he opened it," Anna suggested.

"Assuming he was scared, opening the door makes no sense. That's not what a frightened man would do," Dozer countered.

"What makes less sense is him telling me everything. Baca trusts him."

The three reflected in silence as they sipped their drinks.

"What could Vargas be afraid of?" Anna wondered.

"Maybe something he did pissed Baca off," Dozer speculated.

St. James took a sip of Macallan. "I'd like to know what."

Dozer finished his Imperial and signalled Hanna for another. "So, Vargas told you where Baca operates — not the address, just that it's a warehouse in Alajuela, right?"

"Right."

Dozer squinted. "Where the hell is Alajuela?"

Anna grabbed her cell and typed Alajuela, Costa Rica into Google Maps. "About nineteen kilometres northwest of here."

"Having a separate warehouse for arms is smart," Dozer mused. "Reduces the risk of accidentally blowing up munitions and the office at the same time. Happens more than you might think."

St. James smiled. "Usually, when a criminal mind tries to account for everything except the obvious."

"So, Vargas thinks Baca controls around sixty men, not counting the notaries?" Dozer asked.

"Yep."

Dozer sighed. "Well, I suppose that takes some guesswork out of all this."

St. James shrugged. "Yes. A few more men than the OIJ estimated."

Dozer reflected on the situation. "Baca only lets his men carry weapons on missions. That could come in handy if we have to alter the approach."

St. James paused a moment. "I've thought about that."

"Meaning?" Dozer pressed.

"I wondered if we should attack Baca on his turf. Less chance his men would be armed."

"Wouldn't be catching him trying to kill someone — just a raid Jiménez could have conducted without all this planning."

St. James turned to Anna. "Can you track down Gael Vargas's home address?"

"Do my best."

Dozer frowned. "I'm hungry. Are we eating here or just talking?"

"You're always hungry, Dozer," Anna teased.

Hanna delivered Dozer's second Imperial and handed them a table d'hôte menu.

"Don't often see a menu like this," Dozer remarked.

"Finally met your food match, Dozer?" Anna quipped.

St. James smiled. "No such thing, Anna."

Dozer brushed off their comments. "Mock all you want. This is huge."

"You know you make only one choice for each course, right? You're not expected to eat everything listed there," Anna joked.

Dozer scanned the menu again. "I know."

St. James laughed. "Guess not many pubs offer table d'hôte."

Three bottles of Angélica Zapata Malbec disappeared as they tackled the eight courses.

Dozer glanced at St. James. "Did you talk to Jiménez about his commitment to the mission?"

"We had a good chat today. He said he was all in for the mission but continued to worry about our assessment of Baca's force. The Director spoke to him yesterday as well. I think we're good to go."

No one managed to finish all the table d'hôte. Even Dozer left two courses untouched.

As they left the restaurant, the warm evening air enveloped them, mingling with the aromas of the busy city streets. Dozer looked at St. James. "Do you think Vargas will provide the intelligence we need?"

St. James remained confident. "I'll make sure of it."

The mission ahead held equal parts promise and peril, and with Vargas as their only hope for inside information from Baca's organization, the risk was high.

Approaching the Hotel Presidente, Anna broke the silence. "What if Vargas decides he's better off remaining loyal to Baca? What then?"

Dozer's demeanour clouded. "Then, we adapt our strategy."

St. James reflected. "We'll need to explore other leads if Vargas doesn't come through. This isn't just about getting information; it's about dismantling an entire operation."

Anna's eye caught a near-collision between three cars on the next block. "True, but it would help to identify other sources to back up what Vargas tells us. Make sure he's not lying through his teeth."

Dozer agreed. "We need a safety net. If Vargas becomes spooked or turns out to be a lying liar who lies, we'll need to pivot."

CHAPTER 31

Dozer and St. James took their places at a table, plates piled high with scrambled eggs, sausage, and toast from Hotel Presidente's breakfast buffet. Dozer glanced around the bustling dining room. "Where's Anna?"

St. James unfolded a napkin, laying it across his lap. "Sleeping in. Needed rest after last night's excitement. She did mumble something about not being able to understand how we could eat again so soon."

"I can always eat."

A server approached and poured coffee.

Dozer took a hearty bite of sausage. "Quite the engagement ring you bought for her."

Pride softened St. James's expression. "Should be. Cost the Earth."

Dozer laughed. "I heard she tried on every ring in the place, then picked the most expensive one in the store."

"You heard right."

"The lady has class."

It was Saturday morning in February's third week. The team, minus Smythe, chose a weekend of leisure.

Dozer took a bite of toast. "Spoke to Louis yesterday. He complained about your silence."

St. James smiled with a hint of guilt on his face. "I know. Got an earful from him last night."

"Bet you did."

St. James drank coffee. "He's never been so happy."

Dozer polished off his eggs. "Sandy's good for him. He's a different person. Still not used to seeing him without plaid."

"How is he different?"

"There's a bounce in his step. And he's nicer. Doesn't throw jabs at me anymore. Strangely, I miss the old Louis."

St. James cradled his coffee cup. "I asked if he could pull himself away from Sandy long enough to hack into Baca's systems."

Dozer smiled. "Did he agree? Hard decision for him, I bet."

St. James smiled. "He said he'd try tomorrow morning."

"Excellent."

St. James sipped coffee. "How are things at the office?" He paused and smiled across the table. "Probably raking in money without you there."

Dozer rolled his eyes. "Funny."

As the founder of White Investigations Inc. in Toronto, Dozer managed a reputable team of senior investigators.

"I helped my new COO, Garth Sampson, develop a long-term profitability plan so I can work more with you on international fraud cases."

"That's great. I like that."

"Things are excellent. Garth just landed a big contract with a large international corporation. Key players are being threatened."

"So, he's working out?"

"Very much so."

The two fell into silence for a time.

"Hamilton, did you notice a white Nissan Rogue yesterday?"

"Nope. Why do you ask?"

"It was parked in front when we left the hotel and tailed us back in the afternoon."

St. James sipped his coffee. "Anna wants to change hotels. Wants one with a swimming pool. If the Rogue shows up there, we'll know it's not a coincidence."

"I'll keep an eye out."

When they finished breakfast, Dozer headed to his room while St. James approached the front desk to see about accommodations with pools.

Rhonda, the bubbly lady at the front desk, wore a colourful scarf and her black hair short. "I recommend the Hilton La Sabana, San José's newest hotel."

"Wonderful. Thank you."

Rhonda reserved two rooms for St. James and handed him a confirmation number. "Just off the Avenue of Americas, across from the National Stadium. Tell the cab driver it's the new high-rise Hilton. The Hilton Garden Inn down the street sometimes confuses cab drivers."

"Thank you, kind lady."

St. James returned to find Anna dressed and ready for the day.

***

The three piled into the backseat of a Hotel Presidente cab that deposited them in front the Hilton La Sabana around three that afternoon.

The concierge rushed over to extend a hand to St. James.

"I'm Gabriel. Call me Gabe. Welcome to the newest Hilton and the tallest building in Costa Rica."

A bellboy sauntered over to load their luggage on a cart.

St. James introduced himself, Anna, and Dozer, and they followed Gabe into the high-rise.

"Don't see a reception, Gabe," Anna noted.

"Eighteenth floor."

"That's different," Dozer mumbled.

Gabe smiled. "The first seventeen are business floors — meeting rooms."

Gabe entered an open elevator and told the bellboy to take the next car.

The doors opened on the eighteenth floor, and a breathtaking city view greeted them.

Gabe escorted them to reception, where several guests waited to check in. While guests were being greeted Gabe guided St. James's team to the far glass wall and pointed. "The massive field across the street is our National Stadium."

Dozer's eyes took in the sight. "Brings back memories of my football days."

Gabe's forehead creased. "Professional?"

"University."

Gabe pointed to the right. "Those mountains are part of the Sierra Madre range."

St. James smiled. "Spectacular."

Dozer smiled. "Looks like a bar over there to the right."

Anna clouded. "And the swimming pool?"

Gabe pointed to the ceiling. "Thirty-first floor."

A petite lady, Francesca, wearing a black pantsuit, spoke perfect English as she registered them in two rooms. Dozer signed the registration and presented his passport. "Francesca, is there a toy store nearby?"

St. James raised an eyebrow. "Good Lord, Dozer. What do you want with a toy store?"

Dozer grinned. "Sometimes, I have the urge to play."

St. James threw him a look.

Anna smiled. "That's just Dozer."

"The Toys, Avenida is about a ten-minute cab ride, Mr. Dozer," Francesca advised. "Taxi drivers will know it."

"Thank you, Francesca. Just Dozer, please."

"Very well, Sir."

The bellboy led Anna and St. James to their room on the twentieth floor. Anna directed him to place the bags and tipped generously.

The pristine, all-white room had a pleasant scent and offered a view of the stadium. Dozer's adjacent room mirrored theirs.

"I don't think this room's ever been used," Anna mused.

St. James tossed a suitcase onto the bed to begin unpacking. "Could be."

Anna's hands rested on her hips. "I'll do that."

"I'm trained for it now so you can swim before cocktail hour," St. James teased.

Anna kissed him on the cheek. "Adorable."

"I know."

Anna's warning was playful. "Don't push it. Could come back to bite you."

St. James' eyes sparkled. "Something to look forward to."

Once unpacked, they went to the bar on the eighteenth. St. James glanced around. "No sign of Dozer."

Concern crept into Anna's voice. "Wonder where he could be?"

"Always first to arrive. Not like him to be late," St. James noted.

Anna shrugged. "He'll turn up soon."

Minutes stretched into an hour — still no Dozer.

****

St. James and Anna were showered and dressed the following morning at eight o'clock. Worry over Dozer gnawed at St. James as they headed to the dining room for breakfast.

The elevator doors glided open, and they entered reception.

Anna's face brightened. "Look who's in line!"

St. James frowned as he approached Dozer. "What's the big deal, not showing up for drinks?" St. James's relief mingled with irritation.

Dozer grinned. "On a mission."

St. James was perturbed. "Could have at least texted me."

"Didn't want to spoil the surprise."

Anna and St. James walked behind Dozer to his table. Anna looked at Dozer. "What mission?"

"Secret mission."

"I'll say what I tell Hamilton," Anna teased. "You're trying me."

Dozer replied. "There's a meeting at nine o'clock in the Orion room on the seventeenth. All will be explained."

St. James left the table for the buffet.

Anna trailed behind. "Hamilton, you can't stay angry with him."

St. James's tone reflected his unhappiness. "Let's see what nine o'clock brings first."

St. James and Anna arrived back at Dozer's table. Tension hung like an unwelcome guest.

"I know you're upset with me, Hamilton. But I wanted to test an idea before going public."

St. James crossed his arms. "Telling your teammates what you've been up to is not what I would call going public."

Dozer paused, sipping his coffee. "Look, I'm sorry you're mad. I needed to see if it was worth sharing first."

St. James ate hash browns. "Good to know."

The three ate in silence.

Dozer rose, clapping his hands together. "Hope to see you two at nine."

"We'll be there," Anna assured, her eyes darting between them.

St. James's silence remained.

As Dozer walked away, Anna turned to St. James and said, "Let it go, Hamilton!"

"I don't like secrets."

They stood and walked to Dozer's session, ready to confront whatever revelations awaited.

CHAPTER 32

The Orion room was surrounded by floor-to-ceiling windows on three sides, comfortably accommodating eight people. St. James and Anna arrived shortly after nine and found Dozer seated at the head of the table. Jiménez and Montero sat to his right, with García on his left. Everyone was dressed in colourful shorts and shirts.

A whiteboard occupied the wall behind Dozer, leaving no space for artwork. Anna noticed coffee and pastries on a small table to the left of the larger black table, where two water pitchers stood prominently in the centre. Each placemat was adorned with water glasses, notepads, and pens.

St. James and Anna sat in chairs to García's left after exchanging greetings. "By the look of everyone's clothes, it's easy to see it's Sunday," St. James quipped.

Jiménez smiled. "An agent never sleeps."

Dozer's eyes scanned the faces around the table. "Help yourself to coffee. The pastries are wonderful."

Montero and García rose to accept Dozer's offer.

St. James eyed a long, dark, three-foot-high table nestled against the window opposite Dozer, covered with a king-size bedsheet. "What's under the sheet?"

Dozer smiled. "The mission I mentioned at breakfast."

St. James glanced at Jiménez, who shook his head. "Don't know either."

Montero and García shook their heads, too.

Dozer began. "In previous discussions, we agreed on the general aspects of the mission strategy but never explored specific implementation details.

So, I built a model of Sánchez's place and the surrounding houses for us to discuss where our men might best be positioned. Given the many variables at stake, I thought a model could help us work through the details."

García bristled. "The OIJ can do its job, Dozer."

"I know, García. We both depend on a solid approach — you to make a clean arrest and us to recover assets to cover Global's losses. Hamilton believes it makes sense for us to collaborate. This is my way of contributing — for both of us."

"Let's hear him out, García," Jiménez cautioned.

García lowered his voice. "Sorry, Dozer."

Dozer smiled. "No offence. Everyone's navigating new territory here. We recognize that the OIJ isn't used to working with people like us, just as we are unfamiliar with working with you. There are bound to be bumps along the way."

St. James and Anna exchanged amused glances at this unexpectedly diplomatic side of Dozer.

Montero peeked at his watch. "Can we move things along? I want to spend some of Sunday with my family."

Dozer raised his head, stood, and walked to the mysterious table. He folded back the four corners of the sheet and whisked it away in one smooth motion.

"Wow!" Anna exclaimed as she studied what lay beneath.

The others looked on with amazement.

In the centre of the display was a tiny toy house labelled Sánchez's, flanked by small trees along a scaled-down driveway. A miniature swimming pool sat at the back of the house, surrounded by smaller trees and bushes. Several small-scale houses around represented potential ambush points for Baca.

García's voice carried admiration. "Remarkable replica, Dozer. I have to apologize again. This was a great idea."

Dozer smiled at the compliment.

St. James examined the model, scratching his head. "Must have taken you all night to create this."

Dozer smirked. "Yes. Had to skip cocktail hour to get it done."

St. James threw Dozer a look.

Anna smiled. "Now I see why you asked about toy stores with Francesca."

On the model's right side were tiny blue toy soldiers. On the left, red ones.

"The blue soldiers represent your agents. The red, Baca's men," Dozer explained. "I propose we discuss how to handle the situation — and anticipate Baca's response."

Jiménez agreed. "Excellent suggestion, Dozer."

García offered a faint smile. "Makes sense."

Montero and Anna sat silently.

St. James studied every detail of the model.

Dozer grabbed eight blue soldiers and placed four, spaced apart, three tree rows from either side of the driveway. "Discussed this formation during our previous meetings. When we investigated the property, García and I tested the positioning, and felt it worth considering."

St. James moved closer and pointed out the houses behind the rows of blue soldiers. "We also discussed the potential for Baca to ambush from behind."

Dozer placed the same number of red soldiers behind the blue, several rows further back, close to the next street. "Like this?"

"Yes, like that," St. James confirmed. "Our flank is exposed."

García scowled. "Our flank will be exposed no matter where we place our agents."

Montero agreed. "That's why posting lookout agents on surrounding roofs is so important — provide cover for agents below."

Dozer moved to the model, picked up more blue soldiers and placed them on the roofs of houses behind the dense brush at the rear of Sánchez's house. He positioned three soldiers on roofs behind trees to the right and three more on the roofs behind trees to the left. Uncertainty crept into his voice. "Like this?"

Dozer stood aside, leaning against the window, arms folded, stroking his chin as he stared at the model. "There's a problem."

Anna was curious. "What?"

Dozer looked at García. He reclaimed his seat at the table and held up a notebook. "Notes I made when we scoped out the neighbouring houses."

Montero leaped in. "And?"

"All the houses are bungalows — single-story structures. Trees tower above them, obstructing the view from the roofs. You can't see anything on Sánchez's land except trees. Useless for protecting our men."

Montero's irritation rose to the surface. "Why did you suggest it, then?"

St. James grinned. "That's Dozer's way of showing us why it wouldn't work."

Anna broke her silence. "Then how did Baca's man manage a clean shot at Sánchez?"

CHAPTER 33

García bent down and focused them on a corner of the only roof with a clear view of Sánchez's swimming pool. "Our murder investigation concluded the line of trajectory was from this point. Unlike us, Baca didn't need surveillance over the entire estate. He just needed a clear view of Sánchez in the pool. It didn't matter whether the other roofs had clear visibility."

Jiménez protested. "How come I didn't know this?"

García lowered his voice to a whisper. "With respect, Sir, the information is in the file."

Jiménez frowned, ignoring García. "So, the roof option isn't viable."

Dozer turned to Jiménez. "Not entirely."

Jiménez looked at Dozer. "What do you mean?"

Dozer referred to the same roof. "I suggest we put a man on that roof in the exact location as the man who shot Sánchez."

Jiménez frowned. "What good will a view of Sánchez's swimming pool do?"

St. James smiled. "The agent wouldn't be facing Sánchez's pool. They'd be facing the other direction, outward, toward the street behind. Where there are no trees."

Anna looked baffled. "How does that help our situation?"

Montero realized where Dozer was going. "Like us, Baca has a problem: the trees are an obstruction. He knows only one roof position views Sánchez's house. Stationing a sharpshooter in the same location prevents Baca from using it to kill agents inside the tree line. The trees above the other bungalows prevent a clear shot to targets inside — for Baca's men or ours."

García agreed. "Placing men inside the tree line is a good defensive move."

St. James looked conflicted. He studied the model again, considering the strategy. "But this is not a defensive mission. It's an offence to stop real estate thefts. We have to be more aggressive to win this thing."

St. James's comment quieted the room.

Jiménez's forehead creased.

Dozer's smile was his way of applauding St. James.

Anna thought: *that's my man.*

The others looked to Jiménez for a response.

Jiménez stroked his thin moustache for a moment and frowned. "Thought that's what we were doing, St. James. A strong offence demands a strong defence. They go hand in hand. Things don't always go well."

Jiménez looked at the others. "Mister St. James feels so strongly about the point; we should hear him out." Jiménez turned to St. James. "I'm disappointed in your response."

St. James ignored the admonishment. "We have to think we're attacking Baca. Go on the offensive. Surprise him. Put him on the defensive — not us."

García retorted. "We have to defend Pérez. Can't let Baca kill an innocent man."

Montero laughed. "An innocent man? You're kidding. We've been after Pérez for years."

García frowned. "Yes, but for other crimes. This is setting him up for something he didn't do. He might die for that. It's close to what Chávez described as instigating a crime. Pérez wouldn't steal from his Boss. He's Baca's most loyal notary and his longest-serving one. We are instigating Baca to kill him for something Pérez wouldn't do on his own."

The room went quiet. Everyone considered García's point.

Montero spoke up. "What if Baca sends in scouts first to gauge our defence?"

St. James stared off. "A valid concern. Countermeasures must be implemented to detect and intercept scouting parties."

Pressure mounted in the room, everyone's mind racing through the possibilities. St. James's eyes narrowed as he scanned faces around the table, each reflecting the same grim realization. There were too many variables at play, too many risks they hadn't accounted for. One question lingered: what would be their next move, and would it be the right one?

CHAPTER 34

"Not you again!" Vargas barked as he swung open the door to his shabby office and grudgingly let St. James in. The sharp, smoky scent of burnt coffee hit St. James the second he entered.

Vargas's office was chaotic, papers strewn about as if hit with a sudden windstorm. St. James plopped into the well-worn chair he'd occupied before.

He took in Vargas's dishevelled appearance. His stained tie looked like it had just survived a food fight. An ugly light blue suit clung to him like a second skin.

"Dressed up, I see. Must be meeting a very important client." Sarcasm dripped from St. James's every word.

Vargas scowled. "Just came from a funeral."

St. James feigned sympathy. "Close friend? Fellow Baca-ite?"

Vargas sent a glare to St. James that could slice through rock. "I don't have time for this, St. James."

Unfazed, St. James carried on. "Natural death?"

"Fell out of a fifth-floor window." Vargas's tone was bitter.

St. James put on a laugh.

Vargas's face flushed with anger. "Not funny. He was a good man!"

"By 'fell,' I take it you mean he was helped. What'd he do to piss Baca off?"

Vargas repositioned himself. "What do you want, St. James?"

St. James's tone turned casual. "A favour."

Vargas let out a mocking laugh. "You've got to be kidding."

St. James's eyes brightened. "No. I have reliable information that another Baca notary has been stealing from him."

Vargas straightened his pathetic tie. "Not another one! You'd think they'd learn. Crossing Baca is a dead end. Literally!"

Vargas's eyes veered off. "What does this have to do with me?"

"Nothing. It's about the favour I want."

Vargas growled, suspicion etched on his face. "Why do I think I'll hate this?"

St. James locked eyes with him. "My favour is dangerous."

Vargas's interest piqued, despite his better judgment. "Who crossed Baca?"

"Hector Pérez."

Vargas's disbelief ballooned. "Pérez is Baca's most loyal notary! Find it hard to believe he'd cross Baca. Anyone but him."

St. James watched Vargas's demeanour change. "Afraid so."

Vargas squirmed in his chair. "What do you want from me?"

"Information."

"About what?"

"Baca's timing for going after Pérez."

Vargas's face contorted with anger. His voice trembled. "Jesus! How am I supposed to find that out without Baca accusing me of betrayal?"

"Don't know. I'm sure you'll think of something." St. James's tone dripped with false reassurance.

A loud knock on the office door interrupted them.

Vargas waved St. James out with a flick of his wrist. "A client. You have to go."

St. James rose. "You have my cell number. Call me when you know."

Vargas rose too, a bead of sweat forming on his forehead, his intonation bordering on frantic. "Have you told anyone at the OIJ about our discussions?"

St. James was sincere. "No one. And I don't intend to. I need more information."

Vargas crossed his arms. "About what?"

"What happened to make you so terrified?"

Vargas sighed as if the weight of the world fell on his shoulders. "I paid a bill Baca didn't want paid. He's docking my pay until the money's recovered."

St. James's tone was cold. "You got off easy."

Tension stretched between the two.

St. James's impatience grew. "Where is Baca's headquarters?"

"I told you everything I know."

A second knock came on the door.

St. James was not convinced. "I doubt it."

Vargas's shoulders slumped as he opened the door. He greeted his client with a forced smile. St. James stepped past them into the hall without a glance. The door shut behind him.

In the silence of the hallway, St. James was sure of it: Vargas was holding back.

CHAPTER 35

Anna approached Gabe. "What's the best place to grab lunch within walking distance?"

Gabe's smile was warm and genuine. "Park Café in Rohrmoser is excellent. Delightful location and fabulous food, all situated in a lovely park. Perfect for a stroll afterward."

When St. James and Dozer entered the room, Anna beamed. "Gabe thinks we should try Park Café. Tapas restaurant. Atmosphere's supposed to be wonderful."

St. James nodded. "Okay. Where is it?"

"Fifteen-minute walk."

Dozer's disposition darkened. "Hate that stuff. Plates too small. Still hungry when you finish! It's for old folks who don't eat much — not for a meat-and-potatoes man like me."

Anna smiled. "Time you expanded your dining experiences. Be a little more worldly."

Dozer crossed his arms. "I don't want to be more worldly. I like me the way I am."

St. James smiled. "I like you the way you are, too, Dozer."

Dozer's face lit up. "Does that mean we can skip the tapas place?"

Anna glared at Dozer. "No."

"Shit."

Anna frowned. "All right, you two. Enough of this. Let's go."

Thirty minutes later, they sat at a white linen-covered table in a vibrant garden surrounded by well-trimmed trees. Colourful flowers and neat concrete statues dotted the green grass.

A waitress approached, smiled, and said, "Ready to order?"

"Imperial," Dozer grumbled, still unhappy with the venue.

St. James gave him a disapproving look.

Anna eyed the server. "Pinot grigio, please."

St. James looked at the drink menu. "Too early for Scotch. I'll have an Imperial, too."

When drinks arrived, St. James shifted his weight. "About Vargas this morning. He was scared because he paid a bill Baca didn't want paid. Baca's docking his pay until the money is recovered."

Dozer's face scrunched in disbelief. "Vargas would never pay a bill Baca told him not to pay."

"I don't think Baca told him anything. He's just using Vargas as a scapegoat to avoid self-blame. Bullies never admit they're wrong."

Anna smiled. "So, Baca's the source of Vargas' worry. That's why he didn't hesitate to open the door for you. Baca would never go to Vargas's office to confront him. He'd order Vargas to come to him."

Dozer smiled. "I'll buy that."

"I told Vargas Pérez is the notary stealing from Baca, and he needs to find out when Baca will come after Pérez."

Dozer looked incredulous. "You took a big risk, my friend!"

"He won't say anything. He knows if he does, I'll tell Baca he passed information on to me. That wouldn't end well for him."

Anna's concern was evident. "Hope you're right, for all our sakes."

St. James turned to Dozer. "Tell us about the tactics you and the three amigos devised."

Dozer glanced around, his posture tightening as if sensing eavesdroppers, his delivery dropping. "García will lead thirty agents to Sánchez's house under darkness. Each surrounding roof will have a sharpshooter facing outward. Three agents will be positioned on either side of the treed drive, three rows in, hidden from sight. Three more will be among the trees behind the house, and five will be stationed inside."

St. James looked skeptical. "Thought García only wanted three inside."

"They debated that for a while. Increased the number to five inside and scaled back the driveway to three."

St. James nodded. "What else?"

"The remaining agents will be concealed at the far end of Sánchez's estate, opposite his bungalow, positioned too far back for Baca's men to detect If Baca hides men just outside Sánchez's tree line, they'll be sandwiched between rooftop agents and the ground agents stationed further back."

Anna pushed strands of hair behind her ear, a worried look on her face. "Agents on the ground inside the tree line?"

"Five."

St. James looked puzzled. "Jiménez agreed to that many?"

"Not without a fight. García had to work to convince him the mission would fail without that level of manpower."

Anna eyed a small statue nearby, concern stamped on her features. "What about the surrounding homeowners? Do we have permission to be on their roofs?"

"Montero is handling that," Dozer confirmed. "One of García's agents is organizing medical support for mission day, and another is ensuring the encrypted radios are reliable."

St. James considered the implications. "How many men do they anticipate Baca will bring?"

Dozer's expression was grim. "An army. I pressed for that conclusion with the three amigos. Baca's paranoia will make him assume it's a setup. If it were truly just Pérez at Sánchez's house, he'd kill him and send his men away, no questions asked. But because he's suspicious, he'll think there's more to it."

Anna's concern deepened. "What about the loss of agents?"

Dozer shrugged. "The three amigos agreed on an estimate of five."

St. James was incredulous. "How did they arrive at that?"

Dozer turned to St. James. "Not sure. Might have used some probability formula. I stayed out of that discussion — didn't want to be associated with it."

Anna watched couples stroll through the park, her mind racing with implications. "Smart."

St. James considered this for a moment. "How will it play out?"

Dozer guzzled his Imperial. "Have this homely, jittery notary guy."

Anna grinned. "Saúl Madrigal."

"That's him — bizarre little fellow. Madrigal took the list of real estate that Baca stole, which totals much more than the nineteen million DeSilva paid. He copied the necessary details to transfer the properties from Baca to Global's Reclamation Properties."

St. James swirled his beer. "DeSilva confirmed this morning that the Reclamation Properties subsidiary has been incorporated. I sent the details to the three amigos. They have everything they need to make the transfers."

Dozer drained his Imperial. "Segura will forge Pérez's signature on the documentation once Madrigal finishes his preparation."

The three paused.

Anna nodded. "An excellent starting point. Wish we knew when Baca would come."

St. James sipped his Imperial. "I'll press Vargas on that."

Anna and Dozer exchanged wary glances, their unease discernable.

Dozer squinted. "When?"

St. James finished his Imperial. "All in due course."

Dozer scoffed. "This is the part in every case when I hate working with you."

A playful smirk crossed St. James's face.

Anna frowned.

Realizing that pushing St. James for a more definitive answer was futile, Dozer shifted gears. "We haven't decided how to handle Pérez yet."

St. James scratched his head. "Been thinking about that. We have two options: round up Pérez and put him in front of Sánchez's computer. Alternatively, leave the computer chair empty and ambush whoever comes to kill Pérez before they realize he isn't there."

Dozer finished his Imperial and peered into space, contemplating the options.

The server arrived and distributed plates.

St. James requested the two bottles of wine Anna selected from the list.

Dozer scrutinized his lunch suspiciously. "Another Imperial as well. What is this, Anna?"

Anna smiled. "You wanted meat, so I ordered osso buco braised in red wine, wrapped in aubergine with parmesan risotto."

"Translation?"

"Veal."

Relieved, Dozer dove into his lunch, his mind lingering over Pérez.

St. James watched Dozer take a forkful of osso buco. "Careful, you might learn to like it."

Dozer smiled, shaking his head. "I'll still be hungry after this measly lunch."

Anna sampled her seared tuna.

The server came by, poured wine, and handed Dozer a second Imperial.

Dozer paused. "Prefer to have Pérez in the house."

Anna rested her fork on her plate. "Why?"

"Only way to eliminate the risk."

Anna didn't connect the dots. "What risk?"

St. James focused on his octopus.

"Baca receives the email from Sánchez's computer and realizes his property's been stolen — but not who's stolen it. He'll contact the Registry and discover that Pérez facilitated the transfers, albeit with a signature forged by Segura. Driven mad, he'll hunt Pérez down to kill him. If Pérez isn't at Sánchez's, he could be anywhere — even with Baca, although that's unlikely. Baca would have already killed him if that were the case. If Pérez is murdered elsewhere, it destroys the mission. No longer a reason for Baca to bolt to Sánchez's house."

Anna considered Dozer's conclusion. "Okay. Having Pérez at Sánchez's house keeps Baca fixated on that location. Confirms that Pérez uses Sánchez's computer to orchestrate the thefts. Baca will send men."

St. James agreed. "Right."

Dozer nodded. "We'll grab Pérez the night before Baca arrives."

St. James frowned. "That means someone has to protect him all night."

Dozer was sure. "Jiménez will assign an agent for that."

A flicker of doubt lingered in St. James's eyes. "Don't be too sure. Jiménez will see this as breaking the law a second time — adding kidnapping to theft."

CHAPTER 36

Director Ramírez sat at the head of the table, a formidable presence whose stature exuded authority. His eyes scanned the room, noting the intensity carved on each face.

Today was the defining moment. St. James felt the tension. Their blueprint hinged on gaining the Director's approval.

García took a deep breath and began delivering the amended strategy, leveraging the expertise of his colleagues as he spoke. He outlined estimates for the number of men Baca would deploy, potential OIJ casualties, and the counterattack strategy to thwart an ambush. Each agent's role, positioning, and communication protocols were delineated, revealing the depth of their preparation.

St. James observed a subtle shift in Ramírez's demeanour as the presentation progressed. The stern lines of his face softened. A hint of admiration crossed his features as everything unfolded. Late to the conference, Chávez wasted no time joining the fray, her incisive questions probing the scheme with the precision of a surgeon. The atmosphere morphed from a presentation into a rigorous interrogation. Anna was drained yet engaged.

When García concluded, Ramírez turned to Chávez. "María, how does this align with our legal principles?"

Chávez paused. A thoughtful look crossed her face before a smile emerged. "It's bold, risky, and dangerous." Her tone was both playful and professional. "But I like it. A calculated risk that could yield significant results — if precisely executed."

Ramírez squinted. "What potential repercussions are we facing?"

Chávez's smile broadened. "An ungodly amount. Expect a major retaliation. If we succeed, we will have stuck a significant blow to his criminal network."

Ramírez sought the perspective of Jiménez, known for his cautious approach. Jiménez agreed with Chávez. "We've weighed the risks. The potential benefits do outweigh them, Director."

Ramírez listened to García express his thoughts. "We anticipated the immense risks from the start," García said. "We're prepared for the fallout. Success invites both praise and criticism. We're ready to face that storm."

Ramírez nodded.

The room fell into a hush. Tension thickened as they awaited Ramírez's verdict. Leaning back in his chair, the Director surveyed the room. A slow smile crept onto his face. "I must admit, it's well-conceived. Your effort and dedication shine through. A remarkable improvement."

A wave of relief washed over the group, rekindling their determination. Ramírez's approval was more than a formality. It validated the team's hard work and marked a crucial step toward dismantling Baca's criminal empire.

"For the next steps," Ramírez's tone was resolute: "Meticulous planning and execution are paramount. Perfected training is essential. Every agent must be prepared to navigate the complexities of the mission."

García straightened. "Operatives who don't meet our standards will be reassigned, Sir."

Ramírez regarded them. "Very well. Proceed with your preparations and keep me informed as you progress."

The meeting concluded with cautious optimism. Ramírez's approval granted the green light. The true challenge lay in transforming their carefully devised framework into a decisive victory. The stakes were high, but so was the resolve.

CHAPTER 37

The following day, Segura embarked on her mission to locate a sample of Pérez's signature to forge the real estate transfers. Jiménez, García, and Dozer set out to identify the most capable agents to confront Baca. At the same time, Anna would ensure Madrigal could manage the transfers. St. James floated among the initiatives to ensure everything remained on track.

Dressed in jeans and T-shirts, Segura and Montero made their way to the archives.

"I'm worried we won't find a decent signature specimen," Segura admitted, glancing around the shadowy storage room.

Montero was confident. "We'll find something. Archives are a goldmine for signatures." He flipped on the overhead lights, illuminating rows of dusty boxes and grinned. "Besides, asking Pérez for his autograph isn't exactly an option."

Segura offered a faint smile but carried on in silence.

The room was damp and musty, with boxes stacked precariously from floor to ceiling, leaving narrow pathways barely navigable. Dust motes danced in the shimmering light as Montero displaced boxes, sending clouds swirling around them. Segura had difficulty breathing.

"This place is a health hazard," Montero said, ducking to avoid an overhead beam. "I'll have a word with maintenance about dehumidifiers. We don't want mould ruining important documents."

Segura's mind raced with the implications of her task. Finding a signature was just the beginning. It had to be clear enough to replicate convincingly.

According to the archive registry, Pérez's box was in aisle three, five rows up from the bottom, ten boxes in from the start. Montero discovered a box marked Pérez Nursing Homes in that location. The desired box was nowhere to be seen.

After an hour of fruitless searching, Montero found the right box in aisle ten, three rows from the bottom. "The person who placed the box must be dyslexic," he grumbled. "The aisle, row, and box numbers are mixed up. Waste of time."

Segura sighed as Montero carried the box into a blue, windowless room with a small metal table and two chairs.

A thud broke the stillness.

Segura jumped. "What's that?"

"Old boiler. Sounds worse than it is. Just pushing air through ancient pipes."

Montero sat the box on the table and flipped open the lid. He pulled out six files, gave three to Segura and kept three for himself.

Segura stopped at a contract as she flipped through her files. "There's a signature here."

"Clear enough to use?"

"Bit faded, but I think I can work with it."

Montero's inflexion held a hopeful edge. "So, we're all set?"

Segura blew the dust off the third file. "Not quite. I need more than one specimen to feel confident about his consistent execution. Can't risk not having more specimens."

Montero rifled through his documents and held up a second agreement. "Here's another signature."

Segura scrutinized it, comparing it to her previous find. "Not an exact match, but close enough for initial practice."

Montero was thoughtful. "I remember Pérez was under fraud charges when he signed that first document. He was probably nervous about being arrested. The second one is dated the day after his lawyer arranged his release. You can bet he felt more at ease signing that one."

Segura placed the signatures side by side, studying the differences. "You're right. The second signature is more fluid. Feels more genuine."

Segura forged ahead with her search, uncovering three more signatures, all similar to the one from Pérez's release document. "That's it. I have enough to work with."

Montero's eyes met Segura's. "Let's hope this works. For all our sakes."

***

Jiménez and García sat in Jiménez's office on the second floor of OIJ HQ, overlooking a cluster of government buildings in the square. To their right, a stack of human resource files detailed the career highlights, strengths, and weaknesses of every OIJ agent with over five years of experience.

Dozer lounged at the end of the table, twirling a pen between his fingers as he watched the two men flip through agent personnel records.

"Don't want this individual, Captain," García declared as he slid the agent's file across the table.

Jiménez opened the file and read the first page. "Why not?"

García's eyes locked onto Jiménez's. "Too emotional." The words held the implication of past failures and future risks.

"How so?"

"He's nervous under pressure. I've seen him tumble out of a surveillance van and throw up in front of the suspect's house. Blew an agent's cover and wasted months of work. And that wasn't the only time."

"Oof," Dozer said quietly.

Jiménez lowered the file in front of him. "Your call," he said. "You know him better than I do. I'm more interested in the ones you do want."

García straightened. "Considering the ability to follow orders, shooting accuracy, hand-to-hand combat skills, and overall nerve, I've narrowed it down to thirty candidates." He glanced at the list. "Sixteen are excellent marksmen; the rest are above average. Most have solid hand-to-hand combat skills. I wouldn't hesitate to put them up against any mob."

Jiménez was intrigued by García's thoroughness. "You got the list?"

García handed both Jiménez and Dozer a sheet of paper outlining his selections. "This explains why I picked each one." García's articulation was steady, revealing his passion for the job.

Jiménez ran his finger down the list of names, his mind racing through the implications of each choice, revealing no emotion but weighing the options. The gravity of their situation was perceptible. The right team was the difference between success and failure.

"Don't know anyone on this list, García, so I'm no help," Dozer said.

García was eager to involve Dozer. "Join me for training this afternoon. You can assess their abilities firsthand, with fresh eyes. That's more valuable to me than any file." He knew Dozer's experience would offer insights past evaluations wouldn't capture.

"Sounds good. I'm in!"

Jiménez folded the list and looked up with a nod of approval. "No objections to any names on this list, García. You are free to begin the training."

"Thank you, Captain."

Turning to Dozer, García added, "Today at two?"

Dozer smiled. "It's a date."

***

Anna's eyes pierced Madrigal's. "Have everything you need, Madrigal?"

Nerves shadowed the notary's unassuming air as he fidgeted with the edge of a document. "Believe so."

A look of concern crossed Anna's face. "We need absolute accuracy. Any mistake could have catastrophic consequences."

"Oh, well I feel so much better now," Madrigal said, peering at her ironically.

"I'm sorry, but there's just too much at stake here to pretend otherwise."

"Believe me, I know." Madrigal tried to cease his fidgeting. "Run the plan by me again, please."

Anna thought it curious that an experienced OIJ notary would look to her, a Canadian investigator of financial fraud, for reassurance or procedural advice. But it was what it was.

She sat down nearer to him and tried to make her voice sound soothing. "The plan is simple. You'll prepare the transfer documentation while I'm here." Changing her language, she said, "We'll do it together."

Madrigal nodded and swallowed.

"You'll explain each step as you go and triple-check descriptions and coordinates. I'll do a final review while you read the transactions aloud. If even one letter, number, or symbol is off, the transfers won't go through, and Global won't see its money. Our entire strategy hinges on this."

She noted Madrigal's tension. "But we can do this, Madrigal. And I'm not questioning your ability. Just want to be thorough."

He shifted in his seat. His whole attitude changed, a flash of irritation replacing his former nervousness. "I've done documents like these a hundred times," he said, trying to mask his annoyance.

Anna placed a reassuring hand on his shoulder. "This is not about doubting you. It's about safeguarding the integrity of the transfer process."

"I know that," Madrigal snapped. "Don't talk to me like a child."

"Just trying to be cautious," Anna's tone was calm yet laced with underlying concern.

Madrigal gazed at Anna. The room felt smaller as he wrestled with his pride and his insecurities. "I'll make sure everything is perfect. Just give me a chance." It was a plea for understanding.

CHAPTER 38

Dozer stood next to García in a heavily wooded area outside San José, overseeing training for the thirty men and women selected to confront Baca when he attempted to eliminate Pérez. García thundered through a gruelling training schedule designed to hone everyone's skills — intense hand-to-hand combat, elevating marksmanship to an art form, and mastering quiet and purposeful mission movements.

A junior agent had found the plot of land, nestled amidst dense, Sánchez-like foliage — the perfect setting for García's training regimen. With trees crowding the landscape, it resembled the terrain they would soon face.

"I have a series of synchronized movements, timed manoeuvres, and cooperative tasks for you to practice," García announced when they were organized. "I'm splitting you into two groups. Team one will wear blue armbands and will represent OIJ. Team two will have red armbands representing Baca."

Dozer handed out armbands to each team member. "Team one, you will be led by Agent Martinez. Martinez, I want you to take your team to the left of that stand of trees over there." García pointed to the trees. "Belly down and move in, searching for any sign of Baca as you crawl forward, just like we discussed." García turned to team two. "Agent Chavarría, you will be Baca, leading your men in from the far right, using the first approach we assume Baca may use."

García eyed both teams while Dozer looked on. "Practice this engagement until it's smooth. After that, we'll move on to our second assumption for Baca's strategy."

García pushed both teams to their limits, challenging them to anticipate and counteract every possible move Baca might deploy. Each manoeuvre was designed to strengthen tactical acumen and elevate their adrenaline levels, pushing them in ways Dozer didn't anticipate.

The overarching strategy was clear to Dozer: repetition was everything. García drilled the same training programs daily until each manoeuvre could be executed perfectly for two straight days — necessary to ensure mission readiness.

Not everyone could cope with the quick commands, abrupt shifts in tactics, rapid movements, and precise marksmanship. García turned to Dozer, pointing to three OIJ agents struggling to keep up. "I don't think those three are up to the task. What do you think?"

Dozer stroked his bald head. "Been watching them. They throw the team's timing off when you order the practice manoeuvre for entering Sánchez's property from the left. If that continues, the mission's timing will be off for every step after that. If we're successful, it would be by accident, not by precision."

García chewed his lower lip, evaluating Dozer's comments. "I agree. They do throw off the timing."

"Do you have replacements that could do better?"

"These agents ranked the highest when I measured them against our skill criteria."

Dozer crossed his arms. "Who are the next three on your assessment list?"

García pulled a paper from a uniform pocket and scanned it. "Three excellent females."

"Why did you pass over them?"

"Marksmanship. They scored a little lower."

"Is that the only reason? I mean, are they strong in every other discipline?"

"Very."

"Who's your best marksman?"

García pointed to a woman doing calisthenics several feet away. "Isabella."

Dozer was quiet for a few seconds. "The others were not perfect in every discipline when you began the training. You made them perfect."

"True. But they were the best to start with."

"I know. You'll have more precise movement than you do now if the next three improve execution timing. You've already picked the agents for rooftop duty. So, the next three aren't needed for marksmanship. You could assign them to the ground group at the far end of Sánchez's property."

García reflected on this for a second. "Could make that work. Good suggestion." García pulled his cell from a pocket and tapped the number for his assistant. "She'll arrange a meeting with each of the three next on the list."

García gathered the three underperformers and released them from the mission, praising them for their drive and commitment.

"I hated to do that, Dozer. Crestfallen egos need time to repair."

"I know. If it's any consolation, you did the right thing for the rest of the team, the mission, and the OIJ. Maybe even saved lives. I bet the three knew they weren't keeping up. Probably miserable. You did them a favour."

García nodded. "I feel bad for them, just the same."

***

Six o'clock that afternoon, Dozer and García sat in a pub not far from OIJ headquarters, drinking Imperial. Dozer expressed his admiration for García's training style. "How did you become so good at this?"

"Served with the British SAS for three years before returning to Costa Rica. The training there was brutal. Standards were so high that the failure rate was eighty percent. They send you to the Brecon Beacons for three weeks alone, hiking with heavy backpacks and rifles. If you survive that, you go on to training for hostage negotiations, counterterrorism, and capturing drug trafficking rings. What I put these guys through this week is child's play in comparison."

Dozer signalled the server for another round. García looked at him. "How do you handle training in your company? White Investigations, is it?"

"That's right. Our training programs are similar to yours, but not quite as elaborate."

"Knowing you, it would have to be an excellent program. Consistent training with discipline."

The server placed two more Imperials in front of them.

Dozer eyed García. "Learned a lot from you this week."

García took a pull of Imperial and wiped the froth from his red beard with his shirt sleeve. "What do you mean?"

"Your planning and tactical skills are next level. You mapped out every possible move Baca could make and developed counter moves to neutralize them before beginning to train."

García's smile was faint. "The only way I know how to accomplish two critical objectives."

Dozer drank Imperial. "Objectives?"

"Force the agents to anticipate moves Baca could make rather than learning firsthand in live combat. This gives them an upper hand."

"Second?"

"What my order would be before I give it."

Dozer's forehead creased. "So, you need them to read your mind."

"I need them to internalize the drills until they're automatic."

"What's behind the two-day rule?"

"You mean why do I insist they be able to counter Baca's moves without faltering for two consecutive days before we can move on to another scenario?"

Dozer nodded.

"There's some science to it. The brain needs a certain amount of repetition to store information deeply enough to access it quickly in a crisis. It shortens reaction time and helps ensure the most effective action is taken. Without that, too much is left to chance — leading to mistakes, or worse."

"They respond well to you."

"Not their first rodeo with me. Practice is still necessary. We adjust training to the situation — the mission itself, what's at stake, the sophistication of the enemy, physical environment and terrain, that sort of thing."

Dozer finished his Imperial. "Makes sense."

García sipped the remains of his. "Learned from you, too."

Dozer's forehead rose again.

"You reminded me not to be too focused on original selection criteria. Made me see that I could swap in agents with lesser skills in one discipline to improve the team's overall performance. Flexibility built within rigidity. Huge lesson."

Dozer smiled. "Let's have another beer. All this learning from one another is making me thirsty."

CHAPTER 39

Eduardo fixed his sight on Baca's weathered face. "Boss, I'm concerned." Despite his voice's steady inflection, Eduardo's palms felt clammy at his sides, his heart thudding in his chest. "Our informant's latest intel suggests that Jiménez and his inner circle have been meeting regularly with the Strauss woman, St. James, and Erasmus White. They're plotting to arrest you."

The room's sole light source, a brass desk lamp, cast a warm, amber glow over Baca's worried features. A heavy scent of cigars and aged wood hung in the air.

Baca's reaction was delayed but visceral, sending a shiver down Eduardo's spine as his fist slammed the desk. "I knew it!" he said, frustration and anger transforming his face into a mask. "I felt it when you first mentioned Jiménez engaged that detective fella."

Eduardo grimaced. "Jimmy's been tailing them just like you ordered."

Leaning forward, Baca narrowed his eyes with fierceness. "What has he reported?"

"He tracked them from the Hotel Presidente to OIJ headquarters in the morning and then back at night. They recently switched to the Hilton La Sabana. Jimmy's keeping tabs on them there. Aside from occasional trips to nearby restaurants, they're staying put." Eduardo steadied his hands inside the pockets of his linen pants. "Oh, and the Strauss woman likes to swim."

A quick, evil smile crossed Baca's face, followed by a painful realization. "We're relying only on our OIJ informant?"

"Yes, and García's got a group of federal agents training, too."

Baca's mind raced. "How many?"

"Can't say for sure. It's a wooded area, tough for surveillance. But we estimate thirty."

Baca stroked his square chin and thought. "What about Dozer's brother? May need some leverage now to diffuse the growing threat."

"Lives in Ottawa."

"Hmm. Think we can bring him here?" Baca searched Eduardo's face for reassurance.

"Depends on his passport status."

Baca's stare drifted into the distance.

Unease had crept into his softly lit corner office like a powerful smell.

Sitting behind his enormous mahogany desk, Baca suddenly felt small and vulnerable, not at all like the feared and respected crime Boss he wished to be.

Maybe it was a case of shooting the messenger, but when he looked at Eduardo, he suddenly felt annoyed.

What was the young man good for? Baca wondered. He was presentable, certainly. He could even manage a bit of diplomacy when the need arose. But could he be trusted? Looking at him, Baca couldn't be sure. He trusted Eduardo's judgement, but maybe not his character.

Yet what could he do? Who else knew the business well enough to help him navigate this mess?

Eduardo stood still, awaiting instruction.

Finally, Baca's eyes lit up with menace. "Remember the courier who smuggled that guy down here three years ago? The one who wouldn't give his name?"

"Yes. The cryptic one."

"How'd we contact him without knowing his identity?"

"Negotiated an alliance with a gang leader up there — for cash."

Baca's bearing solidified. "Think we can find him again?"

"I know we can, Boss."

"Good. And Dozer's brother … can we find him?"

"We have enough information to track him down," Eduardo assured. "Name's Denzel. Works at a grocery chain there."

Baca's resolve stiffened. "Get him!"

CHAPTER 40

At eight o'clock that evening, St. James, Anna, and Dozer sat in the Hilton La Sabana dining room, sampling drinks and rehashing their day. Anna swam for an hour that afternoon while St. James stayed in the room, expanding notes on everything they had learned.

St. James sipped his Macallan. "I talked to Louis today. He managed to hack into Baca's systems."

"Yes. He asked for everything I had on Baca before he tried," Anna said. "I sent him what I had but didn't hear back."

Dozer became excited. "So, he's in?"

St. James smiled. "Yep!"

"Wow!" Dozer blurted.

Anna felt put out. "You didn't say anything to me."

St. James smiled. "Wanted to discuss it as a team."

Anna frowned.

"Baca has a hundred and eighteen people on the payroll — seventy-two direct employees; the rest are numbered, not named. I took them to be informants that Baca wants to keep anonymous."

"Interesting," Anna said.

St. James continued. "He's well-organized. Financial statements for each line of business, so to speak."

Anna smiled. "What businesses?"

"Prostitution. Real estate. Identity theft. Miscellaneous."

Dozer smiled at the word miscellaneous.

"Total revenue from all criminal activity last year was over a hundred million," St. James said.

Dozer whistled.

"They're well-managed and well-financed," St. James concluded. "Not to be taken lightly."

Anna sipped her drink. "That'll make Jiménez more nervous."

Dozer agreed.

St. James stared off, deep in thought. "I asked Louis if there was any way we could scoop Baca's cash after the mission, assuming it's successful, that is."

Dozer's forehead furrowed as he drank Imperial.

Anna was incredulous. "We never discussed this!"

"No, we didn't. It's an angle I've been mulling on my own."

Dozer frowned. "You surprise me, Hamilton. You've never taken money to enrich yourself. This isn't you, man!"

"What makes you think I'm doing that?" St. James said.

Anna suddenly understood. "Hamilton has a different plan. Don't you?"

St. James paused to drink scotch. "Thinking about the poor property owners who lost their shirts when Baca stole from them. Wouldn't it be nice if we could take Baca's money and use it to make them whole? They won't get anything from their lawsuits against the crooked notaries. We could set up a fund and have the property owners file claims like we did with the defrauded companies in the German case. Give credit for the plan to Jiménez and the OIJ."

Anna looked at him, proud and intrigued. "I like it. It'll be a helluva boost to the OIJ's public image. Not that anything's wrong with it now."

Dozer chimed in. "Be a huge deterrent to all the other crooks out there, too."

St. James smiled. "Let's agree not to mention this to anyone until we see how the mission goes."

Dozer and Anna agreed to park the idea.

"Okay. What did we accomplish today?"

Dozer recounted the training day, and the role he played in eliminating three poor performers and substituting those who didn't meet all the selection criteria.

Anna sipped her vodka Caesar. "Good on you, Dozer."

Dozer drank Imperial. "What about you two?"

Anna turned to Dozer. "Think I have Madrigal ready to go. Everything's been entered so the titles can be transferred to Reclamation. All he needs to do is hit Send."

"You guys don't trust this fellow. A notary of choice for the OIJ can't be all that bad."

Anna jumped to correct that impression. "He's excellent. Nervous, but excellent. He's so worried about working on a mob case that he has trouble concentrating, which makes him more likely to screw up. But I compensated. Triple-checked everything he did."

"What about Segura? How's she doing with Pérez's signature?"

"Checked in on her this afternoon," Anna reported. "She's interesting to watch."

Dozer's eyebrows rose. "What could be interesting about a signature being forged?"

"You'd be surprised. I thought it would be like watching paint dry, but it was fascinating."

Anna described the whole process, explaining Segura used three whiteboards to practice different elements of the signature.

"She started with the first letter and practiced it until she got the pressure and style as close to the original as possible. Then she moved on to the next letter and repeated the process. When she got to the bottom of the first whiteboard and was satisfied with the quality of each letter, she wrote Pérez's entire signature. Then she compared the quality of the bottom signature with the one she began with at the top, and she was able to measure her progress. She could tell that her work had improved by about twenty-five percent. That was just a start. Nowhere near acceptable to her."

Dozer was glued to Anna's every word, as dull as he thought mastering forgeries could be. St. James had heard it all before and elected to tune out and sip Macallan.

Anna was aware of gushing slightly. "Segura spent an hour studying the curves and loops and the execution of her previous forgery on the first board, compared to Pérez's actual signature, making improvements. She used the second whiteboard to repeat the process, with a much-improved forgery at the top. She anticipated that the same systematic approach on the second board would earn her another twenty-five percent accuracy by the time she reached the bottom."

Dozer was incredulous. "Wow! The discipline's impressive."

"Certainly is." St. James waved to the server for another round.

"Gets better," Anna said, finishing her Vodka Caesar. "She repeated the same process on the third whiteboard, reaching another twenty-five percent improvement. Now, three whiteboards were covered with Pérez's forged signatures. There were improvements on every line, from the forgery at the top of the first whiteboard to the one at the bottom of the third. Segura stood back, satisfied she achieved seventy-five percent accuracy overall."

St. James smiled. "What Segura lacks in personality, she makes up for with methodical work and dedication."

Anna smiled. "In Segura's mind, seventy-five percent is still not good enough."

Dozer shook his head. "What do you mean?"

St. James cut in. "A seventy-five is basically a low B-plus. No self-respecting perfectionist would be happy with that."

Anna nodded and continued. "That's right. She has to continue practicing, but on paper. Segura's been at it for three days and figures another two days will take her to ninety-five percent accuracy."

St. James stared off. "Why the switch to paper?"

"Executing is more real. Normal. She's writing with a pen, not a marker, using paper, not a whiteboard. Where the final forgery will be executed — the one to register the transfers at the National Registry and the one Baca will see. Has to be flawless to pass Baca's eyes."

"At least up to ninety-five percent," Dozer poked.

"In Segura's eyes, when she reaches ninety-five percent, she's achieved the personality of Pérez's signature. In that moment, she basically becomes Pérez. It's a hundred percent in anyone else's eyes, including Baca's."

"An A-plus-plus," St. James said.

Dozer changed the subject. "Hamilton, do you think we're ready to execute the mission?"

"Think it's time to discuss timing with Jiménez and García. Tomorrow's Friday. I'll see if they can spare us an hour in the morning."

"García will want to meet before he hits the training field. He insists on being out there by ten."

St. James glanced at Dozer. "I'll call Jiménez when we return to the Hilton."

CHAPTER 41

Jiménez was all for a Friday session and assured St. James everyone would be present at eight-thirty.

St. James, Dozer, and Anna showed up at eight-fifteen. García and Montero were milling about, nursing cups of strong, black coffee. Madrigal and Segura sat at the table. Segura had a small pile of grapes in front of her, on a napkin, and was eating one every few minutes.

Jiménez breezed in wearing a black suit, crisp white shirt, and blue silk tie — the opposite of a normal casual Friday dress. He brought the meeting to order and turned to García, who wore OIJ fatigues, for a report on the training."

"Yes, Sir," García said. "Progress has been excellent. The agents are working hard and will be ready to execute on Monday or Tuesday. If not, I'll keep drilling them until they can perform all the exercises perfectly two days in a row."

"Excellent." Jiménez turned to Dozer. "Thoughts?"

"García has worked wonders with them. Very impressed with his professionalism and the consistency of his methods."

García reflected appreciation.

Jiménez eyed Dozer. "Think they're ready?"

Dozer didn't hesitate. "Yes, Sir, I do."

"Good!" Jiménez glanced at Madrigal, who jumped slightly at being on the hot seat. "You ready with the property transfers?"

"Yes, Sir. Documents are all completed and ready to file."

"Very well. St. James, are you satisfied that the transfer documents are in proper order for your client's Costa Rican subsidiary?"

Anna interjected. "Yes. I've triple-checked the documents. DeSilva will instruct Global Finance to advance funds and place mortgages on Reclamation's properties when the transfers are registered. Reclamation will transfer nineteen million dollars' worth of the mortgage proceeds to Global Insurance to repay its losses."

"Global Finance will have several million in uncollectible mortgages, just as we discussed during the planning sessions," Montero cautioned.

St. James smiled. "True. As I said, when a few months go by without mortgage payments being made, Global Finance will foreclose and sell the properties to pay off the mortgages."

"Baca could pay off the mortgages before that," García countered.

"He won't know about them unless he conducts a complete title search," St. James retorted. "Don't forget, he's in a rage and only concerned with hunting the person who stole from him. Baca will start by checking the Registry to see who transferred the properties. After dealing with the notary he thinks robbed him, he'll search Reclamation's property titles before actually transferring them back to his companies. That's when he'll realize what's happened. By that time, we'll have him arrested."

"St. James's point is a good one, García," Jiménez supplemented, turning to Segura. "Where are we with the forgery?"

Segura perked up. "Eighty-five percent there, Sir. I'm confident we'll be at ninety-five percent by Tuesday."

"Anna, I know you've been observing. Anything to add?"

"Only that Segura's process for perfecting a signature is brilliant."

Segura smiled for the first time.

"Okay, so we are ready to begin the mission after Tuesday," Jiménez mused, twisting his moustache.

Everyone agreed.

Jiménez turned to St. James and García. "Gentlemen, how do you suggest we kick things off?"

García gestured for St. James to go first.

"I suggest Madrigal file the forged transfers using Sánchez's computer and email account next Wednesday morning. Confirm when the transfers are accepted. That should be immediate. DeSilva will have Finance execute the mortgages for Reclamation Properties when that's done."

Anna's eyebrows rose. "Who signs for Reclamation?"

St. James smiled. "The signing officer is Mùchén Li."

"Who the hell is Mùchén Li?" Jiménez butchered the pronunciation. Anna laughed.

St. James withheld a smile. "Li is the general manager of the Chongqing, China office for Global."

Montero was incredulous. "Couldn't they find someone in New York?"

St. James shook his head. "Since Baca is likely to retaliate violently, Global's legal counsel advised someone from a distant totalitarian country should be the signing officer. Li is close to the authorities in Chongqing and can arrange security for himself. Caught trying to eliminate Li in China, Baca's men would be imprisoned for an indefinite period — maybe even executed. Don't think Baca will want to risk that."

Jiménez shook his head. "Okay. The email from Madrigal informing Baca of his stolen assets will go out Wednesday or Thursday."

"Only when DeSilva confirms the mortgages are in place and the proceeds have been paid to Global Insurance. Too late then for Baca to stop everything." St. James explained. "DeSilva has everything lined up, including a solicitor here in San José. She can make it happen in one day. With any luck, Madrigal can send the anonymous email to Baca no later than Thursday."

García grinned. "I assume Global's solicitor is an honest one."

"Well-investigated, I assure you," St. James confirmed.

"So, by next Friday morning, Baca will learn his most trusted notary, Pérez, just robbed him of several properties," Jiménez mused. "I can hardly wait."

CHAPTER 42

Early Tuesday morning, St. James and Anna headed downtown to rent a car from a local agency. At ten o'clock, they decided on a cream BMW 850i.

St. James preferred cars with horsepower for chasing or evading crooks. The 850's six hundred horses made it perfect.

The rental manager suggested, "Why don't you rent a Mustang convertible? More fun."

Anna stood by quietly.

St. James was in the mood for mischief. "No. Always want a big car — a lot of metal between me and the other guy in case of an accident."

The manager looked at St. James with amusement. "Not many people come in here planning for an accident."

St. James's eye twinkled. "Once, in Denver, I chased two crooks who crashed through a mall like they were auditioning for *Fast & Furious*. Hit a man in a wheelchair and drove him through a lingerie shop window. He crashed into a dressing room where an oversized lady was trying on underwear. Quite a scene. She was fine, but the shoppers got an eyeful."

Anna couldn't believe her ears.

The manager's jaw dropped. "So, you want the extra insurance coverage?"

St. James smiled as he signed the rental papers and grabbed the keys. "Absolutely. Always plan for the worst."

Anna gawked at him as he pushed the vehicle locator button on the key fob to find the 850 in the lot. "What was that all about?"

"Don't like anyone telling me what to drive."

Anna rolled her eyes.

St. James familiarized himself with the car's controls. "Shit, you need to be a genius like Louis to drive this thing."

Anna shook her head. "Don't suppose you want me to drive, do you?"

"No, I've got it. Thank you, darling."

Anna smiled at the old-fashioned moniker and let herself be chauffeured, this time.

After a few laps around the government complex guided by a confused GPS, St. James parked, and they climbed out of the BMW.

Anna entered the building first. "I'll be with Segura if you need me."

St. James kissed her on the cheek. "Catch up with you after I meet with the Director and check in with Dozer and García."

At 10:30, St. James met with the Director, as Ramírez requested. A short, slender receptionist with brown hair led him into the Director's office.

Ramírez's office was spacious, with a grand oak desk, four comfortable dark-brown leather chairs, a matching sofa, and a conference table for eight. The walls were adorned with paintings of Seville and contemporary art from northern Spain. The air smelled of stale cigars. Four university certificates hung behind Ramírez's head. The rest of the wall was taken up by an enormous, flat-screen TV conferencing system.

St. James thought it felt more like a fortress than an office.

Ramírez gestured for St. James to sit in one of the brown leather chairs.

The Director didn't attempt to hide his obesity. His suit coat lay on a nearby chair, revealing his sizable frame. His double chin hung beneath a loosened red tie and open shirt collar. He took a cigar from the desk drawer, stuck it between his teeth, leaned back, and scrutinized St. James.

"Suppose you're wondering why I asked for this meeting?"

St. James was still relaxed, even jovial, after torturing the car rental agent. "Figured you'd let me know."

Ramírez took a moment. "I would like to know what you think of this mission."

St. James hiked his eyebrows. "What do you mean?"

"Is García the best man for the job?"

St. James was incredulous. "A bit late to ask that, isn't it, Sir?"

"Suppose it is," Ramírez's tone was too casual for the gravity of St. James's comment.

"I think Jiménez would be the better one to ask."

"I did ask Jiménez."

St. James was mystified. "García appears to have Jiménez's full backing. Wouldn't have been chosen otherwise."

Ramírez gnawed on the cigar. "One would think."

St. James's irritation showed. "Director Ramírez, a considerable amount of time went into planning this by everyone involved, including yourself. Why raise this now?"

Ramírez ignored the question. "What do you think of Jiménez's judgment?"

St. James was stymied. "Director Ramírez!"

"What?"

"What are you trying to tell me?"

Ramírez dumped his well-chewed cigar into an overflowing ashtray and sighed. "I've never undertaken a mission this massive, this risky, or this public before."

"You've known that from the beginning. Why now?"

"The reality is just hitting me."

Ramírez was not evaluating his agents, St. James thought. He was grappling with torment and self-doubt he could never express to his agents without undermining his authority. This was a confession, for Ramírez, and St. James was the anonymous priest.

St. James closed his eyes for a moment. Then he opened them and sighed. "Okay, Director, let's break this down into smaller pieces and see how we can solve it."

Ramírez's demeanour brightened. "Okay."

"Are you concerned about García's ability to train to the required level for this mission?"

Ramírez thought for a moment. "No."

St. James appeared doubtful. "Is that a hard no?"

"A hard no, yes," Ramírez confirmed. "I'm not concerned about García's training abilities."

"And do you believe the thirty agents he's training can rise to the level required to execute this plan as safely and effectively as possible?"

Ramírez appeared to puff up when talking of his troops. "We have the best law enforcement team in the country, and one of the best in the world."

"So that's a yes?"

"A hard yes," Ramírez confirmed.

"Okay. How do you feel about the strategy?"

Ramírez pulled another cigar from the drawer, unwrapped it, and stared out the window at traffic. After a few seconds, he turned back to St. James. "We scrutinized everything with everyone involved. Challenged every aspect and addressed every weakness. The presentation was flawless. How could I not be comfortable?"

"I want to know if you are confident it will work. Comfortable only carries you halfway. Confidence means you're sure everything has been thought through."

Ramírez weighed this for several seconds, then fixed on St. James's eyes. "I'm confident," he said, returning to his usual gruff tone.

"That leaves the mission's outcome — the number of deaths, public opinion, media reaction — all the risk and reward analysis we did. You're potentially paying a high price to rid Costa Rica of a major threat."

Ramírez nodded, eyes closed for a moment, and St. James continued. "Consider the financial cost of dealing with this level of crime. The hardship for victims, the resources used, and the damage to our — your — reputation. This mission could make a massive difference. Baca is involved in drug smuggling and human trafficking as well as other crimes. OIJ has a chance to tackle all that and make a real positive impact. You have children?"

"Three daughters."

"Think about how many daughters in this country have been forced into prostitution. If insurance fraud isn't enough, think about those girls fighting for their lives. Taking down Baca's racket could eliminate many other crimes and change the nation enormously."

Ramírez processed St. James's words.

St. James stood to leave. Ramírez smiled. "Ever consider running for political office?"

St. James was all smiles. "Couldn't be elected."

"Why?"

"I say what I think."

St. James walked to the door.

"St. James!" Ramírez called.

St. James turned. "Yes?"

"Thank you."

St. James smiled and left.

CHAPTER 43

St. James left Ramírez's office, his mind swirling with commitment and apprehension. Walking down a hall lined with portraits of Costa Rican lawmakers, he couldn't shake the burden of the mission ahead and its potential consequences.

He opted for the stairs to descend one floor, where Segura and Anna were busy working on the forgery. They sat in a tiny room at a small wooden table for four people, loupes on the bridges of their noses, engrossed in perfecting Segura's latest attempts at Pérez's signature.

"Anna, do you see where the loop in the P now seems to be the correct pressure? Not as heavy as before."

"Yes, now that you point it out." Anna sounded proud as if she were forging the signature herself.

St. James stood in the doorway for a moment, amused by the exchange he'd just witnessed.

"Good morning, ladies."

Anna lifted her eyes from her work. "Oh, hi, sweetheart."

"Morning, Mr. St. James," Segura whispered.

"How are we doing with perfecting Pérez's signature?"

"Excellent."

"Nice to have Anna for this," Segura conveyed. "Having someone to discuss loops, pressure, and exaggerated lettering after each attempt makes my job more pleasant."

St. James smiled. "You're progressing well, so I'll see how Dozer and García are doing with the training."

St. James left HQ, powered up the BMW and drove toward the training field.

Segura turned to Anna with a thoughtful expression. "Can't help wondering what all this will achieve. Forging Pérez's signature is one thing, but I worry how this will end. Number of agents we could lose. Innocent people killed."

Anna's forehead wrinkled as she thought about Segura's ponderings. "I know. I have similar worries. The OIJ is competent and has devoted substantial resources to prepare and train for the mission. The task is well thought out. I have faith in Hamilton and Dozer checking everything. We have to trust them."

Sequra agreed. "Right. Let's go back at it."

They adjusted the loupes on their noses and went back to the meticulous task, knowing that mission success depended on Segura's ability to replicate Pérez's signature, at least enough to fool Baca.

**

St. James approached García and Dozer at the edge of the training field. "Where are we, fellas?"

García wiped the sweat from his temple, took a long, thirsty gulp from his water bottle, and sighed. "Ready as we'll ever be."

Dozer wiped the sweat from his face. "Ready for action."

"So, everyone's locked and loaded, right?" The urgency in St. James's voice surprised Dozer, but he and García agreed.

St. James surveyed the agents practicing moves. "Okay. Let's talk about Pérez. We have to get him out of Baca's clutches before Thursday afternoon. Madrigal will then send the 'you've been robbed' email."

García frowned, continuing to combat the heat with sips of water. "Cutting it too close, St. James."

St. James raised an eyebrow. "How?"

García wiped his mouth with the back of his hand, "Can't afford a timing overlap between grabbing Pérez and Baca discovering he's been robbed."

"He won't know who took the property until he talks to the Registry Friday morning," St. James argued.

García grimaced. "True. But it's more convincing if Pérez vanishes a day or two before Baca catches wind of everything. Ratchet up his paranoia. He'd think Pérez was at Sánchez's place, plotting more heists."

Dozer pondered this. "You know what Baca's first move will be, right? He'll call Pérez's wife. Baca's crazy meter will hit the ceiling if she hasn't seen her husband for over a day."

St. James's mind recalibrated his timing. "All right Dozer. Get Pérez out of there on Wednesday morning and stash him at Sánchez's place."

"Okay."

"I'll coordinate a team to watch him until after the shit show," García committed. "My assistant will organize food and security detail. Can't afford any unexpected visitors or nosy neighbours."

Dozer's shoulders squared, "I'll make everything run on my end."

St. James felt a mix of unease and excitement as they hashed out the logistics. Success of the operation hinged on keeping Baca's suspicions at bay, making him believe he was going to eliminate a disloyal notary — when, in reality, Pérez was the bait for the OIJ to arrest him.

García finished his water and tossed the empty bottle into a nearby recycle bin. "Let's make this work, St. James. Come this far. Can't afford not to."

CHAPTER 44

García's cell vibrated while St. James was still on the training field. He glanced at the number. "Director Ramírez. I have to take it."

St. James turned to Dozer.

"What do you think of the training?"

Dozer didn't hesitate. "Put it this way: If we organize another military-like training program, I want García to run it, wherever we are in the world."

St. James grinned. "High praise coming from you."

García clicked off his call with the Director. "He is coming over to address the agents."

Dozer wondered. "Shouldn't Jiménez be here for that?"

García watched the agents doing calisthenics. "Yes, he should. It's protocol for a senior agent to be present when the Director speaks to agents reporting to him."

St. James hesitated. "What are you going to do?"

García smiled. "Nothing. It's up to the two of them to talk. Too dangerous for me to be in the middle of two men who outrank me. Career suicide. Besides, there isn't time. The Director will be here shortly."

In less than forty-five minutes, they spotted Director Ramírez shuffling across the field.

"García, assemble the agents. I wish to speak to them," Ramírez ordered.

"Yes, Sir."

Ramírez stood beside St. James and Dozer, waiting for García to herd the agents he trained. Everyone gathered around the Director. Scanning the faces of the agents who stood before him, Ramírez began to speak.

"Today, we stand on the precipice of history, poised to embark on the most crucial mission ever to be undertaken for the people of Costa Rica. Each of you was handpicked for this monumental task, and I have absolute faith in your ability to rise to the responsibilities you have been assigned.

Under the guidance of Jiménez and García, you have undergone rigorous training, honing your skills to perfection. You have shown unwavering dedication and commitment, and I commend you for your tireless efforts.

Let's not forget the gravity of our mission. The criminals we face have ravaged our nation for decades, siphoning billions from our economy and leaving a trail of devastation in their wake. They preyed upon our citizens, destroying lives with drugs, prostitution, and other heinous crimes. They tested the limits of our resolve, burdening our law enforcement and justice systems beyond measure. Yet, we have been unable to gather reliable evidence to put them away. The mission you are undertaking allows us to collect that evidence.

Today, we stand united against this insidious threat. Guardians of justice. Defenders of the innocent, and champions of freedom. Carry the hopes and aspirations of every Costa Rican who yearns for a better tomorrow, free from the shackles of fear and oppression that come from crime.

Many of you have felt the pain of loss, watching loved ones fall victim to crime. Let that pain fuel your determination and strengthen your resolve, for today, we embark on a mission to reclaim our nation's future.

So, I say to you, stand tall. Stand proud, for you are the vanguard of change. Together, we will confront the darkness threatening our land and emerge victorious.

Thank you for your courage and dedication. May your resolve never waver and may the spirit of Costa Rica guide us on this noble quest. Onward, my friends, for today, we write the first chapter of a new era of justice and prosperity for our beloved Costa Rica!"

García started clapping. Soon, every agent joined in. The applause lasted for more than two minutes without loss of enthusiasm. The Director, moved by their response, glanced at St. James, who applauded him with a double thumbs-up.

CHAPTER 45

The man with no name shook his head. "He didn't utter a single word the entire trip."

Baca turned to Noname. "Cause any trouble going through immigration?"

Baca, Eduardo, Denzel, and Noname sat in Baca's warehouse office. Baca and Eduardo drank coffee, which Noname declined. Denzel only shook his head when offered.

"No. I told the immigration officer he was an individual requiring support, and my sister's son was visiting Costa Rica under my supervision to spend time with family."

Eduardo was incredulous. "Your sister's son? Sister's not…" His sentence trailed off, and an unspoken question stuck in space.

Noname's frustration flared. "No, she's not Black! What gave you that idea?"

The otherwise stern Baca found amusement in the situation — cracked a rare smile at the exchange.

Denzel sat, his posture rigid, eyes fixed on the floor.

Eduardo's concern surfaced as he addressed Denzel. "Are you all right, Denzel?" Denzel sat in terrified silence, rocking slightly to comfort himself.

An impatient Baca tensed with annoyance. "Answer the man, boy!"

Denzel remained quiet. He looked at his feet, at his hands — anywhere except Baca's eyes.

Baca turned to Eduardo. "What's with this kid?"

Eduardo winced. "He's … differently abled, I think the term is, now. You can't expect a typical response."

Baca was still simmering with frustration. "Well, what will you do with him?"

"What do you mean, what will *I* do with him? What were you thinking when you ordered him brought here?"

Baca's eyes gleamed with resolve. "Thought we could use him as leverage. A hostage to pressure Dozer and St. James into backing off their alliance with Jiménez."

Eduardo's skepticism was evident. "If they call our bluff?"

"We show them we're not bluffing. Demonstrate our willingness to do whatever it takes to protect ourselves."

Denzel was a muted enigma. His stillness offered a stark reminder of their dangerous game.

Eduardo sighed. "We need to be careful. Can't afford for this to backfire."

Baca agreed. "We'll handle it. Denzel might be our key to persuading Dozer and St. James to reconsider their stay."

Eduardo's doubt lingered, "From what I've gathered from our informant, they're not easily swayed."

CHAPTER 46

The mission to apprehend Pérez began at eight o'clock Wednesday morning. Dozer and three agents arrived at Pérez's modest house in the east end of San José. They travelled in an inconspicuous car to avoid being spotted by Baca, the man with eyes everywhere.

Anna confirmed Pérez's address for Dozer, and Segura found a picture of Pérez in his file for Anna to pass on to the men. So, they knew their destination and their target. The unknown was whether Pérez would be at home. He could have gone to the office early, or his wife may have sent him on an errand before he left for the day.

Their driver, an OIJ agent six months from retirement, wore a sling on his left arm, but seemed to be having no trouble with the controls. He parked across the street from Pérez's house and left the engine running. The four sat for several seconds, eyeing the house. Modest, but the nicest place on the street.

"Nice grounds," the driver mused, adjusting the vehicle's air conditioning.

The driver observed the crisply edged lawn and the well-maintained gardens surrounding Pérez's property. "You a gardener, Dozer?"

"Touch it, it dies!"

The other agents laughed.

Tapping the steering wheel, the driver attempted small talk: "Gardening's relaxing. Spend most weekends working mine." He lifted his sling arm. "Can't wait to get back to it. Any day now."

The third agent, low key to this point, mused, "Wonder whether that yellow Nissan in the driveway belongs to him or his wife."

The driver eyed the Nissan. "Could check while we wait. Won't mean anything."

Dozer chimed in. "Couples don't care whose name is on the registration as long as the vehicle is in the family and the driveway."

The driver eyed the gardens. "Wonderful variety. Look, Dozer. That's a Guaria Morada orchid — our national flower. Orchids, lobster claws, Bromeliaceae, and Etlingera Elatior — all beautiful, don't you think?"

Dozer rolled his eyes. The agents winked at him, which he took as, *go along with it; we have to listen to this shit all the time.*

The agent pointed toward Pérez's drive. "There he is, walking to his car."

The driver studied Pérez's figure. "Mousy-looking guy."

"I read his file," the second agent advised. "Strong. Not to be underestimated. Those who strived to overpower him paid a price."

Dozer shook his head. "Be surprised if he weighs fifty-seven kilos. We'll be all right."

The third agent reached for the door handle. "Should we get him now?"

Dozer shut the suggestion down. "We're not snatching him from his driveway. His wife might see us, give a description. Senseless to take the risk."

The driver agreed. "We'll follow him. Wait for a better opportunity."

Pérez reversed the yellow Nissan from the driveway and drove past, oblivious to the agents watching.

The driver's swift U-turn put him three cars behind the Nissan. Five blocks later, Pérez pulled into an AM/PM convenience store, parked in front, and walked to the entrance, unaware he was being followed. The agent pulled in moments later and parked along the right side of the store.

Dozer turned to the second agent. "Pérez has never met me, so I'll blend in. What about you?"

The agent hesitated for a moment. "Not that I know of."

"Okay. Let's go."

Dozer veered around one side of the red-and-white concrete block building to enter the store while the agent took the opposite side toward the same door. Inside, they ignored one another, blending seamlessly with other shoppers. They browsed down separate aisles, feigning interest in random items while keeping a vigilant eye on Pérez's every move.

Pérez gathered a few items from the shelves and went to the checkout counter. Dozer and the second agent shadowed him, ensuring they weren't noticed. Pérez pocketed his receipt and exited the AM/PM, bag swinging by his side. Dozer and the agent followed, their footsteps almost imperceptible on the asphalt.

Dozer lunged forward, gripping Pérez's arm like a vise, sending shockwaves of pain and surprise through his compact frame. Pérez's keys dropped to the ground. His bag splashed onto the ground, spilling his purchases: milk, bread, and a sandwich for lunch.

The agent shouted. "You got this, Dozer?" Dozer nodded.

The agent slid into the back seat through the passenger's side and positioned himself to haul Pérez into the car.

Pérez bellowed — "Hey, what is this? Who the hell are you? You don't know who I work for. You're dead men!" Dozer was hustling him toward the back seat, pushing and lifting him to make progress.

Pérez twisted and struggled against Dozer's iron grip, trying to free himself. Dozer sensed the man gaining energy, not running out. Pérez grew more hostile, riding a wave of fresh anger; his limbs flailed, and his body contorted into a frantic, writhing resistance.

"Don't let go, Dozer!" the agent shouted from the passenger's side.

Pérez delivered a hard blow to Dozer's lower body, doubling him over as he staggered backward. Pérez attempted to break free again, but the agent's grip prevented him.

Dozer recovered and sprang forward, catapulting himself toward Pérez. Pérez dodged to one side, and Dozer bounced off the car door, dazed.

Pérez reached through the open car door and grabbed a large metal flashlight loose on the floor in the back seat. He swung it at Dozer with all his might. Dozer grunted in pain, hunched over by the car door. The agent lunged at Pérez, but Pérez broke free and slid along the vehicle's back quarter panel, searching for an escape route.

Seeing the capture spiralling out of control, the agent darted from the rear passenger-side door and intercepted Pérez behind the vehicle. Dozer closed in, locking Pérez in a bear hug from behind. Pérez leveraged Dozer's hold to deliver a forward kick to the agent's groin. The agent cried out. Pérez extended his arms straight up, lifting both legs at the waist, his dead-weight body slipping through Dozer's arms to the ground.

Pérez quickly regained his footing. Booted Dozer's stomach, doubling him over, followed by a kick to the face.

The agent moved behind Pérez, slid his arms through Pérez's underarms, and locked his fingers behind Pérez's neck. Dozer, now upright, delivered a hard blow to Pérez's stomach, winding him, followed by a forceful uppercut, sending Pérez to the ground, unconscious.

The agent flipped Pérez over on his stomach, pulled both hands behind his back, and snapped handcuffs on the limp body. They laid Pérez out on the backseat of the vehicle.

Dozer stood and leaned forward against the car's roof, his head resting on his hands as he tried to catch his breath. The agent adopted the same position on the passenger side, facing Dozer. Dozer lifted his head and peered over the roof at the agent. "What did you say you read in this guy's file?"

Continuing to work on his recovery, the agent lifted his head. "Pérez is strong and not to be underestimated."

Dozer's smile was faint. "Damned accurate!"

CHAPTER 47

Dozer felt a buzz in his pocket and reached for his phone. He tapped to open a message from Albert Swanson, the owner of the food chain where his brother, Denzel, worked.

Swanson's text expressed concern: *This is the second day Denzel hasn't been to work. I'm worried.*

Dozer texted his brother immediately. No answer. Dozer checked in with a family friend who often visited his brother. The friend hadn't seen Denzel in two weeks and knew nothing of his whereabouts.

A tight knot formed in Dozer's stomach as he sat in the Hilton La Sabana bar, waiting for Anna and St. James.

It was 6:30 on Wednesday evening. He sipped an Imperial and tried to distract himself by flirting with Maggie, the bartender, when she wasn't serving other customers.

Dozer opened his contact list, located Swanson's coordinates, and tapped his cell number. Swanson picked up on the first ring.

"When Denzel didn't show up today, I sent a clerk to his apartment. There was no response when he pounded on Denzel's door." Swanson's voice trembled with worry. "The lady next door hasn't seen him for two days. She's concerned."

Dozer struggled to steady himself. "Did you try his cell?"

"Several times. It's turned off."

"I did, too. Nothing." Dozer tried to fend off his growing panic by thinking of things to try. "Denzel left a spare key at your store in case he misplaced his. Do you still have it?"

"In a secure drawer here."

"Good. Can you send someone with a cell phone over to investigate? I want to talk to them while they're in his apartment."

Swanson didn't hesitate. "I'll go myself."

Fifteen minutes later, Dozer's cell buzzed — Swanson. "In the apartment now."

"Okay! Tell me what you see as you move."

Denzel's apartment was a modest one-bedroom in an older four-story brown brick building on Ottawa's Albert Street. The small living room, painted in a faded cream, exuded age and wear. An older Toshiba television occupied one corner, its screen coated in a thin layer of dust. Opposite, a grey, threadbare sofa gave off a damp, musty odour that permeated the room. A matching chair to its right bore the same condition.

In the centre of the room, an Arborite table and two end tables sat askew, surfaces marked with scratches and stains from years of use. Dim lighting suggested the wiring might not have been up to the building code. The room flowed seamlessly into a kitchenette, where metal counters, cupboards, and drawers showed signs of rust and corrosion. The smell of stale pizza mingled with the scent of mildew.

Swanson surveyed the scene as he moved around. "Hope Denzel isn't paying much for this," he mused.

Dozer didn't answer.

"No dirty dishes in the sink. The counter is clean, and his bed is made. Looks like it hasn't been slept in."

Panic gripped Dozer by the throat, but he willed himself to stay calm, for Denzel.

Dozer was listening to Swanson describe other parts of the apartment when St. James and Anna arrived. They swept into the bar in a jovial mood, but as they pulled out stools and made themselves comfortable, they immediately sensed Dozer's distress. He held his phone tightly to his ear and glanced at his friends with a look of helplessness that they couldn't remember having seen before. Anna and St. James exchanged worried glances, both wondering what was unfolding.

Seeing St. James and Anna relieved Dozer, their presence grounding him amid the worry. Maggie hurried over to take drink orders from

St. James and Anna. She noted the strain on Dozer's face. "Everything all right?" she whispered, concern in her tone.

St. James offered a tight-lipped smile, a slight suggestion that everything was okay, though his eyes betrayed his worry.

Anna moved closer to Maggie and whispered, "Not sure."

Dozer held up one finger to ask for quiet at the bar as he spoke. "Mr. Swanson, you mentioned the tables were in the centre of the living room?"

"That's right."

"Not like Denzel. He's a neat freak."

Swanson sputtered. "I know. That's one of the things that makes him such a wonderful employee."

Dozer's suspicion was piqued. "Any sign that the lock was tampered with when you unlocked the door?"

"Not that I could tell, but I'll look at it again."

Dozer heard creaking and shuffling sounds as he pondered the scene and shook his head. "Doesn't matter, anyway. Anyone can buy a lock pick online."

"True. And I can't see any signs that it was tampered with."

Dozer's thoughts changed. "Mr. Swanson, please go to the bedroom."

Seconds later, Swanson said. "I'm here."

"Good. To the right of the bed is a worn chest of drawers."

"I see it."

Unaware of the situation, St. James and Anna observed as Dozer investigated Denzel's apartment through Swanson's eyes.

Maggie placed a double Macallan in front of St. James and a pinot grigio in front of Anna. Both mouthed *thank you* at the same time. Maggie smiled and hurried down the bar.

"Open the top right-hand drawer and tell me what you see," Dozer directed.

Dozer heard the screech of old wood on old wood as Swanson pulled the well-worn drawer. Swanson shuffled several items around, taking inventory to report to Dozer.

With each passing moment, Dozer's agitation grew, suffocating him. His hands clenched into fists, his nails biting into his palms as he fought to keep his emotions in check.

"There're some old bank statements. A couple of letters from someone named Martha."

Dozer interrupted. "Grandmother. She's passed."

"Pocket watch."

"Gift from me."

"An all-in-one screwdriver. What were you expecting me to find?"

"His passport."

CHAPTER 48

Dozer hung up from Swanson and stared ahead in panicked silence. When he had recovered enough to speak, he relayed the unsettling conversation to St. James and Anna. As he spoke, their faces mirrored his growing concern.

St. James sat with a glass of Macallan clutched in both hands, his jet-black hair combed back. The amber liquid swirled as he took a sip. "Jesus. Denzel's passport was not in the bureau drawer?"

Dozer shook his head. "No."

Anna traced the rim of her wine glass. "Would he venture out of the country alone?"

Dozer's response was swift. "Not without calling me first."

Anna nodded and thought. "Is he capable of international travel alone, even with your approval?"

"Maybe," Dozer said, his forehead creased. "Almost." His gaze darted around the lobby, searching for answers that weren't there.

St. James took in the several travellers milling about at reception. "He knows where you are, right? The hotel, I mean?"

"He always knows where I am. It's a rule with us."

"Why not check with the airlines?" Anna suggested. "See if his passport was used for flights out of Ottawa the past few days?"

Dozer's frustration was evident. "They only give that information to the authorities."

St. James grimaced. "And the authorities won't divert resources without good reason."

Anna stared off in thought. "He's been forced by someone — if he won't leave without talking to you, and his passport's gone. Isn't that a sign? Kidnapped?"

Dozer's affirmation was almost inaudible. "That's what I'm afraid of."

St. James's eyes widened. "Who would want to force him out of the country? He doesn't have a single enemy."

Dozer's gaze flicked at St. James and Anna. "But *I* do!"

Anna squinted. "Who among your enemies would be likely to use Denzel to bait you?"

"Any one of them, if they knew Denzel existed."

St. James jumped in. "Who would want something from you badly enough to kidnap your brother?"

"Don't have anything anyone would want. My investigators do the work I used to do at White Investigations."

"If it's not about something you have," Anna ventured, "could it be about vengeance — a past case, possibly?"

"Could be, I suppose. But why now? I'm on vacation in Costa Rica, as far as anyone knows. Besides, if this were about vengeance, they would have killed me by now. They wouldn't need Denzel."

St. James peered out at the Sierra Madre mountains. "Could be something to do with here."

Anna sat up straight. "Remember what Jiménez told us."

Dozer and St. James looked at Anna.

"What?" Dozer blurted.

"Records are kept of those who fly in and out of Costa Rica."

CHAPTER 49

Thursday was execution day for St. James to recover Global's $19 million insurance losses. Dozer withdrew to focus on finding Denzel. St. James and Anna both wanted nothing more than to help their friend locate his brother, but the operation was underway and there was nothing to do but see it through.

At nine, St. James phoned DeSilva. "Mary, it's show time. Segura forged Pérez's signature on the documents. Madrigal transferred the real estate to Reclamation earlier this morning, with confirmation from the Registry that the transfers were accepted."

"Great. I just received the borrowing and director resolutions signed by Mùchén Li. In-house counsel says they are all in order."

"Excellent. Now, you can have Global Finance advance the mortgage funds to Reclamation Properties and instruct your San José notary to register them against the properties we just transferred there."

"How much should I advance under the mortgages?"

"Nineteen million plus an estimated five-hundred thousand in expenses."

"Can I include the one-point-nine million I'll have to pay you?" De Silva sounded hopeful.

"No."

"Why not?"

"Imagine yourself in a witness box."

"Please, God, don't let this be another St. James lesson in morality."

"Now, now." St. James's manner bordered on patronizing. "You wanted to know why. So, you have to listen."

DeSilva hesitated at first. "Okay. Let me have it."

"So, Miss DeSilva, you paid nineteen million in claims you didn't have to pay. You have to say yes, that's correct. Miss DeSilva, are there no investigation procedures to validate claims before you pay them? You would say yes, Sir, there are. Did you follow those procedures, Miss DeSilva? You would have to say no…"

"Too damned busy, St. James, you know that!"

"Too busy to do your job, Miss DeSilva?" St. James persisted. "Didn't do your job, so you had to hire a brilliant detective to fix it."

"I'm hanging up now, Hamilton."

"It's not hanging up if you announce it first."

Click. DeSilva ended the call.

St. James smiled. "Think she has the hots for me."

***

St. James didn't receive confirmation that the mortgages were in place and the funds advanced to Reclamation Properties until six o'clock that evening.

He and Anna enjoyed drinks in the Hilton La Sabana bar. Maggie was on duty.

Dozer came later, full of tension. He signalled Maggie for an Imperial without speaking.

"How did it go?" St. James said.

Dozer didn't acknowledge Maggie when she placed an Imperial in front of him. That earned him an exaggerated frown.

Dozer's face creased with worry. "The airport document showed Denzel landed in Costa Rica the day before yesterday."

"Alone?" Anna wondered.

"No. Escorted by a seatmate, an immense, burly man named Johnston."

St. James cringed. "How'd you find that out?"

"Thanks to Jiménez, the airport general manager agreed to help. He spoke to senior management of the airline Denzel flew with, and they tracked down the pilot and crew of his plane. Ordered them to talk to me."

Anna was anxious. "Have you spoken with them yet?"

"I spoke with the flight attendant in charge of Denzel's flight. She just landed at Heathrow. She remembered Denzel well because he wouldn't eat or answer her questions. He's that way when he's scared. This Johnston guy seemed to care for him. She mentioned no sign of force or harm."

"And you have no idea who he is?"

Dozer looked at Anna. "No clue. But Jiménez is trying to help. He connected with the RCMP to see what they might know about this character. He wants me to wait for what comes from that before doing anything else. All that took the whole day. I'm all yours for the time being."

St. James remained concerned. "Any time you need to go — to deal with Denzel's situation, you go. Anything we can do for Denzel's safe return, you ask. No hesitation. We'll drop everything to help bring him to safety."

"Thanks, man. Appreciate the support. There's nothing you can do at the moment. But I won't hesitate to yell for help if needed."

Anna forced a supportive smile. "In the meantime, we'll pray for Denzel's safe return."

Dozer's typical calm wavered under the weight of Denzel's predicament. Though he kept his emotions in check, a whirlwind of concern and fear for his brother's well-being churned inside.

Dozer's smile back was forced. "Thanks, Anna." He turned to St. James. "Where do we stand with the mission?"

"Just received confirmation from DeSilva that everything is done. Mortgages registered. Money's in Reclamation. And Mùchén Li transferred nineteen and a half million from Reclamation to eliminate Global Insurance's losses." St. James smiled. "Success!"

Anna hoisted her glass of pinot. "To another job well done!"

St. James lifted his glass of scotch. "Here! Here!" Dozer followed along but with little enthusiasm.

St. James read his emails. "DeSilva came through. The bank just confirmed Global's three-point-seven million was deposited into my account. God bless DeSilva."

"To Mary DeSilva!" Anna blurted. Dozer and Anna raised their glasses once more.

St. James's glass followed.

Dozer offered a weak smile. "I'll have my office prepare a bill."

St. James sipped Macallan. "No hurry."

CHAPTER 50

Alajuela

Cameron stood guard at the end of a long row of industrial warehouses, watching cargo loaded and unloaded from trucks with hydraulic lifts. Automobile engines, industrial parts, steel girders, industrial garden equipment, and bales of thick wire.

Cameron recognized most of the workers tending the units — no one he thought was new or a threat. The Boss wanted to know when new faces arrived, what they were doing, and in which unit they were doing it.

His Boss was obsessed with security, but not in the usual way. Forget uniform security personnel or slick suits. He wanted average guys in work clothes. Dressed to seamlessly blend in with others working in the bustling industrial park.

Cameron stood by an ageing blue Volkswagen Golf, dressed like a warehouse foreman in a dark work shirt and grey overalls. He scanned the street. Every sound amplified — a truck rumbling past and machinery's distant hum.

Feet crossed and a Chesterfield Red dangling from his mouth, he looked like he was on a smoke break — and he was. But the cigarette was more than a habit. It was camouflage, a reason to be outside, scanning the surroundings for any signs of trouble.

His job was tedious. He hadn't seen strange or threatening behaviour in weeks.

Cameron couldn't wait for the shift to end. That evening, he was taking the family to dinner — his oldest boy's sixteenth birthday. He checked his watch — ten minutes to go.

Cameron dropped the cigarette and ground it into the dirt with the heel of his boot, then took a final peek in either direction. Satisfied there was nothing of concern, he spun around to enter the building.

A truck revved its engine down the street. Cameron turned. A beige half-ton Ford rolled toward him. Slow at first, continuing to rev its engine as it drifted. The truck picked up speed, forcing everyone in its path to jump aside. Cameron grabbed the AR-15 rifle he stood against the doorway when he left the building — and waited, unsure of the driver's intent. Seconds later, there was no doubt. The truck was coming for him.

Cameron aimed at the driver's side windshield and squeezed the trigger. The windshield shattered. The truck kept coming. Cameron shot again, blowing a hole in the driver's side window. Fifty feet away, the Ford rotated 180 degrees at full speed, now facing the direction from which it came.

The Ford's passenger levelled a shotgun, aimed, and squeezed both triggers. The blast lifted Cameron off his feet, throwing him backward hard against the warehouse door. There he lay. A hole in his chest the size of a baseball.

***

On Thursday afternoon, Baca gathered fifteen of his highest-ranking gang members for an emergency meeting in the Alajuela warehouse.

At the centre of the office portion of the building stood a grand, rectangular table crafted from sturdy, dark birch. Birch filing cabinets, bookcases, and built-in storage nooks imbued the space with old-world charm.

On the other side of the office, a kitchen filled the room with the rich aroma of brewed coffee. The walls of the meeting room were bare, except for a fifty-foot map of Costa Rica that served as Baca's planning tool.

Baca lit a Belmont cigarette and glanced at the group. As the gangsters fell silent, he turned to them and spoke. "Men, we have suffered a loss. Cameron was gunned down at the munition warehouse late yesterday — shotgun to the chest."

Whispers of disbelief spread through the room like a current.

Baca slammed his fist on the table. "Silence!" The room muted instantly as though he had flipped a switch. His sun-drenched, wrinkled face turned blood red, and the scar under his lip deepened as his anger intensified. "These killings must stop!" Baca hammered the table a second time.

He turned to his longest-serving lieutenant, seated on his right. "Ludwig, I want you to take charge of munition warehouse security. Take as many men as you need to fortify the place and arm yourselves with whatever weapons you see fit."

Ludwig displayed a touch of nervousness. "Yes, Sir."

A younger member raised his hand. Baca granted him the floor. "Do we have any leads on who's behind this, Sir?" The young man didn't want his Boss to be angrier than he was.

Baca leaned back, puffing on the Belmont. "Gang out of Panama, as best I can determine — competitor trying to push us out."

A third man spoke. "No one local?"

Baca pondered the pressure of recent events. With a deep breath, he shook his head and eyed a young member. "Ray, start working your way through our informants. Listen to the rumours and gossip — any clue that could lead us to Cameron's killer. Be discreet. We don't want anyone thinking this rattled us."

"Yes, Boss."

"Rest of you, get back to work! Leave. Make money." An order that emptied the room immediately.

Baca turned to Eduardo. "How are you doing with this Denzel character?"

"No trouble. He's locked in the bedroom at the back of the office."

Baca smiled darkly. "He's settling in, I take it?"

"Seems fine so far. I arrange food three times a day, and it's gone when I check on him later, so he must be eating — nothing in the garbage can. No-name grabbed him from his apartment without clothes or toiletries. My son is about the same size, so I bought him a few things. Just what Denzel would need for the foreseeable future."

Baca's mind had drifted elsewhere. "Sounds reasonable."

Eduardo was about to leave to resume his daily responsibilities when Baca turned to him. "Eduardo, send the anonymous note to Dozer's room tonight. Tell him if he wants to see his brother alive again, he must leave Costa Rica within twenty-four hours and have no further communication with the OIJ." Eduardo concurred and left.

Baca turned to his emails. "Jesus! What the hell is this?" He scrolled down to the sixth one. He showed Ludwig his phone. "Take a look at this."

Ludwig read the email, his brow furrowing. "A prank, perhaps, Sir?"

Baca's rage and confusion twisted his features, enlarging his diamond-shaped scar. "No one would dare prank me!"

Ludwig looked up at Baca, fear dominating his dark basset-hound eyes. "Right, Sir. Shouldn't have said that."

Baca let it go and focused on the email: "Look. It came from Sánchez's computer!"

Ludwig reached into the back pocket of his cambric pants and extracted a grey handkerchief. Dabbed sweat from his olive-toned high forehead. "How can that be?" he said, in Spanish. "We killed him."

Ludwig reread the brief email, then paused, his forehead creasing with concern.

I'm transferring property from you. –Anonymous. Ludwig sensed Baca's anger escalating. "Go to the Registry," Baca barked. "Tell them I sent you, and that I want full cooperation — the transferred properties, all the details, and which notary I have to deal with."

Ludwig checked his watch. "It's four forty-five, Sir. The Registro Nacional is closed. Reopens at eight o'clock tomorrow morning."

"Then be on their steps at eight and back here no later than eight-forty-five. I'll call a general assembly for nine-fifteen."

"Yes, Boss. I'll be there at eight."

CHAPTER 51

Baca screamed. "*Hector*? You're telling me *Hector Pérez* stole my properties?" Spit ran from the corner of Baca's mouth. "The only notary I ever trusted. I don't believe it!"

"Afraid it's true, Boss. The Registry clerk gave me a photocopy of the transfer documents." Ludwig pulled the documents from a manila folder, his fingers slick with sweat.

As Baca read each page, disbelief morphed into helpless, white-hot rage. "That's Pérez's signature, all right." He clenched his jaw, a muscle twitching at the corner of his mouth.

Ludwig, once a promising operations manager for an honest company with dreams of a stable life, now found himself caught in the whirlwind of Baca's fury. He stood trembling in the industrial office unit, bracing himself for the storm.

"Where is the bastard?" Baca's eyes blazed with anger.

"Not at work, Sir."

With a roar, Baca hurled a metal folding chair against the wall. Ludwig cringed as it crashed to the floor. "Where is he, then?"

Ludwig stammered. "I sent two men to his house." Baca kicked a filing cabinet. "And…?"

"His wife hasn't seen him since Wednesday morning. No calls or texts. She has no idea where he is."

Baca picked up a chair and threw it hard against the wall. Ludwig jumped. Baca sat down and pounded the table. Ludwig's heart raced in response to the fury radiating from his Boss. After a moment of torment, Baca raised his head. "Wait a minute. The email — it came from Sánchez's computer!"

Ludwig instinctively moved several seats away, wary of Baca's wrath. "What about it, Sir?"

"Pérez made the transfers. The email must have come from him. Nobody's lived there since Sánchez … died."

Ludwig remained silent. He thought about a time when he felt helpless — too scared to speak up against a lousy deal Baca was pursuing. That regret still haunted him.

"He's using Sánchez's computer to steal my real estate. He must be at Sánchez's!"

When Ludwig stood in front of him, not moving, Baca shrieked at him. "What are you waiting for? Assemble my men! I want them in this warehouse within the hour!"

***

Baca stood before a group of dishevelled men scattered around the warehouse. At 9:15 a.m., he paced, chain-smoking, his complexion shading from hazelnut to cherry red.

"I learned this morning that Pérez stole real estate from me. Nobody steals from Elfego Baca and lives to tell the tale!" The overhead fluorescent lights glimmered as he moved.

Disbelief rippled through the crowd. Why would Pérez, Baca's trusted confidante, risk triggering the man's fury, obliterating a long and fruitful partnership? Why would he put himself and his family at risk? Rumours began flying — whispers of a gambling addiction, of a wife unable to control her spending, a son needing special care.

"Silence!" Baca's yell cut through the murmurs, and the room fell quiet.

A hand went up in the second row. "Sir, why are we here if Pérez is the only traitor?"

Baca paused. "Because I have a bad feeling maybe it's not just Pérez. So, I'm assuming the worst."

He glanced at the monitor, where notaries and accountants joined the meeting by Zoom. "You hear that?" He watched heads bob, taking in their reactions.

"This is a shock. Pérez has been with me for many years." Baca fought back his emotion, determination replacing his initial anger. "Pérez's wife hasn't seen him since Wednesday. We don't know where he is. The email came from Sánchez's computer. So, until we know otherwise, our target location is Sánchez's house."

The air smelled of cigarette smoke, mingled with sweat and trepidation.

"Pérez's betrayal has shaken us, but it won't break us. We're going in prepared." Baca's sight locked onto the faces on Zoom. "You're not exempt from this. Everyone needs to be on high alert. I will not tolerate failure!"

Baca turned back to the men in the room. "Ludwig will lead the training. I need every one of you to give it your all. No half-measures. I want everyone ready to raid Sánchez's place on Monday. Cancel your weekend plans."

Murmurs of disappointment and reluctant agreement rippled through the crowd as Baca's words sank in. He raised a hand, silencing them. "We're hitting Sánchez's place hard. Weapons need cleaning, gear needs to be checked, and minds need to be focused. This is not a drill."

Baca turned to Ludwig, nodding for him to take over.

Ludwig stood steady yet tense, his worn leather boots creaking against the concrete floor. He felt the pressure of the moment, the expectations of him to lead and produce results. "Okay, men. The Boss is expecting the worst. We don't know what alliances the traitor Pérez might have formed. Several men could be waiting to ambush us."

A large man in dirty overalls raised his hand. "How many men do you expect, Ludwig?"

"Have no idea. But there'll be forty of us." Ludwig's delivery wavered. Then, he reminded himself he had survived worse.

CHAPTER 52

Anna's research showed Gael Vargas lived in Cerro Colón, an upscale gated community in an area called Ciudad Colón, a half-hour drive from Escazú.

On Friday morning, Gabe fetched the BMW 850 from the Hilton's covered parking area and brought it around to the entrance for St. James and Anna to explore for the day.

It was a perfect day. The weather was delightful — bright sunshine and a warm, gentle breeze — and the air smelled of freshly mowed grass.

Traffic flowed well, and a chorus of honking horns accompanied them as they drove the Próspero Fernández route west from San José, past Santa Ana, to Vargas's enclave.

St. James pulled up to Vargas's community guardhouse when they arrived in Ciudad Colón.

Anna was immediately charmed by the park-like surroundings. "What a beautiful area," she said, then glanced at her iPad. "This website says it's surrounded by nature, with a fabulous view of the mountains — perfect for hiking, horseback riding, and mountain climbing."

St. James drummed his fingers on the steering wheel, not tuned in to Anna's enthusiastic description. "The gates make it hard to see much from here. Seems spacious and well-maintained."

Anna glared at him. "What now?"

"I'll talk to the guy on duty and see about visitor protocol."

"I should go," Anna said.

St. James glanced at her. "Why?"

"Of the two of us, I'm the least intimidating. Might get more information."

St. James considered this. "Okay, I'll wait in the car."

Anna stepped out and made her way toward the guardhouse, a sense of purpose in her stride. With a friendly smile, she introduced herself to Hank, the man on duty. He was dressed in faded blue shorts and a weathered golf shirt. His bald head brought Dozer to mind. Taken by a lady stranger, Hank greeted Anna with a smile.

"What can I do for you, Ms. Anna?" His accent was more Caribbean than Spanish.

"Like to see Mr. Vargas, if possible."

"Have an appointment?"

"No. I'm vacationing here and hoped for an opportunity to visit him."

"He aware you're in Costa Rica?"

"Yes. I met him at his office a few days ago."

Hank sized up Anna some more.

"I can't let you in without his approval, and he's not here."

"Do you happen to know where he went?"

Hank scratched his mossy salt-and-pepper beard. "Owners never tell me where they're going. None of my business. But Mr. Vargas walks his dog every morning this time."

Anna thought about this for a moment. "Your guardhouse faces the street. Vargas must be outside the community if you can see him walking his dog."

"Yep."

Anna wanted more from Hank. "Could you tell me which direction he went? I might try to catch up to him and join him on his walk."

Hank directed her to the woods across the street, where most people walked their dogs.

"Thank you." With a friendly wave, Anna bid goodbye to Hank and returned to the car.

St. James smiled. "Well? Did you use your wiles to locate our source?"

Anna rolled her eyes but gave him the information he wanted. "He's out walking his dog. Should be in the park over there. Let's see if we can find him."

"Okay."

St. James drove to the small parking lot at a trail entrance, where he manoeuvred the vehicle into a spot near a red Toyota Highlander. They climbed out and headed down a trail.

An imposing array of towering trees formed a lush overhead cover. Sunlight filtering through the foliage cast patterns on the forest floor. An atmosphere of tranquility in the wilderness.

A few hundred metres in, they came to a fork in the path. Three smaller paths, offshoots of the original one, fanned out in different directions.

Anna placed her hands on her hips and scanned each path. "Decision time."

St. James examined the trails for signs of heavier and lighter foot traffic. "All three seem beaten down about the same."

Anna looked down at each one. "No clue which to take."

A dog barked several times.

St. James perked up. "Sounds like it's coming from the path on the left."

The barking grew louder. An older woman rounded a corner in the left path, dragged by a golden Labrador retriever on a leash.

"Hello there," said a short, white-haired lady as she approached. "You seem a bit turned around, folks."

Anna smiled. "No, just on the hunt for someone."

The Lab strained against its leash, eager to greet St. James and Anna. The lady released the leash, and the Lab bounded over to Anna. Anna knelt and patted the dog. "What's her name?"

"Happy." The lady smiled. "Brings joy wherever she goes."

Anna stroked Happy's fur and was rewarded with a long session of nuzzling and tail wagging. "What a fitting name," Anna said. "She does spread joy."

St. James was focused on the task. "We're unsure which path to take."

"In search of someone, you say?"

"Yes," St. James confirmed.

"Male or female?"

"Male," Anna answered.

"With a furry companion, I presume?"

Anna observed the path behind the lady. "Yes, he lives in the neighbourhood across the way."

"Oh, I've been a resident there since the beginning. I know most folks. What's his name?"

St. James scanned the paths. "Gael Vargas."

"Ahh, Gael," the lady mused. "I've known him for ages. Has a Doberman pinscher named Sam."

St. James smiled. "Any idea which route he might favour?"

The woman thought. "Gael tends to take the middle path on his way in. That links up with the path to the right, about a kilometre in." She pointed. "He usually comes from that direction. I'd choose the path on the right if I were you. You'll likely run into him and Sam on their way out."

Anna eyed the suggested path. "Thank you ever so much."

"Yes, thank you," St. James echoed.

"You're welcome." The lady wished them luck. Then she and Happy resumed their walk.

As the woman recommended, St. James and Anna pursued Vargas on the right. The path proved rougher and narrower than the entrance, forcing a single-file progression as they navigated around broken branches and soggy patches. Four dogwalkers passed before St. James spotted the greasy-looking Vargas and Sam strolling around a stand of trees.

Vargas came to an abrupt halt, his eyes narrowing as they fixed on St. James with a mix of confusion and aggression.

"What the hell are you doing here? How did you find me?" Vargas demanded, without giving St. James a chance to answer.

St. James snapped back, dripping with sarcasm. "We followed your scent."

Sam howled, and Vargas checked his dog. "Have a mind to unleash Sam and watch him rip your leg off."

"I don't know, Vargas. That might not end well for either of you."

Vargas backed down from his threatening stance. "What do you want, St. James?"

"By now, Baca will have discovered Pérez robbed him."

"Yes. In an earlier Zoom. He was so mad, I thought he would have a stroke."

With reproach, St. James said, "You were supposed to tell me when Baca's men would come for Pérez."

Vargas moved awkwardly. "Must have slipped my mind." He gawked at Anna as if noticing her for the first time. "Who's the bitch?"

Anger flashed across St. James's face. He doubled his fist, drew back, and struck Vargas, knocking him backward over the dog. Sam yelped, more from surprise than hurt.

Anna buried her face in her hands.

St. James gritted his teeth. "Disrespect my fiancée again and you won't get off so easy."

Vargas pulled himself from the ground, brushed debris from his pants and wiped his bleeding nose on a shirt sleeve.

Sam, loosened during the chaos, walked over to Anna and nuzzled her leg.

Vargas rolled his eyes and called his dog back to him. "Baca will come after Pérez early Monday morning, before dawn."

CHAPTER 53

With Denzel's disappearance gnawing at him, Dozer's focus frayed. Jiménez was deep in discussions with the RCMP on Johnston, Denzel's escort to San José, searching for clues. With each passing hour and no solid lead, despair tightened its grip on Dozer's chest. He needed a break, a moment to breathe. St. James and Anna were out, so he decided on a walk.

The elevator doors slid open, and Gabe greeted him. "Morning, Dozer."

Dozer forced a smile. "Morning, Gabe."

Gabe reached into his pocket and pulled out a folded slip of paper. "Some guy left this for you last night."

Dozer took it, unfolded the page, and read: *If you want to see your brother alive again, leave Costa Rica within twenty-four hours and have no further contact with the OIJ.*

His face clouded. Muscles tensed. He clenched his fists.

"Son of a bitch," he muttered.

"What's wrong?" Gabe asked, brow furrowing.

Dozer didn't answer.

"Enjoy your walk," Gabe added, watching him leave without another word.

Outside, the morning air wrapped around Dozer, easing the storm of thoughts racing through his mind. A ceiling of stratus clouds hung low over San José. The temperature hovered near 24°C.

Along the Avenue of the Americas, the familiar smell of exhaust mixed with the aromas of sizzling chicharrónes and sweet, warm chorreadas from nearby food wagons. But the thought of Denzel in danger wiped away any appetite.

His thoughts spun. *Who was Johnston, really? Could the note be from him? Who did he work for?*

He needed to get the note to Jiménez. The OIJ could test it for fingerprints — unlikely to yield anything, but still worth a shot. The walk gave him time to think.

On 6th Street, the noise softened. The chaos of traffic faded to a distant shout from a vendor and the occasional honk.

Then he felt it. A car, following too closely. Too deliberately.

His instincts flared. Without looking back, he adjusted his pace, feigning calm. He reached into his pocket and slid out a compact mirror — a recent purchase for situations just like this.

With a casual stretch, he angled his body and tilted the mirror just enough to catch a glimpse behind him.

Dozer mumbled, "The white Rogue."

Was it Johnston or someone else?

Dozer spotted a man up ahead, washing a car in a driveway. Dozer approached him. "Hey, I'm with the OIJ. Can I ask a favour?"

The man paused, curious but hesitant.

"Without being obvious, can you nod if a white Nissan Rogue pulls up?"

The man agreed, still unsure but willing to help. He nodded.

"Thanks," Dozer said, then suggested to the man that it might be a good time to go inside. The man did as he was asked, casually returning to his home. Dozer moved toward a hedge that lined the driveway. He crouched behind the foliage.

The white Rogue parked across the street. The driver slumped, dark sunglasses masking his appearance.

Dozer crept along the hedge until he was several houses away from the Nissan. By obscuring himself in a group of pedestrians, he managed to cross the street. From there, he crept back to the Nissan along the backs of other hedges and crouched behind the vehicle, buying a few moments to calculate his next move. He peered around the rear of the vehicle and saw the driver looking intently in the other direction.

Grabbing his chance, Dozer slipped along the driver's side below the windows, shoved his arm through the open driver's side window, and gripped the driver's neck. The man's eyes widened in terror, a scream ripping from his throat. He was small enough for Dozer to yank through the open window, flailing with panic.

"Who sent you?" Dozer growled, tightening his grip.

"I — I don't know what you're talking about!" the driver gasped, fear draining the colour from his face.

Dozer hissed, bringing his face inches from the man's. "Don't lie to me! What do you want? Who do you work for?"

The driver struggled for breath, desperation in his eyes. "I swear, I'm just a driver! Someone paid me to follow you! Please!"

Dozer's instincts told him the man was probably terrified enough to tell the truth. "Give me a name," Dozer demanded, his grip loosening.

The driver croaked, "Elfego Baca." The name slipped from his lips like a confession.

Dozer's heart sank. "Baca." The connection was now obvious. Denzel's disappearance was tied to the OIJ case — to Baca. Dozer released the man just enough to let him breathe.

The driver, still gasping, nodded, too terrified to speak another word.

CHAPTER 54

"The man's name is Jimmy Solís," Jiménez announced. "His fingerprints appear in our database as one of Baca's lackeys. Not known to be too bright."

Dozer had texted Jiménez from the street after securing Solís in the Nissan with a rope he found in the trunk. Jiménez wasted no time dispatching two men to pick them up. One drove Solís's car back to OIJ HQ. The other replaced Solís's makeshift restraints with a zip tie and escorted him and Dozer to OIJ headquarters.

Jiménez read the note Gabe had given Dozer as he lit a Delta. "This has Baca's name written all over it," Jiménez said as he took another puff.

Dozer nodded in disgust.

"They're questioning Solís downstairs now. That might yield some connection to the note. But, I doubt it. He may have given up Baca's name to you, but Baca trains his men not to breathe a word about operations. Under penalty of death."

Dozer drank coffee. "Figured as much."

A knock on the door interrupted their conversation.

"Enter," Jiménez barked.

The door opened, and a portly agent named Gómez walked in.

Jiménez took a puff on the Delta. "Get anything out of him, Gómez?"

Gómez hesitated. "Not much, Sir. Pretty loyal to Baca."

Jiménez smirked. "Must have tricked him into telling you something. I'm told he's dumber than a rock."

Dozer grinned. "Must be dumb to let me spot his tail."

"Just that he was ordered to follow Dozer."

Dozer sipped more coffee. "After a little persuasion on the street, he confessed it was Baca."

Jiménez was quick. "Did he say why?"

Dozer shook his head. "No."

Gómez turned to Dozer. "Solís told us it was about needing you to do something. Don't think Baca trusts him with much information."

Jiménez extinguished his cigarette. "Probably not."

Dozer clouded. "Well, I guess that's it then. I suppose you have to let him go?"

Jiménez frowned. "Afraid so. Okay, that's all, thank you, Gómez."

Gómez left the room.

Dozer rose, unease taking hold. "How did you make out with the RCMP on Johnston?"

A thoughtful look crossed Jiménez's face. "Name is Thurston Johnston. Has a record. Rough, small-time crook who does odd jobs that bigger crooks don't want to bother with."

Dozer clenched his jaw, his contempt evident. "Like kidnapping disabled Canadians and sending them to other countries?"

Jiménez's grin was faint. "What will you do now?"

Dozer paused for a moment. "Go after Baca."

Jiménez's demeanour darkened. "Give me a day to think this through before you do anything rash."

Dozer hesitated, holding back his urge to argue. "One day. That's it."

As he prepared to leave, his agitation grew. They'd caught Solís, but Baca's intentions — and Denzel's connection to it all — remained unclear. Dozer couldn't shake the feeling that there was more to uncover, more pieces to fit into the puzzle of Denzel's disappearance.

He hailed a cab and climbed into the backseat, his mind racing. The city's streets blurred past him, but his thoughts stayed with Denzel, circling back to questions that refused to be answered.

***

Eduardo unlocked the bedroom door in the back of Baca's warehouse office, where Denzel White was being held. Eduardo entered the room to find Denzel seated in a black leather chair, his gaze fixed on the floor. Eduardo placed the change of clothes he and his son had purchased for Denzel on the bed.

The walls were soothing earth tones. Two wooden bedside tables flanked a bed draped with a simple, colourful quilt. A ceiling fan whirled overhead, cutting through the tropical heat. In the corner, a small wooden desk was piled with books.

Despite the tranquil setting, the constant sound of truck traffic around the industrial park tormented the room.

Denzel sat with petrified eyes locked on Eduardo. Not a word had escaped his lips since the big man dragged him from his apartment in Ottawa days before.

Eduardo spoke softly. "I brought you lunch — cheeseburger and fries. I'll be back with it in a minute."

Denzel rose from his chair and edged closer to the door as Eduardo left the room.

Minutes later, Eduardo returned carrying a tray of food. Before he could place the tray on the desk, Denzel lunged forward and kicked him hard in the groin. The food went flying and Eduardo cursed loudly. He collapsed to the floor, clutching himself as Denzel unleashed a fury of kicks to Eduardo's head and stomach. Eduardo moaned in pain.

He jumped over Eduardo and yanked the door shut behind him.

Denzel's heart raced as he sprinted down a dimly lit hallway, thoughts of freedom consuming his mind. He spotted a metal door, dashed toward it, and burst through, emerging into the warehouse yard.

He dodged past towering piles of crates and pallets, guards shouting behind him. Veering left, he narrowly missed a wobbly stack of boxes that toppled to the ground in his wake. He gathered speed, stumbled over a loose cable, nearly losing his balance and costing precious seconds.

Sprinting toward the far end of the yard, he glanced over his shoulder. A man rounded the corner of the warehouse behind him. Denzel's pulse quickened.

His legs burned as he closed the gap to a row of looming shipping containers. He darted behind one, pressing his back against the cold metal. His heart hammered in his chest as the man drew closer. Denzel held his breath, praying he wouldn't be discovered.

When the man passed, Denzel edged from behind the container. But before he could move, another guard emerged from the opposite direction. Denzel jerked back, dropping low and pressing himself flat against the ground.

"Did you see him?" one guard barked, scanning the shadows. The other shook his head, frustration etched on his face.

Denzel's breath came in shallow gasps as he darted around the back of containers. His eyes locked onto a mountain of wooden pallets. Without hesitation, he scrambled to the top, concealing himself beneath a layer just below the top.

From his vantage point, he could see the yard layout. Two guards stood near the gate, yelling at one another. He needed a distraction — and fast. What would Erasmus do?

His eyes landed on a stack of lumber piled high, leaning precariously.

He leapt from the pallets and raced behind the lumber, wedging himself between the stack and a small building behind it.

A Baca man spotted him mid-jump.

"Hey!" the man shouted to a second guard, pointing to the pallets. "He jumped from there. Follow me!" The second man joined him, and they searched beyond the pallets.

Denzel crouched low and waited patiently, just as Dozer taught him. He could hear the guards talking, their voices growing louder as they approached his hideaway.

He waited.

The guards drew closer. Their voices dropped to whispers. Denzel couldn't tell how close they were.

He held his breath.

They were directly in front of the lumber now.

Denzel turned to face the building behind him, tightening his back against the lumber pile. He walked his feet up the outside wall of the building and pushed hard against the structure — but the lumber didn't budge.

He pushed harder, extending his legs until he had no leverage left.

Lowering his feet back to the ground, he scanned his surroundings for anything that might improve his leverage. The guards in front continued whispering, debating their next move.

His gaze caught two six-by-six timbers wedged between the lumber pile and the building at the far end. Quietly, he hauled them toward the center of the pile, careful not to alert the guards. He stood them vertically against the building, roughly shoulder-width apart.

Positioning his back against the lumber again, he walked his feet up the two vertical timbers, gaining a modicum of leverage. He pushed with all his might.

He felt movement.

As he pushed harder to generate momentum, the pile leaned further outward. He needed to tip it far enough for gravity to do the rest.

With one final, exhausting push, the pile moved past its tipping point and crashed down on the two guards in front. Their screams pierced the air as the lumber fell. Comrades rushed to rescue them, giving Denzel the precious moments he needed to escape.

He bolted around the far end of the lumber, the exit coming into view in the distance. With a mighty leap, he vaulted over a fence. Landing awkwardly, pain shot through his leg. He scrambled to regain his balance and plunged down a narrow alley, his heart still racing.

Ahead, the alley opened up. Denzel shot toward it, the exit looming closer.

CHAPTER 55

In the late afternoon, the elevator doors opened onto a quiet reception area on the eighteenth floor. Dozer emerged, scanning the room. Francesca stood behind the desk, poised in her black pantsuit, watching him approach.

"Glad to see you, Dozer. Someone's waiting for you out on the balcony."

Dozer looked surprised. "Wasn't expecting anyone."

"The man inquired about an Erasmus White. It took a minute to realize he meant you."

Dozer bolted toward the balcony without a word, leaving Francesca blinking in confusion.

Denzel's face lit up when his older brother appeared. He was on his feet immediately. Dozer closed the distance between them in a second, wrapping Denzel in a fierce bear hug.

Dozer's words were thick with emotion. "Thought something terrible happened. I was scared, Denzel."

Denzel exhaled, his speech barely above a whisper. "I was scared, too."

Dozer held on for a moment longer, unwilling to let go. "I need to know everything. Every detail."

"Okay."

The two headed back inside, where Francesca remained at the front desk.

"Francesca." Dozer smiled. "This is my brother, Denzel. He's staying with me. Whatever he needs, charge it to me."

Francesca smiled, nodding at Denzel. "Welcome to the Hilton La Sabana, Denzel."

Denzel smiled.

Dozer turned to Francesca. "I owe you an apology. I was rude."

Francesca waved him off, her smile widening. "Don't worry about it."

Dozer shook his head. "No. When you said someone was looking for Erasmus White, I knew it was Denzel. He's the only one who calls me that. I was so relieved he was okay. I forgot my manners. I'm sorry."

Francesca's smile softened. "It's fine, Dozer. Really."

Dozer led Denzel into the bar. The place was calm, the evening rush was still a ways off. Maggie hustled over the moment she spotted them.

Dozer nodded toward his brother. "Maggie, this is Denzel."

Maggie's eyes sparkled. "What can I pour for you, Denzel?"

Denzel hesitated, glancing at Dozer. "I can't drink alcohol because of my medications. I have a non-alcoholic beer when I'm out with friends."

Maggie's grin widened. "Got just the thing — Imperial Cero. Zero alcohol."

Dozer gave her a grateful nod. "Perfect."

"For you? The usual?"

Dozer grinned. "Of course."

As Maggie hurried off, Dozer tilted closer to Denzel. "Tell me what happened."

Denzel adjusted in his seat, his fingers fidgeting with the table's edge. "Some big guy broke into my place. Didn't have a key."

Dozer's jaw tightened. "Used a lockpick, most likely. Was it Johnston?"

"Yes, he told me you sent him. That you wanted him to bring me to Costa Rica."

"Bullshit."

"I knew it didn't sound right, but he made me get my passport. He didn't let me pack anything."

Dozer's fists clenched. "Did he hurt you?"

"No." Denzel shook his head. "I didn't talk to him."

"Did he say who sent him?"

"No."

Maggie appeared and sat down the beers. Dozer and Denzel clinked bottles.

"Cheers, Denzel." Dozer's eyes softened. "I'm so relieved you're safe."

Denzel took a sip, his hands steady now. "Johnston told the border men I was a special needs person, and he was taking me to see family."

"Your passport was in order, so they didn't question him. Bastard."

"I was too scared to say anything."

Dozer reached across, placing a hand on his brother's arm. "You did nothing wrong. I'm not mad at you. I'm mad at him."

Relief washed over Denzel as they both drank.

"What happened after you landed here?"

"A driver came. Wanted to blindfold me, but Johnston wouldn't let him."

Dozer's eyes darkened. "What did he say?"

Denzel swallowed hard. "Johnston said, no need. Denzel won't make it out of Costa Rica. That made me mad, Erasmus."

Dozer's grip tightened around his bottle. "Makes me mad, too. Then what?"

"Took me to a place. Looked like a warehouse. But it was an office inside. Johnston handed me over to a guy named Eduardo. Eduardo was good to me. There was another man. Short. Dark skin. Scarred face."

"Baca," Dozer spat, venom in his tone. "That son of a bitch."

Maggie placed another round on the table. "Who are you calling a son of a bitch, big boy?"

Dozer forced a smile, but his mind was elsewhere.

Denzel continued. "Eduardo locked me in a room and brought me food. I did what you taught me, Erasmus."

Dozer's eyes narrowed. "What?"

"I kicked him. Hard. Just like you told me. In the crotch. Then the stomach Then the head. Locked him in the room and ran."

Pride swelled in Dozer's chest. "You did great, Denzel."

Denzel described his escape through the lumber yard, his words tumbling out in a breathless rush, excitement tangled with fear. "Had to keep moving — *had to!* Stay low, real low! Dodged between stacks of pallets — fast, so fast!" His eyes were wide, darting around as if he was still there. "Guards were close, *real* close! I could hear 'em — *crunch, crunch* on the gravel! Voices too, loud ones! But I stayed quiet, just like you taught me, Erasmus!"

His fingers twitched in midair; his body almost vibrating with the memory. "Then — then I saw 'em! Two guards! Their backs were turned!"

His voice dropped, breath quick and ragged. "I ducked behind a container, real fast — then pushed a big lumber stack right over on 'em!" He didn't wait to see what happened. "I bolted. Ran between the stacks, dodging everything. My legs were burning bad, but I knew I couldn't stop. Not yet."

He swallowed a deep breath. "Sawdust and the smell of wet wood." He looked at his brother. "I thought I was dead for sure when one of the guards almost spotted me."

St. James and Anna arrived just as Denzel finished. Anna spotted him first, her eyes dancing as she rushed over and hugged him tightly.

"Denzel!" she exclaimed, her words dribbling out, each overlapping in her excitement. "I can't believe it! What happened? How did you find your way here?" Her hands gripped his shoulders as if to make sure he was actually there.

St. James followed, grinning, shaking Denzel's hand firmly. He nodded in Anna's direction and said, "What she said."

Denzel told the story again from the top. Their eyes grew wider and voices more animated with every word.

St. James tapped Denzel on the shoulder, a sly smile crossing his face. "Your brother taught you well, my friend."

Denzel's eyes shone with pride. "Erasmus's the best."

Dozer downed the remains of his Imperial in one swift motion. "We're not done yet. Baca will pay for this. I'll make sure of it when we execute the mission." His voice was low, the words laced with a cold promise.

Anna frowned, confusion in her eyes. "Why did they take Denzel in the first place?"

St. James shrugged. "Leverage, I imagine. Baca wanted us to back off from helping Jiménez. Denzel was his insurance."

Dozer showed them the note.

St. James glance at it. "That confirms it was Baca in my mind."

Dozer's fist found his brother's arm, a playful punch that held a touch of admiration. "But my brother here outsmarted them."

St. James met Dozer's gaze for a moment, then took a slow sip of Macallan. His eyes narrowed. "Denzel can stay with us while you finish the mission. He'll be safe."

Dozer's gaze drifted toward the dining room. "Let's have dinner."

They stood and walked into the dining room, everyone relieved.

The mission to save Costa Rica from a deadly parasite had taken on a new twist. For Dozer, it was no longer just about the mission — it was personal.

CHAPTER 56

Ludwig assembled a platoon of forty rough men, their faces as coarse as fifty-grit sandpaper, wearing clothes showing neglect.

Ludwig advanced slowly, hands clasped behind his back. "In all likelihood, Pérez is holed up in Sánchez's house transferring the Boss's assets." He gestured to the overhead video display showing an aerial photo of the site.

Ludwig's cell vibrated. *Baca. I have to take this.*

Baca shouted through the phone, his voice dripping with anger. "Denzel attacked Eduardo. Kicked him several times. He's headed for his brother at the Hilton. Send men to bag him."

Ludwig paced the bright room, his mind working through the implications. He took a deep breath. "Sir, with all due respect, we're focusing on the wrong thing. Denzel's escape, as frustrating as it is, changes nothing. He's no longer useful as leverage. He won't be the bargaining chip we thought he was."

Baca's response was sharp. "What are you talking about? He's our ticket to force St. James out of the picture. We can't just let him slip away."

Ludwig paused, choosing his words carefully. "But here's the thing, Sir — *he's already gone.* We've lost our chance. If we go after him now, things will only get worse. Not only will St. James double down on his commitment to Jiménez, but we'll make ourselves look weak."

There was silence on the other end, the tension palpable. Ludwig continued, his voice a little quieter but more insistent. "The priority is the training. We're pushing forward with our operation, and Denzel, as troublesome as he may be, isn't the key. He doesn't change the bigger picture. What we need is to finish what we've started. The fight hinges on getting the training right, and *that's* something we can't afford to let slip. If we go after Denzel now, we risk derailing everything."

Baca muttered something under his breath, clearly agitated, but Ludwig wasn't finished. "You must understand, Sir. If we recapture Denzel, all it does is escalate the situation with Dozer and St. James. They'll turn Denzel's escape into a rallying cry for the people against us. We've already pushed the boundaries with this — if we don't change course, we could ignite something that'll set us back to square one, or worse."

Baca made another pause, this one longer. Ludwig could almost hear Baca weighing options in his head. Finally, Baca's voice came through, quieter now, reluctant. "You're right. It's a mess. But we can't just forget about Denzel."

Ludwig's tone softened, but his argument was firm. "We don't need to forget about him, Sir. We need to refocus. Let St. James and his team handle him. They'll waste resources on something that doesn't matter in the long run. We have a much bigger goal ahead of us. We finish the training, and we control the narrative. We don't let a single man — important or not — take us off course."

There was a long pause as Baca processed Ludwig's words. In the end, he exhaled loudly, frustration giving way to reluctant agreement. "All right. Focus on the training."

Ludwig ended the call. He didn't want to risk further discussion. He knew Baca would never admit the chaos surrounding Denzel had been a diversion. They had to focus on the real prize.

Ludwig turned to the men. "We have intel for Monday. Thirty OIJ agents will be waiting for us." He moved the pointer around the viewscreen. "They'll be positioned here, here, and here."

Gasps rippled through the group, eyes expanding as the implications sank in. "OIJ agents? Nobody told us about that!" one man shouted, fists clenched.

Ludwig locked eyes with him. "Would you like to tell Baca that?" The man fell quiet and looked away.

Ludwig paced slowly as he spoke. "We'll approach from the right, single file against the trees. The OIJ will have people on the rooftops, but the angles between will shield us. Baca will handle our exposure across the street."

A burly man changed his stance. "What about inside the tree line, Ludwig?"

"Agents will be there, and five inside Sánchez's house, protecting Pérez."

"Why's the OIJ protecting Pérez?" Confusion on another man's face. "Should be arresting him."

Ludwig crossed his arms. "Baca's informant says it's a trap."

The man's forehead trenched. "Then why aren't we waiting until Pérez is free?"

Ludwig sighed. "Baca insists we act now to prevent further thefts. Waiting isn't an option in his mind."

A younger man spoke up. "Tackling another gang is one thing. The OIJ is a much greater risk —if we're caught? I have a family."

Ludwig softened his stance. "I understand. Every moment we let the OIJ breathe down our necks is a chance for them to tighten their grip."

The burly man's fists clenched. "We'll be fighting for our freedom, or worse, for our lives!"

Ludwig's jaw tightened, his glare unwavering. "Every mission has risks. We can't wait for them to come after us. We need to take the initiative. Make the first move."

"Why not gather more intel first?" a man on Zoom said. "Trusting that informant could be our downfall."

Ludwig barked back. "Trust is a luxury we can't afford. Baca is insistent. We move now or risk losing more real estate."

The burly man winced. "Are we just supposed to charge in?"

Ludwig stood closer. "No, we'll be strategic and tactical. We'll strike hard and retreat before they know what hit them. We need everyone's full commitment."

A murmur spread through the group, uncertainty in everyone's eyes. Ludwig carried on. "Taking down Pérez sends a message. Nobody should even think about cheating Baca. They'll never get away with it."

"It could be a bloodbath?" the younger man countered.

Ludwig steeled himself. "Nothing will stop Baca. That's why we need to be well-trained and careful. Consider your instincts. If it feels off, we pull back. Right now, we're a force, and we follow orders."

"Even insane orders?" the burly man persisted.

"Even then. We adjust as we go. Watch each other's backs."

Ludwig's eyes swept over the room, searching for resolution. A hint of commitment began to slowly ignite.

Ludwig rallied the group. "All right, let's go over everything again. We have a mission to execute, and we'll do it right."

***

Ludwig split the men into two groups. Gravel crunched beneath their boots as they took their positions. The first team lined up in front of the mock building — a rough structure of plywood and tarps — and crouched low, weapons ready. As they moved silently through doorways and around corners, Ludwig's voice cut through the stillness, sharp and direct.

"Lower and faster," he barked, his eyes scanning each movement. "Your forward pace is too slow. You'll be dead before you reach cover. Use hand signals, not words."

The men stiffened, adjusting their posture, quickening their steps, and exchanging silent gestures. Ludwig nodded, satisfied with the progress, but his eyes never stopped searching for mistakes.

The second group grappled on mats beneath the evergreens. Quesada, a tank-like Tico who had run security ops for Baca for over a decade, was running them through hand-to-hand combat drills that incorporated wrestling, kickboxing, and various martial arts, including Muay Thai and Krav Maga.

Quesada had them focus on strikes, warring, and takedowns. Grunts filled the air as sweaty limbs twisted and bodies hit the ground.

Ludwig wandered over to watch, his arms folded, his face unreadable. "Strength isn't enough," he told the group. "It's about technique and timing. You won't win by just muscling through."

A sharp shout echoed as one man caught another in a hold, pinning him to the mat. Ludwig's gaze hardened. He moved to correct the next fighter, offering subtle adjustments that would make all the difference in a real encounter.

At the half hour mark, both groups shifted to a separate set of drills. Ludwig placed barrels at irregular intervals across the field, simulating cover points. His commands came quickly, forcing men to adapt on the fly as they sprinted, ducking and weaving behind the makeshift shields. The crack of blank ammunition sliced through the air.

Ludwig paced between them, scanning each soldier's reaction, occasionally pausing to offer a gesture that shifted their form. "Focus!" he snapped. "Composure under fire, always."

The exercise shifted as dusk began to settle. Targets were set for live ammunition at varying ranges. Some near. Some far. The men took their positions, happy for a chance to practice real shooting. Ludwig stood behind, watching as they fired at makeshift targets with methodical precision.

When final shots had been fired, Ludwig gathered everyone under the sprawling branches of a massive tree. He stood before them, hands clasped behind his back, his face stern.

"I want to hear from you," he said, his voice steady but urgent. "What worked? What didn't? Talk it out. This is how we improve."

The men exchanged glances, eager to share their thoughts. For the next twenty minutes the men discussed strategy and technique, holds and kicks and even breathing methods. They debated whether to crawl on all four or slither on their bellies, whether to hold fire until fired upon or take the offensive.

What started as grumbling and disappointment on Friday morning had morphed into solid camaraderie by late Sunday. The drills pushed them hard. Sharpened them.

The sky darkened. Ludwig stepped forward again, casting a glance at Quesada, who stood off to the side. "Tomorrow morning brings a full-scale assault. I expect you to bring everything you have to this fight."

The men stirred, anticipation and nerves mingling. They were ready — the weight of the mission made certain by tense shoulders and focused eyes.

Ludwig's voice rang out once more, sharp and commanding. He turned to a senior leader. "Quesada, there can be no mistakes. Make sure everyone knows their role."

"Yes, Sir!" Quesada said, taking one step forward.

Ludwig paused, scanning the faces before him. "Get some sleep. Go to your families. But be back here at one a.m. Baca will be here then."

The buzz of the field hummed with excitement and dread.

The looming mission was nothing short of terrifying.

CHAPTER 57

Under the cloak of darkness Sunday night, García led thirty OIJ agents through the foliage surrounding the heavily treed Sánchez property. They had waited two days at retired agent Henry Araya's house, biding their time until the order came to move.

Clad in black tactical gear, each agent was equipped with night vision goggles, allowing them to pierce the darkness with eerie green light. M16A1 rifles hung on their shoulders, and an M1911 semi-automatic pistol was holstered at each agent's side.

Crouched, the agents advanced cautiously, their movements deliberate and synchronized. They stopped periodically and dropped to their bellies, hearts pounding with adrenaline. Every rustle of leaves or distant snap of a twig was a potential threat.

Advancing several metres without incident, they paused again, watching the dark expanse ahead and listening for signs of life. The night was quiet. Only a faint wind rustling through the bush.

Inside OIJ's headquarters, the atmosphere was charged. Jiménez, St. James, Denzel, and Anna sat huddled in the boardroom, eyes fixed on the massive display that showed all the movements. It flickered with feeds from body cameras and live surveillance redirected by the security company. The stress in the room was high as they focused on the unfolding operation.

García glanced at his second-in-command, Agent Martinez, crouched to his left. He grabbed Martinez's attention and signalled him forward with a left-arm swimmer crawl, directing the men to move around the left flank of Sánchez's property. The agents slithered through the foliage, ghostly silhouettes pressing into the darkness.

"At least the heat's not so bad now," Anna mused in the control room. "Can't imagine lugging that much gear around in the heat of the day."

Denzel rose from a swivel chair and stood next to St. James and Anna. "Where is Erasmus?"

St. James pointed to a screen showing a surveillance feed from inside of Sánchez's house. "Right there, buddy. You can't see him right now because he's hiding, but he's doing great."

Outside the house, a line of agents moved deeper into the shadows. Martinez mirrored García's command, expertly guiding his men toward the tree line, their movements synchronized, every footfall muffled by grass.

García reached for his radio to check in with Dozer and the five agents tasked with securing Pérez inside the house.

"Update?"

"The bait is on the hook," Dozer replied. From a darkened hallway just off the living room, Dozer looked at Pérez, bound and gagged on an L-shaped couch.

The rest of Dozer's team was in position: two agents behind a carved Spanish table in the wood-panelled dining room; another crouched behind an oak computer desk, eyes trained on the entrance. Two more in a cramped storage room near Pérez. Dozer kept a watchful eye on the scene. Breaths were measured as they listened for sounds that might betray their presence.

Montero had secured permission from several of Sánchez's neighbours to station agents on their roofs. Only an elderly woman at the end of the street refused. Without giving away details, Montero persuaded the other homeowners to vacate their homes for the night, at OIJ's expense.

Switching channels, García reached out to Martinez: "Use the treeline like we practiced. Stay down."

Six more agents fanned out along the treed drive, three on either side, each one a shadow behind the growth.

Three agents hid in wait behind the house. The rest faced the tree line, crouched behind bushes several metres away.

García positioned himself at the furthest edge of the tree line, a move calculated to lower the risk of crossfire when chaos erupted. He gazed through the trees at Sánchez's house.

Calculations and probabilities swirled in his mind. Each scenario seemed more harrowing than the one before it. The idea of success was intoxicating, a mix of adrenaline and hope, yet he worried about the human cost.

Memories of fallen comrades flashed through his mind. He remembered the disbelief in their spouses' eyes, the sobbing and the silence that followed as he delivered the heart-wrenching news. Each image sent shivers down his spine, a wave of nausea threatening to overwhelm him.

García took a deep breath and focused on the present. The agents had trained and sacrificed so much to reach this moment. The stakes were high, but so were the rewards. Nailing Baca for real estate theft could knock a pillar out of organized crime in Costa Rica for years, possibly decades, to come. García adjusted his grip on his weapon, the cold metal grounding him as he steeled his resolve. He stiffened himself against the tide of emotions and reminded himself of why they were there — the lives to protect, the justice to serve.

The radio squelched to life, jolting him from his thoughts. "Agents are in place on the roofs, Sir, facing outward as you ordered," Agent Martinez reported.

García's heart raced as he received updates from the others confirming their positions. The operation's success hinged on precise coordination and split-second timing. Surprise was their greatest ally, but the slightest misstep could spell ruin.

The agents waited, patient and focused, surrounded by the faint sounds of distant traffic. Every rustle of leaves and whisper of wind heightened the agents' senses.

Inside the boardroom, Jiménez poured another cup of coffee. "Silence. I hate waiting — always have. Makes me jittery, and that's not a good quality when lives hang in the balance." Jiménez took a sip, trying to ground himself in the familiar comfort of caffeine.

St. James glanced up. "There isn't a man or woman out there or in here tonight who isn't jittery. Anna and I certainly are." Anna wrung her hands together and smiled weakly in agreement.

Denzel sat beside them, his eyes fixed on the screen, trying to absorb what was happening.

St. James spoke almost to himself. "To be jittery is to be human."

Jiménez turned to St. James.

"García believes agents in a fight can't afford to be human. Humans hesitate, and that can be deadly."

The control room went quiet as each person wrestled with their thoughts. Memories of lost comrades tormented Jiménez.

A single gunshot rang out. The four froze. Eyes widened by the sound of a single round. Jiménez's coffee cup clattered to the table.

"My God," Anna whispered.

St. James stared at the screen in disbelief, and Denzel looked at him, utterly confused.

The night had just become infinitely more dangerous.

CHAPTER 58

García's heart raced as the gunshot echoed through the air. An agent fell from a roof. Panic swept over him as he shouted into his radio, "Which direction?"

Martinez roared, "Unknown, Sir!"

An agent shouted, "From the east!"

García tapped the radio on his chin, trying to think. "Just one round?"

Martinez gripped his radio. "So far."

García contacted a ground agent away from the trees. "Action?"

A timid response. "All quiet, Sir."

García ordered, "Agents along the drive, report in!"

Several responded in unison. "No activity, Sir."

The four at HQ were now standing so close to the boardroom monitor that its pixels began to warp and sway in their sightlines. Jiménez held his radio tight. "García, what's happening?"

"Investigating, Sir. I'll come back when I have something."

"García," Jiménez barked.

"Yes?"

"Don't keep me waiting!"

"No, Sir."

Jiménez, Anna, and St. James exchanged worried looks, all of them racking their brains for answers to the same questions. Who knew? How was it possible for someone to pick off an agent wearing black at night, on a secure rooftop location, before anyone other than the OIJ team had entered the house?

St. James was the first to speak. "Something's not right here, Jiménez."

"I agree."

Anna, in shock, was still catching up. "He just fell—"

"No warning, no opposing force," St. James said.

"Nothing to indicate engagement with Baca's troops," Jiménez added. "No sign of anyone."

St. James looked at the captain imploringly, holding onto hope: "Our strategy was sound."

"It was. The chances of them knowing we were here were slim. The chances of them knowing exactly where we placed agents is ten times slimmer."

Anna had caught up. "Someone leaked the details."

St. James winced. "That's my take."

They all took this in, while Denzel stood off to the side, struggling to understand.

"Is Erasmus okay?" he asked. When no answer was immediately forthcoming, Denzel's breath became ragged, and his eyes welled with tears. Anna jolted herself out of her thoughts and moved to console him. "Dozer knows what to do," she said, extending an arm around his wide shoulders. "The whole team is safer because he's there. He'll be just fine." She hoped she was right.

Suddenly Jiménez's hands flew to the sides of his head. He began to pace the control room, frantic with self-blame and disbelief.

"I should have seen this coming." He was muttering to himself, in his own world. "We had it covered ... our *most* trustworthy team." He sat down and stared. "My fault. This is my fault!"

St. James cut through the self-blame. "It's no one's fault, Jiménez! There were many eyes on this. A team effort. And you can't always foresee these things, no matter how much digging you do."

Jiménez glanced at St. James. "I know that. Still hard to accept."

Denzel had left Anna's side and dropped into a swivel chair. He was rocking back and forth, making low sounds under his breath. Anna moved to him again, putting a hand on his shoulder. Together, they studied the visual display unit.

Back behind Sánchez's tree line, García was scrambling to give orders for agents to adapt and respond. He analyzed every movement. "Martinez! Roof agents on their stomachs facing outward, toward the trees?"

"Yes, Sir."

"Ground team, turn a hundred and eighty degrees. Face away from the tree line. Baca's men will come from behind now. Assume they know our plan. Do the opposite."

A chorus of *yes, Sirs* dominated the airways.

"Agents in the rear and along the drive, stay in position. Await further orders."

A roof agent burst into the radio chatter. "Two men running from the house on the far right!"

"Martinez, is that the woman's house where we weren't allowed on the roof?" García shouted.

"Affirmative. But it looks like she allowed those two on her roof. Must be on Baca's payroll."

"Assassins," García responded. "Can Isabella make a clean shot?"

Martinez radioed. "She's getting into position."

"Two spotted behind the front tire of a parked moving van," Isabella confirmed.

"Take the shot when you can!" García ordered.

"Yes, Sir."

A long minute ticked by as Isabella secured herself on the peaked roof and trained her scope on the van below. She steadied her breath and zeroed in on the van's front tire. A man's head poked out from behind the tire, then pulled back, retreating like a turtle into its shell. *Weighing his options*, Isabella thought.

Moments later he re-emerged, edging further, torn between staying put and fleeing. Isabella envisioned his hands against the pavement, ready to bolt from behind the truck. She adjusted her night goggles, slowed her breath, then locked him in with her scope and slowly squeezed the trigger.

The discharge rang out, and the bullet found its mark.

The second man panicked and ran perpendicular to the moving van across the street. Isabella aimed and fired, dropping the man to the pavement face-first.

"Two down," Isabella reported.

"Excellent work, Isabella," García said, and Martinez quickly followed with praise.

"Isabella is a good shot," Anna said admiringly. "We're lucky to have her."

Dozer and the agents listened to the radio exchanges from inside Sánchez's house. Dozer pictured the chaotic scene, wishing he could be out there. After a quick round of comms with his indoor crew, he checked the load in his M1911 semi-automatic pistol, issued to him for the mission by García. He hoped he wouldn't have to use it.

A roof agent radioed the group. "Movement in the bush, due north, thirty degrees."

García brought the radio to his mouth. "See anything?"

"No."

"Stay on it."

García's heart pounded.

Jiménez resumed his pacing. St. James joined Anna and Denzel close to the monitor, eyes fixed on the pixelated scene.

"We have movement to the right," another roof agent announced at 2:45 a.m.

García spoke. "Sighting?"

"No."

***

At 3 a.m., Ludwig guided men armed with sub-machine guns, positioning them in single file, tightly against the outer edge of the trees. Baca positioned himself safely behind Ludwig's men.

Quesada led another group of men from the right. A third Baca deputy, Santos, kept five men at the outer perimeter in case their intelligence needed to be corrected. Trees obstructed the view from the roof. Baca's men stood between the roof agents above and agents on the ground behind. OIJ ground agents now faced away from the trees, opposite the direction planned for the mission.

Through night binoculars, García spotted Baca's movement from the other end of the tree line. "Ground agents! Reverse your position again. Baca's men are closing behind you next to the tree line."

The ground agents turned, but not fast enough; Baca noticed the about-face and ordered his men to drop at the foot of the tree line and fire. Two

OIJ ground agents went down. The rest of the OIJ ground agents returned fire, shooting indiscriminately into the trees, unable to clearly see Baca's men. Their bullets caught more trees than men. The assault scattered a group of screech-owls and separated a large branch from its trunk, sending it crashing to the ground. Baca's operatives, concealed along the tree line, responded with a fresh barrage of gunfire. Shouts punctuated the fight as both sides fought for supremacy.

Pungent smoke from continuous shooting created a suffocating shroud.

An agent on the roof at the far end of the tree line stood, despite orders to remain belly down. Equipped with a silenced pistol, Quesada inched closer, moving with cat-like stealth. He aimed at the agent standing above and squeezed the trigger. The suppressed round delivered a muffled cough. The agent crumpled to the slanted rooftop, rolled off and landed in the garden, the rifle slipping from his lifeless grasp.

The element of surprise had shifted to the attackers, forcing OIJ agents to scramble.

Baca ordered Ludwig to motion Lopez, Fallas, and Quesada through the tree line to take out Pérez. García spotted them moving toward the house and radioed a heads-up to Dozer and the five agents inside Sánchez's.

Gunfire intensified — losses mounted on both sides.

Jiménez shook his head. "Obvious now why they only fired one shot."

Anna appeared puzzled. "Why?"

St. James shook his head in disgust. "Taking out a roof agent meant Baca knew where we placed agents, which means he knew our plan — that we expected him to come along the tree line. He wanted us to know he knew our strategy so we would alter it."

"Reverse-reverse psychology," Anna said.

"Exactly. He wanted us to think he was coming from the other direction, a street away. And we fell for it. We reversed our ground agent direction to defend ourselves with that in mind. All Baca did was stick to our original plan, approaching Sánchez's property along the tree line. Our ground agents now faced the wrong way. Baca tricked us into changing our plan while he stuck with our original one. He played us."

"Like a damn fiddle," Anna mused. She swore so rarely that it caused St. James to look at her in surprise.

Jiménez could barely speak. "Hideous," he finally muttered.

García was still trying to choreograph the gun battle via radio, shouting into his hand piece, urging ground agents to keep the pressure on.

The smell of gunpowder became an acrid stench as the fight raged on.

The OIJ ground agents held their positions as best they could. It was all they could manage. Baca's men had the advantage of better cover.

García radioed. "Martinez, we need a distraction!"

Martinez answered, "Understood. Roof agents, increase cover fire!"

From three different rooftops, OIJ sharpshooters unleashed a barrage of bullets blindly down at the tree line, catching Baca's men by surprise. The attackers scrambled for additional cover.

OIJ ground agents crouched, facing Baca's men, and doubled the OIJ roof agents' blitz.

Jiménez clenched his fists, watching the action unfold on the visual display. "That's it, García! Keep the pressure on!"

St. James was riveted to the display unit. Anna leaned closer, her heart pounding.

Denzel covered his face with both hands, watching the chaotic scene through splayed fingers. He studied Anna's and St. James's faces for clues to how the battle was going.

"Is Erasmus safe?" he asked again. Anna and St. James repeated their mantra: that Dozer was inside the house, safe, and one of the most capable people either of them had ever met.

"I know," Denzel said, pride for his brother showing on his face.

Martinez came back to García: "Disrupted Baca's formation. Gaining ground, Sir."

"Good work. Add more firepower. Don't give them a chance to regroup."

Jiménez watched as the attackers fell back. "Don't let them escape, García. Baca must be captured to end this once and for all."

García frowned, "This isn't over yet."

CHAPTER 59

Ten uncomfortable minutes passed, intensifying Dozer's restlessness. He slipped from the darkened hallway to check on the agents in the house, then moved toward Sánchez's front door. He paused and listened for movement outside.

A massive force smashed the door, sending Dozer backward onto the floor as Quesada, Fallas, and Lopez burst into the room.

From the couch, Pérez heard the commotion and began struggling against the restraints that held his hands behind his back.

Dozer sprang from the floor and launched himself at Quesada. Dozer separated Quesada from his semi-automatic and tossed it to the nearest OIJ agent. He quickly lobbed his own pistol to another agent to keep it out of the intruders' hands, and with a backward kick caught Fallas off guard, knocking the pistol out of his hands.

"What the hell?" Fallas shouted, nursing a hurt wrist.

Lopez still had his gun drawn on the group but looked less confident about using it.

The agents had trained their weapons on Baca's men from three feet away, reluctant to shoot with Dozer among them.

Quesada lunged at Dozer with a wild haymaker. Dozer ducked, pivoted and slammed a right hook into the man's ribs, followed by a kick to his face, snapping the man's head back.

The five agents watched in astonishment, assessing how they could jump in. They waited for an opportunity. Dozer's combat prowess was almost superhuman. They didn't see the need to use their weapons. Dozer was dominating the fight.

Pérez had managed to dislodge his gag by rubbing his face against the couch. He yelled, "What's going on? Boss, are you there? I didn't do it, Boss. I swear I didn't do it."

"Shut up, traitor," Fallas said, still shaking the sting from his hand.

Fallas and Lopez had backed to the broken front door, waiting to see if Quesada got up. Lopez was stunned.

Fallas took a run at Dozer and managed to pin Dozer's arms to his side.

"Need help Dozer?" one of the agents yelled.

Dozer shouted, "No. Got it."

Dozer executed a violent, backward headbutt, smashing Fallas's face. Fallas released his hold and fell backward, blood spraying from his nose.

Lopez charged. Dozer sidestepped the lunge and grabbed Lopez's collar, slamming him face-first into the wall. Lopez's pistol dropped to the floor and Dozer kicked it toward the agents with his left foot. Lopez staggered back, and Dozer landed a vicious kick to the left kidney, followed by a solid fist to the right side. Lopez dropped to his knees in pain.

Quesada crawled from the floor with the support of a chair and pulled himself to standing, blood all down his face. He dropkicked Dozer, slamming him against a wall.

"*Now,* do you want us to help you?" an agent asked, but Dozer raised one finger as if to say, *I'll finish it,* and the men held back.

Quesada hurled himself onto Dozer's back, sending him to the floor. They rolled across the hardwood floor, knocking over two plants and crashing into a glass coffee table. Pérez drew up his feet and wriggled further along the couch, away from the combatants.

Dozer and Quesada jumped to their feet, sweating and breathing heavily. Quesada threw a wild swing as Dozer sprang toward him. Dozer blocked the move with his forearm and jabbed the man's battered face. Quesada stumbled backward and collapsed.

Fallas, still dazed from the headbutt, came back at Dozer and landed a punch to Dozer's stomach, winding him. Dozer recovered and executed a spinning roundhouse kick, connecting with Fallas's temple in one smooth motion. Fallas's eyes rolled back, and he crumpled to the floor, unconscious.

Lopez, recovering from the kidney blow, regained his footing. Dozer rapidly closed the distance and placed a spinning back kick on Lopez's chest. Lopez sprawled backward, crashing into a table.

With all three intruders incapacitated, Dozer stood, his knuckles bloodied and swelling.

The agents rushed to restrain Baca's three disoriented men with zip ties.

"Proud of you, Dozer." St. James said through the command centre's radio.

Jiménez followed. "Great work, Dozer."

In the background, Dozer could hear Denzel saying, "That's my brother! That's my brother, Erasmus White!"

A winded Dozer bent over, his palms resting on his knees, and forced a smile.

"Forgot you guys were watching. Would have thrown in a few fancy moves to impress you."

St. James was mildly sarcastic. "Don't push it, Dozer."

Dozer closed his fingers around the handgun he retrieved from an agent. He checked the load and released the safety, then ran from the house, circling the perimeter toward the rear. Not wanting to be mistaken for a Baca man, he signalled García's three agents as he neared the back corner of the house.

Dozer and the three agents manoeuvred around the far edge of the tree line toward García, who stood like a sentinel, giving orders through his radio.

García peered at Dozer. "Pérez still under our control?"

"Yes. Your men have arrested the three Baca men sent to kill him."

"Excellent."

Dozer spotted a Baca man crawling toward García from behind. He motioned García to step aside, lifted his M1911 semi-automatic, aimed at the approaching assailant, and squeezed the trigger, rendering the man lifeless.

Without skipping a beat, García commanded the rooftop agents to intensify their suppressing fire further. A ferocious storm of gunfire erupted from above, raining bullets down upon the tree line once more, forcing Baca's men to scatter for more cover.

García barked orders at agents in the driveway. "Advance toward the tree line!"

The agents moved despite the perilous hail of bullets flying close, taking cover where possible.

Baca began to realize the overwhelming force against him. Calculating his odds of survival, he retreated further into the trees and disappeared, leaving his men to García's mercy.

He moved along the inner edge of the tree line toward the driveway, pausing to assess surrounding risks.

Baca's remaining men in front of the tree line were surrounded, outmatched, and forced to surrender with García's relentless onslaught.

García's words crackled over the radio once more as the smoke dissipated and the gunfire subsided. "All hostiles are neutralized. We have control!"

Jiménez, St. James, and Anna exchanged triumphant fist pumps. Denzel had gone from excitement to terror to overwhelmed, all in ten minutes. He scanned the screen for any sign of his brother.

Baca pulled out his cell phone as he neared the driveway and texted a message. He spotted agents abandoning their posts through the trees flanking the driveway. He ducked down and waited, wary of potential stragglers. He made his way down the right side of the drive, using the same cover that had sheltered the agents just minutes before.

CHAPTER 60

St. James sat in the rented BMW 850i, tapping the steering wheel to the beat of a Spanish pop song playing softly on the radio. Parked across the street, he peered through the windshield, eyes narrowed. Scanning the surroundings, he waited for Dozer to emerge from Sánchez's drive.

His eye caught a swift movement along the tree line to the left.

Baca.

A lime-green Porsche sped toward him, slowing as it approached. Within metres, the passenger door swung open, and Baca dove into the moving vehicle. Dozer sprinted behind the car until it sped off, leaving him squinting at the license plate.

Dozer dashed toward the BMW. Igniting the engine, St. James leaned over, pushed the passenger door open, and shifted into gear. The car drifted forward, offering Dozer a chance to jump in. Instead, Dozer ran to the driver's side.

"I'm driving. Get in the passenger seat," Dozer yelled.

With no time to argue, St. James climbed into the passenger's side and pulled the door shut.

Dozer jammed the accelerator to the floor, and the BMW shot forward. A cloud of tire smoke billowed behind them as the car fishtailed onto Nacional Secundaria. Horns blared as three unsuspecting drivers were forced off the road.

St. James grinned. "You may have pissed off a few drivers back there."

Dozer let the tension fade from his smile.

"García's agents arrested twenty Baca men."

St. James was incredulous. "Only twenty?"

"The other twenty were killed. OIJ lost twelve. I saw Baca disappear through the trees just before the arrests. Chased him down the drive."

"Twelve agents killed. García expected no more than five. Ramírez won't be happy."

Dozer glanced at his side mirror, searching for a gap in traffic. Spotting a slim opening, he darted into it. Several horns blared at the reckless move. Dozer gripped the steering wheel with white-knuckled intensity as he fought to keep pace.

The Porsche zoomed ahead, threading traffic, avoiding several accidents with little to spare. Turning left onto a side street that looped around and back onto Nacional Secundaria, it sideswiped a yellow Hyundai Palisade backing out of a drive.

St. James couldn't suppress his fear as the BMW raced through the packed streets in the rapid pursuit of the lime-green Porsche. Every swerve, every near miss, played at his frayed nerves until he was gripping the sides of his seat.

Dozer eyed the Porsche ahead. "They spotted us!"

The Porsche careened around a corner, barely missing a group of pedestrians crossing the street. Dozer floored the accelerator, his eyes narrowing as he pushed the BMW to its limits to navigate the tight turn.

Baca's driver turned sharply onto another loop street toward the Korean Embassy, destroying a well-kept private lawn to avoid children playing early morning soccer in the street. Dozer, seconds behind.

The vehicles weaved in and out of side streets, the distance between them expanding and contracting like an accordion.

The BMW slipped behind. Dozer accelerated to regain ground.

St. James pointed ahead. "Woman on the left, pushing a carriage!"

"See her!" Dozer swerved to avoid the carriage, mounting a curb and veering toward a sidewalk café. Patrons leapt from their seats, barely escaping the crash that reduced patio tables and chairs to splinters.

St. James whipped his head around as the café chaos receded behind them. "Faster, they've almost disappeared."

Dozer gunned the BMW, sending bits of wood and debris flying from its engine bonnet.

The Porsche made a sharp turn at the next intersection. Dozer followed, narrowing the gap.

The Porsche slammed to a halt in front of the green light at the 105 intersection, its engine revving, stalling for time until the light turned yellow and then red against the BMW. The Porsche surged through the red light onto the 105 at greased lightning speed. Dozer wasn't losing the Porsche over a traffic light. The BMW raced through, accelerating onto the 105 at 165 kmh, crisscrossing lanes to avoid traffic.

A Cadillac SUV ploughed into the BMW's passenger side, slamming the door hard into St. James's right arm. The impact spun the BMW into a slow, 360-degree rotation. Dozer slammed the brakes, then pushed the accelerator to the floor, avoiding traffic barreling toward them behind. The SUV mimicked Dozer's manoeuvre and pursued the speeding BMW.

St. James winced.

"All right, Hamilton?"

St. James held his shoulder. "Think so. Arm hurts, but hey, it's still attached."

Dozer monitored the SUV's movements through the rear mirror. "Baca phoned for backup. That SUV is his. Wouldn't be chasing us if it wasn't."

"Wonderful."

The Porsche swerved onto an off-ramp to the 167, followed by a right turn into a subdivision just past the Taco Bar Escazú. Dozer trailed close behind. The SUV fell back four car lengths for reasons Dozer couldn't fathom.

Dozer slammed on the brakes.

St. James yelled, "What the hell are you doing?"

Dozer faced the back window, his arm resting on St. James's headrest. "Brace yourself."

The SUV rounded the turn. Dozer shifted into reverse, flooring the accelerator. Tires screeched as the BMW roared backward, crashing into the front end of the SUV, driving its bumper into the radiator, buckling the BMW trunk. Dozer pulled the car into drive and accelerated. The BMW struggled to disengage from the SUV. It broke free, ploughing through a row of potted plants lining the sidewalk, sending ceramic shards flying in every direction.

St. James winced as the BMW shuddered from the impact. Dozer regained control and accelerated.

"Where did you learn to drive, demolition derbies?"

"Harlem."

"Didn't know you lived in Harlem."

The BMW surged to 175 kmh. Scanning the side streets for potential threats, Dozer manoeuvred through congested traffic, missing a taxi's rear bumper as it swerved to avoid a collision.

"I didn't. Worked with the NYPD to crack a car-jacking ring. Learned this to stay alive."

"Here, I thought I knew you."

"Hardly!"

The Porsche veered into a narrow alley scarcely wide enough for a sports car. Mirrors on both sides scraped brick walls, leaving a trail of sparks behind. Too large to follow, the BMW bolted straight.

St. James yelled, "Down the alleyway back there."

"Get him out the other side."

Turning onto the next street, Dozer spotted the Porsche emerging from the alley. Dozer accelerated.

The Porsche shot up a ramp at full speed onto Autopista Prospero Fernandez. Dozer followed, switching to the middle lane to close a three-car gap. A red Dodge Ram loomed in the passenger side mirror, fast approaching on the inside.

"Coming fast up the inside."

St. James nodded. "Got it."

Light rain dampened the windshield. The automatic wipers swooshed back and forth. "Gonna get slippery," Dozer yelled.

The Dodge drew parallel and drifted closer.

Dozer's eyes moved back and forth between mirrors.

The Dodge pushed the BMW into another lane, colliding with a blue Jaguar, triggering a five-car pile-up. Dozer yanked the BMW back, slamming the Dodge into a guardrail. The Dodge charged again, forcing a Mini Countryman into the third lane.

"Hope we live through this," St. James yelled, one hand on the door handle and the other stabilizing him with the dash.

"Hope so, too!"

The rain intensified. The BMW swerved. Dozer struggled to maintain control.

Dozer was laser-focused, his grip on the wheel tightening as sweat dripped from his forehead.

"Stop screwing around, Dozer. Get this guy off our backs," St. James blurted.

Dozer cast St. James a penetrating glare and manoeuvred the BMW into the truck, wedging it against the guardrail. The vehicles interlocked, charging forward as one, slewing on the wet pavement, accompanied by the screeching of metal on metal. The Dodge's front end snarled against a broken rail section, wedging between the BMW and the barrier. The stopping force flipped the truck over the guardrail and onto a grassy incline. It rolled several times with the BMW's passenger door attached.

"We'll lose Baca altogether if we stop. Cars behind coming too fast," Dozer yelled.

Lunging from the guardrail, the BMW glanced off a maroon Chrysler and spun counterclockwise into the third lane. Dozer struggled to bring the BMW back under control. Police sirens screamed in the distance.

Dozer increased the pace. "We're out of Baca's sight. He'll think the Dodge got us instead of the other way around."

St. James leaned away from the doorless passenger's side, gripping his seat to fight against the wind suction at 175 kmh.

Dozer's grin was tense. "What are you telling the rental people?"

St. James glanced at Dozer. "That I'll buy the car. Pay full price as if there wasn't a scratch on it. Offset the cost against your bills."

Dozer scowled. "*My* bills? It's your case!"

St. James smirked at Dozer. "You're driving. I'm only a passenger."

Dozer spotted a green Porsche coming into view several cars ahead. "Forget it! There's Baca."

"Taking another exit. Headed for the parking garage on the right," St. James shouted.

"Stupid shit. He'll corner himself."

The Porsche took the exit and darted into the multi-story parking facility, tires screeching against the concrete as it vanished into the structure.

"Speeding up the down ramp," St. James barked. "Not a smart move."

"Stupid shit."

The garage reverberated with the din of screeching tires and roaring engines.

A yellow half-ton Chev lunged into the Porsche's front end on its way to the exit. The driver reversed, pulling the half-ton back from the sports car, climbed down from the cab, and pulled his driver's license and insurance card from a wallet.

The Porsche took advantage of the gap and bolted around the truck, leaving the driver standing behind, stunned, scratching his head. The Porsche charged up onto the roof of the parking building.

The rain fell harder.

The Porsche sped around a tight corner, scraping the door of a parked black Audi.

Dozer manoeuvred the BMW, avoiding two SUVs.

The Porsche accelerated, roaring as it sped toward the short wall at the rooftop's edge. The driver slammed the brakes just in time, sending a cascade of water from the rain-soaked surface over the small wall. The BMW ground to a halt centimetres from the barrier.

The Porsche reversed, misjudging a pillar's distance, crunching metal echoing through the garage.

The BMW squeezed through a narrow gap, scraping a pillar and sending sparks flying.

St. James shook his head. "How do we finish this?"

"Badly!"

CHAPTER 61

The Porsche made it to ground level without crashing into another vehicle, but not without ripping out a section of the pay booth and terrifying the attendant inside. The attendant bolted from the damaged booth, jumping up and down, waving his fist, cursing, and blocking the BMW's exit from the garage.

Dozer blared the horn, inching forward, poised to nudge the man aside. The attendant pounded the BMW engine bonnet. Dozer laid on the horn again. The attendant pounded several more times before moving. Dozer rolled the car into the street, searching for the Porsche.

"Go right," St. James barked.

Dozer turned right, holding the BMW to the city speed limit.

"You watch the side streets on the left," St. James yelled. "I'll watch the right. Couldn't have gotten too far."

Dozer made two turns onto side streets on a hunch. "Should have run over that attendant. Save time."

St. James forced a smile. "A murder charge might have delayed us a bit longer."

Dozer yelled, "Shit."

"What's wrong?"

"We're going the wrong way on a one-way street."

St. James's face tensed further. "Oh!"

The BMW charged forward, weaving between oncoming cars, trucks, and motorcycles, narrowly avoiding several collisions and leaving a trail of angry drivers behind.

A taxi swerved to avoid the BMW, grazing a brown Lexus parked on the side, launching it forward, sending several motorcycles toppling like dominoes.

St. James closed his eyes, unable to watch. "This is insane!"

Dozer remained focused. His mind fixed on dodging each oncoming vehicle as it neared.

Close to the Hilton La Sabana, St. James spotted a Porsche matching the colour of Baca's entering a parking lot. "Stadium."

Dozer yanked the wheel to exit onto the Avenue of the Americas and drove into the stadium grounds, several car lengths behind the Porsche.

St. James grabbed the dash. "Getting boring, Dozer. Haven't hit anything for five minutes."

Dozer's smile was slight. "Matter of time, my friend."

The Porsche spun around the stadium at excessive speed, rotated 360 degrees, straightened, and darted back onto the avenue, turning south onto Hungria Libre Street with Dozer tight on its tail. The Porsche swerved onto the sidewalk.

Dozer slammed the brakes, avoiding three teenage girls, skidding to a stop just before a storefront, barely missing a street vendor's cart. The Porsche made the green light, but Dozer was held back by traffic. He made the right turn with St. James leaning in. "Don't see them."

Dozer bit his lower lip. "About ten cars ahead. They're turning into someplace."

St. James shouted, "Push into the left lane."

Dozer forced a brown Hyundai to the curb, ignoring a red light and forcing a pedestrian back onto the sidewalk. A city bus ploughed into a line of cars waiting at the light, accordioning several vehicles.

St. James watched the carnage happen. "Surprised the police haven't caught up yet."

"Soon."

St. James signalled ahead. "There. The carwash."

Dozer wheeled the BMW into the carwash, stopped, and searched for signs of the Porsche. Along one wall, three young people were washing large SUVs. Dozer pointed to a redheaded lady. "Put your window down and ask that woman."

St. James's laugh was uncontrollable.

Dozer faced St. James, "What's so funny?"

"Don't have a door, let alone a window!"

Dozer shook his head. "Man, I'm focused on keeping us alive, not your door!"

St. James swung around, placed a foot on the concrete floor, and spoke to a redhead in overalls, wiping down a GMC Suburban with a chamois. "Excuse me, miss. See a banged-up green Porsche come here?"

Too frightened, the lady didn't answer.

"Somebody's threatened her," Dozer whispered.

The redhead shifted her eyes from right to left several times, holding them a tad longer to the left than the right, toward a new grey Lincoln Navigator. St. James picked up the signal. "Behind that big Lincoln."

Dozer eyed the vehicle.

St. James smiled his thanks to the woman.

Dozer rolled the BMW slowly down the Navigator's passenger side toward the rear. An engine roared to life, and Baca's Porsche raced past the Lincoln on the driver's side, out the carwash entrance before the less nimble BMW could turn.

Dozer made a three-point turn around the Navigator and zigzagged out of the carwash.

Dense traffic prevented the Porsche from speeding through an intersection three blocks ahead. It sped over the adjacent crosswalk and through the intersection, ignoring the red light and colliding with a motorcycle waiting for the light to change. The rider flew through a store window. The Porsche knocked over a mailbox and two waste receptacles.

St. James watched the Porsche rip up the sidewalk. "We can't make it over the sidewalk. We'll lose him."

Dozer remained still.

The light changed. Two lanes of vehicles moved forward through the intersection, but not fast enough for Dozer. Dozer accelerated, wedging the BMW between a yellow Jeep and a black Buick, parting them like the Red Sea, ripping the side mirrors off each and scraping paint from all three vehicles. The Buick driver cursed in Italian. The Jeep driver sat, stunned.

Dozer matted the accelerator.

"Jesus, Dozer," St. James yelled, bracing himself with both hands on the dash.

St. James eyed an ambulance working its way through traffic.

The Porsche rocked as it leapt onto the street from the sidewalk on the other side of the intersection, forcing a silver Volvo into a fire hydrant, sending water gushing into the air.

Approaching a sharp turn, Dozer slammed the brakes. The BMW went into a controlled skid, tires screeching, fishtailing around the corner, avoiding an oncoming bus.

"You're gonna kill us!" St. James yelled.

"Not today," Dozer said, too casual for the situation.

The Porsche slewed right onto a wet one-way avenue east, causing a delivery truck to jackknife, spilling its trailer load of canned dog food over the street.

Police sirens from the north grew louder.

The BMW held its course as it roared onto the avenue, weaving around carnage in the Porsche's wake. Forcing its way into the far-left lane, the Porsche displaced several vehicles and ran a red light before making an abrupt left turn.

A massive black dump truck surged from a side street, ramming the Porsche and flipping it onto its roof. The Porsche skidded through the entrance of San José's central market. Screaming customers vaulted to one side as the slow-moving metal devastation scraped toward them like lava.

A trail of police cars with flashing lights and blaring sirens came from all directions.

Dozer limped the battered BMW to the curb. They climbed out and ran toward the now unrecognizable Porsche. St. James went to the passenger's side. Dozer approached the driver's door. St. James stooped, felt for Baca's pulse, then stood and looked at Dozer over the undercarriage. "Dead!"

"This one, too!" Dozer shouted.

CHAPTER 62

The clang of the metal door echoed through the holding cell at the Policía Municipal de San José as it closed with a forceful thud.

A short, wiry police officer with a stern countenance and deep facial lines glared at his two prisoners with disdain. His bright eyes narrowed, scanning them from head to toe, lingering on their dishevelled appearances.

"Because of you two," he said, his gravelly voice seemingly scraping against the walls, "there won't be an available tow truck in San José for two weeks."

St. James couldn't help thinking that the officer seemed to be taking their actions personally. He scanned the solid grey walls of the small, windowless lockup. His eyes lingered on the cots along opposite walls, each covered with grey blankets and separated by a basic toilet.

"Hope Jiménez arrives soon; this place gives me the creeps. Like being trapped in a forgotten cellar beneath the city streets," St. James admitted, trying to mask his unease.

Dozer stood, his grip on the bars tightening as his mind wandered through a labyrinth of thoughts. Hours passed with no sign of Jiménez. The skinny, offended policeman appeared at around six o'clock with a food tray. St. James and Dozer jumped at the metallic screech as he scraped the tray against the bars. The policeman's gaze flicked back and forth between his two captives, never settling long enough to afford Dozer or St. James any status beyond reprobates.

"If it were up to me, you'd go hungry. One of the cars you crashed was my son's. He's in the hospital with a broken leg and a concussion." The policeman turned and left.

St. James attempted to lighten the oppressive mood. "Do you sense he blames us for the accidents?"

Dozer ignored the humour and grabbed a plate from the tray. St. James did the same, grimacing at the mushy spaghetti.

Dozer swirled some of the pasta around his fork, his appetite waning. "Almost killed us a dozen times today," he said finally.

St. James offered reassurance. "Come on, Dozer — you handled everything like a pro. Lucky to have you and your skills behind the wheel."

Dozer's stare became distant as he relived the day. "Delayed remorse always follows a wild car chase, where every split-second decision carries the weight of life. A ghostly replay in my head."

St. James's demeanour stiffened. "I'm sorry. Didn't realize there was such a thing as a ghostly replay."

Dozer's thoughts were still trapped in the shadows of his mind.

St. James and Dozer heard a voice from the other side of the cell door. "Don't know whether to hug you two or leave you here," Jiménez said as he entered the room. "You've destroyed half the vehicles in the city. It'll take ten people at least a month to handle the paperwork."

St. James smirked. "They kept getting in our way."

Jiménez's frown resembled that of a stern headmaster. "Took me two hours to convince the local police to release you into my custody. They demanded the OIJ be on the hook for everything you've done. Director Ramírez is wild."

Dozer returned to the present, his mood like a thundercloud ready to burst. "I couldn't care less if Ramírez is wild! He knew this mission carried immense risk, with no guarantee of success. Both you and Ramírez should realize that we put our lives on the line for this country. Helped end property thefts and other criminal operations by removing the head serpent. So what if there are irate drivers and angry insurance companies? Today's operation didn't claim any innocent, civilian lives, as far as we know — only those involved on either side of the mission. I don't want to hear your whining. You've been freed of Baca without squandering hundreds of millions on legal fees for his conviction. Ramírez is ahead of the game, no matter the damages. Baca's no longer a burden to the Costa Rican people. Consider yourselves damn lucky the mission was a success!"

Jiménez stood there, mouth agape, speechless, waiting for Dozer to finish. St. James stood by, admiring Dozer's impassioned speech.

The police officer emerged from the outer office, stared at St. James and Dozer, then unlocked the cell for Jiménez. "You're free to go, but only in the OIJ's custody."

Jiménez ushered them from the cell to the outer office, where he signed the necessary release papers.

No one spoke during the drive back to OIJ headquarters. The atmosphere was thick with a swirling cocktail of angst, guilt, and blame.

***

As plump as he was, Ramírez still managed to loom menacingly over Jiménez and García. His eyes blazed with fury as they stood before him, their faces full of apprehension, their shoulders slumped under the weight of his anger.

"It'll take years to untangle the mess you've created!" Ramírez's voice thundered through the office. "The mayor is breathing fire, demanding answers. Do you have any idea the damage that's been done to our reputation? The media is tearing us apart, painting us as incompetent fools, incapable of maintaining order!"

He clenched his fists. "Let's not forget the insurance companies! Sharpening their knives, ready to carve us up in court. We're facing financial ruin because of this mission!"

His eye swept over Jiménez and García, disappointment and scorn formed on his features. "I'll be lucky to hold onto my position after this disaster. If I don't, neither will you. Like the mess you left today, your careers will be in ruins!"

St. James and Dozer exchanged uneasy glances, distressed by Ramírez's wrath bearing down on their colleagues. Guilt gnawed at their insides despite their best intentions.

St. James seized the opportunity to interject when the Director paused his tirade. "Sir, chasing Baca was our initiative, not the OIJ's. OIJ didn't know about it until the chase was underway. We saw an opportunity to prevent Baca from escaping, and we took it. So we alone are responsible for the mess."

"Even so, you were operating under the direction of the OIJ, so the responsibility lands on my shoulders, no matter what." The Director sighed, frustration coming out of every pore. "How am I to fund all the damage, let alone justify causing it?"

Dozer exchanged a glance with St. James, asking permission to speak. Despite St. James's subtle shake of the head, Dozer forged ahead. "Sir, I have a suggestion."

Ramírez squinted. "A suggestion? I don't care!"

Jiménez cleared his throat, speaking up in support. "Perhaps, Sir, we should spend our time strategizing how to handle everything for an honourable way out of this."

Ramírez's incredulous gaze fell on Jiménez. "Honourable way out! You've got to be kidding!"

Jiménez was resolute. "No, Sir, I'm not. You made your assessment of our performance clear. We need time to plan our way out."

Jiménez turned to Dozer before Ramírez could respond. "You have a suggestion?"

Dozer was determined. "Continuing to dwell on past events only prolongs negativity in the city. I suggest we highlight the OIJ's contribution to eradicating a parasite from your society: the extensive negative impact of Baca's criminal activities over the years. Calculate the financial burden of his crimes on the Costa Rican people — stolen real estate, investigations, and court proceedings.

Quantifying these costs will illustrate the immense relief from eliminating such criminal activities from your country. Compare that to the total damage incurred today. I'm willing to wager that one year's savings with Baca gone will offset today's damages."

García's skepticism was apparent. "Who's going to believe that? Everyone will say we fudged the numbers."

St. James shook his head. "Audit the analysis — independently. Present an unassailable case."

Jiménez nodded. "Then we hire a public relations firm to communicate the results. Craft a narrative that frames your actions and the mission positively."

Dozer's smile was cautious, but his determination shone through. "Run a campaign to show the success of the mission, not its cost. People need to see the bigger picture."

Ramírez's mind churned with conflicting emotions. Instinctively, he knew they were right — dwelling on the catastrophe would only deepen the wound. But he was still furious at Dozer and St. James for their rampage through San José. His initial instinct was to push back against the idea and maintain control, but the fire in his agents' eyes sparked something within him.

Ramírez stared off, considering the suggestion. He could feel his thoughts untangling and his anger subsiding as the plan's promise sunk in. "All right. Lay out the facts and the true impact of our action against Baca's reign of terror."

The office seemed to exhale a collective breath as Ramírez's encouragement swept the room.

The atmosphere morphed from panic to anxiety to practicality as they discussed a possible strategy. Ramírez, though still harbouring reservations, found himself swept up in the energy of his agents' resolve. With the basic strategy hashed out, a sense of purpose began to take root.

García sat back in his chair, skepticism still lingering. "What if we don't have the resources to pull this off?"

Jiménez brushed off the concern. "We'll make do with what we have. It's not ideal, but we'll find a way. We always do."

García shrugged. "I guess we've faced worse odds. We can do this. We've come this far; we can't back down now."

Hours passed in a blur as they worked to set things right. As the sun began to fade, they emerged with the outline of a comprehensive strategy.

Ramírez observed his agents. "We have our work cut out for us. I'm confident we're going in the right direction."

CHAPTER 63

St. James and Dozer stood before Anna, absorbing her anger and concern as her emotions surged. Guilt and remorse intensified with each syllable.

Denzel sat quietly in a corner of St. James's hotel room, sleepy and bewildered.

Anna was red-faced. "It's a wonder you didn't end up in jail."

St. James attempted levity. "Just for the record, sweetheart, we did end up in jail."

Anna's scream reverberated down the hallway, prompting a concerned knock on their door by another hotel guest.

"Everything all right?" a man shouted from the hall.

"Yes," Dozer yelled back. "Just being verbally ripped to shreds by my buddy's fiancée."

The man mumbled something unintelligible and shuffled off.

It took several minutes for Anna to calm down, her initial fury giving way to concern and compassion as she processed the day. St. James and Dozer took turns recounting the chaotic chain of events, from Baca's attempted escape to their many collisions and near misses, subsequent arrest, and emotional outbursts.

"Well, I guess I can see how it all could happen," Anna conceded as she grappled with the implications. "You couldn't let Baca escape."

A fresh wave of anger overtook her when she imagined St. James wrapped around a telephone pole or crushed under the BMW. "You nearly died ten times. Not to mention all the people you injured and nearly killed."

Dozer was hanging his head. "The ghostly replay," he said under his breath, confusing Anna. St. James said nothing, for there was nothing to say.

Anna wiped away her tears and let the morbid imaginings pass. "How did Ramírez react?" she asked.

Dozer's smile was faint. "Not well!"

Anna rolled her eyes, her lingering anger tempered by a hint of amusement. "Not surprised."

"Can we go back to normal now?" St. James's request was almost a plea.

Anna weighed the request. "Very well," she said, still cool.

Dozer rubbernecked between Anna and St. James. "What now?"

Anna reversed Dozer's gaze. "Louis phoned this morning."

St. James straightened. "What's up?"

"He's on his way back to Ottawa."

Dozer grimaced. "Why?"

"Sandy woke yesterday morning with an epiphany. She remembered having a husband in California."

Shock hijacked St. James and Dozer.

St. James cringed. "Bring him here. He'll need support."

"Did my best to persuade him to come. But he was determined to go back to Ottawa. He's sad and embarrassed. A lot of hurt in his voice."

St. James stared off. "I can imagine."

"Poor guy," Dozer murmured. "I'll phone him in the morning."

Anna's earlier anger dissipated completely as Louis's situation sank in. "Going through something like that … bound to take its toll."

Dozer shook his head. "Must have cut deep."

Anna sighed. "Take time to heal."

St. James couldn't shake the image of Louis, alone and broken.

They were silent for a few minutes, buried in their thoughts. Anna was the first to speak. "Some wounds run too deep to heal. And some scars never fade."

CHAPTER 64

St. James and Dozer hailed a taxi to the car rental office on Tuesday morning. They were determined to sort out the aftermath of the BMW they wrecked the day before.

The cacophony of honking horns and chatter from pedestrians hurrying along the overcrowded sidewalk dominated the atmosphere as they climbed out of the taxi.

"Dozer, do you think they've invented a 'sorry-we-totally-destroyed-your-car' insurance?" St. James quipped.

"If they haven't, we should pitch the idea."

Arriving at the rental agency, they found the same manager surveying the BMW wreckage with disbelief engraved across his face.

"Do you think he'll recognize us?" Dozer whispered as they approached.

St. James smirked. "I'm sure he'll never forget the guys who turned his luxury car into modern art."

As they got closer, the manager's eyes widened. "You! What were you thinking?" His hands flew to the top of his head in frustration.

St. James decided to play along. "Morning!" He leaned in jovially and read the man's name tag. "Matt, is it? Lovely day for some paperwork, don't you think?"

The manager's face flushed. "Some paperwork? I'll be drowning in reports for a month! Head office will threaten to pull the franchise! I feared it was one of our cars when I saw the late-night news. When they showed a picture, I couldn't tell what it was! Do you have any idea what you've done to me?"

Dozer contained his amusement. "Hey, at least you don't have to rent it anymore. Silver lining, right?"

The manager glared at them. "What's that supposed to mean? Why wouldn't I want to rent it? It's a BMW. It was one of our best vehicles. You know what? Never mind. You're insane."

"Now, now," Dozer began, but Matt held up his hand to stop him. "You have no idea the mess you've created."

St. James glanced at Dozer, who was struggling to stifle a laugh.

The police had run the BMW's dented license plate and discovered it was a rental. They'd arranged for it to be winched onto a flatbed and transported to the rental agency overnight. The vehicle's twisted metal and shattered glass witnessed the previous day's chaos, starkly contrasting its former sleek luxury.

The rental manager circled the wreckage as if trying to make sense of senseless.

Dozer's grin seemed permanent. "Other than a few dents, it's in perfect shape."

The manager was stunned, glaring but speechless.

St. James decided to piggyback on Dozer's exaggeration. "Now you know why I wanted the extra insurance."

"Extra insurance? The insurance company will use your negligence as an excuse not to pay! You've unleashed a nightmare on me!"

Dozer continued to struggle, suppressing his laughter.

Worried the manager might have a heart attack, St. James interjected. "Would it be easier if I just bought the car from you at full list price?"

The red drained from the manager's face. "Well ... ah ... yes," he stammered. "That would be much better. Then we wouldn't have an insurable interest. The problem would be yours."

St. James pulled a chequebook from his jacket pocket. "Let's go inside, find the original price, and settle this. I'll even add an extra thousand for you to send the car to a junkyard."

The rental manager couldn't believe his ears. He led them to a cluttered desk covered with stacks of paper. St. James scanned the room, amused by its disarray, while Dozer propped himself against the doorframe, grinning.

After a few minutes of shuffling through papers, the manager located the original purchase price and handed St. James a faded invoice.

St. James scribbled the figure onto the cheque with practiced ease and added the promised extra thousand without hesitation. He handed the completed cheque to the manager.

The manager smiled for the first time. "I'll take care of the rest."

As they walked out, St. James let out a sigh of relief. "Well, that's one way to solve a problem."

Dozer grinned. "Yep. We officially made our mark on San José."

CHAPTER 65

García went through an emotional wringer. Every visit to the homes of fallen OIJ agents left him drained, heavy with grief and guilt. As he sat in his car afterward, the weight of the family meetings pressed down on him, a physical force that made it hard to breathe.

The faces of the spouses and families he met haunted him, their pain carved into his memory. The homes had been filled with tears, cries of anguish, and raw despair, all now echoing in his mind, a living torment he couldn't escape. Each conversation was a brutal reminder of the sacrifices made in the fight against Baca, a criminal and a tyrant who had plagued the country far too long. With each visit, García felt the gravity of responsibility increase.

García felt relief and dread as he prepared to visit the twelfth house. Relief that these visits would soon be over and he could begin to find some semblance of closure. Dread at the thought of facing yet another grieving family.

Taking a deep breath, he gathered his strength, climbed out of the car, and steeled himself for what lay ahead. As he approached the house, García prayed for the strength to endure the final family. He knew resilience would carry him through, no matter the burden.

***

St. James and Dozer taxied to HQ from the rental office to work with Jiménez on a communication plan explaining the long-term benefit of the mission's success.

St. James couldn't shake his conflicting thoughts as they made themselves comfortable in Jiménez's office. On one hand, there was a sense of accomplishment. They had neutralized Baca. The days of hard work, dedication, and risk-taking to make it happen had paid off. Yet a nagging edginess consumed him.

Chasing Baca through the streets of San José was beyond dangerous. It bordered on suicidal. Anna would never let him forget that. The aftermath loomed large in his mind. The potential repercussions of their actions cast a shadow over the victory. The thought of innocent bystanders caught in the wake of crashing cars now weighed heavily on his conscience. The damage inflicted on the city streets only added to his guilt.

Jiménez lit a Delta, leaning back as he exhaled the smoke. "Our communication people are looking at a draft communiqué — something for us to review. Here's an outline." Jiménez handed St. James and Dozer a copy and gave them time to digest it.

St. James smiled. "This is excellent!"

Dozer grinned. "Exactly what's needed."

Jiménez was pleased with their response: "When the communications people send the first draft of the details, I want your input. All eyes should be on this, just as they were with planning the mission."

Dozer was enthusiastic. "Pleasure to help."

Jiménez butted his cigarette. "The Director wants a monument erected in honour of the fallen agents, each name boldly inscribed — a ceremony with the families front and centre to the monument. Costa Rica will acknowledge their loss as Costa Rica's loss. Their loved ones died for a noble cause. The Director will acknowledge them as war heroes."

St. James slapped his hands together. "Splendid suggestion, Sir."

Dozer brightened. "You must tell us when this takes place. We want to be here for it."

Jiménez smiled. "You're at the top of the invitation list." Jiménez paused and changed the subject. "What loose ends do we have to talk about?"

St. James altered his thinking. "What are you doing with Pérez?"

"He's downstairs being interrogated. I'm told he's singing like a bird, with his boss dead. Baca's remaining men have been charged and will be tried. They're likely headed for prison."

Dozer stroked his chin. "Good."

St. James's eyes veered off. "Then there's Vargas. The personality of a rattlesnake, but we would never have known when Baca was coming for Pérez without him. Is he a threat, with Baca dead?"

Jiménez winced. "Probably not. Definitely part of Baca's gang. But losing his accounting license should be punishment enough."

Dozer agreed.

"I have a proposal," St. James said.

Jiménez' forehead furrowed. "What?"

"With Baca's empire crumbled there is considerable cash and other assets at stake in his various companies. Smythe, my computer expert, hacked into Baca's records for the purpose of having this discussion. Baca's cash increased by over a hundred million US dollars last year. His real estate holdings are valued at over five hundred million. Plenty of wealth to share with homeowners who lost their property — maybe not enough to pay everything, but probably a healthy portion."

Jiménez was listening intently and looking pleased. "What about your client? Have they been made whole?"

"Completely. Global has been reimbursed for its insurance losses. So, we've achieved our goals, and with Baca and most of his men either dead or on their way to prison, I think you've achieved yours. Correct?"

"Correct."

"But a few of Baca's men are still out there. We can't let those crooks got their hands these assets."

"Amen to that," Jiménez said. "But I don't know how we could prevent it."

"There may be a way, depending on Costa Rica laws. We can include Chávez in those discussions."

"What do you have in mind?"

"Chávez might be able to get a court order freezing Baca's assets."

Jiménez looked puzzled. "On what basis? We have no legal right to Baca's assets."

"Maybe on behalf of the Costa Rican people you do. All of Baca's assets were realized by defrauding and abusing Costa Ricans, or those interested enough in Costa Rica to buy property here. The courts may be convinced it's fair and just for those assets to be seized and used to compensate those harmed."

Jiménez twisted his moustache. "Interesting concept. But a Judge may not go for it."

St. James smiled broadly. "If not, I bet the government would allow it. Works well for politicians at election time. And it goes a long way to creating a halo over the OIJ's head. Not only did you bring the crooks to justice, but you also made sure there would be some money for the victims."

"Win, win, win, all around," Jiménez mused, seeing the plan's full potential.

"We did something similar during our last case in Germany. We created a fund from the swindler's spoils and used it to compensate companies he had pilfered from."

Jiménez stared off. "Appealing."

"It would be easier for the Director to approve this than it was for the mission that brought the assets to our attention in the first place."

Dozer, who had been quiet up until now, leaned forward, his expression thoughtful. "The mayor would get off the OIJ's back, and the favourable press would help minimize any negativity from the car chase. A win for our communication plan."

Jiménez smiled, clearly pleased. "I like it. I'll take it up with the Director." St. James gave a faint smile. "Excellent. Let me know if I can help."

Jiménez nodded. He eyed the two men. "I guess your work here is done. I suspect you'll be heading back up north soon."

St. James leaned forward. "Not yet. Still something to be done."

CHAPTER 66

Jiménez was surprised by St. James's pronouncement. "What do you mean there's still work to be done? We have the vehicle mess and paperwork in hand. García is leading the public relations campaign. You've just laid out a plan to make the OIJ look like Robin Hood. What else is there?"

St. James was authoritative. "There's one final piece to this puzzle before we close the case."

Frustration crossed Jiménez's face. "What are you talking about? We tied up the major issues. What more could need your help for?"

St. James was insistent. "We need to know how Baca learned of our plan."

A hint of sarcasm crept into Jiménez's tone. "And how do you propose we do that?"

"Gather everyone, and we'll piece the story together." St. James's demeanour was calm and unwavering.

Jiménez glanced at Dozer, who shrugged. "Just St. James's way of tying up loose ends. He likes to see a case through to its absolute conclusion."

With a reluctant sigh, Jiménez relented. "Fine. I'll arrange a conference room for this afternoon."

***

At three o'clock, Montero strode into the boardroom. Jiménez, just back from a smoke break, absently traced his fingers along his moustache, his nerves visible as he anticipated St. James's next move.

García sat opposite Montero, his eyes wide, almost bulging. Segura took the seat beside him, her face unreadable. Madrigal fidgeted nervously in his chair. St. James, Dozer, Anna, and Denzel completed the circle, the tension thickening.

The door swung open, and Director Ramírez stepped inside, a knowing smile playing at his lips. "When Jiménez told me about this meeting, I thought I should attend. Anyone object?"

Jiménez's voice was calm, sincere. "Glad to have you join us, Director."

The agents fell silent, the Director's presence accepted without a word.

Jiménez gestured toward St. James. "Your show," he said, though doubt lingered in his tone.

St. James stood, radiating confidence as he addressed the room. "As you all know, Global Insurance asked us to investigate claims made by notaries for transferring real estate without the owners' consent. This investigation led us to you, Captain Jiménez, and ultimately to Baca, the likely mastermind behind the thefts."

García and Montero exchanged a glance, displeasure noticeable. Segura's gaze remained fixed ahead, unwavering.

"When a roof agent was shot before the fighting began," St. James continued, "it was clear that Baca knew about our operation. Otherwise, how could he have known where we placed agents? He misled us into positioning ground agents away from the tree line, letting his men move behind us undetected."

St. James paused, reaching for a bottle of water in the center of the table. He took a slow sip, tension looming over the room.

Montero adjusted his chair, tapping his fingers impatiently on the armrest. Madrigal glanced at his phone, clearly disinterested in having the mission read back to him like a children's bedtime story. García drummed his fingers on the table, deep in thought.

But the room's disengagement only seemed to aggravate St. James. He halted his speech and turned on the agents, eyes full of indignation.

"I can't believe you aren't more interested in who betrayed us," he barked, his voice sharp. "Agents were killed because your strategy was compromised. Doesn't that bother you?"

A shock of surprise flickered across Ramírez's face as the room stirred to life.

"This behavior is unnatural, given the circumstances," St. James snapped.

A murmur of disbelief rippled through the room.

St. James's voice grew more clipped. "Do you want to know why you lost so many agents?"

Jiménez frowned but remained steady. "It bothers all of us, St. James. We'll figure out who betrayed us, but it takes time. We need to be sure of the facts. This isn't something that can be done overnight."

St. James's eyes scanned the table, disappointment clear in his gaze. "Very well. If you don't want to hear who among you is a traitor, my team and I will catch the first flight back to Canada."

A thick silence settled. The agents exchanged uneasy glances, the awkwardness of Jiménez's weak dismissal weighing down the atmosphere. Dozer and Anna's contempt was unmistakable. Ramírez, visibly frustrated, intervened.

"Jiménez," Ramírez's voice cracked like a whip, "St. James and his team have given everything to the OIJ. They've risked their lives and played a crucial role in eliminating the country's greatest threat."

He turned his gaze to the agents around the table, his stare cutting through them. "They've sacrificed. And yet we're dismissing their contribution because of some internal procedure?"

Ramírez's voice snapped into a shout. "Show some goddamn respect!"

The outburst stunned everyone. The room fell into shocked silence.

Ramírez looked back to St. James. "Go ahead. Take all the time you need. Nobody's going anywhere until you've been heard."

St. James nodded, his posture relaxing slightly. "Thank you, Director." He turned his attention to García. "I ruled you out as a possible mole. Your reaction to delivering the bad news to the fallen agents' families told me everything I needed to know. Your heart is with the agents. You would never sacrifice them intentionally."

Dozer leaned in. "The passion García put into training told me the same."

García exhaled in relief, meeting Dozer's gaze. "Thank you."

St. James ignored García, his focus now shifting to Madrigal. "You, on the other hand, were too nervous to be a mole for Baca."

Madrigal looked more unsettled than usual.

Montero's tone was sharp. "What makes you think it was one of us?"

"The plan was password-protected and encrypted," St. James replied, calmly. "Only those with the approved fingerprints could access the document. And those approved were limited to people in this room."

Montero raised an eyebrow. "Computer security people could have accessed it."

Dozer and Anna exchanged glances, amusement flickering in their eyes. Denzel sat, ecstatic to be reunited with his brother.

"True," St. James agreed, "computer security experts could have accessed the plan, but they didn't."

"How do you know," Montero challenged.

"I interviewed the computer services manager. She showed me proof of everyone who accessed the files. And no one outside this room opened them."

Montero looked unconvinced, but the seed of doubt was planted.

Jiménez shifted in his seat, the weight of Ramírez's earlier reprimand still pressing on him. Segura, for her part, seemed entirely uninterested in the unfolding drama.

St. James locked eyes with Montero. "At first, I considered you the mole.

But after working with you, following the detail you generated for the mission plan, it became clear that you couldn't be the one."

The room fell silent. The air seemed to thicken as the uncertainty settled over them all. Jiménez's pulse quickened as he tried to anticipate St. James's next move.

CHAPTER 67

St. James sat back in his chair, sipping water. "Anna investigated every corner of Baca's world, examining every connection. It was uneventful until she uncovered Hector Pérez's past."

St. James glanced at García, who could have been more readable. "Early in our mission planning, you mentioned that Pérez was Baca's most trusted notary. We used his name as bait, hoping Baca would be enraged enough to try to kill Pérez when he learned his trusted employee turned against him."

García nodded.

St. James continued. "Anna uncovered more about Pérez than we realized."

Jiménez's impatience was evident. "What does this have to do with identifying our mole?"

"That will become clear soon," St. James assured.

García and Montero exchanged a glance, questioning the direction of the conversation. Anna's eyes sparkled with anticipation.

Undeterred by the skepticism, St. James continued. "Anna, please tell the agents about your investigation."

Anna smiled and nodded before saying, "Pérez took a lover, a decision that led to major issues. He and his lover bought a house beyond their means, affordable only if they pooled their resources. Pérez was married, and this house was meant to be their secret rendezvous."

St. James paused, letting the gravity of the situation sink in. "When Pérez ended the relationship, he left his lover with an unaffordable mortgage. This betrayal left her bitter and struggling financially," he said.

Anna continued. "Bitterness turned to vindictiveness. Baca learned of her plight and offered to solve her financial problems in exchange for her loyalty to him. To avoid losing her house, she accepted Baca's offer…"

"Isn't that right, Segura?" St. James interjected.

Segura's face went pale. "No! That isn't true!"

The room erupted in chaos. Montero was overcome with disbelief. "Are you telling us you were involved with our decoy? How could you do this to us?"

Segura's silence was her only answer.

Ignoring the outburst, St. James glared at Segura. "Who suggested Pérez's name as the decoy?"

Segura's voice trembled. "García."

García remained calm, his face grim, grappling with anger.

"No," St. James corrected. "It was you who proposed Pérez's name as our decoy. García only provided the information regarding Pérez's arrest for property theft five years ago after you suggested him."

Stillness fell as everyone absorbed St. James's words.

"My God," Ramírez whispered, his horror obvious.

Jiménez's eyes broadened in shock. "Jesus." His trust in Segura instantly evaporated.

Segura's face twisted in fear and shame, her palms slick with sweat, realizing her colleagues now regarded her with outrage.

García clenched his jaw and gripped the table, knuckles white, unable to meet Segura's tear-streaked eyes.

"How could you?" Montero's voice was raw. "After everything we've been through together."

St. James's tone cut through the murmurings. "Segura was not Pérez's lover."

Confusion replaced anger as everyone struggled to reassess Segura's culpability.

"Then who was?" Montero demanded.

The room fell into an expectant silence. St. James took a deliberate sip of water.

Anna jumped in. "My investigation revealed Segura has a sister. Gabriela." Anna's voice was measured. "Gabriela was the one involved with Pérez, wasn't she, Segura?"

Segura's eyes fell to the table, her quiet a glaring confession.

St. James nodded, his voice steady. "Pérez left Gabriela in ruins. Drowning in debt. Her life spiraled after he ended their relationship."

Montero's eyes narrowed, but he said nothing.

"Baca saw her vulnerability," St. James continued, his gaze never leaving Segura. "He offered her a way out — a financial lifeline — in exchange for her loyalty. Gabriela took it. For her, it was simple. Survival."

A tense silence lingered. Segura flinched, her hands shaking as she wiped tears from her eyes.

"Gabriela's desperation led her to confide in you, Segura, hoping you would help — perhaps even leak details of our mission," St. James said. "You loved your sister and wanted to do something. Together, the two of you schemed. You proposed using Pérez — Baca's most trusted notary — as our decoy, pretending he planned to steal Baca's property. Gabriela hoped this would enrage Baca so deeply that he would see Pérez's betrayal as unforgivable — and kill him. That would give her the revenge she craved.

"At the same time, she knew the money Baca promised her in exchange for loyalty could save her home from foreclosure. But Baca's loyalty came at a price: any intelligence she could gather from you, whenever he demanded it. And unfortunately, that included our entire plan to finally arrest him."

A murmur of disbelief rippled through the room.

"Hatred and money —two of the strongest motivators," St. James added, his eyes scanning each agent's face.

Montero's disdainful eye fixed on Segura. "How could you betray us and the families of our fallen?"

Segura buried her face in her hands, sobbing.

St. James paused, waiting for silence. The agents froze in disbelief, struggling to process Segura's betrayal.

García's fists clenched. "You put our lives at risk. Didn't you realize what would happen?"

Segura lifted her head, eyes red and swollen. "I didn't think it would go this far! I was just trying to help my sister. Gabriela was in so much pain—"

"Pain doesn't excuse your treason," Montero snapped, cutting her off. "You had a duty to us, this team and the OIJ. Yet you passed on sensitive information, our mission plan, to your sister, knowing she would divulge it to Baca."

Jiménez felt his anger rise. "We trusted you, Segura. You knew the stakes and chose to betray us."

St. James intervened, his voice calm but sharp. "This isn't just betrayal. It's about how Baca operated. He preyed on the vulnerable, turning them into pawns. Segura, your sister was a pawn, and you unwittingly played right into her hands, once Baca owned her."

"I never wanted this!" Segura cried.

St. James moved closer, his gaze piercing. "Consider the consequences. Agents killed. Families destroyed. Leaking information put us all in danger — no one is here to protect individuals at the team's expense."

The room fell still. Each agent grappled with their emotions.

Ramírez spoke with authority. "Montero, arrest her!"

CHAPTER 68

Montero read Segura her rights while a police officer closed the handcuffs around her wrists. Segura's tears flowed freely, her guilt and fear clouding her face as she hung her head, her body trembling. The air felt thick. Oppressive.

Jiménez's voice broke the silence. "Get Gabriela in for questioning and probable arrest. We'll need to move quickly." He glanced at Segura one last time before turning away.

As Segura was led out of the room, the weight of the moment settled over the agents. The room fell into an unnatural stillness.

Ramírez stood frozen, his gaze fixed on Segura's retreating figure, his eyes wide with disbelief. His voice was low, strained. "I never imagined … never thought someone would betray us like this. It's … hard to process." His voice cracked slightly. "Even harder to accept."

Jiménez lowered his head, his expression tight. "I'm at a loss for words. Just … devastated."

García's hands shook as he spoke. "We're all at a loss for words," he murmured, his voice full of disbelief.

The others sat in stunned silence, the weight of disappointment crushing the air. The room felt too small now, too crowded with unspoken emotions.

Ramírez's face twisted in anguish, and his voice was barely above a whisper. "OIJ's hard-earned reputation … torn apart in an instant. This whole mission … it was supposed to be a success." His hands gripped the edge of the table. "Now it feels … hollow."

His mind raced. How could they salvage their reputation? How would they face the families of fallen agents? The questions gnawed at him, but the answers seemed out of reach.

St. James, Anna, and Dozer exchanged glances, each feeling the weight of the moment. Denzel stared blankly, struggling to comprehend the magnitude of what had just unfolded.

García turned to Jiménez. "What now, Sir?"

Jiménez glared, searching for the words. "For now, we keep this under wraps. We need time to manage the mess. Make sure the mission's success is recognized." His eyes took in the door as Segura disappeared from sight. "For now, I need a drink." He exhaled slowly. "We'll meet tomorrow in the boardroom. Come with a clear head."

Everyone nodded, their faces etched with grim resolve.

As they left the room, St. James lingered for a moment. "What about my team?"

Jiménez's eyes were vacant, distant. "This morning, I was ready to commend you all for a job well done, to shake your hand and send you off. Now? Well, that seems... premature."

***

The Sky Lobby was quieter than usual as St. James, Anna, Denzel, and Dozer stepped out of the elevator. Maggie was already behind the bar, pouring their drinks. Her eyes met theirs.

"Everything okay?" she asked, her voice soft.

Anna took a long sip of her pinot, her gaze distant. "Rough day," she muttered, the weight of the hours pressing on her.

Maggie wiped down the bar with a red cloth. "Want to talk about it?"

Dozer shook his head, his hand gripping the can of Imperial a little too tightly. "Nope."

St. James remained silent, focusing on his glass.

Maggie smiled gently, sensing the tension. "If you change your mind ... I'm a good listener."

St. James looked at her, his eyes carrying a mix of gratitude and pain. "Thanks, Maggie. Just ... a long day."

Anna shifted in her seat, glancing between St. James and Dozer. She let out a heavy sigh. "We need time to process all this. The betrayal … it's just…" Her voice trailed off.

St. James rubbed his forehead, eyes clouded with exhaustion. "The fallout from Segura's betrayal will be major. But we can't let it derail everything we've accomplished."

Maggie returned to check on their drinks.

Dozer's phone buzzed, cutting through the tension. He answered quickly, his face slowly draining of colour. The seconds stretched on, and the change in his expression was enough to freeze the others in place.

"Thank you for letting us know," Dozer murmured, his voice hollow. He closed his cell and stared at it, his hand trembling slightly.

St. James's eyes narrowed. "What was that about?"

Dozer's jaw clenched. He looked at the can in his hand, squeezing it with force. "It's … it's Segura. She … she asked for some clothes and personal effects from home before being locked up. A female agent escorted her home. While the agent took a call from García, Segura … she went to the basement." He paused, swallowing hard. "She had a pistol there. She … she ended it. She chose to die rather than face disgrace and prison."

Anna's face went pale. Her hands flew to her mouth, and she shook her head in disbelief. "Jesus," she whispered.

St. James stared into his glass of Macallan, the news hitting him harder than he thought it would. His grip tightened on the glass, and for a moment, he didn't speak. The silence between them stretched, each grappling with their thoughts.

Dozer's voice broke the silence first, low and distant. "I never thought … she'd be that broken. We knew she was guilty, but … this?" He trailed off, shaking his head.

Anna rubbed the back of her neck and let out a long, frustrated breath. "I don't know how to feel about this. How didn't we see this coming?"

Dozer's eyes flickered toward her, his voice barely above a whisper. "Maybe we didn't want to see it. She … she was good at hiding everything else."

Anna turned away, staring into her drink, her lips tight. She wasn't sure what was harder to deal with — the betrayal, or the fact that they hadn't stopped the suicide.

The silence lingered longer now, suffocating. The weight of the situation hung over them, a collective heaviness they couldn't escape.

St. James sat motionless, his fingers drumming the side of his glass. He watched the liquid swirl inside, his face unreadable. Then, after what felt like an eternity, he sighed deeply and looked up at the others, the coldness in his eyes unmistakable.

"Sorry to sound callous," he said, his voice cutting through the silence, "but this … this solves OIJ's betrayal problem."

Dozer's eyes widened. "How the hell do you figure that?"

St. James sipped his scotch, unphased by Dozer's disbelief. "Segura's death will be framed as mental illness. An unexpected loss. Far removed from the mission's success. My guess? OIJ public communications will make sure the two events are presented as separate, unrelated incidents."

Dozer stared at him, stunned. "You're something, you know that?"

St. James met his gaze and flashed a slight, devilish grin. "I know."

Anna slipped off her stool without a word, her movements sharp and deliberate. It caught St. James by surprise.

"Where are you going, Anna?"

She didn't look back. "To pack. I have a wedding to plan."

St. James shrugged, as if it was the most casual thing in the world. "That reminds me. I have to go to New York."

Dozer finished his second Imperial and raised an eyebrow. "What for?"

St. James leaned back, the faintest hint of a smile playing on his lips. "DeSilva promised to kiss my ass in Times Square if I got her nineteen million back."